# THE CAMELOT CHRONICLES

# THE CAMELOT CHRONICLES

HEROIC ADVENTURES
FROM THE TIME OF KING ARTHUR

EDITED BY MIKE ASHLEY

WINGS BOOKS
New York • Avenel

This 1995 edition is published by Wings Books,
distributed by Random House Value Publishing, Inc.,
40 Engelhard Avenue, Avenel, New Jersey 07001,
by arrangement with Robinson Publishing  Ltd.

Random House
New York • Toronto • London • Sydney • Auckland

Printed and bound in the United States of America

Library of Congress Cataloging–in–Publication Data

The Camelot chronicles: heroic adventures
from the time of King Arthur / edited by Mike Ashley.
p.   cm.
ISBN 0-517-12450-5
1. Arthurian romances—Adaptations.  2. Knights and knighthood—Fiction.
3. Adventure stories, English.  4. Adventure Stories, English.
5. Kings and rulers—Fiction.  I. Ashley, Michael.
PS648.A78C36   1995
813.008'0351—dc20                                    95-9765
                                                       CIP

8 7 6 5 4 3 2 1

## Copyright Acknowledgements

"Belle Dame, Sans Merci" by Vera Chapman, (c) 1992 by Vera Chapman. First printing, used by permission of the author.

"The Oath of the Saxon" by Peter Tremayne, (c) 1992 by Peter Tremayne. First printing, used by permission of the author.

"The Storming Bone" by Ian McDowell, (c) 1991 by Ian McDowell. First published in *Amazing Stories*, September 1991. Reprinted by permission of the author.

"Blueflow" by Don Wilcox, (c) 1992 by Don Wilcox. First printing, used by permission of the author.

"The Brotherhood of Britain" by Keith Taylor, (c) 1992 by Keith Taylor. First printing, used by permission of the author.

"Morte d'un Marcheant" by Maxey Brooke, (c) 1992 by Maxey Brooke. First printing, used by permission of the author.

"Sir Borlays and the Dark Knight" by Anthony Armstrong, (c) 1933 by Anthony Armstrong Willis for *The Strand Magazine*, December 1933.

"Sir Agravaine" by P.G. Wodehouse, (c) 1914 by P.G. Wodehouse for *The Man Upstairs and Other Stories*. Reprinted by permission of the author's estate and the Random Century Group on behalf of the publisher, Barrie & Jenkins.

"The Romance of Tristan and Iseult" by Hilaire Belloc, (c) 1913 by Hilaire Belloc. Reprinted by permission of the agent for the estate, the Peters Fraser & Dunlop Group, Ltd.

"The Coming of the Light" by Phyllis Ann Karr, (c) 1992 by Phyllis Ann Karr. First printing, used by permission of the author, and the author's agent, Owlswick Literary Agency.

"Told By Moonlight" by Darrell Schweitzer, (c) 1992 by Darrell Schweitzer. First printing, used by permission of the author.

"The Quiet Monk" by Jane Yolen, (c) 1988 by Jane Yolen. First published in *Isaac Asimov's Science Fiction Magazine*, March 1988. Reprinted by permission of the author, and the author's agent, Curtis Brown Ltd.

"The Sad Wizard" by John T. Aquino, (c) 1985 by John T. Aquino. First published in *Fantasy Book*, December 1985. Reprinted by permission of the author.

"To Camelot" by Theodore Goodridge Roberts, (c) 1934 by Theodore Goodridge Roberts for *The Leather Bottle*. "Mountainy Madness" by Theodore Goodridge Roberts, (c) 1992 by Mrs Dorothy Roberts Leisner. Both printed by permission of Mrs Dorothy Roberts Leisner.

# CONTENTS

To all those seeking Camelot,

Be true to yourself.

# TO CAMELOT

In Quest of Beauty I rode far,
With dreams for guide, and a falling star,
A leaping stag and a golden bee:
I found you under a wishing-tree.

I know the road to Camelot,
By leafy glade and ferny grot;
You know, by flash of song and wing,
the silver birds of which I sing.

In Beauty's service still I ride
by grassy track and curling tide.
Now every wood has its wishing-tree
And every rose her golden bee.

—Theodore Goodridge Roberts

# INTRODUCTION

I am delighted to be able to assemble a further volume of Arthurian stories, following my earlier selection, *The Pendragon Chronicles*. As before, I have sought to provide a balance between the traditional tales of knightly valour and chivalry and the more historical reality of the Arthurian world. The stories also bring a blend of humour, mystery and mysticism.

I am particularly pleased that eight of the stories presented here have never previously been published, and four of those were written especially for this volume. In addition there are a variety of stories of all ages, many of which have not been reprinted since their original publication.

Camelot is the name most closely associated with Arthur's castle and capital, though the name came late to Arthurian lore. It first appeared in the romance *Lancelot* by that greatest of Arthurian chroniclers, Chrétien de Troyes, writing in the latter half of the twelfth century. Even then Chrétien makes only one reference to Camelot, and does not say where it stood. Malory, whose *Morte d'Arthur* ushered in the Tudor revival of interest in Arthurian legend, equated Camelot with Winchester. Visitors to Winchester today will indeed see on exhibit in the Great Hall a Round Table, but there is no reason to believe it is Arthur's. Scientific tests on the table back in 1977, which included tree-ring and carbon-dating, suggested a date of manufacture at some time around the early fourteenth century. It existed at the time Caxton printed Malory's epic work, and was probably sufficient reason for linking Winchester with Camelot.

The most popularly accepted site for Camelot is Cadbury Castle in Somerset. Here stood an ancient hill fort as far back as the Iron Age. Fortifications were renewed over the centuries, including one at the time ascribed to King Arthur, around 500 A.D.. Archeological excavations at the site have discovered sufficient evidence to support the tradition that the place was once the political court of a High King. Whether or not it is the Camelot of legend will probably never be proved, but it has a strong claim.

Of course, Arthur had other courts throughout the land, most notably Caerleon on the River Usk in South Wales. This site was used in the history by Geoffrey of Monmouth—not too surprising seeing that Geoffrey came from a neighbouring town, and held allegiance to his Welsh ancestry in those harsh years just after the Norman conquest. Writers using Geoffrey as their source tend to set Arthur's adventures at Caerleon.

That isn't too important. The real location of Camelot is more ideological than geographical. It has come to symbolise a haven of peace in a world of turbulence—a city of dreams. It is that world, whether at Camelot, Caerleon, Tintagel, Carlisle (or Caerduel) or other Arthurian sites, that the authors have brought back to life in this volume.

On the surface, the Arthurian world might seem a simple one. King Arthur, having defeated the Saxons at Badon, ruled during a period of peace in which courageous knights set out on valorous quests in an age of apparent chivalry. But it doesn't take the reader long to realise that the Arthurian world was nothing like that—not even the legendary one.

Arthur's knights are portrayed as a bloodthirsty, psychotic brigade who murder and plunder without qualm. They are plagued by emotional and mental instability and undertake quests, not so much for valour as for redemption.

Arthur was likewise plagued by nightmares—his was the classic tragedy of love and betrayal. First there was his incestuous son Mordred, whom he believed would one day cause his death. Despite this Arthur loved and trusted Mordred, only ultimately to be betrayed. That same anguish applied to Arthur's wife Guinevere who proved faithless to Arthur with a succession of knights, most notably Lancelot. The emotions roused by these webs of passion and deceit would ultimately prove the undoing of Arthur, and the downfall of ancient Britain.

It is that conflict that is caught in the fiction here. On the surface Camelot is a city of dreams, but within is a city of nightmare. I hope you are prepared. The tour starts here.

Mike Ashley,
Walderslade,
February 1992

# DRAMATIS PERSONAE
## A guide to Arthurian characters

*In The Pendragon Chronicles I presented a short guide to the Arthurian characters and names you were likely to encounter, and I'm doing the same here. There are so many names in Arthurian lore that it's not always easy to know whether you've just encountered someone of significance or not, and when those names can be subjected to so many alternative spellings, it can become very confusing. I hope the following helps. It does not include minor characters or those invented by the writers.*

**Aelle.** Saxon invader and first king of the South Saxons. He is also recorded as the first Bretwalda, or overlord of the Saxons. Reigned between c. 477–491 A.D., and is thus contemporaneous with Arthur. He defeated the Britons at Anderida (Pevensey) in 477, and again in 485. In 491, however, the British overwhelmed Aelle and his name vanishes from the chronicles.

**Aglaval/Aglovale.** Knight of the Round Table and brother of Sir Percevale. He carries out King Arthur's wishes in the punishment of Guinevere and is killed by Lancelot.

**Agravaine.** Son of King Lot and Morgause of Orkney, and brother of Gawain, Gaheris and Gareth. Sided with Mordred in the plot to reveal the adultery between Lancelot and Guinevere.

**Ambrosius Aurelianus.** Historically "the Last of the Romans", he governed Britain in the last half of the fifth century and helped stem the tide of Saxon advance in the days immediately prior to Arthur. In Arthurian legend he is sometimes depicted as Arthur's uncle.

**Arthur/Artorius/Artos.** High-King of Britain, son of Uther Pendragon and Igraine, raised as foster-son of Ector of the Forest Sauvage and foster-brother of Sir Kay. Founded the Fellowship of the Round Table, married Guinevere. By his half-sister Morgause he fathered Mordred who later waged war against him, resulting in the final battle at Camlann where both Arthur and Mordred fell.

**Aurelianius,** see Ambrosius.

**Bors.** Son of King Bors and cousin to Sir Lancelot. He was one of the three successful knights in the search for the Holy Grail.

**Bran.** A hero of Welsh legend, who lived at about the time of Christ. His story is recounted in the Daughter of Llyr episode of *The Mabinogion*. Bran led an expedition against the King of Ireland, in which Bran is mortally wounded. He ordered that his head be cut off and buried on the Hill of Ravens (Tower Hill in London—Bran means raven) as a protection against the future invasion of Britain. The legend still lives on, of course, in the belief that if the ravens ever leave the Tower of London, England will fall. Bran is recorded as the father of Caractacus, king of the Britons at the time of the Roman invasion in 43 AD.

**Brandiles.** A knight of the Round Table, son of Sir Gilbert. He came into conflict with Gawain who had seduced Brandiles's sister and defeated his father and brothers.

**Breunor/Brewnor/Bruno le Noir.** A knight noted for his untidy appearance. When he first arrived at Camelot he was nick-named "La Cote Mal-Taile" by Sir Kay and sent to serve as a kitchen scullion until he proved his worth. The story has some parallels with that of Gareth Beaumains.

**Cae/Cei,** see Kay.

**Cissa.** Son of Aelle, king of Sussex, and his companion in his battles against the British.

**Constantine.** Arthur's cousin and son of Cador, King of Cornwall. A close and trusted knight he became King Arthur's successor, after defeating the sons of Mordred. There was an historical king Constantine of Dumnonia (Devon and Cornwall) in the early sixth century, though he was a murderous, deceitful king.

**Dinadan.** A Knight of the Round Table noted for his wit and humour.

**Drustan,** see Tristan.

**Elaine.** There are three Elaines in the Arthurian cycle: **Elaine of Garlot** the half-sister of King Arthur; **Elaine de Astolat,** a maiden who fell in love with Sir Lancelot; and **Elaine of Corbenic,** daughter of King Pelles and, by Lancelot, the mother of Sir Galahad.

**Ewaine,** see Owain.

**Gaheris.** Third son of King Lot and brother to Agravaine, Gareth and Gawain. Half-brother of Mordred.

**Galahad.** Son of Sir Lancelot and Elaine of Corbenic and the purest of all the Knights of the Round Table. With Sir Bors and Sir Percevale, he was one of the successful Grail Knights. He was the only knight able to sit at the "Seige Perilous" seat of the Round Table.

**Gareth.** The youngest son of King Lot of Orkney and brother of Gawain, Gaheris and Agravaine. He first arrived anonymously at Camelot and was given the nickname "Beaumains" by Sir Kay, owing to his fine hands.

**Gawain/Gwalchmai.** The eldest son of King Lot of Orkney and brother of Gareth, Gaheris and Agravaine. He was one of the strongest knights of the Round Table. He features in the earliest legends of Arthur and appears in the Celtic texts as Gwalchmai, meaning the Hawk of May. He undertook the challenge of the Green Knight, Sir Bertilak.

**Gorlas/Gorlois.** Duke of Cornwall, husband of Igraine, and father of Morgan le Fay, Morgause and Elaine of Garlot.

**Gorvenal.** The servant of Tristan who later became king of Lyonesse.

**Griflet/Girflet/Jaufry.** One of Arthur's earliest and youngest knights who is wounded by King Pellinore. He recovers and becomes the hero of his own quest with Brunissende.

**Guinevere/Gwynhwfar.** Daughter of Leodegrance, King of Cameliard, and wife of King Arthur. Her adultery with Sir Lancelot causes the downfall of the Fellowship of the Round Table. She was condemned to death by Arthur but rescued by Lancelot and ended her days in a nunnery.

**Gwalchmai**, see Gawain.

**Gwyn ap Nudd.** A Welsh deity who seems originally to have been King of the Underworld. He is later seen as King of the Fairies. He is in perpetual battle against Gwythr for the hand of Creudylad, daughter of King Llud.

**Igraine/Igerna/Ygraine.** Wife of Duke Gorlois of Cornwall and, by him, mother of Morgan le Fay, Morgause and Elaine. Seduced by Uther Pendragon and became mother of Arthur. Later married Uther.

**Iseult/Isolde/Isolt/Yseult/Ysolt.** Wife of King Mark of Cornwall but lover of her husband's nephew, Tristan of Lyonesse. Not to be confused with Iseult of Brittany whom Tristan married after his banishment from Cornwall.

**Kay/Kai/Cai/Cei/Caius.** Son of Sir Ector and foster-brother of Arthur. He becomes the king's High Seneschal and is noted for his sour temperament. In the earliest legends Kay is an heroic knight, but in later versions he becomes Arthur's irrascible steward.

**Lamorack of Gaul.** Son of King Pellinore and one of the strongest knights of the Round Table. He became the lover of Morgause after the death of King Lot and was killed by Gawain and his brothers.

**Lancelot/Lancelet/Launcelot/Lancot.** Son of King Ban and greatest of the Knights of the Round Table. His castle was called the Joyous Gard. His love for Guinevere led to the downfall of the Fellowship of the Round Table. After the deaths of Arthur and Guinevere he became a hermit.

**Lanval/Launfal.** One of the Knights of the Round Table who is beloved by Guinevere. When rebuffed she beseeches Arthur to punish him. He is saved by his beloved lady of Avalon.

**Leodegrance.** King of Cameliard and father of Guinevere.

**Linet**, see Lunetta.

**Lot.** King of Orkney who opposed Arthur for the crown of Britain. He was the husband of Arthur's half-sister Morgause and father of Gawain, Agravaine, Gaheris and Gareth. He was killed by King Pellinore and his sons.

**Lunetta/Lynette/Linet/Lunet.** Sister of Lady Lyonesse and Sir Gringamore of the Castle Perilous. She led Sir Gareth on his first quest. Although she later falls in love with Gareth she is given in marriage to his brother Gaheris. In Celtic myth she is the mistress of the Lady of the Fountain.

**Margawse/Margause**, see Morgause.

**Mark/Marc**. King of Cornwall and husband of Iseult.

**Medraut**, see Mordred.

**Mellicene/Mellicent**. A lady-in-waiting on Guinevere at the court of King Leodegrance.

**Merlin/Merdyn/Myrddyn**. Magician and adviser of King Arthur. He was the offspring of a girl and a demon of the air and was raised in a nunnery. His prophecies began in the last days of King Vortigern. He later raised Stonehenge. He put a glamour on Igraine so that she mistook Uther Pendragon for her husband Gorlois. Merlin became guardian to the young Arthur and later contrived the episode of the sword in the stone so that Arthur was recognised as the future High-King. He created the Round Table. He became enamoured of the enchantress Niniane, who imprisoned him in a cave.

**Mordred/Medraut/Modred/Modreuant**. The incestuous child of Arthur and his half-sister Morgause. He later attempted to seduce Guinevere and claimed the throne of Britain. He met in mortal battle with Arthur at Camlann.

**Morgan le Fay/Morgana/Morgaine**. Daughter of Gorlois and Igraine and half-sister of King Arthur. She was educated in the sorcerous arts and became Arthur's major enemy, forever seeking the downfall of the Round Table. By hiding the scabbard of Excalibur, which had previously protected Arthur, she rendered him mortal. She was the mother of Owain.

**Morgause/Margawse**. Daughter of Gorlois, sister of Morgan le Fay, wife of Lot of Orkney, and mother by him of Gawain, Agravaine, Gaheris and Gareth. She was also the mother of Mordred by Arthur, her half-brother.

**Morholt/Marhaus**. The brother of Iseult, who is slain by Tristan in combat.

**Nimue/Nymue/Niniane**, see Vivian.

**Owain/Ewen/Uwaine/Yvain**. Historical hero who, in Celtic and Arthurian legend, becomes the son of Morgan le Fay and King Urien.

**Palomides/Palamides.** A Saracen who becomes one of the greatest Knights of the Round Table. A suitor for Queen Iseult he later becomes involved in the ceaseless search for the Questing Beast.

**Parsival,** see Percivale.

**Pelles.** The King of the Grail Castle and possibly synonymous with the Fisher King. He was the grandfather of Sir Galahad and is sometimes named as the brother of King Pellinore.

**Pellinore.** King of the Isles and one of the mightiest of the Knights of the Round Table who, in an early episode, overpowered Arthur and would have killed him had he not been enchanted by Merlin. He was involved in the search for the Questing Beast. He was the father of Sir Lamorack and, in some versions, also of Sir Percivale. He killed King Lot and was, in turn, killed by Sir Gawain.

**Percivale/Parsival/Parzival/Peredur.** The knight most closely associated with the quest for the Holy Grail. Early legends have him raised in the wilds of Wales, but later legends link him with King Pellinore.

**Peredur,** see Percivale.

**Riothamus.** A British king who ruled about 470 A.D. who has been linked with Arthur. He assisted the Romans against the Visigoths.

**Sagramore/Segramore.** Knight of the Round Table, son of the King of Hungary, and descended from the emperors of Constantinople. He served as Guinevere's body-guard.

**Taliesin.** A legendary bard and prophet who has become closely linked with Merlin.

**Tristan/Tristram/Drustan.** Son of King Melodias of Lyonesse and nephew of king Mark of Cornwall, whose wife, Iseult, he fell in love with. Banished from Cornwall he entered King Arthur's court as one of the mightiest knights, until forced to flee to Brittany, where he married another Iseult.

**Uther Pendragon.** High-King of Britain and father of Arthur, by Igraine.

**Vivian/Nimue/Niniane.** An enchantress who is perceived in a number of roles in the Arthurian legend. She is called the Lady of the Lake, the foster mother of Lancelot, who gave Excalibur to Arthur. She also became the lover of Merlin whom she imprisoned in a cave. She is seen by some as a sister to Morgause and Morgan and thus equated with Elaine of Garlot.

**Vortigern.** King of Britain whose reign preceded Ambrosius in the mid-fifth century. He invited Hengist to Britain to rid the land of Saxons, but Hengist in turn conquered Kent. Merlin first appears in Vortigern's reign.

**Ygraine,** see Igraine.

**Yseult,** see Iseult.

**Yvain,** see Owain.

# BELLE DAME, SANS MERCI
## by Vera Chapman

*Vera Chapman (1898–), who was present in*
The Pendragon Chronicles *with her complete
novel* The King's Damosel, *sets us on the
road to Camelot with an episode from the
days before Arthur's birth. Here we see the
workings of Arthur's three elder half-sisters,
Vivian, Morgause and Morgan, whose lives
would ultimately seal Arthur's fate. The story
is a self-contained extract from Vera's unpub-
lished novel,* The Enchantresses.

On the small, heavily-fortified peninsula Tintagel, in the castle, dwelt the three daughters of Ygraine, Duchess of Cornwall: Vivian, Morgause and Morgan. Their mother was also destined by the workings of time and fate to be the mother of King Arthur.

The three were born triplets, but were all entirely different. All destined by descent and fate to be witches, or at least magicians; Vivian, chestnut-haired, adhered closely to the White Magic of the old Druids; Morgause, golden, lazy, pleasure-loving and easily led, could follow either White or Black Magic; but Morgan had hair as black as her heart and her magic.

For a time Merlin had been their tutor, and taught them reading and much else besides. All the winters and the stormy springs and autumns they were close-shut in their narrow ridge of rock, but in the summer they were sent to a more generous

10

county, on the sunny mainland, where the last of Anderida Wood stretched out green fingers towards the coast; there in a comfortable farm-grange, with Olwen their old nurse, they spent their summers.

# I

Britain was a lawless place in those days. Since the Romans had left there was no real rule or authority, nor much communication between one region and another. Cut off by unrepaired roads and dangerous wildernesses, small communities drew in upon themselves, knowing little of the world outside, or even of their neighbours. Small landowners set themselves up as petty lords, and dispensed justice or injustice as they saw fit—for one good ruler a dozen bad ones. Might was right; tyranny and cruelty abounded. In many places fierce foreigners in long black ships came raiding in, and often these were hardly worse than the tyrants they replaced. The men of peace—the monks and the priests of the old British Church—died martyrs or fled away from the burning churches into the mountains westward.

And here and there, in all this confusion, it was not to be wondered at if things still more evil survived. In the darkest impenetrable woods, in the clefts of the mountains, in the honey-comb caves underground, strange creatures still lurked, survivors from earlier times, great worms, batwinged birds—some, it might be, not altogether of this world, half in and half out of the Shadowland. Hauntings and baleful influences. Such things always thrive on thoughts of hatred. Time had been, when the Christian priests of the British Church, saying their Masses daily in the white decorated villas, had kept these things at bay, and before them, the white-clad Druids had warded them off with their good magic. But now it was said that some of the barons even protected and nourished the monsters—and who dared say what they nourished them on.

But there were still, in one place and another, families and little groups who remembered better things. One such family was that of Bors and his brothers Ector, Torion and Lioncel, who lived on the edge of the Anderida Forest. Their father, Briareus, and their mother Elena, remembered better times, and their grandfather Constans remembered the Romans. In their moated grange—a farmhouse solidly built of wood, surrounded by a deep moat,

and able to stand a siege if necessary—they did their best to keep
alive the old civilised ways. They had their priest, who said Mass
daily in their little chapel, for the family and a few friends—Brian,
Ulphius, Brastias—some of them with their wives, and all young.
Meeting often, they would wish with all their hearts for better
things, and talked of banding together to root out injustices,
Sometimes they would take action together to right some of the
worst wrongs, but their power was little, and whether others were
like-minded with themselves in other places, they had no means
of knowing.

Two legacies they had from the Roman days, besides their
house: a few pieces of the fine Roman armour, in particular the
towering helmets and the breastplates; and a breeding strain of
tall black horses, taller by many hands than the stocky British
ponies. It was said that the ancestors of those horses came from
Rome, long ago—certainly they were not like any other horses
ever seen in these parts, or, as far as was known, in Britain. A
man on one of those horses could command respect.

So sometimes, mounted on those same black horses, these
young men would ride out, in twos and threes, or singly, in
search of wrongs to right, a monster to exterminate, or a victim
to rescue.

So Torion, the youngest brother of the four, had ridden out one
day alone, in search of adventure. Setting out from the borders
of Anderida on his tall black horse, he had ridden south and
west . . . He had heard of a strange wild region in the extreme
west, where the land stretched out into the sea, and then was no
more—Land's End.

In a late afternoon he came to a place he had heard spoken
of as Dozmary Pool. "Douce-Maree"—sweet lake. But all that
was sweet about it he found, was that it was not salt. A desolate,
weedy, slimy pool, with a sinister feel about it. Something bad
there. Searching carefully, he found it—a nasty thing of the lizard
kind, not very large but undoubtedly dangerous, lurking in a dim
crevice in the most stagnant corner of the lake—the bones that
surrounded its lair showed how dangerous it was. There were
human bones among them.

He dealt with it effectively, as he had done with others—his
horse was as used as he was to such encounters, and knew how
to help him. True, it was no easy fight, nor without danger—but
it was done, and he left the obscene carcass, with the birds already
beginning to collect, and rode away with a sense of mission
accomplished. He was tired now, and would have welcomed

an inn, but there seemed none in sight over the bare treeless landscape. He pressed on, as the sun began to sink.

The rough road that he was following began to go downhill, and just as the sun's rim dipped ahead of him he saw a light in a hollow below. It seemed to be coming from within a wood. All day he had seen no woods, and this seemed reassuring—there would be people there, woodcutters, perhaps a village. He pressed on.

Descending the hill, he lost sight of the light, but the woods closed in upon him. Then he began to hear music, very faint and far off—at first more rhythm than tune, just the deep pulsations of drums and tabors and possibly of feet—then the melody of country pipes was added to it. Music! Who was dancing in the woods at sunset? Well . . . there were country revels, shepherds' dances, huntsmen's celebrations—it need be nothing stranger. But could it—and his heart beat a little faster—could it perhaps be the Little People, of whom he had heard in fireside tales still seen in many places, a weird and beautiful sight, but dangerous? What an adventure if it were . . . He spurred his horse forward.

At last he found the elusive gleam of light, red and flashing, the light of a bonfire. And a gap through the trees, on a slight rise, showed him the picture at a distance—people, women from their long hair, dancing in a ring round a fire. But still too far off to see clearly. Oh yes, surely it must be the Little People—yet not so little.

He closed in on them—then a turn round a screen of thick bushes suddenly brought him close to them, and he almost cried out in amazement. They were all stark naked.

Beyond all doubt he had fallen among witches.

Nothing alluring about their nakedness. Young and old they were, some comely and some hideous, all sorts and kinds, their unbound hair golden or black or grey—the ruddy light of the fire played upon their skins, snow-white or red or tawny—all terrifying. They surrounded him, not touching him but menacing—hands like claws at the ready, teeth bared, eyes glaring. The music had ceased abruptly, and he heard only a low growling noise, like threatening cats. His horse stood still, shivering and running with sweat, its ears laid back. He could do nothing.

A voice spoke over the heads of the crowded women.

"What shall we do with him?"

"Tear him to pieces," several voices chorused.

"Too quick and easy!" said another voice.

"Shall we," said the first voice, "do as Diana did to Acteon?—

No hounds with him—shall we let his horse be his executioner?" The voice paused, and then went on, "No, not the horse. Why should we destroy the dumb brute? We've no quarrel with beasts, only with men.—This we will do—we will loose the Barghest upon him from behind. It has fasted long and is hungry."

"Yes, yes, the Barghest," the others assented, in a shrill chattering of voices. "The Barghest! The Barghest!"

They drew back from him, still not touching him—he could not understand it, for they seemed to be letting him go. One of them turned his horse's head with a jerk to the bridle, and motioned him to go on.

"Go!" some of them shouted. "Go in peace—the kind of peace, we'll give you! Go, and the Barghest attend you—"

He urged his horse into a canter until he was well away from the witches. The thought of them made him shudder and feel slightly sick. What was it they said? "The Barghest." What was the Barghest? Dimly he recalled fireside tales. Oh yes, the bear-ghost, or the ghost-bear, that some of the old people in the cottages were afraid of. Not a bear, though—they mostly spoke of a dog, a black dog, on certain lonely roads. Packmen and pedlars were frightened by it—but as roads grew worse, and men travelled less, and drew in more to their own homesteads, the bogies outside were forgotten—there were enough horrors in the dark corners of their own houses. Outside were *"They"*—and nobody liked to speculate much on what *"They"* were, or give them names to bring them closer. But there was a house he knew, an old house, that had a stone pavement, and worked in the pavement in a pattern of little stones, the picture of a black dog and the word "Cave"—"Beware." The owner of the house hadn't liked it, and had covered it up with a floor of trodden ashes.—"Cave." . . . He shuddered.

Then, as he slackened his horse's pace to a walk, along the dark pathway, he heard the footsteps behind him. Plod, plod, plod—soft and deliberate. Following him. He turned—awkwardly in his cumbersome armour—and where a faint gleam of the rising moon illuminated the road, he saw it, and laughed aloud with relief. A dog, a small dog, no more than a spaniel, trotting in the dust of the road. Well, was this all that their Barghest amounted to? A nasty little dog, though—it yapped at him and showed little sharp teeth and hostile eyes. He took up the bunch of twigs he kept by the saddle to brush flies away, and waved it at the little dog, saying "Shoo" or "Boo" or something of the kind, and it turned and plodded away out of sight . . . So, that was that, and he laughed again and went on his way.

It must be after midnight, and he was tired and very anxious to reach shelter. He was accustomed to camp out if needful, but this dark wood, that seemed to go on and on, offered no good camping-place. He would have to press on in hope weary as he was. And then—he heard the footsteps again. Oh, curse the silly little dog! He turned to wave it off again—and there it was, but—bigger this time. A hulking great hound, like a farmer's lurcher as black as the other, and with the same menacing eyes and teeth. This would heed no fly-whisk. He drew his sword and waved it at the beast—which silently turned and went away. Oh well, very strange, and very disquieting—but better go on. Perhaps he had got rid of it this time.

No. After a mile—plod, plod, plod, behind. He could feel his horse begin to tremble. This time, looking back, the thing that was following him was bigger than any hound he had ever seen—long-legged, straight-backed. drooping-jowled, with a tail that curved away like a bow—all black as night, great luminous eyes gazing down on him—why, the brute must be as tall as a horse . . .

Wildly he waved his sword. Without any sign of fear, the beast turned, flourishing its long tail, and retreated up the road. He went on, uneasily. Not to canter, not to gallop—if he did, would *that thing* come thundering after him?—Plod, plod, plod—would he never shake off those accursed footsteps? He turned again—the thing was no longer a dog but a bear, huge and shaggy, on its hind legs, taller than a man, against the rising moon.

Now he thrust towards it with the point of his sword—and again, quietly, it was gone. As he faced forward again in the saddle, he was sweating cold and panting, and his horse pulled against the rein and would have bolted. Then suddenly from the side of the road a woman came.

She was wrapped and veiled in soft floating grey, and all that he could see of her was that she seemed slender and young, and her hair was dark red. She stepped up close beside him and spoke in an urgent whisper, as if something might overhear them.

"You must turn and fight it," she said. "If you go on walking away, it gets bigger every time. It will be bigger next time—and the time after that you can't think—turn and fight it. I will help you. Give me your sword."

"Give you my sword? Never!"

"You must if I am to help you. Oh, be quick!"

"But you're one of the witches."

"I am not a witch, though I was amongst them. Oh give me your sword, for God's sake!"

"My sword is consecrated, and I may not."

"I tell you—give me your sword in the Name of the Father, and of the Son, and of the Holy Ghost."

"And how shall I fight if I do?"

"Take your spear. I will hold your sword behind you as a cross. It is the only way."

He turned his sword, which he was still holding, and gave it to her by the hilt; she took it and turned it crosswise, holding it by the blade. He set his spear in its rest as to charge, and wheeled about as he heard the plodding footsteps again.

The thing that advanced on him was horrifying ... Larger than a bear—larger than any beast he had ever seen or heard of—black and shaggy, tusked like a boar, fiery-eyed, with luminous foam dripping from its open jaws—It came upright, menacing with its uplifted paws—

"Now charge!" the woman said, holding the cruciform sword steady. He gave the spur and the familiar toss to the reins, as if in the tourney, and the good horse carried him forward right into that mass of fur and flesh—the long spear found its mark, he heard the beast shriek, and felt the drag of its weight on the spear—and then the impulse of the beast's charge carried it, struggling, up the length of the spear, as a wounded boar will do. But a boar-spear has a strong bar across it to deal with just such a struggle, and Torion's spear had not—Up and up the beast struggled, the claws thrashing in front of it—the horse, plunging in terror, was within its range, but its armour saved its eyes and it breast. Torion was dimly conscious that the woman behind him was holding up his sword, from which light streamed, and as the light shone, the monster's struggles grew weaker—and ceased. It fell, dragging the spear to the ground, out of Torion's grasp.

"Quick now," she said, handing him the sword. "Cut its head off."

Dismounting, he did so—and stood back amazed as the whole great beast began to dissolve away, like a pool of water drying under the sun. A small shrinking black pool, and then—nothing. The woman stepped forward, and put her foot—brown, bare and firm—on the spot where the last vestige had vanished.

And the first faint light of daybreak began to creep through the woods.

And now he looked down at the woman, and really saw her. And saw that she was the most beautiful girl he had ever seen.

Her dark-red hair was lighter and more glowing as the daylight visited it. Her eyes were what he noticed the most—so large and deep-set and haunting, a strange bluish-green, like turqoises, or like the sky seen through beech-leaves in spring. Her mouth was like a wild rose, and her face, pale and softly flushed, was like a wild rose too, its shape and form something more than merely perfect. She stood by his horse's head, caressing it with her long white hands, soothing it, smoothing away all its fear.

He tried to speak, his voice choked with emotion.

"Lady—"

"Yes?" She looked up at him smiling "Yes?"

"Oh lady . . . what am I to call you?"

"My name is Vivian", she said "I am one of three sisters, and we come from the castle of Tintagel—Well? What could you ask me? What can I do for you?"

"Lady," he said, completely lost, "oh, fairest lady—I love you, I adore you, I worship you—"

"That is sweet of you," she said with a disarming smile. "Say no more. I think you are not quite yourself yet. You must be very weary, are you not?"

"Oh, not too weary to know—to know that you are—you are—"

"Come now," she said, "no more talk. I will take you where you can find rest and refreshment. Let me sit behind you and I will guide you where you should go."

Her brisk tone pulled him together—unaided she sprang to the crupper behind him, and piloted him through forest paths—but to feel her slender body pressed to his back was almost more than he could bear. She leant over his shoulder and whispered directions to him.

"You must attend to me," she said sternly, "or I'll slap your face. Stop being a silly boy or we'll never get there."

They reached the boundary of the forest, beyond which was bare downland and the sea; and at the forest's edge was a peasant's hut. Vivian slipped quickly to the ground and knocked on the door; an elderly woman came out.

"My lady! You're here early."

"Bless you, Mother Woodedge. I know I can always count on you. This knight needs food and a bed, and stabling for his horse. Both horse and man have fought a battle. Will you see to him?"

"Why, willingly, my lady. Come in, Sir Knight, and welcome. Be you wounded? No;—thank the Powers. Come your ways, sir."

In the hut they shared frumenty with cream and honey.

"Now tell me your name," said Vivian

My name is Torion, the son of Briareus—we live on the other side of Anderida Forest. I and my brothers and some friends are vowed to ride as far as we may range, to rid the land of monstrous beasts and tyrannous men."

"You've made good riddance of one such, to-day," she said.

"With your help. But the land is full of them. We can do so little."

"I know," she said. "Our tutor Merlin has many times told us."

"Merlin?" he said, looking sharply up. "I have heard the name. Your tutor? Whence comes he?"

"Why—I don't know. He's just—our tutor."

"I should like to meet him. We have heard—our father Briareus has told us—that there are other men like us in the land, who would like to see better things and better ways—if only we had a leader—perhaps a man will come some day—"

"Perhaps a man will come. You must have faith, and be ready."

"We shall.—But, lady—may I not see you again—perhaps to talk of Merlin?"

"I think not," she said. "Not for the present. I must go home, and you must go and sleep now. You need sleep."

"Oh, how can I sleep for thinking of you?"

"Look," she said, and pointed one finger at him. "For this time only—as you think of me you will sleep, deeply and sweetly. Now good rest to you," and she got up from the bench, and went quickly out of the hut—he was already reeling with drowsiness, and the old woman came and led him away to a soft pallet of dried ferns, and helped him off with his armour—he was asleep while still in her hands.

And Vivien took her way home to the farm, walking thoughtfully in the fresh morning. Oh, a charming young man—and one of the right kind, such as Merlin was seeking. But not a lover for her. For herself, now, there was only one man in the world, and that was Merlin.

## II

The homestead where the three girls spent their summers had grown, in those five years or so, into a comfortable farm-house—the girls now had a pleasant "bower," or upper room, with a window with shutters, and outside they had made a little enclosed garden. Into this garden in the fresh morning, Vivian came walking—a little dazed for lack of sleep—and found her sisters, also rather sleepy, but at least having had a few hours in bed.

"Well, Vivian dear," said Morgause, with a yawn, "you left us after the dancing. Oh, I hope you found a nice partner to walk home with. Took you all night, didn't it?"

"Oh, she found a partner, right enough," said Morgan. "*And* spent all night with him—and yet she wasted her time. She didn't sleep with him."

"She doesn't have to *sleep*,", said Morgause, giggling.

"No, I *didn't* sleep with him," said Vivian, red-faced.

"I know you didn't," said Morgan. "More fool you."

Vivian rounded on Morgan. "How do you know?"

"How? You ought to know. You have the clear-sight like the rest of us. I was with you and saw everything."

Vivian's face was alight with anger.

"You saw? You followed me with the Sight? Oh, do I never have any privacy? Am I never safe from you?"

"My dear," said Morgan very condescendingly, "you must improve your art. If you don't know better how to safeguard your mind against me, why, I can't help it."

"Oh . . ." Vivian was speechless with mortification, and turned away. But Morgan pursued her.

"That's a lovely young man of yours, and you wasted your opportunity like a fool. Couldn't you take the good fortune that came your way? I would, I tell you."

Morgause cackled with appreciation. "Morgan, do you know why she wouldn't take him?"

"Oh, I know," said Morgan.

Vivian looked from one to the other, seeing only persecutors.

"It's because she's besotted on Merlin," said Morgause. "Our old tutor Merlin. Old enough to be her father—or her grandad. Oh yes, grandad's darling! Perhaps he'll leave you all his money when he dies?" . . . and her voice ran off into a shrill ringing laugh.

Overwrought and overtired, Vivian broke down in uncontrollable tears.

"Oh, I hate you, I hate you both," she sobbed. "But Morgan is the worst." So she ran from them, and back into the wood to seek a quiet place to weep.

' Torion, after sleeping nearly the clock round, sat soberly by the door of the woodland hut, eating bread and cheese, and talking to Mother Woodedge.

"The young lady," Mother Woodedge said, "Ah, that's the Lady Vivian. Oh, she's a good lady, the very best. I don't know where we'd be if it wasn't for her. She saved my boy from Uther Pendragon's men, when they was after him for poaching and would have hanged him—the Pendragon is terrible hard on any that takes his deer, and we were in sore need. How she saved him I don't know—the Pendragon's men tramped right past him where he was hid, well nigh on top of him and never seemed to see him. Some says it's powers she has—that she's in with those we call the Good Neighbours, not to name no names. I've seen them with her a time or two. But she's not a witch, no, she's not a witch, Her two sisters they're witches I'd say, and I'd never do aught to offend them—they all go to visit the witches down-along in the wood from time to time—but *she*'s not a witch, not the Lady Vivian."

"But where do they come from, those ladies?"

"Why—all we know is, they're some great lord's daughters from far over to southward, but more than that we don't know—and those that know mustn't tell. But she's a good lady. What she gives us in the summer sees us through the winter so we don't starve, and she puts a blessing on the place as well, on my little cow and my bees and my apple-trees, and on what the dog gets in the woods. Sometimes we think she's like one of those the old tales tell about—the great ladies of the woods in time gone by. There was one they called Nimue. They said she made the flowers grow in the spring and the beasts bring forth young . . ."

So when the goodwife was gone, he sat and thought, always of Vivian. In his thoughts there was never any forward-looking, never any plan of life. What would he ask of her? Not to be his bride—one has no such thoughts about a heavenly manifestation of beauty . . . Only to admire her, to bathe his eyes in her sight, to lose himself in contact with her . . . In bodily contact?—Oh, dear God, what intoxication—perhaps to die in that moment . . .

"Will she come back here, do you think?" he asked.

"Why, yes, in a day or a week or so, while the summer lasts."

"Then, goodwife, would you be so kind as to let me stay here till I see her again?"

"Surely, sir—you bide here as long as you've a mind to. My son and my goodman are up-along in the woods, and will be for a while, and I'm glad of company. That's if the heap of fern in the shippen be good enough for you."

"Oh, excellent, goodwife—I ask for no better."

"And our food's nothing much—"

"I shall not eat."

"Oh, never say that! Don't be a fool, lad. Of course you'll eat. What good will you be to a lady if you fall over with faintness when next you see her?"

And so she coaxed him, almost forced him, to eat her good frumenty, and clotted cream, and her eggs and butter, though he hardly knew what he did.

And on the third day he saw her coming, riding on a white horse.

She dismounted, and almost ran to him, her hands outstretched, her face aglow with delight.

"My dear friend! I had to come and see how you fared. You're well? Mother Woodedge has looked after you? Come, I have so much to tell you. Let us walk in the woods. No, not ride—I love to walk. Let me show you where the bluebell glades are. Have you forgotten that it is May?"

In a daze of bliss he followed her, hardly finding a word to answer. It was indeed May, and now he realised it, and tasted the beauty of the time, as she led him through it and pointed out to him all its charms and graces. Things he would never have noticed before—not only the bluebells, though they made a heaven of the ground they sprang from, but the first little sparks of crimson that were the campions, setting off the blue; wood-anemones, and the great green trusses of wood-spurge; late-flowering wild cherries overhead, and the blush-pink of the crab-apples; Solomon's Seal, and lilies of the valley. Enchantment after enchantment—and he saw each one as an adornment to her and with her beauty, this new gentleness and warmth and kindness . . .

And at last, deep in the untrodden woods, she led him to a little dell, roofed over with the stretching boughs of beech-trees, where last year's brown beech-leaves, and of many years gone by, lay in a thick rustling drift. Here she stood still, and saying nothing, took off her long grey mantle and laid it on the beech-leaves. Underneath the mantle she wore only a light, translucent dress. Her arms reached out to him, and she drew him down to the beech-leaf bed.

It was late morning and the sun was high, shining through the opened lattice window where the girls were sleeping. Vivian was awakened by the sound of Morgan laughing.

"What are you laughing at, Morgan?"

"Why—you, among other things. Thank you very much, dear Vivian, for the loan of your beautiful lover."

"What do you mean?" Vivian exclaimed, jumping out of bed and looking down at Morgan, who lolled against her pillows.

"Why, dear sister, as you wouldn't take pity on the poor man, I did. There in the woods—I took your shape, and of course he thought it was you."

"You didn't! Morgan, did you, did you?"

"Indeed I did, and he enjoyed it and so did I. You were a fool not to take your chance when you had it."

"Morgan . . ." Vivian could find no words. Indignation and anger choked her. In the other bed, Morgause, lying snug and listening, chuckled to herself.

"You certainly don't deserve him," Morgan went on. "So wrapped up in dreams of old Merlin, you couldn't take pity on a fine young fellow—oh, he's a grand lover, I can tell you—"

"Be quiet!" cried Vivian, her cheeks crimson. "Morgan—how could you do such a thing? I'll never speak to you again . . ."

"Ha, ha," said Morgan, and turned back to her pillow.

He was watching the path to the hut, and as soon as Vivian came in sight on her white horse, he ran to her, holding her stirrup as she dismounted, and would have taken her in his arms, crying "Oh my lady, my dear love . . ."

She slipped from his arms, and put him from her gently.

"No, my dear man, no. Not like that—"

"But, my lady—after last night—surely . . .?"

"No, no, no." she thrust him away with one long slim hand. "You are mistaken. It was not I—last night."

"Not you? Oh, what do you mean?"

"That was my sister Morgan—she took my shape. Don't you

understand—that was not I, at all. I was not there. It was my sister Morgan."

He started back from her, incredulous.

"What are you telling me? That it was not you, not you yourself? My dear love, in my arms? Oh, no, no. I can't believe it. Lady, you are lying to me."

"I am not lying . . . I was not there—oh, my poor friend, I have told you, I cannot give you my love, for it is given to another. I was not there last night—"

Amazement, frustration, rage, followed in waves across his face.

"You are lying to me. You are false to me. You have deceived me. Why, why? Oh, my God—you were so kind, so loving to me yesterday—why?—and now to-day you—deny that we . . . Oh my love, do you think I don't know that it was you? How could I be mistaken? Oh, your lips, your breasts, all your lovely body—surely, surely—"

His hands groped for her—she stepped back, eluding his grasp, and he followed her.

"Do not drive me mad. Why should you torment me thus? Have I displeased you—have you been persuaded to deny our love? Has someone—you say you have another lover—by the flames below, if you have played me false—and in so short a time—"

There was a mad blaze in his eyes. He made a quick lunge forward and seized her wrist.

"Don't touch me," she said. "Let me go. Oh, I've told you—I feel kindly to you—"

"Kindly!" he scoffed.

"I do feel kindly to you, but I do not and cannot love you. It was my sister Morgan, who is a witch—"

"And so are you!"

"My sister Morgan, who took my shape and came to you yesterday. This morning she told me—"

"Lies! All lies!" he dragged on her wrist, trying to pull her close to him.

"No, let me go . . ." She was afraid of him now. His right hand gripped her hard, and his left was groping towards her neck, her face—his eyes had a red glare. With a sudden effort she broke free from him and jumped away out of range. He did not try to follow her. Instead, he hid his face in his hands, and then lifting his face again, uttered a great cry.

"Betrayed! Deceived! Betrayed!" and turning, dashed madly away into the woods.

At first she did not dare to follow him, being afraid of his burning eyes and clutching hands. Then she grew anxious for him, and tried to trace where he had gone, but could not, although she knew the woods about as well as anyone could know them—but every way she went she found nothing but disappointment and frustration; and she began to recognise the signs of a stronger magic working against her. She gave it up, and went back to the farmstead.

# III

"Vivian," said Morgan two days later. Vivian did not reply—she could not yet bring herself to speak to Morgan.

"Vivian, I think you had better listen to what I have to say," Morgan persisted.

"Say on then."

"If you want to see your fine lover again, you'd better go to the foot of Chough's Crag. And go at once, before the tide comes in."

"What do you mean?"

"What I said."

"What have you done, Morgan you devil?"

"I? I've done nothing. Anything, that was done, he did himself—

Chough's Crag was known to the sisters—it was a high cliff above sea, with a sheer granite face, of terrifying height. Below it were jagged rocks at low tide, and at high tide deep swirling water.

Vivian left her horse tethered to a fence half a mile inland—nearer the sea was not safe—and hastened down by twisting paths to the rocky shore.

He was there. His body lay, shattered and twisted on the rocks, the dead face turned to the sky. But Vivian, with her clear-sight, could see the shadow-body of the man, standing upright above the earthly body. Tall, drooping and forlorn it stood, a dark and yet a tenuous shape—and as it looked at her, the eyes took fire, and glowed out like lamps. The woman in her mortal body, and the man in his ghost-body, confronted each other, and behind them the sun drew towards the west and the sea was reddening.

He moaned, and stretched his arms towards her.

"Lady, oh lady, I am so glad you have come. Oh, Lady Vivian, my love—my eyes are cleared, and now I know you told me the truth. I still love you—I love you more than ever. Stay with me now and do not leave me."

"I must not stay with you," she said, and her voice was choked with tears. "And you must not stay here. For I am still in the mortal body, but you are free from it, and must go yonder," and she pointed to the west. "Out there I can see gates, and there are helpers who wait for you."

"Where must I go?" he said, and his luminous spectral eyes were full of fear. "To Judgment—and to the flames of hell?"

"No, no, dear man. Judgment there must be, and payment no doubt, but not as you think. HE is very merciful. You need not be afraid. Look! The Presences in the west are kindly and helpful. Go on the shining path, and be happy."

"Then come with me. I will not go unless you do."

"But, dear man, I cannot come with you. I am in the body, and I have to stay in the body. You are out of the body, and you must go."

"I will not go without you."

"I have told you—I cannot come."

"I will not go from here."

"Oh, do not be so foolish! Can you not understand? Soon the tide will come in, and your poor bones that lie there will be overwhelmed by the waters. Then, either you will follow them, and be tossed to and fro without rest, or you will haunt here under the cliff, in darkness and misery, until you see reason and go on your way. Why must you make yourself a miserable wraith? Go in peace where they wait for you."

"Not without you," he said,

She considered, frowning, deeply troubled. Then at last she resolved what to do. Since an illusion had wrecked him, an illusion should save him.

She drew out one hair of her head—long and dark-reddish chestnut—and wincing a little from the pain, plucked it out. Then she held it before her, blowing in the wind. It took a shape, an outline—and as her thought worked upon it, the outline thickened and grew solid, until there stood there a simulacrum of herself, perfect in every detail—perfect down to the least roughness of a fingernail. It spoke in her voice, as she herself stepped back out of sight.

"Come then, my love," it said. "I will lead you on your way, and will not forsake you. Give me your hand and let us go into the Land of Light."

And the ghost-body of Torion put its hand trustfully into the hand of the simulacrum of Vivian. As the sun dipped, sending a long red path across the sea—they took the westward path. Far off, the real Vivian could see, against the sun, the pillars of a gate, and beyond them certain tall solemn presences. Torion would be safe.

The tide was coming in. She laid the limbs of Torion's earthly body straight and seemly, with his hands crossed over his breast, though she knew the sea would not leave them so for long—and she sprinkled sand for earth, and made the sign of the holy Cross over the body—but she knew that the man himself was elsewhere.

Then she went home in the twilight, and she wept bitterly as she rode.

# THE WINNING OF A SWORD

by Howard Pyle

*Howard Pyle (1853–1911), was an American writer and artist who established a reputation for his children's books which he both wrote and elaborately illustrated. These began with* The Merry Adventures of Robin Hood *in 1883. His best known books are the three inspired by the Arthurian legends:* The Story of King Arthur and His Knights *(1903),* The Story of the Champions of the Round Table *(1905) and* The Story of Sir Lancelot and His Companions *(1907). The following story about how Arthur finds his famous sword Excalibur, is taken from the first of these.*

## In the Valley of Delight

Now it fell upon a certain pleasant time in the Springtide season that King Arthur and his Court were making a royal progression through that part of Britain which lieth close to the Forests of the Usk. At that time the weather was exceedingly warm, and so the King and Court made pause within the forest under the trees in the cool and pleasant shade that the place afforded, and there the King rested for a while upon a couch of rushes spread with scarlet cloth.

27

And the knights then present at that Court were, Sir Gawaine, and Sir Ewaine, and Sir Kay, and Sir Pellias, and Sir Bedevere, and Sir Caradoc, and Sir Geraint, and Sir Bodwin of Britain and Sir Constantine of Cornwall, and Sir Brandiles and Sir Mador de la Porte, and there was not to be found anywhere in the world a company of such noble and exalted knights as these.

Now as the King lay drowsing and as these worthies sat holding cheerful converse together at that place, there came, of a sudden, a considerable bustle and stir upon the outskirts of the Court, and presently there appeared a very sad and woeful sight. For there came thitherward a knight, sore wounded, and upheld upon his horse by a golden-haired page, clad in an apparel of white and azure. And, likewise, the knight's apparel and the trappings of his horse were of white and azure, and upon his shield he bore the emblazonment of a single lily flower of silver upon a ground of pure azure.

But the knight was in a very woeful plight. For his face was as pale as wax and hung down upon his breast. And his eyes were glazed and saw naught that passed around him, and his fair apparel of white and blue was all red with the blood of life that ran from a great wound in his side. And, as they came upon their way, the young page lamented in such wise that it wrung the heart for to hear him.

Now, as these approached, King Arthur aroused cried out, "Alas! what doleful spectacle is that which I behold? Now hasten, ye my lords, and bring succor to yonder knight; and do thou, Sir Kay, go quickly and bring that fair young page hither that we may presently hear from his lips what mishap hath befallen his lord."

So certain of those knights hastened at the King's bidding and gave all succor to the wounded knight, and conveyed him to King Arthur's own pavilion, which had been pitched at a little distance. And when he had come there the King's chirurgeon presently attended upon him—albeit his wounds were of such a sort he might not hope to live for a very long while.

Meantime, Sir Kay brought that fair young page before the King, where he sat, and the King thought that he had hardly ever seen a more beautiful countenance. And the King said, "I prithee tell me, Sir Page, who is thy master, and how came he in such a sad and pitiable condition as that which we have just now beheld."

"That will I so, Lord," said the youth. "Know that my master is entitled Sir Myles of the White Fountain, and that he cometh from the country north of where we are and at a considerable distance from this. In that country he is the Lord of seven castles and several noble estates, wherefore, as thou mayst see, he is of considerable consequence. A fortnight ago (being doubtless moved thereunto by the lustiness of the Springtime), he set forth with only me for his esquire, for he had a mind to seek adventure in such manner as beseemed a good knight who would be errant. And we had several adventures, and in all of them my lord was entirely successful; for he overcame six knights at various places and sent them all to his castle for to attest his valor unto his lady.

"At last, this morning, coming to a certain place situated at a considerable distance from this, we came upon a fair castle of the forest, which stood in a valley surrounded by open spaces of level lawn, bedight with many flowers of divers sorts. There we beheld three fair damsels who tossed a golden ball from one to another, and the damsels were clad all in flame-colored satin, and their hair was of the color of gold. And as we drew nigh to them they stinted their play, and she who was the chief of those damsels called out to my lord, demanding of him whither he went and what was his errand.

"To her my lord made answer that he was errant and in search of adventure, and upon this, the three damsels laughed, and she who had first spoken said, 'An thou art in search of adventure, Sir Knight, happily I may be able to help thee to one that shall satisfy thee to thy heart's content.'

"Unto this my master made reply 'I prithee, fair damsel, tell me what that adventure may be so that I may presently assay it.'

"Thereupon this lady bade my master to take a certain path, and to follow the same for the distance of a league or a little more, and that he would then come to a bridge of stone that crossed a violent stream, and she assured him that there he might find adventure enough for to satisfy any man.

"So my master and I wended thitherward as that damoiselle had directed, and, by and by, we came unto the bridge whereof she had spoken. And, lo! beyond the bridge was a lonesome castle with a tall straight tower, and before the castle was a wide and level lawn of well-trimmed grass. And immediately beyond the bridge was an apple-tree hung over with a multitude of shields. And midway upon the bridge was a single shield, entirely of black; and beside it hung a hammer of brass; and beneath the shield was written these words in letters of red:

Whoso Smiteth This Shield
Doeth So At His Peril.

"Now, my master, Sir Myles, when he read those words went
straightway to that shield and, seizing the hammer that hung
beside it, he smote upon it a blow so that it rang like thunder.

"Thereupon, as in answer, the portcullis of the castle was let
fall, and there immediately came forth a knight, clad all from
head to foot in sable armor. And his apparel and the trappings of
his horse and all the appointments thereof were likewise entirely
of sable.

"Now when that Sable Knight perceived my master he came
riding swiftly across the meadow and so to the other end of the
bridge. And when he had come there he drew rein and saluted my
master and cried out, 'Sir Knight, I demand of thee why thou didst
smite that shield. Now let me tell thee, because of thy boldness,
I shall take away from thee thine own shield, and shall hang
it upon yonder apple-tree, where thou beholdest all those other
shields to be hanging.' Unto this my master made reply. 'That
thou shalt not do unless thou mayst overcome me, as knight to
knight.' And thereupon, immediately, he dressed his shield and
put himself into array for an assault at arms.

"So my master and this Sable Knight, having made themselves
ready for that encounter, presently drave together with might
and main. And they met in the middle of the course, where my
master's spear burst into splinters. But the spear of the Sable
Knight held and it pierced through Sir Myles, his shield, and it
penetrated his side, so that both he and his horse were overthrown
violently into the dust; he being wounded so grievously that he
could not arise again from the ground whereon he lay.

"Then the Sable Knight took my master's shield and hung it
up in the branches of the apple-tree where the other shields
were hanging, and, thereupon, without paying further heed
to my master, or inquiring as to his hurt, he rode away into
his castle again, whereof the portcullis was immediately closed
behind him.

"So, after that he had gone, I got my master to his horse with
great labor, and straightway took him thence, not knowing where
I might find harborage for him, until I came to this place. And
that, my lord King, is the true story of how my master came by
that mortal hurt which he hath suffered."

"Ha! By the glory of Paradise!" cried King Arthur, "I do
consider it great shame that in my Kingdom and so near to my

Court strangers should be so discourteously treated as Sir Myles hath been served. For it is certainly a discourtesy for to leave a fallen knight upon the ground, without tarrying to inquire as to his hurt how grievous it may be. And still more discourteous is it for to take away the shield of a fallen knight who hath done good battle."

And so did all the knights of the King's Court exclaim against the discourtesy of that Sable Knight.

Then there came forth a certain esquire attendant upon the King's person, by name Griflet, who was much beloved by his Royal Master, and he kneeled before the King and cried out in a loud voice: "I crave a boon of thee, my lord King! and do beseech thee that thou wilt grant it unto me!"

Then King Arthur uplifted his countenance upon the youth as he knelt before him and he said, "Ask, Griflet, and thy boon shall be granted unto thee."

Thereupon Griflet said, "It is this that I would ask—I crave that thou wilt make me straightway knight, and that thou wilt let me go forth and endeavor to punish this unkindly knight, by overthrowing him, and so redeeming those shields which he hath hung upon that apple-tree."

Then was King Arthur much troubled in his spirit, for Griflet was as yet only an esquire and altogether untried in arms. So he said, "Behold, thou art yet too young to have to do with so potent a knight as this sable champion must be, who has thus overthrown so many knights without himself suffering any mishap. I prithee, dear Griflet, consider and ask some other boon."

But young Griflet only cried the more, "A boon! A boon! and thou hast granted it unto me."

Thereupon King Arthur said, "Thou shalt have thy boon, though my heart much misgiveth me that thou wilt suffer great ill and misfortune from this adventure."

So that night Griflet kept watch upon his armor in a chapel of the forest, and, in the morning, having received the Sacrament, he was created a knight by the hand of King Arthur—and it was not possible for any knight to have greater honor than that. Then King Arthur fastened the golden spurs to Sir Griflet's heels with his own hand.

So Griflet was made a knight, and having mounted his charger, he rode straightway upon his adventure, much rejoicing and singing for pure pleasure.

And it was at this time that Sir Myles died of his hurt, for it is often so that death and misfortune befall some, whiles others laugh and sing for hope and joy, as though such grievous things as sorrow and death could never happen in the world wherein they live.

Now that afternoon King Arthur sat waiting with great anxiety for word of that young knight, but there was no word until toward evening, when there came hurrying to him certain of his attendants, proclaiming that Sir Griflet was returning, but without his shield, and in such guise that it seemed as though a great misfortune had befallen him. And straightway thereafter came Sir Griflet himself, sustained upon his horse on the one hand by Sir Constantine and upon the other by Sir Brandiles. And, lo! Sir Griflet's head hung down upon his breast, and his fair new armor was all broken and stained with blood and dust. And so woeful was he of appearance that King Arthur's heart was contracted with sorrow to behold that young knight in so pitiable a condition.

So, at King Arthur's bidding, they conducted Sir Griflet to the Royal Pavilion, and there they laid him down upon a soft couch. Then the King's chirurgeon searched his wounds and found that the head of a spear and a part of the shaft thereof were still piercing Sir Griflet's side, so that he was in most woeful and grievous pain.

And when King Arthur beheld in what a parlous state Sir Griflet lay he cried out, "Alas! my dear young knight, what hath happened to thee to bring thee unto such a woeful condition as this which I behold?"

Then Sir Griflet, speaking in a very weak voice, told King Arthur how he had fared. And he said that he had proceeded through the forest, until he had discovered the three beautiful damsels whereof the page of Sir Myles had spoken. And he said that these damsels had directed him as to the manner in which he should pursue his adventure. And he said that he had found the bridge whereon hung the shield and the brazen mall, and that he had there beheld the apple-tree hung full of shields; and he said that he smote the shield of the Sable Knight with the brazen mall, and that the Sable Knight had thereupon come riding out against him. And he said that this knight did not appear of a mind to fight with him; instead, he cried out to him with a great deal of nobleness that he was too young and too untried in arms to have to do with a seasoned knight; wherefore he advised Sir Griflet to withdraw him from that adventure ere it was too late. But, notwithstanding this advice, Sir Griflet would not withdraw but declared that he would certainly have to do with that other knight in sable. Now at the very first onset Sir Griflet's spear had burst into pieces, but the spear of the Sable Knight had held and had pierced through Sir Griflet's shield and into his side, causing him this grievous wound whereof he suffered. And Sir Griflet said that the Sable Knight had then, most courteously, uplifted him upon his horse again (albeit he had kept Sir Griflet's shield and had hung it upon the tree with those others that hung there) and had then directed him upon his way, so that he had made shift to ride thither, though with great pain and dole.

Then was King Arthur very wode and greatly disturbed in his mind, for indeed he loved Sir Griflet exceedingly well. Wherefore he declared that he himself would now go forth for to punish that Sable Knight, and for to humble him with his own hand. And, though the knights of his Court strove to dissuade him from that adventure, yet he declared that he with his own hand would accomplish that proud knight's humiliation, and that he would undertake the adventure, with God His Grace, upon the very next day.

And so disturbed was he that he could scarce eat his food that evening for vexation, nor would he go to his couch to sleep, but, having inquired very narrowly of Sir Griflet where he might find that valley of flowers and those three damsels, he spent the night in walking up and down his pavilion, awaiting for the dawning of the day.

Now, as soon as the birds first began to chirp and the east to brighten with the coming of the daylight, King Arthur summoned his two esquires, and, having with their aid donned his armor and mounted a milk-white war-horse, he presently took his departure upon that adventure which he had determined upon.

And, indeed it is a very pleasant thing for to ride forth in the dawning of a Springtime day. For then the little birds do sing their sweetest song, all joining in one joyous medley, whereof one may scarce tell one note from another, so multitudinous is that pretty roundelay; then do the growing things of the earth smell the sweetest in the freshness of the early daytime—the fair flowers, the shrubs, and the blossoms upon the trees; then doth the dew bespangle all the sward as with an incredible multitude of jewels of various colors; then is all the world sweet and clean and new, as though it had been fresh created for him who came to roam abroad so early in the morning.

So King Arthur's heart expanded with great joy, and he chanted a quaint song as he rode through the forest upon the quest of that knightly adventure.

So, about noon-tide, he came to that part of the forest lands whereof he had heard those several times before. For of a sudden, he discovered before him a wide and gently sloping valley, a-down which ran a stream as bright as silver. And, lo! the valley was strewn all over with an infinite multitude of fair and fragrant flowers of divers sorts. And in the midst of the valley there stood a comely castle, with tall red roofs and many bright windows, so that it seemed to King Arthur that it was a very fine castle indeed. And upon a smooth green lawn he perceived those three damoiselles clad in flame-colored satin of whom the page of Sir Myles and Sir Griflet had spoken. And they played at ball with a golden ball, and the hair of each was of the hue of gold, and it seemed to King Arthur, as he drew nigh, that they were the most beautiful damoiselles that he had ever beheld in all of his life.

Now as King Arthur came unto them the three ceased tossing the ball, and she who was the fairest of all damoiselles demanded of him whither he went and upon what errand he was bound.

Then King Arthur made reply: "Ha! fair lady! whither should a belted knight ride upon such a day as this, and upon what business, other than the search of adventure such as beseemeth a knight of a proper strength of heart and frame who would be errant?"

Then the three damoiselles smiled upon the King, for he was exceedingly comely of face and they liked him very well. "Alas, Sir Knight!" said she who had before spoken, "I prithee be in no such haste to undertake a dangerous adventure, but rather tarry with us for a day or two or three, for to feast and make merry with us. For surely good cheer doth greatly enlarge the heart, and we would fain enjoy the company of so gallant a knight as thou appearest to be. Yonder castle is ours and all this gay valley is ours, and those who have visited it are pleased, because of its joyousness, to call it the Valley of Delight. So tarry with us for a little and be not in such haste to go forward."

"Nay," said King Arthur, "I may not tarry with ye, fair ladies, for I am bent upon an adventure of which ye may wot right well, when I tell ye that I seek that Sable Knight, who hath overcome so many other knights and hath taken away their shields. So I do pray ye of your grace for to tell me where I may find him."

"Grace of Heaven!" cried she who spake for the others, "this is certainly a sorry adventure which ye seek, Sir Knight! For already, in these two days, have two knights assayed with that knight, and both have fallen into great pain and disregard. Ne'theless, an thou wilt undertake this peril, yet shalt thou not go until thou hast eaten and refreshed thyself." So saying, she lifted a little ivory whistle that hung from her neck by a chain of gold, and blew upon it very shrilly.

In answer to this summons there came forth from the castle three fair young pages, clad all in flame-colored raiment, bearing among them a silver table covered with a white napkin. And after them came five other pages of the same appearance, bearing flagons of white wine and red, dried fruits and comfits and manchets of white fair bread.

Then King Arthur descended from his war-horse with great gladness, for he was both hungry and athirst, and, seating himself at the table with the damsels beside him, he ate with great enjoyment, discoursing pleasantly the while with those fair ladies, who listened to him with great cheerfulness of spirit. Yet he told them not who he was, though they greatly marvelled who might be the noble warrior who had come thus into that place.

So, having satisfied his hunger and his thirst, King Arthur mounted his steed again, and the three damsels conducted him across the valley a little way—he riding upon his horse and they walking beside him. So, by and by, he perceived where was a dark pathway that led into the farther side of the forest land; and when he had come thither the lady who had addressed him before said to him, "Yonder is the way that thou must take an thou wouldst enter upon this adventure. So fare thee well, and may good hap go with thee, for, certes, thou art the Knight most pleasant of address who hath come hitherward for this long time."

Thereupon King Arthur, having saluted those ladies right courteously, rode away with very great joy of that pleasant adventure through which he had thus passed.

Now when King Arthur had gone some ways he came, by and by, to a certain place where charcoal burners plied their trade. For here were many mounds of earth, all a-smoke with the smouldering logs within, whilst all the air was filled with the smell of the dampened fires.

As the King approached this spot, he presently beheld that something was toward that was sadly amiss. For, in the open clearing, he beheld three sooty fellows with long knives in their hands, who pursued one old man, whose beard was as white as snow. And he beheld that the reverend old man, who was clad richly in black, and whose horse stood at a little distance, was

running hither and thither, as though to escape from those wicked
men, and he appeared to be very hard pressed and in great danger
of his life.

"Pardee!" quoth the young King to himself, "here, certes, is
one in sore need of succor." Whereupon he cried out in a great
voice, "Hold, villains! What would you be at!" and therewith
set spurs to his horse and dropped his spear into rest and drove
down upon them with a noise like to thunder for loudness.

But when the three wicked fellows beheld the armed Knight
thus thundering down upon them, they straightway dropped their
knives and, with loud outcries of fear, ran away hither and thither
until they had escaped into the thickets of the forest, where one
upon a horse might not hope to pursue them.

Whereupon, having driven away those wicked fellows, King
Arthur rode up to him whom he had succored, thinking to
offer him condolence. And behold! when he had come nigh
to him, he perceived that the old man was the Enchanter
Merlin. Yet whence he had so suddenly come, who had only
a little while before been at the King's Court at Carleon,
and what he did in that place, the King could in no wise
understand. Wherefore he bespoke the Enchanter in this wise,
"Ha! Merlin, it seemeth to me that I have saved thy life.
For, surely, thou hadst not escaped from the hands of those
wicked men had I not happened to come hitherward at this
time."

"Dost thou think so, Lord?" said Merlin. "Now let me
tell thee that I did maybe appear to be in danger, yet I
might have saved myself very easily had I been of a mind
to do so. But, as thou sawst me in this seeming peril, so
may thou know that a real peril, far greater than this, lieth
before thee, and there will be no errant knight to succor thee
from it. Wherefore, I pray thee, Lord, for to take me with
thee upon this adventure that thou art set upon, for I do
tell thee that thou shalt certainly suffer great dole and pain
therein."

"Merlin," said King Arthur, "even an I were to face my
death, yet would I not turn back from this adventure. But
touching the advice thou givest me, meseems it will be very
well to take thee with me if such peril lieth before me as thou
sayest."

And Merlin said, "Yea, it would be very well for thee to
do so."

So Merlin mounted upon his palfrey, and King Arthur and he

betook their way from that place in pursuit of that adventure which the King had undertaken to perform.

## The Battle with the Sable-Knight.

King Arthur and Merlin rode together through the forest for a considerable while, until they perceived that they must be approaching nigh to the place where dwelt the Sable Knight whom the King sought so diligently. For the forest, which had till then been altogether a wilderness, very deep and mossy, began to show an aspect more thin and open, as though a dwelling-place of mankind was close at hand.

And, after a little, they beheld before them a violent stream of water, that rushed through a dark and dismal glen. And, likewise, they perceived that across this stream of water there was a bridge of stone, and that upon the other side of the bridge there was a smooth and level lawn of green grass, whereon Knights-contestants might joust very well. And beyond this lawn they beheld a tall and forbidding castle, with smooth walls and a straight tower; and this castle was built upon the rocks so that it appeared to be altogether a part of the stone. So they wist that this must be the castle whereof the page and Sir Griflet had spoken.

For, midway upon the bridge, they beheld that there hung a sable shield and a brass mall exactly as the page and Sir Griflet had said; and that upon the farther side of the stream was an apple-tree, amid the leaves of which hung a very great many shields of various devices, exactly as those two had reported: and they beheld that some of those shields were clean and fair, and that some were foul and stained with blood, and that some were smooth and unbroken, and that some were cleft as though by battle of knight with knight. And all those shields were the shields of different knights whom the Sable Knight, who dwelt within the castle, had overthrown in combat with his own hand.

"Splendor of Paradise!" quote King Arthur, "that must, indeed, be a right valiant knight who, with his own single strength, hath overthrown and cast down so many other knights. For, indeed, Merlin, there must be an hundred shields hanging in yonder tree!"

Unto this Merlin made reply, "And thou, Lord, mayst be very happy an thy shield, too, hangeth not there ere the sun goeth down this even-tide."

"That," said King Arthur, with a very steadfast countenance "shall be as God willeth. For, certes, I have a greater mind than ever for to try my power against yonder knight. For, consider, what especial honor would fall to me should I overcome so valiant a warrior as this same Sable Champion appeareth to be, seeing that he hath been victorious over so many other good knights."

Thereupon, having so spoken his mind, King Arthur immediately pushed forward his horse and so, coming upon the bridge, he clearly read that challenge writ in letters of red beneath the shield:

> Whoso Smiteth This Shield
> Doeth So At His Peril.

Upon reading these words, the King seized the brazen mall, and smote that shield so violent a blow that the sound thereof echoed back from the smooth walls of the castle, and from the rocks whereon it stood, and from the skirts of the forest around about, as though twelve other shields had been struck in those several places.

And in answer to that sound, the portcullis of the castle was immediately let fall, and there issued forth a knight, very huge of frame, and clad all in sable armor. And, likewise, all of his apparel and all the trappings of his horse were entirely of sable, so that he presented a most grim and forbidding aspect. And this Sable Knight came across that level meadow of smooth grass with a very stately and honorable gait; for neither did he ride in haste, nor did he ride slowly, but with great pride and haughtiness of mien, as became a champion who, haply, had never yet been overcome in battle. So, reaching the bridge-head, he drew rein and saluted King Arthur with great dignity, and also right haughtily. "Ha! Sir Knight!" quoth he, "why didst thou, having read those words yonder inscribed, smite upon my shield? Now I do tell thee that, for thy discourtesy, I shall presently take thy shield away from thee, and shall hang it up upon yonder apple-tree where thou beholdest all those other shields to be hanging. Wherefore, either deliver thou thy shield unto me without more ado or else prepare for to defend it with thy person—in the which event thou shalt certainly suffer great pain and discomfort to thy body."

"Gramercy for the choice thou grantest me," said King Arthur. "But as for taking away my shield—I do believe that that shall be as Heaven willeth, and not as thou willest. Know, thou unkind knight, that I have come hither for no other purpose than to do battle with thee and so to endeavor for to redeem with my person all those shields that hang yonder upon that apple-tree. So make thou ready straightway that I may have to do with thee, maybe to thy great disadvantage."

"That will I so," replied the Sable Knight. And thereupon he turned his horse's head and, riding back a certain distance across the level lawn, he took stand in such place as appeared to him to be convenient. And so did King Arthur ride forth also upon that lawn, and take his station as seemed to him to be convenient.

Then each knight dressed his spear and his shield for the encounter, and, having thus made ready for the assault, each shouted to his war-horse and drave his spurs deep into its flank.

Then those two noble steeds rushed forth like lightning, coursing across the ground with such violent speed that the earth trembled and shook beneath them, an it were by cause of an earthquake. So those two knights met fairly in the midst of the centre of the field, crashing together like a thunderbolt. And so violently did they smite the one against the other that the spears burst into splinters, even unto the guard and the truncheon thereof, and the horses of the riders staggered back from the onset, so that only because of the extraordinary address of the knights-rider did they recover from falling before that shock of meeting.

But, with great spirit, these two knights uplifted each his horse with his own spirit, and so completed his course in safety.

And indeed King Arthur was very much amazed that he had not overthrown his opponent, for, at that time, as aforesaid, he was considered to be the very best knight and the one best approved in deeds of arms that lived in all of Britain. Wherefore he marvelled at the power and the address of that knight against whom he had driven, that he had not been overthrown by the greatness of the blow that had been delivered against his defences. So, when they met again in the midst of the field, King Arthur gave that knight greeting, and bespoke him with great courtesy, addressing him in this wise: "Sir Knight, I know not who thou art, but I do pledge my knightly word that thou art the most potent knight that ever I have met in all of my life. Now I do bid thee get down straightway from thy horse, and let us two fight this battle with sword and upon foot, for it were pity to let it end in this way."

"Not so," quote the Sable Knight—"not so, nor until one of us twain be overthrown will I so contest this battle upon foot." And upon this he shouted, "Ho! Ho!" in a very loud voice, and straightway thereupon the gateway of the castle opened and there came running forth two tall esquires clad all in black, pied with crimson. And each of these esquires bare in his hand a great spear of ash-wood, new and well-seasoned, and never yet strained in battle.

So King Arthur chose one of these spears and the Sable Knight took the other, and thereupon each returned to that station wherefrom he had before essayed the encounter.

Then once again each knight rushed his steed to the assault, and once again did each smite so fairly in the midst of the defence of the other that the spears were splintered, so that only the guard and the truncheon thereof remained in the grasp of the knight who held it.

Then, as before, King Arthur would have fought the battle out with swords and upon foot, but again the Sable Knight would not have it so, but called aloud upon those within the castle, whereupon there immediately came forth two other esquires with fresh, new spears of ash-wood. So each knight again took him a spear, and having armed himself therewith, chose each his station upon that fair, level lawn of grass.

And now, for the third time, having thus prepared themselves thereof assault, those two excellent knights hurled themselves together in furious assault. And now, as twice before, did King Arthur strike the Sable Knight so fairly in the centre of his defence that the spear which he held was burst into splinters. But this time, the spear of the Sable Knight did not so break in that manner, but held; and so violent was the blow that he delivered upon King Arthur's shield that he pierced through the centre of it. Then the girths of the King's saddle burst apart by that great, powerful blow, and both he and his steed were cast violently backward. So King Arthur might have been overcast, had he not voided his saddle with extraordinary skill and knightly address, wherefore, though his horse was overthrown, he himself still held his footing and did not fall into the dust. Ne'theless, so violent was the blow that he received that, for a little space, he was altogether bereft of his senses so that everything whirled around before his eyes.

But when his sight returned to him he was filled with an anger so vehement that it appeared to him as though all the blood in his heart rushed into his brains so that he saw naught but red, as of blood, before his eyes. And when this also had passed he perceived the Sable Knight that he sat his horse at no great distance. Then immediately King Arthur ran to him and catching the bridle-rein of his horse, he cried out aloud unto that Sable Knight with great violence: "Come down, thou black knight! and fight me upon foot and with thy sword."

"That will I not do," said the Sable Knight, "for, lo! I have overthrown thee. Wherefore deliver thou to me thy shield, that I may hang it upon yonder apple-tree, and go thy way as others have done before thee."

"That will I not!" cried King Arthur, with exceeding passion, "neither will I yield myself nor go hence until either thou or I have altogether conquered the other." Thereupon he thrust the horse of the Sable Knight backward by the bridle-rein so vehemently, that the other was constrained to void his saddle to save himself from being overthrown upon the ground.

And now each knight was as entirely furious as the other, wherefore, each drew his sword and dressed his shield, and thereupon rushed together like two wild bulls in battle. They foined, they smote, they traced, they parried, they struck again and again, and the sound of their blows, crashing and clashing the one upon the other, filled the entire surrounding space with an extraordinary uproar. Nor may any man altogether conceive of the entire fury of that encounter, for, because of the violence of the blows which the one delivered upon the other, whole cantels of armor were hewn from their bodies and many deep and grievous wounds were given and received, so that the armor of each was altogether stained with red because of the blood that flowed down upon it.

At last King Arthur, waxing, as it were, entirely mad, struck so fierce a blow that no armor could have withstood that stroke had it fallen fairly upon it. But it befell with that stroke that his sword broke at the hilt and the blade thereof flew into three several pieces into the air. Yet was the stroke so wonderfully fierce that the Sable Knight groaned, and staggered, and ran about in a circle as though he had gone blind and knew not whither to direct his steps.

But presently he recovered himself again, and perceiving King Arthur standing near by, and not knowing that his enemy had now no sword for to defend himself withal, he cast aside his shield and took his own sword into both hands, and therewith smote so dolorous a stroke that he crave through King Arthur's shield and through his helmet and even to the bone of his brain-pan.

Then King Arthur thought that he had received his death-wound, for his brains swam like water, his thighs trembled exceedingly, and he sank down to his knees, whilst the blood and sweat, commingled together in the darkness of his helmet, flowed down into his eyes in a lather and blinded him. Thereupon, seeing him thus grievously hurt, the Sable Knight called upon him with great vehemence for to yield himself and to surrender his shield, because he was now too sorely wounded for to fight any more.

But King Arthur would not yield himself, but catching the other by the sword-belt, he lifted himself to his feet. Then, being in a manner recovered from his amazement, he embraced the other with both arms, and placing his knee behind the thigh of the Sable Knight, he cast him backward down upon the ground so violently that the sound of the fall was astounding to hear. And with that fall the Sable Knight was, awhile, entirely bereft of consciousness. Then King Arthur straightway unlaced the helm of the Sable Knight and so beheld his face, and he knew him in spite of the blood that still ran down his own countenance in great quantities, and he knew that knight was King Pellinore, who had twice warred against King Arthur.

Now when King Arthur beheld whom it was against whom he had done battle, he cried out aloud, "Ha! Pellinore, is it then thou? Now yield thee to me, for thou art entirely at my mercy." And upon this he drew his misericordia and set the point thereof at King Pellinore's throat.

But by now King Pellinore had greatly recovered from his fall, and perceiving that the blood was flowing down in great measure from out his enemy's helmet, he wist that that other must have been very sorely wounded by the blow which he had just now received. Wherefore he catched King Arthur's wrist in his hand and directed the point of the dagger away from his own throat so that no great danger threatened therefrom.

And, indeed, what with his sore wound and with the loss of blood, King Arthur was now fallen exceedingly sick and faint, so that it appeared to him that he was nigh to death. Accordingly, it was with no very great ado that King Pellinore suddenly heaved himself up from the ground and so overthrew his enemy that King Arthur was now underneath his knees.

And by this King Pellinore was exceedingly mad with the fury of the sore battle he had fought. For he was so enraged that his eyes were all beshot with blood like those of a wild boar, and a froth, like the champings of a wild boar, stood in the beard about his lips. Wherefore he wrenched the dagger out of his enemy's hand, and immediately began to unlace his helm, with intent to slay him where he lay. But at this moment Merlin came in great haste, crying out, "Stay! stay! Sir Pellinore; what would you be at? Stay your sacrilegious hand! For he who lieth beneath you is none other than Arthur, King of all this realm!"

At this King Pellinore was astonished beyond measure. And for a little he was silent, and then after a while he cried out in a very loud voice, "Say you so, old man? Then verily your words have doomed this man unto death. For no one in all this world hath ever suffered such ill and such wrongs as I have suffered at his hands. For, lo! he hath taken from me power, and kingship, and honors, and estates, and hath left me only this gloomy, dismal castle of the forest as an abiding-place. Wherefore, seeing that he is thus in my power, he shall now presently die; if for no other reason than because if I now let him go free, he will certainly revenge himself when he shall have recovered from all the ill he hath suffered at my hands."

Then Merlin said, "Not so! He shall not die at thy hands, for I, myself, shall save him." Whereupon he uplifted his staff and smote King Pellinore across the shoulders. Then immediately King Pellinore fell down and lay upon the ground on his face like one who had suddenly gone dead.

Upon this, King Arthur uplifted himself upon his elbow and beheld his enemy lying there as though dead, and he cried out, "Ha! Merlin! what is this that thou hast done? I am very sorry, for I do perceive that thou, by thy arts of magic, hath slain one of the best knights in all the world."

"Not so, my lord King!" said Merlin; "for, in sooth, I tell thee that thou art far nigher to thy death than he. For he is but in sleep and will soon awaken; but thou art in such a case that it would take only a very little for to cause thee to die."

And indeed King Arthur was exceeding sick, even to the heart, with the sore wound he had received, so that it was only with much ado that Merlin could help him up upon his horse. Having done the which and having hung the King's shield upon the horn of his saddle, Merlin straightway conveyed the wounded man thence across the bridge, and, leading the horse by the bridle, so took him away into the forest.

Now I must tell you that there was in that part of the forest a certain hermit so holy that the wild birds of the woodland would come and rest upon his hand whiles he read his breviary; and so sanctified was he in gentleness that the wild does would come even to the door of his hermitage, and there stand whilst he milked them for his refreshment. And this hermit dwelt in that part of the forest so remote from the habitations of man that when he rang the bell for matins or for vespers, there was hardly ever

anyone to hear the sound thereof excepting the wild creatures
that dwelt thereabout. Yet, ne'theless, to this remote and lonely
place royal folk and others of high degree would sometimes come,
as though on a pilgrimage, because of the hermit's exceeding
saintliness.

So Merlin conveyed King Arthur unto this sanctuary, and,
having reached that place, he and the hermit lifted the wounded
man down from his saddle—the hermit giving many words of
pity and sorrow—and together they conveyed him into the holy
man's cell. There they laid him upon a couch of moss and unlaced
his armor and searched his wounds and bathed them with pure
water and dressed his hurts, for that hermit was a very skilful
leech. So for all that day and part of the next, King Arthur lay
upon the hermit's pallet like one about to die; for he beheld
all things about him as though through thin water, and the
breath hung upon his lips and fluttered, and he could not even
lift his head from the pallet because of the weakness that lay
upon him.

Now upon the afternoon of the second day there fell a great
noise and tumult in that part of the forest. For it happened
that the Lady Guinevere of Cameliard, together with her Court,
both of ladies and of knights, had come upon a pilgrimage
to that holy man, the fame of whose saintliness had reached
even unto the place where she dwelt. For that lady had a
favorite page who was very sick of a fever, and she trusted
that the holy man might give her some charm or amulet
by the virtue of which he might haply be cured. Wherefore
she had come to that place with her entire Court so that
all that part of the forest was made gay with fine raiment
and the silence thereof was made merry with the sound of
talk and laughter and the singing of songs and the chattering
of many voices and the neighing of horses. And the Lady
Guinevere rode in the midst of her damsels and her Court,
and her beauty outshone the beauty of her damsels as the
splendor of the morning star outshines that of all the lesser
stars that surround it. For then and afterward she was held
by all the Courts of Chivalry to be the most beautiful lady in
the world.

Now when the Lady Guinevere had come to that place, she
perceived the milk-white war-horse of King Arthur where it
stood cropping the green grass of the open glade nigh to the
hermitage. And likewise she perceived Merlin, where he stood
beside the door of the cell. So of him she demanded whose

was that noble war-horse that stood browsing upon the grass at that lonely place, and who was it that lay within that cell. And unto her Merlin made answer, "Lady, he who lieth within is a knight, very sorely wounded, so that he is sick nigh unto death!"

"Pity of Heaven!" cried the Lady Guinevere. "What a sad thing is this that thou tellest me! Now I do beseech thee to lead me presently unto that knight that I may behold him. For I have in my Court a very skilful leech, who is well used to the cure of hurts such as knights receive in battle."

So Merlin brought the lady into the cell, and there she beheld King Arthur where he lay stretched upon the pallet. And she wist not who he was. Yet it appeared to her that in all her life she had not beheld so noble appearing a knight as he who lay sorely wounded in that lonely place. And King Arthur cast his looks upward to where she stood beside his bed of pain, surrounded by her maidens, and in the great weakness that lay upon him he wist not whether she whom he beheld was a mortal lady or whether she was not rather some tall straight angel who had descended from one of the Lordly Courts of Paradise for to visit him in his pain and distresses. And the Lady Guinevere was filled with a great pity at beholding King Arthur's sorrowful estate. Wherefore she called to her that skilful leech who was with her Court. And she bade him bring a certain alabaster box of exceedingly precious balsam. And she commanded him for to search that knight's wounds and to anoint them with the balsam, so that he might be healed of his hurts with all despatch.

So that wise and skilful leech did according to the Lady Guinevere's commands, and immediately King Arthur felt entire ease of all his aches and great content of spirit. And when the Lady and her Court had departed, he found himself much uplifted in heart, and three days thereafter he was entirely healed and was as well and strong and lusty as ever he had been in all of his life.

And this was the first time that King Arthur ever beheld that beautiful lady, the Lady Guinevere of Cameliard, and from that time forth he never forgot her, but she was almost always present in his thoughts. Wherefore, when he was recovered he said thus to himself: "I will forget that I am a king and I will cherish the thought of this lady and will serve her faithfully as a good knight may serve his chosen dame."

## Excalibur the Sword

Now, as soon as King Arthur had, by means of that extraordinary balsam, been thus healed of those grievous wounds which he had received in his battle with King Pellinore, he found himself to be moved by a most vehement desire to meet his enemy again for to try issue of battle with him once more, and so recover the credit which he had lost in that combat. Now, upon the morning of the fourth day, being entirely cured, and having broken his fast, he walked for refreshment beside the skirts of the forest, listening the while to the cheerful sound of the wood-birds singing their matins, all with might and main. And Merlin walked beside him, and King Arthur spake his mind to Merlin concerning his intent to engage once more in knightly contest with King Pellinore. And he said, "Merlin, it doth vex me very sorely for to have come off so ill in my late encounter with King Pellinore. Certes, he is the very best knight in all the world whom I have ever yet encountered. Ne'theless, it might have fared differently with me had I not broken my sword, and so left myself altogether defenceless in that respect. Howsoever that may be, I am of a mind for to assay this adventure once more, and so will I do as immediately as may be."

Thereunto Merlin made reply, "Thou art, assuredly, a very brave man to have so much appetite for battle, seeing how nigh thou camest unto thy death not even four days ago. Yet how mayst thou hope to undertake this adventure without due preparation? For, lo! thou hast no sword, nor hast thou a spear, nor hast thou even thy misericordia for to do battle withal. How then mayst thou hope for to assay this adventure?"

And King Arthur said, "That I know not, nevertheless I will presently seek for some weapon as soon as may be. For, even an I have no better weapon than an oaken cudgel, yet would I assay this battle again with so poor a tool as that."

"Ha! Lord," said Merlin, "I do perceive that thou art altogether fixed in thy purpose for to renew this quarrel. Wherefore, I will not seek to stay thee therefrom, but will do all that in me lies for to aid thee in thy desires. Now to this end I must tell thee that in one part of this forest (which is, indeed, a very strange place) there is a certain woodland sometimes called Arroy, and other times called the Forest of Adventure. For no knight ever entereth therein but some adventure befalleth him. And close to Arroy is a land of enchantment which has several times been seen. And that is a very wonderful land, for there is in it a wide and considerable lake, which is also of enchantment. And in the centre of that lake there hath for some time been seen the appearance as of a woman's arm—exceedingly beautiful and clad in white samite, and the hand of this arm holdeth a sword of such exceeding excellence and beauty that no eye hath ever beheld its like. And the name of this sword is Excalibur—it being so named by those who have beheld it because of its marvellous brightness and beauty. For it hath come to pass that several knights have already seen that sword and have endeavored to obtain it for their own, but, heretofore, no one hath been able to touch it, and many have lost their lives in that adventure. For when any man draweth near unto it, either he sinks into the lake, or else the arm disappeareth entirely, or else it is withdrawn beneath the lake; wherefore no man hath ever been able to obtain the possession of that sword. Now I am able to conduct thee unto that Lake of Enchantment, and there thou mayst see Excalibur with thine own eyes. Then when thou hast seen him thou mayst, haply, have the desire to obtain him; which, an thou art able to do, thou wilt have a sword very fitted for to do battle with."

"Merlin," quoth the King, "this is a very strange thing which thou tellest me. Now I am desirous beyond measure for to attempt to obtain this sword for mine own, wherefore I do beseech thee to lead me with all despatch to this enchanted lake whereof thou tellest me." And Merlin said, "I will do so."

So that morning King Arthur and Merlin took leave of that holy hermit (the King having kneeled in the grass to receive his benediction), and so, departing from that place, they entered the deeper forest once more, betaking their way to that part which was known as Arroy.

And after awhile they came to Arroy, and it was about noon-tide. And when they had entered into those woodlands they came to a certain little open place, and in that place they beheld a white doe with a golden collar about its neck. And King Arthur said, "Look, Merlin, yonder is a wonderful sight." And Merlin said, "Let us follow that doe." And upon this the doe turned and they followed it. And by and by in following it they came to an opening in the trees where was a little lawn of sweet soft grass. Here they beheld a bower and before the bower

was a table spread with a fair snow-white cloth, and set with
refreshments of white bread, wine, and meats of several sorts.
And at the door of this bower there stood a page, clad all in
green, and his hair was as black as ebony, and his eyes as black as
jet and exceeding bright. And when this page beheld King Arthur
and Merlin, he gave them greeting, and welcomed the King very
pleasantly saying, "Ha! King Arthur, thou art welcome to this
place. Now I prithee dismount and refresh thyself before going
farther."

Then was King Arthur a-doubt as to whether there might not
be some enchantment in this for to work him an ill, for he was
astonished that that page in the deep forest should know him so
well. But Merlin bade him have good cheer, and he said, "Indeed,
Lord, thou mayst freely partake of that refreshment which, I may
tell thee, was prepared especially for thee. Moreover in this thou
mayst foretell a very happy issue unto this adventure."

So King Arthur sat down to the table with great comfort of
heart (for he was an hungered) and that page and another like
unto him ministered unto his needs, serving him all the food upon
silver plates, and all the wine in golden goblets as he was used to
being served in his own court—only that those things were much
more cunningly wrought and fashioned, and were more beautiful
than the table furniture of the King's court.

Then, after he had eaten his fill and had washed his hands from
a silver basin which the first page offered to him, and had wiped
his hands upon a fine linen napkin which the other page brought
unto him, and after Merlin had also refreshed himself, they went
their way, greatly rejoicing at this pleasant adventure, which, it
seemed to the King, could not but betoken a very good issue to
his undertaking.

Now about the middle of the afternoon King Arthur and
Merlin came, of a sudden, out from the forest and upon a fair
and level plain, bedight all over with such a number of flowers
that no man could conceive of their quantity nor of the beauty
thereof.

And this was a very wonderful land, for, lo! all the air appeared
as it were to be as of gold—so bright was it and so singularly
radiant. And here and there upon that plain were sundry trees
all in blossom; and the fragrance of the blossoms was so sweet
that the King had never smelt any fragrance like to it. And in
the branches of those trees were a multitude of birds of many
colors, and the melody of their singing ravished the heart of the

hearer. And midway in the plain was a lake of water as bright as silver, and all around the borders of the lake were incredible numbers of lilies and of daffodils. Yet, although this place was so exceedingly fair, there was, nevertheless, nowhere about it a single sign of human life of any sort, but it appeared altogether as lonely as the hollow sky upon a day of summer. So, because of all the marvellous beauty of this place, and because of its strangeness and its entire solitude, King Arthur perceived that he must have come into a land of powerful enchantment where, happily, dwelt a fairy of very exalted quality; wherefore his spirit was enwrapped in a manner of fear, as he pushed his great milk-white war-horse through that long fair grass, all bedight with flowers, and he wist not what strange things were about to befall him.

So when he had come unto the margin of the lake he beheld there the miracle that Merlin had told him of aforetime. For, lo! in the midst of the expanse of water there was the appearance of a fair and beautiful arm, as of a woman, clad all in white samite. And the arm was encircled with several bracelets of wrought gold; and the hand held a sword of marvellous workmanship aloft in the air above the surface of the water; and neither the arm nor the sword moved so much as a hair's-breadth, but were motionless like to a carven image upon the surface of the lake. And, behold! the sun of that strange land shone down upon the hilt of the sword, and it was of pure gold beset with jewels of several sorts, so that the hilt of the sword and the bracelets that encircled the arm glistered in the midst of the lake like to some singular star of exceeding splendor. And King Arthur sat upon his war-horse and gazed from a distance at the arm and the sword, and he greatly marvelled thereat; yet he wist not how he might come at that sword, for the lake was wonderfully wide and deep, wherefore he knew not how he might come thereunto for to make it his own. And as he sat pondering this thing within himself, he was suddenly aware of a strange lady, who approached him through those tall flowers that bloomed along the margin of the lake. And when he perceived her coming toward him he quickly dismounted from his war-horse and he went forward for to meet her with the bridle-rein over his arm. And when he had come nigh to her, he perceived that she was extraordinarily beautiful, and that her face was like wax for clearness, and that her eyes were perfectly black, and that they were as bright and glistening as though they were two jewels set in ivory. And he perceived that her hair was like silk and as black as it was possible to be, and so long that it reached unto the ground

as she walked. And the lady was clad all in green—only that
a fine cord of crimson and gold was interwoven into the plaits
of her hair. And around her neck there hung a very beautiful
necklace of several strands of opal stones and emeralds, set in
cunningly wrought gold; and around her wrists were bracelets
of the like sort—of opal stones and emeralds set into gold. So
when King Arthur beheld her wonderful appearance, that it was
like to an ivory statue of exceeding beauty clad all in green, he
immediately kneeled before her in the midst of all those flowers
as he said, "Lady, I do certainly perceive that thou art no mortal
damoiselle, but that thou art Fay. Also that this place, because
of its extraordinary beauty, can be no other than some land of
Faerie into which I have entered."

And the Lady replied, "King Arthur, thou sayest soothly, for
I am indeed Faerie. Moreover, I may tell thee that my name is
Nymue, and that I am the chiefest of those Ladies of the Lake
of whom thou mayst have heard people speak. Also thou art to
know that what thou beholdest yonder as a wide lake is, in truth,
a plain like unto this, all bedight with flowers. And likewise thou
art to know that in the midst of that plain there standeth a castle
of white marble and of ultramarine illuminated with gold. But,
lest mortal eyes should behold our dwelling-place, my sisters and I
have caused it to be that this appearance as of a lake should extend
all over that castle so that it is entirely hidden from sight. Nor may
any mortal man cross that lake, saving in one way—otherwise he
shall certainly perish therein."

"Lady," said King Arthur, "that which thou tellest me causes
me to wonder a very great deal. And, indeed, I am afraid that in
coming hitherward I have bcen doing amiss for to intrude upon
the solitude of your dwelling-place."

"Nay, not so, King Arthur," said the Lady of the Lake, "for,
in truth, thou art very welcome hereunto. Moreover, I may tell
thee that I have a greater friendliness for thee and those noble
knights of thy court than thou canst easily wot of. But I do
beseech thee of thy courtesy for to tell me what it is that brings
thee to our land?"

"Lady," quoth the King, "I will tell thee the entire truth. I
fought of late a battle with a certain sable knight, in the which
I was sorely and grievously wounded, and wherein I burst my
spear and snapped my sword and lost even my misericordia, so
that I had not a single thing left me by way of a weapon. In this
extremity Merlin, here, told me of Excalibur, and of how he is
continually upheld by an arm in the midst of this magical lake.

So I came hither and, behold, I find it even as he hath said. Now, Lady, an it be possible, I would fain achieve that excellent sword, that, by means of it I might fight my battle to its entire end."

"Ha! my lord King," said the Lady of the Lake, "that sword is no easy thing for to achieve, and, moreover, I may tell thee that several knights have lost their lives by attempting that which thou hast a mind to do. For, in sooth, no man may win yonder sword unless he be without fear and without reproach."

"Alas, Lady!" quoth King Arthur, "that is indeed a sad saying for me. For, though I may not lack in knightly courage, yet, in truth, there be many things wherewith I do reproach myself withal. Ne'theless, I would fain attempt this thing, even an it be to my great endangerment. Wherefore, I prithee tell me how I may best undertake this adventure."

"King Arthur," said the Lady of the Lake, "I will do what I say to aid thee in thy wishes in this matter." Whereupon she lifted a single emerald that hung by a small chain of gold at her girdle and, lo! the emerald was cunningly carved into the form of a whistle. And she set the whistle to her lips and blew upon it very shrilly. Then straightway there appeared upon the water, a great way off, a certain thing that shone very brightly. And this drew near with great speed, and as it came nigh, behold! it was a boat all of carven brass. And the prow of the boat was carved into the form of a head of a beautiful woman, and upon either side were wings like the wings of a swan. And the boat moved upon the water like a swan—very swiftly—so that long lines, like to silver threads, stretched far away behind, across the face of the water, which otherwise was like unto glass for smoothness. And when the brazen boat had reached the bank it rested there and moved no more.

Then the Lady of the Lake bade King Arthur to enter the boat, and so he entered it. And immediately he had done so, the boat moved away from the bank as swiftly as it had come thither. And Merlin and the Lady of the Lake stood upon the margin of the water, and gazed after King Arthur and the brazen boat.

And King Arthur beheld that the boat floated swiftly across the lake to where was the arm uplifting the sword, and that the arm and the sword moved not but remained where they were.

Then King Arthur reached forth and took the sword in his hand, and immediately the arm disappeared beneath the water, and King Arthur held the sword and the scabbard thereof and the belt thereof in his hand and, lo! they were his own.

Then verily his heart swelled with joy an it would burst within his bosom, for Excalibur was an hundred times more beautiful than he had thought possible. Wherefore his heart was nigh breaking for pure joy at having obtained that magic sword.

Then the brazen boat bore him very quickly back to the land again and he stepped ashore where stood the Lady of the Lake and Merlin. And when he stood upon the shore, he gave the Lady great thanks beyond measure for all that she had done for to aid him in his great undertaking; and she gave him cheerful and pleasing words in reply.

Then King Arthur saluted the lady, as became him, and, having mounted his war-horse, and Merlin having mounted his palfrey, they rode away thence upon their business—the King's heart still greatly expanded with pure delight at having for his own that beautiful sword—the most beautiful and the most famous sword in all the world.

That night King Arthur and Merlin abided with the holy hermit at the forest sanctuary, and when the next morning had come (the King having bathed himself in the ice-cold forest fountain, and being exceedingly refreshed thereby) they took their departure, offering thanks to that saintly man for the harborage he had given them.

Anon, about noon-tide, they reached the valley of the Sable Knight, and there were all things appointed exactly as when King Arthur had been there before: to wit, that gloomy castle, the lawn of smooth grass, the apple-tree covered over with shields, and the bridge whereon hung that single shield of sable.

"Now, Merlin," quoth King Arthur, "I do this time most strictly forbid thee for to interfere in this quarrel. Nor shalt thou, under pain of my displeasure, exert any of thy arts of magic in my behalf. So hearken thou to what I say, and heed it with all possible diligence."

Thereupon, straightway, the King rode forth upon the bridge and, seizing the brazen mall, he smote upon the sable shield with all his might and main. Immediately the portcullis of the castle was let fall as afore told, and, in the same manner as that other time, the Sable Knight rode forth therefrom, already bedight and equipped for the encounter. So he came to the bridge-head and there King Arthur spake to him in this wise: "Sir Pellinore, we do now know one another entirely well, and each doth judge that he hath cause of quarrel with the other: thou, that I, for mine own reasons as seemed to me to be fit, have taken away from thee thy kingly estate, and have driven thee into this forest solitude: I, that thou has set thyself up here for to do injury and affront to knights and lords and other people of this kingdom of mine. Wherefore, seeing that I am here as an errant Knight, I do challenge thee for to fight with me, man to man, until either thou or I have conquered the other."

Unto this speech King Pellinore bowed his head in obedience, and thereupon he wheeled his horse, and, riding to some little distance, took his place where he had afore stood. And King Arthur also rode to some little distance, and took his station where he had afore stood. At the same time there came forth from the castle one of those tall pages clad all in sable, pied with crimson, and gave to King Arthur a good, stout spear of ash-wood, well seasoned and untried in battle; and when the two Knights were duly prepared, they shouted and drave their horses together, the one smiting the other so fairly in the midst of his defences that the spears shivered in the hand of each, bursting all into small splinters as they had aforetime done.

Then each of these two knights immediately voided his horse with great skill and address, and drew each his sword. And thereupon they fell to at a combat, so furious and so violent, that two wild bulls upon the mountains could not have engaged in a more desperate encounter.

But now, having Excalibur for to aid him in his battle, King Arthur soon overcame his enemy. For he gave him several wounds and yet received none himself, nor did he shed a single drop of blood in all that fight, though his enemy's armor was in a little while all stained with crimson. And at last King Arthur delivered so vehement a stroke that King Pellinore was entirely benumbed thereby, wherefore his sword and his shield fell down from their defence, his thighs trembled beneath him and he sank unto his knees upon the ground, Then he called upon King Arthur to have mercy, saying, "Spare my life and I will yield myself unto thee."

And King Arthur said, "I will spare thee and I will do more than that. For now that thou hast yielded thyself unto me, lo! I will restore unto thee thy power and estate. For I bear no ill-will toward thee, Pellinore, ne'theless, I can brook no rebels against my power in this realm. For, as God judges me, I do declare that I hold singly in my sight the good of the people of my kingdom. Wherefore, he who is against me is also against them, and he who is against them is also against me. But now that thou hast acknowledged me I will take thee into my favor. Only as a pledge of thy good faith toward me in the future, I shall require it of thee that thou shalt send me as hostage of thy good-will, thy two eldest sons, to wit: Sir Aglaval and Sir Lamorack. Thy young son, Dornar, thou mayest keep with thee for thy comfort."

So those two young knights above mentioned came to the Court of King Arthur, and they became very famous knights, and by and by were made fellows in great honor of the Round Table.

And King Arthur and King Pellinore went together into the castle of King Pellinore, and there King Pellinore's wounds were dressed and he was made comfortable. That night King Arthur abode in the castle of King Pellinore, and when the next morning had come, he and Merlin returned unto the Court of the King, where it awaited him in the forest at that place where he had established it.

Now King Arthur took very great pleasure unto himself as he and Merlin rode together in return through that forest; for it was the leafiest time of all the year, what time the woodlands decked themselves in their best apparel of clear, bright green. Each bosky dell and dingle was full of the perfume of the thickets, and in every tangled depth the small bird sang with all his might and main, and as though he would burst his little throat with the melody of his singing. And the ground beneath the horses' feet was so soft with fragrant moss that the ear could not hear any sound of hoof-beats upon the earth. And the bright yellow sunlight came down through the leaves so that all the ground was scattered over with a great multitude of trembling circles as of pure yellow gold. And, anon, that sunlight would fall down upon the armed knight as he rode, so that every little while his armor appeared to catch fire with a great glory, shining like a sudden bright star amid the dark shadows of the woodland.

So it was that King Arthur took great joy in that forest land, for he was without ache or pain of any sort and his heart was very greatly elated with the wonderfulness of the success of that adventure into which he had entered. For in that adventure he had not only won a very bitter enemy into a friend who should be of great usefulness and satisfaction to him, but likewise, he had obtained for himself a sword, the like of which the world had never before beheld. And whenever he would think of that singularly splendid sword which now hung by his side, and whenever he remembered that land of Faëry into which he had wandered, and of that which had befallen him therein, his heart would become so greatly elated with pure joyousness that he hardly knew how to contain himself because of the great delight that filled his entire bosom.

And, indeed, I know of no greater good that I could wish for you in all of your life than to have you enjoy such happiness as cometh to one when he hath done his best endeavor and hath succeeded with great entirety in his undertaking. For then all the world appears to be filled as with a bright shining light, and the body seemeth to become so elated that the feet are uplifted from heaviness and touch the earth very lightly because of the lightness of the spirit within. Wherefore, it is, that if I could have it in my power to give you the very best that the world hath to give, I would wish that you might win your battle as King Arthur won his battle at that time, and that you might ride homeward in such triumph and joyousness as filled him that day, and that the sunlight might shine around you as it shone around him, and that the breezes might blow and that all the little birds might sing with might and main as they sang for him, and that your heart also might sing its song of rejoicing in the pleasantness of the world in which you live.

Now as they rode thus through the forest together, Merlin said to the King: "Lord, which wouldst thou rather have, Excalibur, or the sheath that holds him?" To which King Arthur replied, "Ten thousand times would I rather have Excalibur than his sheath." "In that thou art wrong, my Lord," said Merlin, "for let me tell thee, that though Excalibur is of so great a temper that he may cut in twain either a feather or a bar of iron, yet is his sheath of such a sort that he who wears it can suffer no wound in battle, neither may he lose a single drop of blood. In witness whereof, thou mayst remember that, in thy late battle with King Pellinore, thou didst suffer no wound, neither didst thou lose any blood."

Then King Arthur directed a countenance of great displeasure upon his companion and he said, "Now, Merlin, I do declare that thou hast taken from me the entire glory of that battle which I have lately fought. For what credit may there be to any knight who fights his enemy by means of enchantment such as thou tellest me of? And, indeed, I am minded to take this glorious sword back to that magic lake and to cast it therein where it belongeth; for I believe that a knight should fight by means of his own strength, and not by means of magic."

"My Lord," said Merlin, "assuredly thou art entirely right in what thou holdest. But thou must bear in mind that thou art not as an ordinary errant knight, but that thou art a King, and that thy life belongeth not unto thee, but unto thy people. Accordingly thou hast no right to imperil it, but shouldst do all that lieth in thy power for to preserve it. Wherefore thou shouldst keep that sword so that it may safeguard thy life."

Then King Arthur meditated that saying for a long while in silence; and when he spake it was in this wise: "Merlin, thou art right in what thou sayest, and, for the sake of my people, I will keep both Excalibur for to fight for them, and likewise his sheath for to preserve my life for their sake. Ne'theless, I will never use him again saving in serious battle." And King Arthur held to that saying, so that thereafter he did no battle in sport excepting with lance and a-horseback.

King Arthur kept Excalibur as the chiefest treasure of all his possessions. For he said to himself, "Such a sword as this is fit for a king above other kings and a lord above other lords. Now, as God hath seen fit for to intrust that sword into my keeping in so marvellous a manner as fell about, so must He mean that I am to be His servant for to do unusual things. Wherefore I will treasure this noble weapon not more for its excellent worth than because it shall be unto me as a sign of those great things that God, in His mercy, hath evidently ordained for me to perform for to do Him service."

So King Arthur had made for Excalibur a strong chest or coffer, bound around with many bands of wrought iron, studded all over with great nails of iron, and locked with three great padlocks. In this strong-box he kept Excalibur lying upon a cushion of crimson silk and wrapped in swathings of fine linen, and very few people ever beheld the sword in its glory excepting when it shone like a sudden flame in the uproar of battle.

# THE STORMING BONE
## by Ian McDowell

*In* The Pendragon Chronicles *Ian McDowell's
"Son of the Morning" introduced us to the
young Mordred, the incestuous son of Arthur
and his half-sister, Morgause. In "The Storming
Bone", McDowell continues the story showing
the growing feelings of Mordred to the world
about him.*

This is the story of how I killed my mother's husband and how
she helped me do it, after she was dead.

Notice I said "mother's husband" and not "father." My real
da, and uncle, too, to his pious shame, is Arthur Pendragon, High
King of all the Brits and higher holy hypocrite. He only figures in
this story by his absence; the tale of him and me's not done yet,
and won't be, I fear, until we're both provender for worms.

No, I speak of Lot Mac Conag, King of the Orkneys and
thwarted would-be king of more than that, the father of my
brother and lord of the house where I was born. I've a terrible
memory for faces, but his I'll carry to the grave. I've only to shut
my eyes to again see the high, pale brow, pursed mouth, long
ascetic nose and perpetually startled eyes, all giving him a look of
sanctimonious hauteur mingled with righteous indignation, like
a prelate who's just been buggered by a Jute.

Mother's face lurks in that darkness, too, her Breton features
flat and swarthy as any Pict's, all wide cheekbones and black
commanding eyes. If I can't remember a time when Lot was
young, Queen Morgawse never seemed to get older than twenty.
But then, you expect that in a sorceress. And, if her husband

was craftier than he appeared, she was more unstable. Born of an Armorican princess and unwanted by her father (Uther cast aside offspring like old shoes), she'd been raised in the proper Latin household of her uncle, Ambrosius Aurelanius. The two strains, Roman and Breton, did not mix well in her.

Believe me, I should know; I suffered the discomfort of her attempts to raise me in the Quadrium et Trivium *and* the old ways of earth and fire and blood. Poor Morgawse should have been either a Roman matron or a Druid queen, not the wife of a petty island warlord with thwarted designs upon her father's throne.

I've called Lot craftier than he looked, a weasel-sly man with a fine eye for the main chance, but such craft does not always pay off. Uther, my maternal and paternal grandfather, had been the first Brit High King since the Romans came, and Lot's marriage to my mother should have made Orkney's sour lord the next in that royal line. So much for high hopes; a man everyone thought a common soldier proved to be another of Uther's forgotten bastards. When Arthur turned up to catch the falling crown, all of Lot's royal ambitions proved worth less than a crofter's fart.

That draught would have been bitter enough, but the very man who'd so thwarted Lot, his wife's brother, also turned out to be the incestuous father of Orkney's youngest son. My da, I mean. Our family history does tend to sound like something out of a complicated bawdy joke, doesn't it?

Enough preamble; direct narrative's the thing. I'll begin *in media res*, with wind and rain and music from a bone.

I stared out past the tower's crenelated edge, at the muddy courtyard and crumbling curtain wall, the squat hump of bare earth and rock that rose, then sloped down to the steeper slope of the cliff, and beyond that, the sea, all grey-green swells rolling up into ivory streaks of foam. There were no clouds in the iron sky, rusting now at its lower border, where the sun was corroding onto the waves. No wind, either.

I lifted the flute to my lips. It was not very impressive, just a hollow cylinder with two holes drilled near one end and runes scrawled across its lacquered surface. Actually, they only looked scrawled; I'd copied them very carefully from an old black stone in Mother's sanctum.

The bone the flute had been carved from was not immediately identifiable as human, but it was; a radius, to be precise. Two days before, it had been safely sheathed in the fat right arm of Wilf, a household slave who'd pilfered the larder once too often.

It had taken me a long time to slice and boil and scrape the fleshy matter from his severed forearm, then whittle it down into its present shape.

Now, to see if it worked. I put it to my lips and blew, changing the sound by covering and uncovering the holes and worming my tongue into the hollow where marrow used to be. The notes came clear and muffled, dull and sharp, as I learned to shape them.

No wind started yet, but the stillness felt strained and transient, like a man holding his breath. I blew three sharp notes and three soft ones. They hung in the air, trilling echoes spreading out like ripples in a pool. Out past the sloughing waves, a spot appeared on the horizon, an ink drop in a puddle of spilled wine. It spread through the ruddy smear of the sunset, darkening the stain.

A mottled tern came wheeling up over the lee, coasting on the sudden gust that broke like a wave around the cliff's sheer face. Then I felt it too, gentler at my higher elevation, like a woman running her fingers through my hair. Salt stung my eyes and I could smell all the miles of ocean that lay between me and the churning blackness where the sea-rim met the sky.

"Careful," said Queen Morgawse as she joined me at the parapet's worn edge, the breeze pressing her red linen gown against her tall slim body and catching her unbound hair, spreading it like black wings around the olive triangle of her face. She reached out and plucked the bone flute from my hand. "A wrong note might summon more storm and sea than you'd easily put down again. Carelessness could make another Atlantis of your homeland."

Some homeland, I thought, turning towards the tower's leeward side and looking out across the peaty hills. Her patronizing tone irritated me; I wasn't a child, to be scolded against burning myself on the oven. "Jesus, Mother," I said in a voice of bruised innocence. "I'm not such a fool as that."

"Don't swear by the carpenter, Mordred. You're no Christian yet, I hope."

I was in no mood to argue theology. "Throwing his name about doesn't mean I worship him." Sitting on the crenel, I dangled my feet in empty air. "I don't worship much of anything, really. Except you and King Lot, of course."

"Don't bait me," she snapped, annoyed for once by my guying flattery. "You hated Lot even when you thought he was your father."

For no good reason, this was getting nasty. Good; I hadn't been in the mood for a magic lesson, anyway. "I loved him as much as you ever did," I said sweetly.

I might have regretted that remark if she hadn't pretended to ignore it. "You were pleased to worship something once, you know," she continued lightly. "It's a fine thing you weren't playing with storms then; when your worship stopped, you'd have gladly drowned all Orkney like a bag of unwanted kittens."

With her customary skill at salting old wounds, she was referring to the turbulent day when Arthur discovered who he and I were, only to recoil from that knowledge and from me. Not that I'd ever loved him as much as she liked to claim.

"Playing, is it?" I said, drumming my heels against the tower face. "I'm only practicing what you taught me. And what you're talking about is over and done with, isn't it, so why don't you just bloody well leave off?"

Not looking at her, I wasn't conscious of the change until she walked up behind me and gently gripped my shoulders, then bent to kiss the nape of my neck. Not this again, I thought, my neck hairs bristling. Now that I was all grown up, I reminded her too much of the one man she'd wanted and couldn't have, at least not more than once.

"Yes," she said, in the husky, yearning voice she was too wont to use on me these days. "It's long past. You're a man, now, and can be trusted with the art. And with much else, besides."

On the horizon, the storm I'd summoned was breaking up, the black clouds dissipating without my music to sustain them. Mother's fingers stroked the back of my neck. Even if I hadn't been pissed at the mention of Arthur, I'd still have sought refuge in the continued fight.

"Oh, fine," I snapped, slipping from the crenel, shaking off her insistent hands, and stalking to the opposite parapet, to look again at the clean sea and feel its salt upon my face. "Toss me another bone; that one's gnawed clean. Magic's a game for women and disillusioned clerics. I can do well enough without it."

She seized me by the upper arm and turned me around with that damnable peasant strength of hers, waving the bone flute so close to my face I thought she'd rap my nose with it. "It's a game that can shape the world. Would you cast *that* aside?"

"Yes," I replied, emphasizing my point by taking the bone from her hand and tossing it over the tower's edge. "As readily as that. Soldiers shape the world, mother. Poets and rhetoricians, too, sometimes. Alexander, Aristotle, Homer—they did well enough without your carrion music."

She briefly smiled—I think she was pleased that I could still throw her precious classicism back at her. Then came the stem, matronly look that sat so uneasily upon her earthy Breton face. "This is no age for rhetoricians or for poets; you know that. Soldiers, yes. The age breeds them the way dung breeds flies. Go to my brother and be one, then. He'd not refuse your service, no matter his protested shame."

She turned away, her anger mounting. "Right, then. Forget my 'toys'; leave me to this cold island and its colder lord. Gawain is Arthur's man already, never coming home except to collect the royal taxes. Now that he's got them, he'll be leaving again, tomorrow or the day after. Go back with him. Have your fine squadron of a hundred horse and forget about me. I'll languish here, a Queen of peat and driftwood, while my sons chop up Saxons for pious Arthur and his carpenter god. Go on with you, then. I don't care."

My guts felt all twisted up, and once again I almost hated her for having such a tight grip on my feelings, and hated myself for allowing her to tear them this way. I started to accuse her of being maudlin, but my hand was reaching out, acting on its own, and she was hugging me, her arms locked tighter around my ribs than those of a drowning sailor clutching a floating spar. I steadied myself against her fierce, unexpected sobs and wondered what to say.

"She's getting worse," I said as I cut low at Gawain's legs, a trick I'd learned from the commander of Lot's Jutland mercenaries. He parried with difficulty, and the shock ran up my lead-weighted wooden practice sword. "Her moods vary by the minute," I continued when I'd caught my breath. "She sobs at trifles now."

Gawain spat in the cold dust of the inner courtyard and leaned on his oaken blade. He looked up at mother's slab-sided tower, almost as if he expected her to be watching from the roof. "Losing you isn't a trifle, boyo, and that's what she's scared of. Ignore her tears and get on with your life. It's all you can do."

Too tired to have another go at him, I dropped my sword and sat on the cold ground. "I wish I could. She changes so bloody fast—haughty one minute, weepy the next. I spend half my time wanting to put the boot to her, half feeling like a total shit for wanting to. We're not getting on at all."

I didn't tell him of how she sometimes touched me, or worse, of the feelings stirred in me by that touch. Despite his family background, Gawain was no one to understand how love gets twisted up.

My burly half-brother pulled off his padded leather helmet and squatted beside me, shaking coppery bangs out of his deceptively mild brown eyes. There were lines around those eyes, I noticed. That shouldn't have been surprising, for I had just turned eighteen and Gawain was a decade and a half older than me, making him almost Arthur's age. Still, it was a shock to realize that my growing up meant my brother was getting old.

"It's not her that's the problem," he said, drawing idly in the dirt with the point of his wooden sword. "It's you. You need to leave this place. Come back to Camelot with me."

I laughed. "What a thought; Arthur welcoming me with open arms."

"Maybe not, but he'd have you. He's not what he was. It's the prospect of his wedding, I think. He's been a happy man since he met her."

I tried to imagine what sort of woman Arthur might marry. A pious little would-be nun, maybe, considering his obsession with expunging his past sins. "Oh, yes, marriage is a balm, isn't it? Think of Mother and King Lot."

Gawain rested his chin upon his dusty knees. "That's different. There was never any love there."

True enough. Not for the first time, I tried to picture Morgawse and Lot in bed together, performing the act they must have performed at least once, only to recoil from the thought. "I hate him, you know."

Gawain looked at me hard. "Arthur?"

"No. There's nothing left for him. Lot. I hate the shriveled old turd. When I was a boy, I often wanted him dead. I'm sorry he's your father."

Gawain stood up. "Let's not talk family here." Shrugging off his padded leather gambeson, he clapped for a serf, who came trotting up with clean, white surtunics for us both. A red dragon wriggled across the front of Gawain's, the symbol of Arthur's united Britain. "Fetch horses," he commanded.

Later, we rode the broken strand beyond the lee, where our hooded otter-fur cloaks barely protected us from the salt wind that knifed in across the breakers. Above us, the sheer black palisades of the cliff tumbled upwards into a grey sky, all scudding pale cloud and paler, wheeling birds. Pulling ahead, I reined my dappled mare towards the base of the cliff, where a stack of storm-chiseled basalt was undergoing the centuries-long process of becoming a separate pinnacle of rock. A hundred feet above us, it was still attached to the bluff, but here, at sea level, there was a gap of at least a dozen yards between it and the cliff's face, forming a natural arch. This had been our secret place when we were boys.

"Don't hate Father," Gawain said as he joined me in the damp shade. "He's not a bad man, just full of disappointment."

"Full of more than that, I think," I said, relaxing in the saddle and removing my hood, for its inwardly turned fur was making my ears itch. "You don't live with the man."

"And you don't have to," he said, slipping fluidly from the saddle and standing beside his roan gelding, one hand on the uneasy horse's flank while the other caressed the huge column of glistening rock. "That doesn't change what I said. Orkney's to blame, not him. These islands were fine enough for our pirate ancestors, kicked out of Ireland for robbing their neighbours instead of the Brits, but they're no place to build a kingdom. Our cattle die and more and more of our folk slip off to the mainland each year. By the time I'm into my patrimony, I'll be lord of a few hardy crofters and maybe a dozen sheep. Father had his chance for more, once, and lost it. Now Orkney dwindles, and him with it. It's hard to be a good man when everything is slipping away."

"Including your son," I said with some of the same acid I'd used in arguing with Mother.

"I saw an out, and took it. You can, too. What's the word—pragmatist? Be a pragmatist. It's the only way to live." There may have been a tinge of sorrow in his voice.

I didn't dismount, though my legs needed stretching. "Mother never had that choice."

Gawain looked at me, his face gone hard. "She made all her choices a long time ago. Now she's stuck with them. Leave her to her boredom and folly. It's not good for you to remain here, now that you're a man. She sees too much of Arthur in you."

I was glad of the dim light, for my face was burning. So . . . simple, stout Gawain didn't understand such things? Well, I was younger then, and people could still surprise me. Suddenly, I needed sunlight, and no one near me. Muttering something, I don't know what, I spurred my mare out onto the misty beach. Gawain followed on foot, shouting, but the wind caught his words and carried them away.

Later, calm and inside of myself again, I turned back towards the palace. The wind was even fiercer there, as I rode over the plank bridge that spanned the great ditch and crossed under the stone and timber gatehouse, Lot's addition to the earthwork erected by his father. Dismounting, I let a serf take my horse and entered the inner courtyard, which was surrounded on three sides by the horseshoe-shaped great hall and on the forth by a timber palisade. Mother's tower, where she spent so much of her time these days, was joined to that palisade, but I was too close to that square, sandstone building to see if she was watching from its creneled roof.

Someone shouted Gawain's name. I looked about, expecting to see him coming up behind me, but he wasn't there. Instead, I saw King Lot approaching from the opposite direction, striding bowleggedly through a flock of hooting geese, his purple robe hiked up almost to his knees in a vain attempt to keep its ermine trim free of the mud and shit of the courtyard. I wanted to laugh out loud at the sight of his sticklike calves and pale, scabby ankles, but the look in his eyes stopped me. Yes, he could rule me like that, with a frosty, fishy glance. I often meant to stare defiantly into his seemingly weak face, only to see the soft, pop-eyed cod mask slip away and reveal the hungry pike beneath.

His vision was not as sharp as it once had been. "Ach, it's you," he said with bland distaste. "I took you for my son."

"I'm sorry to disappoint you," I said as coolly as I could. "Sometimes it seems my only talent."

He ignored the sarcasm. "Where's Gawain?"

"Out riding." I started to step past him.

"And my wife?"

Now why did he ask that? I shrugged and pointed at her tower. "Where she always is, I suppose."

"Yes, where she always is," he muttered. "I think it time I changed that. Go now and tell her there will be no supper there for her tonight. She must sit at table like a proper Queen." He swayed a bit, and I caught the ale on his breath. It was unusual for him to be drunk this early in the day, but not unheard of.

I bit back my anger at being asked to deliver messages like a servant. "What's the occasion?"

His look turned even more sour. "Gawain sails for Camelot tomorrow morning. It's bad enough he'll have half my treasury in his strongbox; I'll not have him telling his master Arthur that the royal house of Orkney is in disarray. Tonight, my wife will share my table and my bed."

I tried to keep my face calm, not pausing to wonder why

I should have trouble doing so. Why was he demanding his conjugal rights now?

"What's the matter, Gertruda got her period?" Gertruda was the captured Saxon serf who was his most frequent bedmate.

A flood of color rushed through the gullies of his face. "She died this morning," he said with unaccustomed softness.

Out riding, I hadn't heard the news. I didn't ask how it happened; serfs wore out all the time. "I'm sorry."

I must not have sounded it, for his face quickly hardened again. "I doubt that, but you would be wise to curb your insolence. I'm in no mood."

Any pity I might have felt didn't last long, and the contempt came slinking back in. "Of course, My Lord. Anything you wish."

He still blocked my way. "These are hard times, Mordred. Hoofed plague rages among my livestock, driving my herders to the mainland. I've a mad and spiteful wife who'd think Byzantium too mean a kingdom, yet who prefers a cot in an empty tower to the royal bed and who once was randy enough to roger her own brother. My true son devotes his life to that pious usurper, coming home only to collect the imperial taxes. On top of this, I'm saddled with the upkeep of an incestuous bastard with an insolent mouth. This last problem would seem the easiest to solve."

He prodded my sternum with a grubby-nailed finger. "My own father would simply have had you killed. In these more civilized times, exile is still a happy possibility. So, rather than compounding my daily quota of irritation, why don't you go fetch your dear mother down to dinner?"

With that, he turned unsteadily upon his heel and stalked stiffly away. Honking, the flock of geese changed direction and flowed like a river about me, until a sway-back dog chased a piglet through their ranks, scattering them. I stood there, hating him, hating myself. The wind stirred about me, lifting dust and feathers, then settled, beaten back by a sudden soft drizzle of rain. Walking to the wall, I hit it, several times, hard enough to drive splinters into my bloody knuckles.

I wished I hadn't thrown the bone flute away, wished I had it with me now, so that I could scramble atop the wall and call the waves until they folded over the entire island and scoured it clean, bearing palace, people and peaty hillsides all down to the cold bosom of the sea.

The dried head of one of Lot's ancestors dangled on a leather cord from the ceiling of mother's chamber, grinning and swaying in the bar of sunlight that shone in through the single narrow window. Every time I looked at it I could taste cedar oil, a memory of the time when I was eight years old and Gawain had dared me to kiss its lipless mouth.

Mother reached out and gave it an idle spin. "If you were Lot's son, you could make strong magic with our smiling friend here, did you know that?" I did, of course, but didn't interrupt her pedantry. "The flesh and bone of one's own kin makes for powerful raw material, and there's plenty of it in the royal cairn. It's too bad I could never interest your brother in the art. What have you done to your hand?"

I was wrapping a strip of linen around my damaged knuckles. "Gawain caught me there with a practice sword." Better change the subject. "I just heard Gertruda died. Did you kill her?"

"What a tedious question." She sat on a three-legged stool and frowned. "That's not for what the draught was intended, no. It was that damned eternal sniffle of hers. You wouldn't expect a northern girl to be so susceptible to head colds."

"Well, you ended her sneezing, but the other results aren't so happy. Lot now expects you to share his bed tonight."

She smiled absent-mindedly, not at all the reaction I'd expected. "Perhaps I'll do that."

I felt obscurely disappointed. "He also requests your presence at dinner. Gawain is leaving in the morning, and Lot thinks we should appear a happy family."

She rose and stretched. "But of course. Now, whatever should I wear?" Unpinning her simple grey linen gown, she let it fall to her ankles and stepped out of it. Her breasts hardly sagged, though her stomach drooped slightly and bore the signs of childbirth. When she turned around I could see her buttocks were still as firm and flat as a boy's. Coughing, I regained enough control to turn away.

"Now how can you help me find something to wear if you stand there staring at the wall?" she said coyly. Cursing under my breath, I fled, leaving her with no audience but the dangling, grinning head.

I met Gawain at the entrance to the great hall and drew him aside. "Look, I'm sorry I left you behind like that today. You were right. I can't stay here. I'll sail with you in the morning."

His gaze was unreadable, but his embrace seemed warm

enough. "Lugh and Jesus be praised. You're good to be out of this, boyo. Think of the times we'll have together."

I nodded without enthusiasm. "Too bad we can't leave now. Be ready for a turbulent night. Gertruda's died, and now Lot's taken it into his head to want Mother in his bed again. She took the news incredibly well, but I doubt her humor will last."

He shrugged. "Then follow my lead and retire early. There's no need for us to be part of any unpleasantness. Shall we go in? It's cold here, and I'm hungry."

I doubt he found the supper very satisfactory, consisting as it did of seaweed boiled in milk, several salted dogfish, and a few scraps of mutton in jellied hamhocks. It was clear that the meal's niggardliness was intended as a statement, for Lot leaned back in his chair and grinned.

"I'm sorry that I cannot afford a more generous feast, Gawain. What with your uncle's gouging taxes, I'm lucky to be able to provide what you see before you."

Gawain looked embarrassed. I knew he disliked collecting Arthur's levies almost as much as Lot disliked paying them, if that was possible. "Don't worry, Father," he said mildly. "I'm used to campaign rations, so this is luxury indeed."

But Lot was not in a conciliatory mood. "Nonsense. The Saxons have kept within their borders for the past ten years. You've been lounging at Camelot, where I hear Arthur's men live like Romans, stuffing themselves on snails, liquamen, and dormice. Tell me, has he installed a vomitorium yet, or do you just puke it all up in the corner before staggering back to the table to gorge yourselves some more?"

Gawain stiffened. "I don't have to listen to this."

Flickering light from the great hearth played across Lot's bald patch as he bent to pick up a joint of mutton he'd carelessly dropped on the floor. "Ach, but in your father's house you do. Isn't that right, Mordred?"

Mother's entrance prevented me from having to answer. For some reason, she'd decided to be resplendent in a blood-colored linen gown with an ornate collar of raven feathers.

"Ah, dear wife," said Lot. "I was afraid you would be unable to join us. Unfortunately, there's not much left. I was explaining to our son how your sanctimonious brother is depleting the royal treasury."

Ignoring him, she bent to kiss Gawain on the cheek, then me upon the mouth. Lot didn't seem to notice, but Gawain did.

"Hello, Mother," he said, giving her a hard look. "Sorry to be rude, but I must retire early. Father's spoiling for a fight, and I don't much fancy giving him one."

"Run along then, dear," she said as she sat down. "I'm sure the rest of us will do well enough without you. We can quarrel with the king by ourselves, can't we, Mordred?"

"He won't be doing it after tonight," said Gawain testily. "He's coming back to Camelot with me."

Mother didn't make a sound, just sat very straight and began to radiate a chill. I'm not speaking metaphorically; the air around her grew palpably colder. Well, at least this sorcerous hauteur was better than the weeping I'd seen this morning.

For his part, Lot only grunted and picked a piece of gristle from his beard. "And why shouldn't he, then? If my high and mighty brother-in-law can command the loyalty of *my* son, it's about time he commanded it of his own. May you both prosper in his service, and rot in Hell with him when the Saxons finally rise up to chop you down. The worms and ravens will be grateful, I'm quite sure."

Mother hissed like a snake, and her face went uncustomarily pale, but she still said nothing coherent, just sat there, radiating cold. Lot clapped for one of the serfs, a paunchy, balding lout with a rheumy eye and an old brand on his cheek.

"Ho, Sergius, fetch out the heart-of-wine. Our dear little Mordred has decided to soldier with the Brits. Let's drink his health and wish him a glorious career."

Trying to avoid Mother's freezing face, I watched Gawain rise stiffly to his feet. "Forgive me for not staying for the toast, but I'm tired and want my bed."

Lot waved dismissively. "Away with you, then. But your brother must stay and drink. I want him to have pleasant memories of my table." He was clearly enjoying this, and it wasn't hard to figure out why. Anything that upset his wife was likely to please King Lot.

Gawain nodded meaningfully to me as he left. I would have liked to follow him, but somehow Mother's presence stopped me. As much as I did not want to remain there with her, I did not want to leave her alone with Lot, either.

Heart-of-wine is potent stuff, being the fiery liquid left unfrozen in a wine cask that's been buried in a snowdrift for a few days. Lot had already consumed a bucketful of barley ale. Before much longer, he was lolling in his chair, his mouth open and his sweaty red face looking as though it were about to collapse in upon itself at any minute, like a wet, ruddy, half-deflated bladder.

Occasionally, he would stir, his head nodding forward and then snapping back with spastic regularity, like some sort of broken-necked doll.

I could no longer avoid Mother's gaze. The frozen mask had cracked and melted at some point. Now, her cheeks were flushed and a tear trailed from the corner of one eye.

"I don't blame you for leaving," she said at last. "There's no home for you here, is there?"

"Now, Mother, don't say that."

She shook her head. "It's true. I shouldn't cry. We lose things all our lives. This had to come."

I bowed my head. "I'm sorry."

She drained her cup and stared emotionlessly at her husband. "He can sleep here, I think. Will you help me up to bed, Mordred?"

"Your tower?" Obscurely, I hoped she'd chosen to defy Lot's wishes in that regard. After all, she'd done so often enough before.

She rose, a bit unsteadily, for she had drunk deep of the heart-of-wine, too. (Me, I'd barely touched it.) "No. I think I relish the chance to sleep in the royal bed alone. It is more comfortable than the cot in my tower. Will you help me on the stairs?"

I stood and trudged wearily to her. She gripped me about the waist and rested her head upon my shoulder. As I guided her towards the stairs, she began to whistle an old Breton cradle song. It was dark on the upper landing, and no serfs appeared with burning tallow to light our way. She seemed to enjoy our stumbling passage, and she interrupted her whistling to giggle and press herself more tightly against me. I was tempted to shove her into the wall, but refrained.

Four candles blazed in the royal bedroom, burned down almost to their holders. Mother stepped away from me and stood in the center of the chamber, no longer swaying. She reached up and untied her hair, swept it forward over her face like a veil, then back again.

"Stay with me these few hours before your departure, Mordred. There's not much night left, and I'm lonely."

I turned to go. "No, Mother, I can't do that. I'll say good-bye to you in the morning." I'd almost reached the door when a gust of air blew it shut. The candles did not gutter.

She reached out and took my forearms from behind, and I allowed myself to be turned around to face her again. "Remember how you lay with me, when you were small and sick with fever? I feel a fever now, and it's not of the body. Please lie with me again."

I looked at some point on the wall behind her, knowing better than to meet her eyes. "Don't think I don't know what you're asking of me. Stop it now. Just stop."

She reached out, took my chin, and tilted my head till my gaze met hers. "I'm going to die on this island, Mordred. You won't be coming back. Leave me with something, then. Some memory of you, and of your father. Don't deny me that." Then she kissed me. And I let her do it.

I was surprised when she stepped back, a cool Roman smile on the lips that had just touched mine. "See? That wasn't so bad. It's family tradition, after all. I couldn't have him more than once, but he gave me you. Do you hate him? What better way to strike back? At Lot, too, for that matter. Let's try it again."

With that, she unpinned the brooch that fastened her gown at the shoulder. It fell about her feet. Taking my hand, she drew me close again. I felt her nipples against my chest, even through the coarse weave of my tunic. When her teeth closed on my lower lip, I actually became aroused. At that, her tongue wormed its way into mouth and she gripped my buttocks and pulled me into a tighter embrace.

That was the worst of it, that I could feel my arousal, pressing against her through the skirt of my tunic. I think, I hope, I pray (but to whom?) that I would have shoved her away from me, just the same. Maybe. The choice wasn't mine to make, for the door flew open and Lot stepped into the room.

There was spittle in his beard and his eyes were red and gummy, but his brain was awake and raging. In one hand he held a long white object, twisty like a unicorn's horn. It was an old gift from some former Saxon ally, the tooth of a narwhale.

"Bitch. Whore. I'm going to kill you."

I'd stepped away from her, not heeding his threat, just wanting to be somewhere else. She faced him, her gown still gathered about her ankles, somehow regal despite her awkward nakedness.

"Go away, you paltry little man. Before I say a word that will enter your brain and burn there like a drop of molten lead. Go!"

She hissed the last word like an angry swan and he did indeed step back, for he could never stand up to her when she was raging. She might have faced him down, but she made a crucial error.

Rather than relying on her magic, or even her mere presence, she took a step towards him. Comically, horribly, her feet tangled in her gown and she stumbled to her knees. He laughed, a dry barking sound, and, taking two steps forward, struck her full in the face with the thick end of the narwhale staff.

Her head snapped back and her arms flailed the air and there was blood coming from her mouth. Jamming the tip of the staff into her midriff, he leaned into it, shoving her backwards as it went into her. Pinned against the floor with her heels beneath her backside, she flailed wildly and drummed her head against the boards. Then she was still and there was blood all over everything.

I'd stood there, paralyzed, watching it all, suddenly aware that my breeches were soiled. My mother had been murdered before my eyes and my only reaction had been to piss myself.

Maybe before I die I'll do another thing that will shame me as much as that.

Pointlessly, now, the paralysis was gone, and I ran at him, screaming. He wasn't even able to bring up the staff; I smashed into him and we fell across her body and struggled there, both of us rolling about in her blood. My hands were about his throat when the palace guards pulled us apart.

Not much after that is clear. The room was full of guards and serfs—I couldn't see Lot for the forest of pop-eyed, candlelit faces. Somewhere, though, I could hear him making hoarse rasping sounds that might have been words. I made for the noise, but Gawain stood in my way. I tried to push past him, only to find myself being half dragged down the hallway, screaming, by my brother. His lips were moving, and though I couldn't hear anything, some part of me made out that he was saying "Jesus Jesus Jesus Jesus," over and over and over.

He practically threw me into my own room, shut the door behind us, and stood there with his back against it. I threw myself against him, but it was in vain, and at last I sank to my knees at his feet, sobbing.

"It's all right, boyo," he said tonelessly, stupidly, like a man dazed. "There's nothing we can do for her." Squatting clumsily beside me, he held me and we wept together. Some time later, I remember us standing, facing each other, his face very white, with lines in it like gullies, making him look much older. "Tomorrow we'll be away from this," he kept saying.

I walked to the wall and hit it, hard, several times. He didn't try to stop me. The pain helped, but not enough. So I smashed my forehead against the plaster, with enough force that a chip cracked off to reveal the timber underneath. On my brow's third impact with the wall, my legs crumbled and I slid to the floor. I don't think I'd actually managed to stun myself, but I was all used up and could only swoon. After that, merciful nothing for a time.

Maybe not so merciful. In the blackness, I was aware of Mother beside me in my bed, bloody and naked and dead, whispering something in my ear. She whispered it over and over and over again. *Do this*, she said, *if you want to be rid of him and me.* The words were still echoing in my head when I woke up.

Sunlight came in through the window. There was a fresh bandage on my head, and someone had taken my bloody clothing away and wiped me clean. Lot was standing in the doorway, with Gawain between him and me.

At last, the King of Orkney spoke. I heard weariness and a hangover in his voice, but no real emotion.

"It's done with. She's in the cairn now and there's no help for it. She was mad and now she's at peace. Hate me, if you like, for killing her. I don't care what you think."

I looked at him and didn't feel anything.

"Your ship has sailed," he continued. "There will be another soon. Avoid my sight until then." With that, he turned and left.

Gawain knelt beside me. "Look," he said, stumbling over his words. "I know it must be hard for you. Just remember, soon you'll be someplace away from here and clean."

I sat up, which hurt. He gently pushed me back. "There's something I must do before I go," I said.

"No." He said it softly, his face very close to mine. "Swear you won't. He'll have his Jutes with him at all times until you're gone. If you try to kill him, you'll die. I've lost my mother, Mordred. I don't want to lose my brother, too."

"Bastard," I said. I meant him as much as Lot.

"Swear you won't." His grip on my forearm was painful.

"All right, I swear. Now let go of me."

He did. I shut my eyes. Eventually, he left, shutting the door behind him. I lay there for some time, sleeping and waking. Food was brought to me, and water. After a while, my head didn't hurt so much, and I could move with less difficulty.

Somewhere, I was almost grateful that Lot had killed her. Rage at him was a clean, cool thing, not like the feelings she'd stirred up. I immersed myself in it quietly, sensing it slip over me like the water at the bottom of a well. Gawain visited me sometime after the next sunrise, but we didn't say much to each other. Then I was alone again.

I hoped I'd be strong enough to do what I needed to do before the next ship came.

The sun had set just beneath the lee and the air was full of chittering bats. I stood before the royal cairn, a high, steep-sided mound, overgrown with brown moss and roofed in peat, with stone slabs and heavy timbers projecting here and there like exposed ribs. A hundred yards or so behind me, I could hear the changing of the guard on the palace's landward palisade. If they saw me, no one hailed.

With a leather sack in one hand and an expensive wax candle in the other, I approached the mound. Gnarled faces leered at me from the driftwood posts erected in a circle around the mound. Stepping past those carved sentinels, I put down my burdens and crouched in front of the block of square red sandstone that effectively plugged the entrance.

Grunting with the strain, and splitting a seam in the crotch of my breeches, I finally managed to heave it aside. A dry, dead smell wafted up at me and by the light of the candle I could see a low passage slanting away into the darkness.

Picking up the candle and the sack, I crawled inside. The passage's floor was rough and wet and there was no room to stand erect. I was conscious of the great weight of stone and wood and earth above me, and my stomach clenched like a fist.

The interior of the cairn was a long chamber, perhaps fifty feet in length, at least thirty feet wide, and a good eight feet high. Standing, I looked about. The stones were roughly fitted and dripped moisture. Hordes of spindly, pale crickets fled the candlelight, leaping and skittering across the uneven floor. Slugs were everywhere, even gleaming like gelid stars from the dark timbers above my head. Skulls grinned from shadowed niches set halfway between the floor and dripping ceiling, while more complete remains were carefully laid out on low slabs that lined the four walls like granite cots. All except the nearest slab bore bare, desiccated bones and strips of rotten cloth.

A blanket of fine white ermine covered her from foot to chin. Small, round spiders and more crickets rustled in the pale fur and crawled across her bloodless face, to disappear in her still luxurious hair. Her eyes had fallen in, and her black lips were drawn back to expose grey gums. When I moved the blanket to uncover her right arm, the air became much fouler, and I had to bite down on the clove of garlic I'd brought with me for that purpose.

Gripping her hand, which felt like a leather glove filled with cold lard and dry sticks, I took a heavy skinning knife out of my sack and began to saw away at the crook of her arm. Slicing through the muscles and tendons, I cut around to the elbow. Then, putting the knife down, I produced a small hatchet and chopped away at the ligaments and bone until I was able to wrench the forearm free.

More sawing and chopping removed the hand. Shoving the point of the knife into the exposed cross-section of the wrist, I slid the blade down between the ulna and the radius, separating the two bones. This last took some effort. I was soon drenched in sweat and, despite the garlic, choking on the filthy air.

Still, I was able to make myself do a fairly complete job of it, whittling most of the soapy flesh away from the radius in long strips before wrapping it in calfskin and putting it back into the sack with the hatchet and the skinning knife. Gingerly, I tucked the right hand, the ulna, and the larger strips of sinew back under the concealing blanket, doing my best not to look at her drawn, dead face. After memorizing the location of the exit, I blew out the candle and scrambled hurriedly back up into the outer air.

Later, in the top room of her tower, I boiled the remaining flesh away from the bone in a small kettle, carved off the knobby end joints, shoved out the remaining marrow, widened the hollow with an auger, and drilled the necessary holes. Further carving and then the lacquering took me well into the next afternoon. I welcomed the exhaustion, for it made it easier not to think.

The monolith stood several leagues from the palace, a good hour's ride down the coast and then another twenty minutes' canter up the rising ground inland. There were no nearby traces of the Picts, or whatever other ancient people had reared it; the gorse-and bracken-carpeted hills rolled away from me on all sides, bare of everything but clumps of bluebell and horned poppy and the occasional limestone outcropping. I'd come here often as a boy, to pretend I was lord of the peaty wasteland, the crown of the monolith the highest turret of my palace.

One side of the roughly squarish, ten-foot-high pillar of red sandstone had been sculpted into the crude likeness of a frowning visage, which nature had decorated with the scars of wind and rain and pockmarks of greenish lichen. An old, dead god of the harvest or the sea, maybe, though he faced the wrong direction for the latter.

Standing on tiptoe to grip the furrowed brow and using the open mouth for a foothold, I hauled myself atop the monolith and sat cross-legged on its rough, flat crown. Facing away from its stony inland gaze, I looked out towards the invisible ocean and untied the lambskin pouch that hung at my belt. When I gently emptied the bone flute out onto my lap, the fresh lacquer gleamed in the still sunlight, while the etched symbols seemed to crawl across its surface like a column of marching ants.

I ran my finger over the polished bone. It was so easy to think of it as something like porcelain or wood, something that had never been sheathed in soft flesh and smooth skin and delicate black hairs. Damn you, you crazy bitch, I thought, that I should think of you this way after you are dead. Lifting the bone flute to my mouth, I ran my lips across its smooth surface in something like a kiss, then blew into it, producing a single shrill note.

It was audible for a long time, and when it faded it seemed to take all other sounds with it—the rustle of the wind-stirred bracken, the cries of the wheeling birds, the snorting of my tethered mare, the dull moan of the distant, unseen sea. No clouds rolled across the sun, but the clear brightness faded, giving way to the kind of daylight one sees through dirty glass. The air about me grew cold and heavy and very still, like the waters of a deep pond.

I blew again, repeatedly, varying the notes, building them, weaving them into a textured pattern. The tune was muffled and distant, something heard beyond the next hill or inside a seashell or at the bottom of a well.

Ripples spread through the pond that was the air around me, expanding outward, then crashing in upon themselves, reverberating, swirling into currents and cross-currents. My mare raised her head and nickered and dug her hooves into the turf. The stubby grass began to bristle and hiss and whisper. With a suddenness that drove my breath back down into my chest, clouds erupted like boils upon the colorless ligament of the sky, coalescing patterns of scudding shadow across the far hillsides. A dozen yards away, a flock of rock pigeons exploded from the short heather and disappeared inland, fleeing the dark turbulence that came beating in from the direction of the sea. The first rumble of thunder was low and distant, but it echoed in the ground beneath my feet.

I stopped trying to form a tune and simply blew shrilly into the bone, but the notes continued, shaping and building upon themselves. Rearing, my horse tore free of the shrub to which I'd tethered her. She paced back and forth for a moment, almost as if she was dancing to the music, rolling her eyes and whinnying; then she wheeled and galloped for the crest of the rise behind me. I didn't even turn my head to watch her go.

The air was full of salt and I could hear the rising cacophony of surf upon the distant rocks. Night seemed to have fallen on the seaward horizon; the sky above the ridge was dark and heaving and folded in upon itself like tumbled layers of billowing wet black cloth. If it looked this bad from here, the view from the palace ramparts was sure to make the sentries piss their breeches. I hoped Lot was on the battlements or looking out a window, anyplace where he could see the approaching storm.

Bracing my feet against the wind, I stood, holding the flute high above my head. The air blew through it and it continued playing, a crazy wild music, fit for the Last Judgment or Ragnarok or the Hunt of the Hounds of Arawn. I shut my eyes and listened and felt the raw tension of the chaos straining to erupt around me.

Thunder crashed deafeningly close and it was as if a bucket of water had been dashed in my face. There was no transition at all, no preliminary sprinkle; the rain was suddenly falling everywhere in great unbound sheaves, buffeting me, pressing my instantly sopping clothing against my body and threatening to rip my cloak from my back. As the wind increased, the water came sweeping along in near-vertical gusts, carrying with it clods of peat and loamy clay torn from the hills and ridges that lay between me and the surging, unseen ocean. Before I could be hurled off, I half slid, half fell down to the monolith's landward side, where I huddled in the new-made mud and pressed myself against its carven face.

The flute played on by itself, quivering in my clenched fist like a live thing. Impossibly, its tune remained audible above the din; indeed, I could feel it trilling in my bones. Suddenly, I wondered about everything I'd done in the last two days, about what I'd ever intended to accomplish. I thought of great waves surging over the rocks at Brough's Head, of torrents of intermingled water, earth and air smashing into the palace's frail stone, of the palace serfs and the guards and of Gawain, all the people who did not deserve to be smashed or drowned. I'd called up a rage greater than my own, a fury that dwarfed mine and left me powerless to control it. There was no catharsis in this, only crippling fear. If the tempest kept on increasing in strength, it would indeed scour the island clean. Perhaps that had been my crazed intention, but now I found myself quite unready for the reality.

Frantically, I thrust the flute down into the soft mud between my knees, but its song continued, now apparently originating just above my head. I looked up at the carved face on the monolith. Its features, in the chaotic light, seemed to have sharpened, become more feminine, with Mother's high cheekbones and imperious brow. And its lips were pursed as if it was whistling.

Screaming "No, stay dead!" I lifted the flute from the mud and smashed it into the graven face, again and again, until I was pummeling the stone with a bloody fist full of shards of polished bone, some of which were driven deep into my palm. "I don't want your vengeance anymore, not if it kills me, too!"

The wind roared and beat against the monolith with enough force to make it rock and sway. There was one final crash of thunder, so loud I thought the sky was coming down, and then a silence so sudden and deep I was sure I was deaf, maybe even dead.

After a timeless interval, I rose unsteadily and looked about me. Bare earth showed through where grass and peat and heather had been torn from the battered hillsides, and for as far as I could see, the remaining vegetation was sodden and beaten flat. The sky was still black and low, but it was beginning to be pierced here and there by shafts of ruddy light. There was no trace of rain, and the silent wind was gentle as a caress.

Sometime later, I walked beside the sea, which rolled in upon the strand like a whipped dog creeping back into its kennel. The sand and shingle and even the cliffs were strewn with clumps of glistening weed, with driftwood and dead fish everywhere, while great rocks that had once lain beneath the swells were now scattered beyond the tide line like pebbles tossed by an idle child. I walked aimlessly to and fro and watched the waves and then walked some more, until I finally set my sopping, muddy feet in the direction of the palace.

Long before I got there, a dot rounded the bluff and swelled into an approaching rider. It was Gawain, astride a very nervous gelding. His wet hair hung in his eyes, his harness was in disarray, and his clothes were as soaked as mine, if not so filthy.

He reined and looked at me. "You're alive, at least," he said with weary relief.

"I am," I answered, still not quite believing it.

"Father's dead."

Three syllables, spoken softly and without apparent emotion.

I did not, I think, feel joy, but something that had been wound very tight now loosened within me. *You got him, you bitch*, I thought, *you got him after you were dead. Though you had to use me.*

I sat on a weedy rock and looked at my damaged hand. Eventually, the question came.

"How?"

Gawain shifted in his saddle but did not dismount. He didn't look at me, either, but out at the sullen waves. "He'd been drinking constantly. It got worse after you disappeared from the palace. Then the storm came."

He did look at me then, but I couldn't read his face. Magic was the world I'd shared with Mother; would he acknowledge its existence?

No. "He began to rave. He said he could hear Mother in the storm, calling to him, mocking him. Everybody went down into the cellar, but not him. He ran out into the courtyard, shouting for her forgiveness. I followed, but got out just in time to see the Queen's tower come tumbling down on top of him. I doubt they've dug him out yet."

I patted his horse, trying to think of what to say. "You're King now."

He shook his head. "Not me. Not here. The Picts can have these islands again for all of me."

"Back to Camelot, then?" As if he'd ever really left.

"Yes. Maybe soon. If the ship rode out the storm."

I found myself hoping it had. Someplace clean, and away from all this, he'd said. Good. Maybe marriage had changed Arthur after all. Even if it hadn't, there was nowhere else to go.

We looked at each other. At length, he reached down and pulled me up behind him. There was nothing for it but to ride back, along the ravaged shore.

# THE OATH OF THE SAXON
## by Peter Tremayne

*Peter Tremayne is the pen name reserved for his fiction by journalist, literary detective and Celtic historian, Peter Berresford Ellis (1943–). Amongst his recent scholarly works are A Dictionary of Irish Mythology and A Dictionary of Celtic Mythology, both of which will be of interest to Arthurian devotees. The following story continues the relationship between Arthur and Mordred (here called Modreuant) which McDowell considered in the last one.*

*Tremayne's tale derives its theme from an old Welsh triad which states that Arthur's eventual downfall, and the victory of the Saxons, was ordained when he ordered that the head of Bran the Blessed, Britain's talisman against invasion, be dug up—on the basis that Britons should not rely on magic to protect them from the Saxons.*

He came back to consciousness with a sense of disbelief followed almost immediately by an anguish that he was not dead. He lay chill and shivering, aware that it was twilight, aware of a throbbing ache in his temples and a pain in his right thigh. He tried moving, to ease into a sitting position, but he felt sick and giddy and contented himself to lay back on the cold ground. His eyes, flickering from side to side, could distinguish little beyond the dark prone outlines of those warriors who had died around

79

him. He could hear voices calling in the distance, soft groaning sounds and an occasional shriek of anguish.

Night was fast approaching.

But he realised that his chill was due to the fact that he lay naked.

He cursed softly in his discomfiture.

The jackals had already stripped him of his clothes, armour and weapons; the jackals of battles—human vultures who descended on the battlefield after the survivors have departed. They must have thought him already dead and robbed him. He turned his eyes again and realised that the corpses which lay around him had also been stripped.

There came the rustle of a movement nearby.

He could not help but flinch for he was helpless and unarmed now. He had no defence against the marauders who plundered the dead and dying after each battle. These carrion-crows of the battlefield were liable to cut a dying man's throat in their eagerness for plunder.

Oh Woden! Why had he not been allowed to die with Wocca, his *eorldoman*? Why had he not been granted a good death which even his own *ceorls* had been allowed, proved by their shattered and mutilated corpses strewn around him? Had he not earned the right to sit with Woden in the *Wael-haell*, the hall of slain heroes? Why had he, thane of Wocca's *tun*, in the land of the East Saxons, been shamed with survival?

He could still hear the victorious battle cry of the Wealhas, the foreigners, as they raced down on Wocca's lines of warriors. Defeat was at hand, for the foreigners had slaughtered a thousand Saxon warriors in this fearsome conflict and only Wocca's band had been left to defend the honour of Woden, god of battles.

How the Saxon army had, that morning, confidently marched against the Wealhas, crying with joy to Woden to bless their arms. They had been told that the Wealhas had chosen a new leader called "The Bear", a leader who had seen no more than twenty-one summers—one so young and inexperienced was bound to lead the Wealhas to defeat against the battle-hardened hosts of Woden. Cissa, of the West Saxons, had marched at their head; Cissa, who was already styling himself *Bretwalda*, ruler of the island of Britain. But their confidence and supplication to Woden had proved useless for Woden had hidden his face from them. As the tide of battle turned against them, Saxons fled the field crying that the young "Bear" of the Wealhas had single-handedly slain so many Saxon thanes that there was no counting them. Then

Cissa himself had fled the field. Only Wocca, his thanes and *ceorls* had been left on the field to protect the flight of king of the West Saxons. And in spite of their cries to the gods of valour, to Woden, to Tiw and to Thunor, a great wave of Wealhas swept down on them like a mighty ocean tide and they had perished . . . all, except he—Wulfgar, thane of Wocca's *tun*. Now shame was his portion.

A shadow fell across him and Wulfgar flinched and managed to raise an arm to ward off the inevitable death blow.

It did not fall.

Instead a voice exclaimed as if in amazement. Then another voice intervened, sharp and commanding.

Wulfgar lowered his arm and gazed up into the dark shadows. Figures stood looking down at him. The sharp, commanding voice spoke again. Obviously a question.

"I have no understanding of your Weilsc tongue," grunted Wulfgar, his voice painful from the thirst.

There came a dry mirthless chuckle.

"Then it is fortunate that I have enough of your Saxon speech to make myself understood. Be you thane or *ceorl*?"

"I am Wulfgar, thane of Wocca's *tun*," replied the Saxon warrior, unable to keep the pride from spilling into his voice.

A second voice intervened but Wulfgar's questioner shook his head.

"No, no. We will take and tend this Saxon's wounds for he may be useful to us." The reply was given in Saxon obviously for Wulfgar's benefit.

"If I am to be made a slave, then I prefer that you give me a sword that I may kill myself, Wcalha," he rejoined. "This I owe to Woden and thus shall I obliterate my shame."

The questioner chuckled again, this time with wry humour.

"It is not your destiny to be a slave nor to take your life. You will be useful to me."

He turned and snapped an order and out of the grey shadows of twilight two burly warriors came and lifted the Saxon thane as if he were but a child. The sudden movement caused a sharp pain in his right thigh and Wulfgar found himself swimming in a sea the colour of pitch. He was conscious of nothing else.

When he came too again he was lying in a stone building with rays of sunlight beaming in through the high open windows. He lay on a wooden cot with a thick woollen blanket over him. He felt as if he were waking from a long, deep sleep. His throat was dry and his tongue seemed to cleave to the roof of his mouth.

He tried to find some saliva to ease the discomfiture but only succeeded in making a groaning sound.

In one corner of the room a figure rose, clad in brown homespun from poll to ankle.

Wulfgar was aware that a cup of water was placed at his lips. He drank from it eagerly, gulping at the cold, crystal liquid. Then he lay back, exhausted by the effort, recovering his breath. It was then that he saw the face of the figure bending over him. A woman. His eyes widened in astonishment for she had pale, almost translucent skin, dark eyes of such changing shades that he could not tell whether they were black or brown. Beneath the hood of her robe, he could just see strands of raven black hair. Around her neck she wore a single piece of jewellry in the shape of a silver cross on which was placed a tiny figurine.

He found himself unable to suppress an immediate animal desire for the woman. He was incapable of understanding the compulsion behind his reaction at the sight of her.

"Where am I?" Wulfgar demanded, trying to concentrate his thoughts.

"You are at the priory of Cunotigern, of blessed name," she replied in the same language with a soft, musical accent which betrayed the fact that Saxon was not native to her speech.

"A Christian temple?" Wulfgar suddenly remembered that the Wealhas worshipped a god called Christ which they depicted as being executed on a cross.

"A church," corrected the girl.

"And who brought me hither from the *slatrefeld*?"

The girl frowned. "The field of slaughter'?" she echoed, translating into her own language. "Ah, you mean the battlefield where our warriors defeated your Saxon hordes? Why, the chieftain Modreuant brought you here."

The Saxon bit his lip, digesting the information.

"Is he the one they call 'The Bear'?"

The girl laughed pleasantly.

"No. no, he is not the High King. He is not Artios, whom you call 'The Bear'."

"Why did this Modreuant save me? To make me slave or to be a sacrifice to your gods?"

The girl pursed her lips in a pitying grimace.

"We do not make slaves of people nor do we sacrifice to our God, Saxon."

Wulfgar frowned as he sought to digest this information. Everything about these Wealhas was indeed foreign to his upbringing and the Saxon way of life. That they did not believe in the same gods, in Woden, Tiw, Thurnor, and Frig, he knew. But all gods surely demanded sacrifice? And for a people not to have slaves and serfs . . . why that was simply ridiculous.

He caught sight of the girl smiling gently as she watched the puzzled expressions on his face and his face darkened. Was she mocking him?

"Do you belong to this thane of the Wealhas?" he demanded brusquely.

"Belong? Ah, do you mean . . . am I Modreuant's wife?" The girl grimaced with apparent amusement. "No. Modreuant is my brother. And I am spouse to no mortal man. I am a bride of Christ, and in his service. I serve in the order of the blessed Cunotigern."

"Are you a priestess, then?" his eyes widened slightly.

"I am Creirwy, the prioress of this abbey. And enough questions, now, Saxon, or you'll not be fit to see Modreuant when he comes. I will prepare a broth which will help you regain your strength."

The girl stood up to leave the room. Wulfgar observed her lithe attractive figure and felt the strange pang of desire again.

Wulfgar's cracked lips split into a lascivious grin. Priestess or no, among the Saxons a good warrior would have made her happy.

"Among my people you would not feel the need to waste your life in devotions to the dead," he said, his wolfish look making his meaning clear.

Creirwy coloured hotly.

"Fortunately, Saxon, we are not among your people," she snapped in annoyance as she left the room.

Wulfgar tried to struggle up. The next thought was to attempt to make an escape from these Wealhas. But even as he tried to raise himself he realised that he was far too weak to even traverse the distance from bed to door.

Modreuant came to see him two days later when Wulfgar was up and able to walk in the grounds of the priory, though he still limped from the wound in his right thigh, which was now healing thanks to the herbal poultices Creirwy applied daily. He still had thoughts of escape but among the priests and priestess, as he considered those who dwelt in the priory, he saw that there were also many armed warriors. So he had spent time with Creirwy, the prioress, trying to learn as much as possible about these strange people and growing more desirous of her. He hoped he could find a way of escape. And such thoughts were tempered with the idea of taking the girl with him.

Modreuant, the brother of Creirwy, was short, swarthy and young. Wulfgar placed his age at no more than twenty years. He was, like his sister, black of hair and eyes, but with a sharp, calculating look and a thin, mean looking mouth. Wulfgar noticed that his clothes and weaponry were rich in adornment and estimated that he was a thane of high standing among the Wealhas. Two armed warriors, eyes watchful, accompanied him together with a man of pudgy face, dressed in the same brown robes which the Wealha priests wore, bearing a silver cross hung on a leather thong around his neck and also having his hair cut in the same outlandish fashion as the other male priests he had seen. Their skulls were shaven in a line from ear to ear. Wulfgar learned from Creirwy that the Wealhas called this a tonsure and that it was a mark of their priestly calling. The females, however, did not shave their heads but simply kept them covered as a sign of respect to their gods. The pudgy face man had eyes that were pale, so pale that Wulfgar had to look carefully to assure himself of their colour. They were ice-grey. Wulfgar found himself shivering slightly under their cold scrutiny.

"Well, Wulfgar, thane of Wocca's *tun*," greeted Modreuant in his well modulated Saxon, "the prioress, my sister, Creirwy, tells me that you are well recovered. Is it so?"

Wulfgar shrugged.

"As you see, Wealha," he said, indifferently.

The pudgy face man sniffed in annoyance.

"Mind your manners, Saxon. We are not foreigners in our own land. We are Britons."

Modreuant made a gesture with his hand and smiled grimly.

"Let the Saxon call us what he will, Drem. Britons or Wealhas, we are still their masters. The Saxons have tasted our mettle now and know defeat. It will not be long before we drive them out of this island back to the lands from whence they have come."

Wulfgar raised his head defiantly.

"We have been here in this island long enough to claim it as our own by right of sword, Wealha! I was born in this island at Wocca's *tun* in the country of the East Saxons."

The man named Drem sneered.

"And your father? Where was he born? You Saxons invaded our island of Britain scarcely a generation ago but it will not take us another generation to ensure that you return back across the seas to your own lands. Britain is our land and we will fight for it. Already our new High King, Artios, whom you call 'The Bear', has sent your Saxon warriors fleeing back to their hovels in despair. Soon he will bring a greater army against you and will drive you all back into the sea."

"We took the land by the sword and will keep it by the sword, as is a warrior's right", replied Wulfgar, spiritedly.

"Then we shall take it back by the sword, as is our right," was Drem's riposte.

"Enough!" Modreuant's face took on a look of annoyance. "I did not come here to waste words in argument."

Wulfgar turned to examine him, trying to make his face a mask of indifference.

"And why did you come? Why did you save me from the scavengers on the field of slaughter? Your sister claims that I am not to be your slave nor am I to be sacrificed to your gods. Why, then, was I saved?"

Modreuant did not answer immediately but stood rubbing his chin as he examined the warrior as if deep in thought.

"I have need of the service of a Saxon thane."

Wulfgar gave a grunt of surprise.

"What makes you think I will serve you? I would rather die."

"That can be arranged," interrupted Drem.

Modreuant ignored him. He smiled at Wulfgar. It reminded the Saxon of the sneer of a wolf before it pounced on its prey.

"You may have observed that I speak your Saxon tongue well. I had some good teachers. They taught me many things about you Saxons; about your beliefs and superstitions."

Wulfgar's eyes narrowed as he wondered what point Modreuant was coming to.

"For example, Saxon, what if I had you bound hand and foot and thrown into the river to drown?"

Wulfgar's eyes widened slightly. He had no need to look closely into Modreuant's eyes to see whether the man was capable of carrying out such a threat. A shiver chilled his body.

"Give me a sword and let me die on its steel," he whispered. The pleading tone in his voice was obvious.

Modreuant laughed mockingly.

"See? I know your beliefs, Saxon. You are a thane. And Saxon thanes must die with sword in hand and the name of his god of battles, Woden, on his lips. If he does not then he has no means to enter the *Wael-heall*, the hall of the slain, to live with Woden in the life hereafter. Is this not so?"

Wulfgar hung his head in defeat. Modreuant's knowledge placed Wulfgar at the Wealha's mercy. He knew it.

Not to die with sword in hand and Woden's awesome name on his lips denied him a place in the hall of slain heroes! His soul would go down into the terrible blackness of non-existence.

Modreuant smiled as he saw the little beads of sweat stand out on the Saxon's brow. He sensed his power over the man.

"Now, Saxon, what is the most binding oath that a Saxon thane can swear?"

Wulfgar bit his lip. His mind worked feverishly as he tried to wrestle against his feelings of utter powerlessness. Yet he was still a Saxon thane and would not meekly submit to a mere Wealha!

"We swear by . . . by the fire of Thunor," he muttered.

Modreuant glanced grimly at the priest called Drem and his lips thinned in a curious smile. Then he signalled to his two warriors who came forward with their swords drawn.

"Come with us," Modreuant said, turning and leading the way from the cluster of stone priory buildings. They followed the pathway in silence. Modreuant strode in front, followed by Wulfgar with the two warriors guarding him at each shoulder. Then Drem trailed on behind. It was a short walk over the hill and, as they crossed the shoulder of it, Wulfgar saw a broad, silver ribbon of river immediately below them. Modreuant led the way to the bank. He paused gazing at the rippling expanse of water.

"This river was once sacred to one of our ancient goddesses, Sabrann, in the days before we turned to the one true God," Modreuant explain softly, addressing himself to Wulfgar. "Sabrann was the patroness of truth. Some still believe in her powers for it was said that she would drown a liar who set foot in her domain."

Wulfgar licked his lips nervously. There was a similar goddess among his own people who was the daughter of Woden.

"Why bring me here, Wealha?" he muttered.

"You said that the most sacred and binding oath of a Saxon thane is to swear on the fires of Thunor. Is that not so?"

Wulfgar nodded uneasily and wondered if the man were mocking him.

Modreuant's eyes flickered to the two warriors and he gave an imperceptible nod. Within a trice Wulfgar found his left arm bound across his back to his right ankle and a strip of cloth stuffed in his mouth so that he could not cry out. The two warriors still held him upright.

"I have heard, Saxon," went on Modreuant in even tones,

"that your most sacred oath is actually to swear on the great battle sword of Woden and your warrior's honour—not on the fires of Thunor. We must discover the truth of this."

He said something sharply in his Weilsc tongue and Wulfgar found himself swung upwards by the two warriors and then he was flying through the air. He hit the cold waters of the river and sunk beneath their surface almost at once. The chill waters closed darkly over his head. His mind cried in despair. No, no! He could not bear such an end, trussed like a fowl, without a sword, and unable to cry on Woden's name. Now his soul would never enter the hall of the slain, nor feast in eternity with the heroes and the gods.

He began to struggle in a frenzy inspired by the fear of such a terrible death but he soon lost consciousness in the blackness of the waters.

Then he was laying prone on the bank, the gag removed, and crying for breath while Modreuant and his companions looked down at him in scornful fashion.

"Do you say that I am wrong, Saxon?" taunted Modreuant. "What is your sacred oath? To Woden or to Thunor?"

Wulfgar heaved several breaths before he could speak and resigned himself to admit the truth.

"You are right, Wealha," he gasped. "It is as you say . . . the oath on the great battle sword of Woden, and our honour, is sacred to us."

Again Modreuant gestured and again Wulfgar found the strip of cloth in his mouth and his trussed body being propelled into the river. This time he lost consciousness more quickly. Then once more he lay on the muddy embankment with Modreuant gazing dispassionately down at him.

"I swear I do not lie," moaned Wulfgar as soon as he had breath.

"I doubt it not," nodded Modreuant in satisfaction. "But you will now swear fealty to me, Saxon. You will swear to be loyal and resolute to me in a quest that I shall presently send you on. You will swear that you will fulfil that quest. Unless you swear, your soul shall never reach your hall of the slain. So let this be a further warning."

Before Wulfgar had time to digest what Modreuant had said, he found himself plunging yet again into the dark, chill waters. For a third time he passed out.

When he finally came to his senses he had been untied but the two warriors held their sword points at his throat.

"Now, Saxon," this time it was Drem who spoke, "kneel before Modreuant and swear on the battle sword of Woden and on your honour as a warrior to be loyal to him and fulfil the task he will apprise you of."

"I will swear," gasped Wulfgar, "but then, for pity's sake, allow me to die sword in hand and Woden's name on my tongue. For my shame is great."

"If you do not swear, then you will die as a dog whelp and your soul will be plunged into oblivion." replied Modreuant. "If you swear, I have plans for you other than death, thane of Wocca's *tun*."

"I so swear, then. I swear to be loyal to Modreuant, thane of the Wealhas, until I have completed the task he instructs me to undertake. By Woden's great battle sword and by my warrior's honour! I so swear!"

"And now I trust you, Saxon," grinned Modreuant triumphantly, "for a thane who breaks such an oath will be outcast from the hall of the slain and enjoy no life hereafter."

Wulfgar bent his head in submission.

"It is so. I am yours to command, thane of the Wealhas."

"Now I shall tell you about the task you must perform for me."

Two weeks later, Wulfgar, resting in the shade of a copse, with Drem and a taciturn warrior called Mud, swore he would never understand the Wealhas. The task which Modreuant had commanded him to do was, superficially, a simple one. And one that seemed no great betrayal of his people. He had to accompany Drem and Mud into the ruined city of London. Wulfgar, as a Saxon thane, was able to pass Drem and Mud through any Saxons stopping and questioning them. The once great capital of Britain was now in Saxon held territory. Twenty years before, the hosts of Woden had driven the Wealhas and their king, Emrys, out of the city, scattering them west and north, and shattering its sturdy walls, sending it great buildings tumbling down and putting everything to the torch.

Why Drem and Mud should want to risk their lives for Modreuant by undertaking such a hazardous journey into Saxon territory was beyond him. He could understand Modreuant's strategy in forcing him to accompany them, so that he could pretend that they were his *ceorls* when questioned by Saxon guards, thereby ensuring that they would not betray themselves. The fact that he was a thane, to which position all Saxons except kings and those of equal rank deferred, allowed their journey into the rubble of the great city to be an easy one.

Yes; a simple task. To ensure, to the best of his ability, Drem and Mud reached London, did what they had to do, and escort them safely back to the priory of Cunotigern.

Wulfgar had always avoided the cities of the Wealhas and was uncomfortable and restless under the great walls of stone or brick, thrusting up black against the sky and casting gloomy shadows in whose depths no one knew what frightfulness lurked. The older Saxon folk, those who had driven the Wealhas from such places, talked of them as being haunted by demons and dark spirits which lurked there, waiting for vengeance. He knew the ruins were inhabited by bats, screech owls, ravening wolves and otherworld creatures, gliding like fearsome shadows under the fallen lintels and masonry.

As they had ridden through the decaying ruins, he had seen Drem's cold eyes examining the devastation.

"*Londo*," Drem had observed. "In our language *londo* means the wild place, and this place was so named before the coming of the Romans, when it was simply a small trading settlement by the banks of the sacred Tamesis. The wild place. Well, it has now returned to what it once was."

Wulfgar had bitten his lip, feeling uncomfortable. He had always been taught that the Wealhas were an inferior people, fit only to slaughter or be slaves to the Saxons. Yet even as he looked at the ruins he had realised just how awesome such buildings must have been compared to the crude wooden buildings in which the Saxons dwelt. Even a thane's hall was of no great size compared to these stone palaces of the Wealhas.

Drem had known precisely where he was going. He had conducted the way to the east of the ruined city, towards a hill which rose in the south-east corner. It was crowned by a small, almost demolished fortress. He called it the Hill of the Ravens. They had stabled their horses by the walls of the ruined fortress in the gathering dusk. Wulfgar was surprised when Drem, not waiting for the light of morning, had began to examine the surrounding hillside. It was mostly overgrown with bushes, wild grasses and young trees pushing through the rubble of what had been buildings. Wulfgar had waited nervously and impatiently while Drem seemed to scour the hill as if looking for something. Finally, he had halted at a spot underneath the threatening shadow of a large oak tree. Then he had signalled Mud to come forward and the silent man began to dig.

Wulfgar had sat quietly dozing now and then as the long hours passed. Drem had lit a torch as darkness fell, black and chill, in order to facilitate Mud's digging. Wulfgar was still dozing when a stifled exclamation brought him wide awake. He saw both Drem and Mud retrieving some object from the hole they had tunnelled into the earth below the giant tree.

"What is it?" he demanded, as Drem, almost trembling with excitement, bundled the object into a sack.

"That is not for you to know, Saxon," Drem snapped coldly. "Your task now is to conduct us in safety back to Modreuant at the Priory of Cunotigern."

Momentary anger had coursed through the thane's frame.

"I could slay you both," he had hissed, "and be back with my own people within a few hours."

"And loose your right to sit in your *Wael-heall* when death eventually finds you?" Drem had sneered. "No; you are bound by your oath."

Wulfgar had bitten his lip.

The Wealha was right. He had sworn to fulfil this task or be doomed for all eternity. He had hesitated only a moment more and then shrugged.

"Then let us go. There is an old gateway out of the city below this hill to the south, it opens onto the river."

Wulfgar was surprised when Drem shivered slightly and closed his eyes.

"Belinos' Gate! No, no! Not that way. That is the gateway of the dead."

Wulfgar had frowned.

"What do you mean, Wealha?"

"In the time before we turned to the one true God, Belinos was the god who ferried our souls to the Otherworld. When a chieftain's death occurred in this city, his body was taken out through Belinos' Gate to be burnt on the banks of the great river Tamesis. We will not leave through that gate."

"Then you Wealhas still believe in omens and evil spirits?" Wulfgar had grinned cynically.

Drem sniffed disdainfully in reply.

"If one believes in good, as we do, it follows that one must believe in evil."

They had ridden out of the city with the grey light of dawn creeping into the sky behind them. The sack, with its mysterious contents, was strapped carefully to Drem's saddle. Many times Wulfgar was tempted to peer into it. For the Wealhas to risk their lives for such a prize, he presumed it was some rich treasure left buried in London by a thane of the Wealhas when the Saxons forced them to flee from the city. But at no time did Drem open the sack nor did Wulfgar have the opportunity to examine the contents.

Now they were back in the country of the Wealhas, resting in a copse with Wulfgar none the wiser for his adventure. A strange people, indeed.

The following day the three men rode down into the valley in which the priory of Cunotigern stood by the great winding strip of the Sabrann river. Modreuant was waiting impatiently for their return and as they dismounted he called out excitedly to Drem. The priest replied, his pasty face animated and he held up the sack as if displaying a triumph.

Wulfgar had no knowledge of what their excited Weilsc talk meant. He cleared his throat to attract attention.

"I have kept my oath to you, thane of the Wealhas," he interrupted their conversation. "I have fulfilled the task which you set me. Am I now released from my oath?"

Modreuant turned from Drem, his eyes hooded suddenly and he smiled thinly.

"Ah, the Saxon," he said, as if seeing Wulfgar for the first time. "You seem to have done well. But I would keep you here a while longer before your service to me is done."

Wulfgar made to protest but found two warriors at his sides, their sword points place at his neck. A word from Modreuant and he was led to a stone building and thrown in. The door slammed enclosing him in the gloom of the cell. Wulfgar cursed loudly in the name of his gods. So this was how the Wealhas kept their word!

It was some hours before the door opened. In fact, night had long since fallen and Wulfgar felt a gnawing hunger in his belly.

His eyes widened as he saw the slim figure of Creirwy standing in the doorway. She carried a tray on which there was food and a wooden cup and jug.

"You have made my brother, Modreuant, very happy, Wulfgar," she smiled, setting down the tray before him.

Wulfgar glowered and grabbed at the food without any preamble.

"He is not an honourable man," he said, his mouth full. "I fulfilled my oath and completed his task. He should have released me to return to my own people."

"No doubt he will," she replied lightly. "But first he has to be sure that he has been served well."

"And how will that be? I do not even know what it was that Drem dug up on that hill in the ruined city."

He took the cup of mead and swallowed noisily.

Creirwy sniffed disapprovingly.

"No harm to tell you," she said tightly. "It was something which may help my brother Modreuant replace Artios as High King."

Wulfgar's brows came together and he paused in his eating.

"I would have a better explanation," he demanded. "Are the Wealhas dissatisfied with this king they call 'The Bear'?"

A look of anger contorted the girl's face.

"The High Kingship should have been Modreuant's," the girl replied, her voice rising with emotion. "Artios is our uncle by blood, but even so he is scarcely older than my brother Modreuant and I. It was Modreuant who was trained in the arts of kingship. The crown was his by right. Yet when the time came for our people to approve of Modreuant, as is our custom, they chose Artios, who won the day by trickery. Artios and his unctuous advisor Myrddin, who is not even of the Church, were able to persuade the people. Artios was chosen as High King! Well, what is won by a trick may be retaken by a better trick. My brother has ridden to the fortress of Artios at Camulos this night. Artios has set in train his own downfall!"

Wulfgar pursed his lips, little wiser, except for the knowledge that these Wealhas could argue and plot among themselves.

"But what was it which the priest Drem dug up in the city? Some great treasure, no doubt? But I can't see what it has to do with Modreuant's dispute with his uncle."

Creirwy smiled triumphantly.

"The contents of Drem's bag is indeed a treasure to the people of Britain and one which will cause the downfall of Artios. When the people of Britain learn that it has been removed from the Hill of Ravens, they will turn their allegiance to Modreuant."

"But it was Modreuant who ordered it to be dug up," Wulfgar was increasingly bewildered.

"At the order of Artios . . . or so the story will be told."

Wulfgar gave up the puzzle. "So your brother and Drem have gone to show this prize to your king?"

The girl shook her head. She was full of excited confidence.

"No. That which you brought back from London is too precious to leave this priory now. Drem guards it in the chapel until Modreuant and his warriors return."

"So?" Wulfgar exhaled slowly and thoughtfully. He began to study Creirwy speculatively.

The great hall of the fortress of Camulos, the powerful fortification which still bore the name of the ancient war god of the Britons from the days before they embraced the faith of the one true God, was almost deserted. Only three men occupied positions before the central hearth of the hall, in which a fire crackled. A young man, richly attired, sprawled in a wooden, high-backed chair, hands together, fingertips to fingertips, a thoughtful frown on his pale, youthful face as his blue eyes studied the dancing flames. His hair was of burnished copper and cut shoulder length, surmounting a handsome face with a firm chin line. He was hardly more than twenty-one summers in age.

An elderly man, white of hair, in rich long robes with a golden chain at his neck, stood to one side, one hand resting lightly on the back of the young man's chair.

Modreuant made up the trio and stood to the other side of the fireplace, his thin lips pressed in a sneering smile.

"Is this true, Artios?" the elderly man asked, his tone serious.

The young man heaved a sigh and then spread his hands in a gesture of resignation.

"I cannot deny that I said it, Myrddin. And in truth, I suppose I meant it."

The elderly man shook his head as if in disbelief.

Modreuant chuckled softly.

"Well, I cannot see what the problem is. After all, you are High King, Artios, and your will is paramount."

"Not so, the people are greater than the High King," snapped the man called Myrddin.

Modreuant sniffed disparagingly.

"Why so?"

"It is the people who ordain the king, not the king the people. You, more than anyone, should know that fact."

"The people will do as they are told," replied Modreuant, his tone sharp.

The young man, Artios, raised a hand wearily.

"Let's not quarrel, Modreuant. The fact is that I said it and you have taken me at my word. The fault lies with me."

"What is wrong in saying that Britons, being firm in the faith of Christ, should not rely on superstitions and magic to protect them against the invasions of the Saxons?" demanded Modreuant.

"What is wrong in saying that they should put their trust in their swords and shields and in the ability of their High King to drive the Saxon from our shores?"

Myrddin stared hard at the dark, triumphant eyes of Modreuant.

"Nothing . . . if said generally between friends. But when translated to the irresponsible action of removing sacred relics . . .!" He made a gesture with his hand. "We Britons have an older faith which goes back to the dawn of time and which, while we now temper it with the new beliefs, we cannot discard overnight. For countless centuries the story has been handed down that the relics of Bran the Blessed, brought back from Ireland by his faithful companions and buried on the Hill of the Ravens, would protect Britain against all foreign invasion and eventually secure our victory against any invader."

Modreuant pursed his lips derisively.

"We know the tale, Myrddin. A tale told by old men to excite the imagination of children. Did it protect Britain from the coming of the Romans?"

Myrddin's eyes narrowed.

"It did. Was not the great Caesar, Julius, twice thwarted when he tried to conquer these lands?"

"But when the Romans came again one hundred years later," Modreuant smiled, "they came with such armies as defeated our great King Caradoc and they stayed."

"Yet where are the Romans now, Modreuant? We are still here but they have long gone and their empire is but a fading memory. The tale of Bran the Blessed may have some truth in it. And if it does not, the important thing is that the people believe in it. Children are taught it with their mother's milk. Bran, son of Llyr, was the greatest ruler of our people in the days at the dawn of time, a time which was and yet may come again. For tens of hundreds of years our people have held sacred his relics as talisman against misfortune."

Modreuant sighed in exasperation.

"I but heard my uncle's wish, stated clearly, that the people should not rely on magical charms and fetishes," snapped Modreuant. "I have a witness. Drem, who is a churchman . . ."

"And your creature," snapped Myrddin.

"Creirwy, prioress of Cunotigern's Priory, was another witness. Do you impugn my sister?"

Myrddin raised his eyes to the ceiling in eloquent expression.

Modreuant went on: "Knowing my uncle's wish, I had Bran's relics dug up and brought here so that the people will know that it is only Artios they should rely on—Artios and the one true God."

He paused, glancing triumphantly at the worried face of Artios.

"Now we should proclaim to the people what has been done so that they might know they are ruled by a strong king who answers only to the one true God."

Myrddin's face was white. "Perhaps, Modreuant, you brought the relics hither by guile so that people, alarmed at such a desecration and angered at this affront to their ancient belief, will turn from Artios . . . and who would be his natural successor?"

Modreuant's hand slipped to his sword hilt, a flash of anger on his brow.

"By the . . ." he began, but Artios intervened.

"Myrddin!" he cried, rising from his chair and placing himself between the elderly man and Modreuant. "Quarrel not over me. I have already admitted my responsibility. I did say what I did say. There is no denying it. Modreuant merely acted on what he thought were my wishes. I must accept responsibility."

He turned to Modreuant.

"Where are the relics of Bran the Blessed now?"

"Safe at the Priory of Cunotigern."

The young king hesitated and turned to Myrddin.

"You have counselled me wisely this last year, Myrddin. Through your advice I have become High King of Britain and met the Saxons in our first great victory. For the first time since my predecessor, Natan-leod, perished with five thousand of his best warriors under the swords of the Saxons at the marsh which now bears his name, we Britons have stood up to the invader and demonstrated that our annihilation will not be an easy task. For that, I, and all Britons, owe you more than we can repay. I acknowledge that you have a wisdom beyond understanding and the ability to scan the future. Tell me, Myrddin, what may come of this?"

The old man sighed and hunched his shoulders.

"I have already examined the stars in their courses and it bodes ill for the future of our people if the relics of Bran the Blessed are not returned to the Hill of the Ravens immediately."

Modreuant laughed harshly and dismissively, at the same time giving at sideways glance at Artios.

"Keep such tales for the children at the time of their putting to bed. We are warriors in this hall."

Myrddin ignored him.

"Your destiny, Artios, is partly your own to control, my young Bear," he smiled indulgently at the High King. "Your skill will give you many victories yet over the Saxons. But the day must come, and may it be a long time coming, when, because of this desecration and your acceptance of responsibility for it, the stars that now shine down on us will look down on your own blood staining a battlefield . . . and not just the blood of Artios," the old man turned to gaze evenly at the black haired Modreuant. "Your blood as well shall stain the same field and ravens shall scream as foreigners begin to trample over the flower of Britain's valour."

"What evil talk is this?" snapped Modreuant. "Such talk is treason to the High King!"

"Treasonable action carries more guilt than treasonable talk," replied Myrddin dryly.

"Yet it is you who talk of my death, Myrddin," interrupted Artios his voice almost inaudible.

"Yes. But I do not plot it. If the relics be not returned, young Bear, I cannot intervene to stop what is written in the heavens." Myrddin replied. "So, Artios, let your own warriors ensure the return of the relics." He glanced significantly at Modreuant. "And let everyone here take oath that no word is to be spoken of this matter again."

"Then you place great store in this magic? More than a faith in the one true God?" pressed Artios.

Myrddin smiled softly.

"There are many things which are not given to our understanding, young Bear. This is my advice. Send your warriors to return the relics of Bran the Blessed or we will one day see a nation descended from the Saxons ruling this island while our children's children will be pressed in the remote places, into the fastnesses, scarce daring to speak nor observe their own language and customs. They will be as slaves in their own lands, dried chaffs of wheat blown hither and thither by the whim of the Saxons."

Artios lowered his head and sighed.

"So be it," he said softly. "The relics must be returned."

It was almost too easy. Wulfgar waited until Creirwy had turned to open the door of his cell and then he acted. He sprung forward and clasped his hand across the girl's mouth, preventing her from crying out and forced her to the ground to pinion her struggling form under the weight of his body. It took several moments to rip some linen to bind and gag her. He left her trussed on the bed and peered out into the gloomy twilight. The buildings of the priory seemed deserted.

Wulfgar's lips thinned into a triumphant smile.

The girl had said that Drem was guarding the treasure in a place called the chapel. Wulfgar knew she meant the main temple, a large building in the corner of the priory. Keeping to the shadows, the thane of Wocca's *tun* moved quietly around the buildings until he came to the large structure of the temple.

His first thoughts had been simply to seize a horse and flee from the priory but the idea grew—why should he return to Wocca's *tun* empty handed and with the shame of having been made to take an oath to Woden to serve the enemies of his people? He would take back this fabulous treasure for which the Wealhas had risked so much. Not only the treasure, but he would take back the priestess for his own pleasures to appease his anger at being made to supplicate to the gods of the Wealhas and be shamed in the eyes of Woden.

He moved to the door of the temple building and found it slightly ajar.

He halted frowning.

A single voice was chanting in curious rhythms. He peered inside. The building was deserted except for a figure kneeling before a richly decorated table at the far end of the hall. A large silver cross, the symbol of the Wealhas' gods, stood on it between two tall lighted candles. Before the table, a little to one side, was the sack which Drem had brought from the ruined city. And there was Drem himself, on his knees, head bowed before the table, chanting away to his gods.

Wulfgar could have roared with laughter at his luck.

Woden was with him!

His footsteps were noiseless as he moved quietly up the aisle behind Drem. He was almost within reach when Drem's voice halted. Perhaps he had been alerted by a sixth sense, or a shadow falling across him, or even by the spluttering of one of the altar candles caused by the draught from the door. He swung round and his eyes widened as he saw Wulfgar poised above him.

"Your oath!" he cried out, as if producing a talisman. "You gave your oath!"

Wulfgar merely laughed at the Wealhas' naivety.

Drem made a grab for Wulfgar's legs but the thane of Wocca's *tun* kicked out, a swift kick which caught the priest in the throat. The man's head jerked back and his body went sprawling into the

table, sending the symbol of the Wealhas' gods crashing down.
In a trice, Wulfgar was at the throat of the priest but it took
only a moment's glance to see that the man was dead, his neck
broken.

Smiling grimly, the Saxon grabbed the knife carried in the
priest's belt and the sack which he had been guarding.

The way to the stables he knew well enough having been
shown it when he began his journey with Drem and Mud to
the ruined city. He paused at the door of the temple. The din
of the falling cross had apparently roused no one in the priory
from their slumbers.

He crossed to the stable and it was a matter of moments for
his skilled hands to saddle two horses, tying the sack securely to
the pommel of the one he had chosen for himself.

The eye of Woden was on him for he opened the stable door
and observed the silence throughout the buildings of the priory.
He went back to the cell in which he had been confined and
grinning, lifted the struggling body of Creirwy from the bed
and threw her bodily across his broad shoulder. He returned
to the stable and deposited her on one of the horses, tying her
legs to the stirrups and her hands before her on the pommel to
secure her.

He was about to mount the other horse when the light of
flickering torch glinted on something standing against the wall.

Woden's luck, again!

A discarded sword stood balanced against the wall. He caught
it up and tested its balance. It was not such a weapon as he
would wish but it was better than Drem's little knife which he
now carried at his belt. He raised the weapon above his head
with a grin and softly mouthed "Woden!" He was a man again!
A warrior and thane of Wocca's *tun*. Now he could be absolved
from the shame of serving the Wealhas.

With a light heart, he scrambled onto his horse, clutching up
the lead rein of the horse on which Creirwy sat, still struggling
against her bonds.

With a thump of his heels against the flanks of his mount,
Wulfgar sent it charging forth out of the doors of the stables,
followed by its companion. Across to the entrance of the
priory—gates that were never closed according to the Wealhas'
religious customs—and into the darkness of the open countryside
he urged the horses. As the beasts clattered over the stone flagged
courtyard through the gates, Wulfgar heard a cry of alarm. A
figure leapt before him out of the darkness in an effort to stop

him but he urged him mount onwards, at the same time swinging back his sword arm in a long, curving slash. He heard a cry of agony fading behind him as he sped onward. Then he felt a breath of wind, heard a hiss, as someone let loose an arrow.

Moments later, Wulfgar was urging the horses into the dark shelter of the forest and galloping along its darkened pathway, away from the priory of Cunotigern.

Instead of heading eastward, directly towards the lands held by the Saxons, Wulfgar, in order to trick the Wealhas, turned southwards, avoiding places of habitation.

It was three days later that the thane of Wocca's *tun* found himself encamped on a cliff top overlooking a broad stretch of grey sea. It was a lonely spot. Yet the noise was enough to make his head throb. He felt oppressed by the scream of gulls and the powerful pounding of the restless seas on the rocks just below the cliff edge. He was confident now; confident that he had managed to evade any Wealhas following his trail.

"We will soon be in the lands of Cissa and the West Saxons," Wulfgar confided cheerfully to Creirwy who lay bound on the far side of the fire he had made. He had just finished a meal of a hare which he had snared the day before. Feeding the girl was always difficult. She was an absolute wildcat. He would have removed her bonds some time ago, if only to make the journey easy on himself, but she fought him at every opportunity. Mealtimes were especially difficult. No sooner had he released her hands so that she might eat then she was attempting to escape. If only he did not find her so attractive. He could be rid of her with one quick push over the cliff and his journey home would be so much easier.

He sighed deeply and stirred uneasily at his thoughts. "By this evening we shall be at Cissa's *tun*," he went on. "We shall ride along these cliffs due eastward now. And after several more days we will eventually find ourselves at Wocca's *tun*." Except, he suddenly thought, Wocca and his thanes had all been slaughtered except himself. He would be *eorldoman* of his people now. Wulfgar's *tun*. It had a better ring about it.

"May you rot for betraying your oath to your god," snapped Creirwy in reply. "You hold him in little regard to disregard your promise to serve my brother."

Wulfgar chuckled with amusement.

"I took oath only to escort Drem and Mod to the ruined city and bring them safely back to Modreuant at the priory of Cunotigern. I did so. Nothing else was promised. When I completed my task, had your brother allowed me to leave, I would have left in peace. For at that time my oath to serve him ended. I was under no oath when he made me prisoner and so I could escape when and as I willed."

Creirwy glowered in anger at the warrior.

"You had no right to rob and kill Drem."

"I had every right," Wulfgar replied. "I had every right to compensate myself as I saw fit for the misfortune your brother visited on me."

He looked at the girl's resentful face, her bosom heaving with the anger of her breath and her lips slightly parted. Wulfgar shivered with desire. By Frig, goddess of love, the young warrior had never felt such passion as when he gazed down on the helpless Wealha girl. He licked his dry lips as he fought to control his lustful thoughts.

"Yes Kerry," (he could never wrap his tongue properly around the Weilsc name Creirwy), "I have every right to compensate myself according to the custom of my people."

Creirwy's eyes widened slightly at the change of tone in his voice. She was woman enough to realise the desire raging in his mind.

"You have Drem's sack," she said nervously. "Why not take it and go?"

He smiled, suddenly giving up the struggle within him.

"But I also have you. Therefore I am even richer."

Fear shone for a moment in the girl's eyes as the Saxon warrior moved towards her and stood over her prone form.

"No!" she gasped.

Her agitation seemed to excite him further.

Wulfgar dropped to his knees by her recumbent figure and placing a hand behind her head, steadying it from twisting from side to side by tangling his fingers in her hair, he slowly brought her face towards his, his mouth meshing savagely against her own. For several minutes the girl tried to struggle in his powerful grasp and then she relaxed. To the Saxon's surprise, she struggled no more, she did not attempt to cry out nor try to fight against him. Instead, he found she was pressing forward against him. She seemed to bend her face eagerly to his, mouth open, tongue darting.

He pulled back to stare down at her in bewilderment.

Her eyes were sparkling, cheeks flushed and a smile of lascivi- ous desire masked her face. He felt his throat go dry with craving to possess the woman. He felt desire and triumph.

So the priestess was a woman after all!

The Saxon thane bent his head again.

"No, Wulfgar!" she said softly, twisting her head from his.

He hesitated, frowning. What trick was this now?

"It is unfair," purred Creirwy. "My hands are bound. Unloosen my bounds so that our joy in this moment may be mutual."

Wulfgar, trembling with his passion, eagerly plucked at the knife in his belt, Drem's knife, and slashed at the bonds which held Creirwy's wrists. She came into his arms eagerly, willingly . . .

The blow was like a hard punch to the stomach. For a moment he hesitated wondering if he had knocked himself against a rock. He reached down a hand, suddenly feeling the warm liquid spilling over his clothes.

In disbelief he rolled away from the girl, staring downwards.

The handle of Drem's knife was sticking out of his stomach.

He raised his eyes to Creirwy in confusion.

The girl's face was utterly changed. The eyes burned with venomous hatred, the lips were twisted back so that the teeth were barred like fangs.

"Saxon pig!" hissed the girl. "You think to violate me? Live like a pig and so die like one!"

A pain shot through Wulfgar's frame, starting in the depth of his wounded stomach and making every nerve vibrate in agony.

He suddenly knew that he was going to die. The day seem to be growing dark and he glanced around for his sword.

He saw it, resting by the saddle of his horse and made to move towards it but he fell on his face.

He stretched out an arm . . . his fingers clasping at the air.

Creirwy had leapt to her feet, loosening the remaining bonds and stood over him, fists clenched.

Wulfgar raised a pale, sweating face up to her, eyes wide and pleading.

His dry lips tried to form words.

His hand motioned to his sword.

The girl frowned at the sudden transformation of the Saxon's face from brutal warrior into a frightened young man. Some compassion stirred in her causing her to automatically reach forward and lay a hand on the sword.

Hope leapt into Wulfgar's dying eyes.

"Woden!" he gasped, reaching out a hand to take the sword.

Creirwy hesitated a moment more and than her fear and anger drowned out all other emotion.

"Saxon pig!" she hissed and threw the sword from her, out of his reach.

Wulfgar gave an animal like cry of pain and fear and fell back.

It took a while before Creirwy realised that he was dead.

"That was no way for a Saxon thane to die," grunted a voice behind her.

Creirwy swung round, a cry strangling with fear in her throat. Three Saxon warriors stood with drawn swords by the edge of the trees.

One of them was chuckling sourly as he surveyed the scene.

"Perhaps we should have given him his sword, Wuldor, and allowed him to rest in *Wael-heall*?" another of the trio asked, though with a sneer in his voice.

The man called Wuldor spat.

"There are too many thanes in *Wael-heall*, Aedwig," he replied. "It is time that the thanes move aside and allow us poor *ceorls* a place with Woden in the life hereafter."

The others chuckled at his jest. The one called Aedwig raised his sword and cried "Woden!", falling backward in the manner of a man struck down. Then he scrambled to his feet guffawing at his crude humour. His beady eyes fell on the trembling girl.

"But what have we here . . . a Wealha woman?"

Creirwy had stood frozen in terror at the appearance of the rough clad, evil looking Saxons.

Now, spurred by desperation, Creirwy sprang towards the horses. She could have reached them just ahead of the Saxons, for their reactions were slow, had not, for some inexplicable instinct, she tried to make a grab for Drem's sack as well.

The extra few seconds were enough to allow the man called Wuldor to grab her. She twisted in his powerful arms screaming and clawing at his face; drawing long weals of blood on his cheeks. In anger, the burly *ceorl* raised her bodily above his head in both hands and, with one mighty jerk, he threw her from him. Her screaming form disappeared over the edge of the cliff, plunging down to the rock strewn sea below.

Wuldor's companions came to his side. Aedwig shook his head sadly.

"A waste, Wuldor. A waste. She was young and attractive and could have satisfied all our wants for a while."

Wuldor spat again in disgust and raised a hand to his bleeding face.

"She was a Wealha bitch. We can find more like her."

His companion Aedwig turned towards the sack.

"She wanted that sack badly enough. Maybe it was the thane's loot, some treasure from a Wealha temple?"

He made a move towards it.

Wuldor reached out a hand to push Aedwig aside so that he might pick up the sack first.

Aedwig bit his lip in annoyance. Although Wuldor was chief of their band, he was chief by their sufferance and too often he behaved as if he were a thane rather than just a fellow *ceorl*. One day he would be challenged. Aedwig bit his lip and then gave a mental shrug. One day. But not today.

They watched as Wuldor scooped up the sack and plucked eagerly at the thongs which held its neck together. He opened it and peered eagerly in.

Wuldor stared at the contents of the sack, his eyes wide in disbelief and disgust.

An ancient, stained human skull grinned up with sightless eyes. It was still earth encrusted, the mud and dirt clung obstinately to it.

"What is this?" he breathed softly. "There is no treasure?"

The others peered over his shoulder in anger.

"What would the Wealha bitch want with an ancient skull?" demanded Aedwig.

Wuldor shuddered suddenly.

"Maybe she was a witch. Woden's curse on her and this sack!"

He took it to the cliff edge and whirled it once, twice and again around his head before sending it flying out over the cliff edge into the foaming seas below.

# BLUEFLOW
## by Don Wilcox

*Now for some slightly lighter relief. Don Wilcox (1905–) was a prolific writer of science fiction and fantasy for the pulp magazines back in the 1940s. When the pulps faded away in their losing battle against paperbacks and television. Wilcox turned to other professions. Now, living in retirement in Florida, he turns his hand to portrait painting. Because of his artistic temperament I asked Don to write an Arthurian story featuring the magical talents of a painter. The following is the result. It also introduces us to the darkening clouds of Guinevere's relationship with Lancelot.*

A wandering artist who loved walking by moonlight strayed through a strange forest from midnight to dawn with no certain destination. At daylight, reaching the edge of a meadow, he removed the packets of paints and brushes from his shoulders, placed them on the ground, and lay down to sleep. He awakened when the noon sun was beating down on him, warm and friendly.

He looked up to see an old man standing near, gazing at him. What a long white beard. What bright eyes, gleaming through the wrinkles of the mysterious old face.

The old man spoke. "Good noon, my friend." Low, gentle voice. "Are you not a stranger here? Are you lost?"

"Never lost," the artist replied. "Just roving through forests to explore more of this beautiful world." He rose up on one elbow and brushed his ruffled hair.

104

"I see that you have brought paints and brushes. An interesting way to travel."

"I am a painter, as you have probably guessed. Some people believe I am a great artist. They call me Master Artist Blueflow." He sat up while explaining his name. Friends had given it to him when he was a child. "It's a fitting name because I flow, mentally, with the skies of ever-changing blue." He came to his feet and gestured toward the sky. "Always flowing blue. Sunset, sunrise, noon. Peaceful days and storms. I have made a list of eighty blues. I even have names for them—and of course there are many more."

The old man looked down at the display of paints: twenty-one colors arranged in three rows of little leather cups.

"I hope to watch you paint someday. Permit me to ask, doesn't the sun make your cups of paint go dry? You must have to mix fresh fluid daily."

The artist smiled. "You have guessed one of my problems. You yourself must be a painter."

"I happen to be a magician, as the people of this land will tell you. My name is Merlin. I have many powers. If you wish, I could freshen your paints at this moment." His upraised hand suddenly held a container of liquid. "I feel sure you would like the results, Mr. Blueflow. If you wish—"

The master artist was cautious. "Your offer has the sound of a gift. I should return the favor somehow. Perhaps you wish me to paint your portrait."

"A portrait of me?" The old man laughed. "I am quite a complex subject. Do you think you could do me justice?"

The artist smiled with amusement. "Quite honestly, no. I would probably paint your beautiful beard in five minutes. You may have taken fifty years to grow it. Indeed I would not be doing you justice."

"A generous answer, my friend. However, portrait painting must be expensive. Let's try to reach a bargain. Have you observed yonder brown building at the edge of the trees? It's a travelers' lodge. There you could sleep, eat, bathe and rest to suit your needs for a day or two. I will gladly pay for your lodging. Later, you may undertake to paint me if you wish."

The plan sounded agreeable, and Master Artist Blueflow immediately went to the lodge.

The following day he asked the people where he could find the elderly man with the white beard. They answered that he had left early on business. To return soon? No one knew. He was never predictable.

Blueflow said, "I must find him to paint his picture. I owe it to him." Then someone brought a slab of wood, finely polished, ready for painting. The lodge keeper explained, "The old man left this for you in case you want to start the painting in his absence."

"I'll start at once," Blueflow said.

He began. The paints were surprisingly fresh and responsive and the brushes moved fast. Some of the people at the lodge gathered near, watching, guessing that he might start the background during the subject's absence. To their surprise he did more. He painted, with a few touches, the shape of the head; with a few careful strokes he suggested the features; then with amazing delicacy came the mysterious wrinkles around the burning bright eyes. Soon the slightly bent shoulders appeared. And finally the magnificent white beard with its tinges of blue shadows began to take form. In less than half an hour the painting was almost complete. The colors of the garments were, at the start, a reminder of the clothes the old man had worn the previous day.

How did the artist do it? He explained briefly. This was a skill that he had acquired with years of self-training. To memorize a face. To hold it in his mind and paint from the mental image.

Suddenly he did something that puzzled the onlookers. He began changing the color of the shirt. One of the watchers spoke.

"Excuse me, Mr. Blueflow, but I recall he was wearing a yellow shirt last evening. Did you forget? I see you're now changing it to green."

The artist turned to glance across the room. "Your memory is correct, my friend, but I just now caught the strange feeling that the old man has returned and has asked me to paint it green. Am I mistaken?"

Someone else spoke up. "The fact is, he did come in, just two minutes ago, and paused for a moment to watch."

Blueflow nodded. "That was the feeling that I caught through the air. Where has he gone?"

"Into his room, but—pardon me—in truth he was still wearing the same yellow shirt from yesterday."

"Strange," Blueflow said. "These mental messages—" He broke off, for at that moment the old man returned from his room. And now he was wearing green. The viewers pointed, puzzled. "Look, he's changed." It was something the artist had felt!

Old Merlin came up briskly, saw the completed painting, and exclaimed in celebration. "Mr. Blueflow! Mr. Blueflow! You've already done me. And I like it! Every detail! Even my clothing! How on earth could you do it?" Merlin whirled with a grand gesture; he spun with such excitement that his flying beard created a small whirlwind. He was laughing, lifting his arms in tribute to the artist's victory. "I'm going to give a banquet for you tonight—and all of you are invited!"

# II

Before Artist Blueflow left the following morning he had been treated to many stories about the greatest, most noble king. And the Round Table where the most valorous knights came together. And the oath of knighthood that was lifting this part of the world to new levels of excellence. This was a morning for such a wandering artist as Blueflow not to talk but to listen. To listen in admiration. These good words had filled him. He would not forget the hospitality of these friendly people.

While walking along the paths beyond the meadow he saw many knights in armor riding out in various directions. Not toward combat, he was told, but for practicing their skills across the open lands. One rode near to offer him a ride to the castle, which was over the hills. No, thank you, it was pleasant to walk. Others volunteered to help him with his luggage. "No, thank you, I always carry my paints personally."

"Will we see you painting sometime? We have heard about your painting of Merlin." "Will you paint the king or the queen?"

Their praise-filled conversation revealed a very favorable circumstance: it was well known at Camelot that the great King Arthur wanted a painting of himself and his queen. It should be as tall and as wide as necessary to represent the two of them, life-size, sitting together.

Blueflow asked, "Are there no artists in King Arthur's domain?"

The answer was, yes, a few. Two, especially, were honored for their skills. These were two friendly rivals. Each had been requested to do the double portrait, but somehow the plan had languished. Blueflow was puzzled over it.

Hiking up the long slope, he now caught sight of the vast castle against the sky. The towers of pink, gold and blue were like a great fantastic mountain moulded into architecture. "I am arriving," he said to himself. "Will I indeed have a chance to paint some of the royalty?"

Portcullis and drawbridge were ready; the way was open. At once he was inside, following mazes of walkways among the sand-colored walls. His path led him outward into a long curving balcony. From various doorways came voices of people at work. To his left he looked down on the wide parade grounds that extended to the east. Again the knights on horseback could be seen, sometimes racing, drilling in formation, practicing their skills. On his right, a few spectators were looking down from tower windows. Fragrance filled the air, flowing over the open lands. Blueflow paused, resting his arms on the railing, enjoying the scene.

Someone was walking toward him, calling to him. He was a slender young man dressed in an ill-fitting outfit of light green. He was not in knight's clothing but was perhaps in the service of some castle department. He gave a pleasant wave and introduced himself. He said he had been asked to find this stranger and guide him.

"My name is Breunor. I believe you are the artist who has gained fame for himself by painting Merlin the Magician. Your reputation has arrived ahead of you. Some of the knights who were at the lodge yesterday while you were painting came back to the castle and told King Arthur about you."

"The great King Arthur? He knows about me?"

"He is interested in your abilities. He has long wished for a portrait of himself and his beautiful Queen Guinevere. Last night at the lodge, after you retired following the banquet, the two best-known artists at this castle, hearing of your portrait of Merlin, rode out to the lodge and saw—"

"Saw the portrait that I painted?"

"Saw and were enthusiastic. They came back to talk with our king about you. As a result, the king has been making plans this morning. He is a man of action. He has decided to put you to work at once."

"Are you leading me to his throne? Am I to have the privilege of meeting him?"

"Unfortunately he is very busy at this hour. He is administering oaths to the newly selected knights. It's a very sacred and emotional ceremony—but I see you have your painting equipment at hand."

"Always."

"This is good. You will begin painting at once. The scene is being arranged on this east balcony, on the curve a few steps ahead. But first we'll pause for a bit of food and drink, and by that time the queen will be ready."

"Do you have the panel on which I'll paint?"

"Fortunately, yes. The perfect size for the two subjects, king and queen, life-size, sitting together. It's the panel that was previously prepared for one or the other of the two artists. Quite ready but untouched."

Blueflow gave his guide a questioning look. "Tell me what happened, Mr. Breunor. Was there a conflict between the two of them? I'm a man of peace. Am I about to walk into a fight?"

Breunor laughed. "Peace, I assure you. These two artists defer to each other like a couple of comedians. When the offer of the job was in the air, each preferred that the honour go to the other. They would have done the painting jointly if it could have been done. The block was that the king himself was always too busy. He could never find time to stop and pose. And Queen Guinevere herself realized that her hope was futile. But now, suddenly, following the reports of your success with Merlin, the king feels sure. Are you now ready to go to the scene and set up your paints?"

"Ah—didn't you mention—"

"Oh, forgive me. Food and drink before you start. Of course. This way, please."

# III

Beautiful Queen Guinevere, protected from the glare of the early afternoon sun, sat in a cushioned chair, waiting for the artist she had been promised. She was dressed in pink, white and lavender, and adorned with jewelry. She was slightly ill-at-ease, as some of her friends may have noticed. Not from the task of posing, however, but because her usual lady-in-waiting was not with her, having gone on a short vacation. This abrupt event had been planned only this morning. All of which explained the presence of a "substitute" lady-in-waiting, a tall, nervous one who was adjusting the queen's clothing.

"She's visiting here this week—the tall one in the dark purple and green. She came from a distant village. Her name is Mellicent.

Years ago she was Guinevere's companion, and this week she's reenacting her old role of self-importance. It was her idea to bring three guards with her because she doesn't trust knights. If she worries over imaginary dangers, try to overlook it."

Blueflow hardly noticed what was being said. For the moment he was transfixed. Guinevere's beauty held him. The descriptions that he had heard were not exaggerated. Yes, she was stunningly beautiful. All right, stop acting paralyzed, he scolded himself. She is already posed, waiting. He lined out his paints and brushes in the order he liked.

More explanations from Breunor? Something of secret importance that should be confided to him?

"Her beauty has such drawing power—"

Low voice. Was this something that Blueflow really needed to know?

"—such drawing power that one of our great knights—the very popular knight named Lancelot—highly skilled—yes, and handsome—but that's another story. I'll not burden you—"

The half-whispered words were left unfinished. Blueflow gave complete attention to what he was doing. No more digressions. The queen was sitting perfectly. His paints were fresh and the brushes were swift. Start where? With the cascade of golden brown hair that framed her face? He was beginning. Several people were gathering too close. That substitute lady-in-waiting, Mellicent had promised to hold them back. She started to scold them—yes, they began to respond. Good, some free working space around him now. The brush was in action. The panel had been well mounted, the surface was smooth and clean. With a light purple stroke Blueflow drew a nearly vertical dividing line, a guide to his separation of the space. Here was where the shoulders of the king and the queen would touch, and where the king's hand would reach over to touch hers as they sat close together. All the space on the left side would remain untouched until sometime when the king would come and pose.

When would that be? Optimistically, Breunor had said that possibly a small party of knights, together with the king himself, might ride along the parade grounds within view of the balcony sometime this afternoon. If so, the king might be persuaded to stop for a few minutes. A stairway of eighteen or twenty steps led up from the parade ground level. This visit could give Blueflow at least a passing glance at the great man himself.

Were the onlookers coming too close again to Blueflow's paints and brushes? Should he speak to the lady-in-waiting? No, better not. It might bruise her feeling of authority. He sensed that this whole occasion was felt by her to be an imposition, and he was the cause of it.

Who were these gathering spectators? Some were bringing chairs, crowding up around the area of action. Those ladies dressed in finery were probably the wives of knights, turning the event into a game. There were quieter onlookers too, by now the people on the left, dressed in dull brown and gray. They were some of the palace workers. Their chores had brought them to this east porch and here they had stopped to watch.

At the other side were three uniformed guards who stood stiffly by the stone railing. From Breunor's words, Blueflow knew they were not a part of Camelot, but were Mellicent's private protection, her three-man army from her distant village. Their presence gave Mellicent self-importance, no doubt.

Blueflow was painting now with a swift hand. The crowd was attentive. Whispers but no talking. Paint, paint, paint! Catch quick glimpses of his subject, perfectly posed. What his eyes saw his skilled hand converted into brush strokes.

For nearly an hour the spectators were entranced. Even Mellicent. She hovered near, frozen in fascination.

Finally Blueflow stepped back to see the picture from a little distance. He added a few touches and the work was done. Mellicent gave a slight gesture to the onlookers. Yes, he was finished. "But don't crowd. Make way for her highness."

Queen Guinevere rose, radiant with pleasure, and stepped forward. To Artist Blueflow she smiled and nodded. He bowed. Now all began to speak soft words of praise. Breunor tapped Blueflow on the shoulder and whispered, "Wonderful, my friend."

Quite abruptly the praise was cut short. Mellicent spoke with a tone of command. Enough of confusion. She ordered the onlookers to stand aside.

"Back to your seats, everyone. This artist is only half done. Give him room."

What was going to happen next? Everyone wondered.

"All right, Mr. Artist." Mellicent assumed the role of a general commanding the battle to continue. "Go ahead. You're wasting time."

Blueflow gave her a puzzled look. "What are you trying to tell me?"

"Pick up your brushes and go on with the job—the second half—the portrait of the king."

Blueflow frowned. "Miss Mellicent, don't you realize we need the king himself to be here, to pose? We must wait. He may come sometime this afternoon."

Mellicent's voice was edged with suspicion. "Are you trying to dodge us? We know about you. We've heard how you painted Merlin the Magician while he was absent. They say you did it from memory. Let's see you do the same for our king."

Blueflow was shaking his head slowly. "Miss Mellicent, I was able to do that only because Merlin's face was fresh in my mind. But I have never seen King Arthur."

"You're dodging. You're lying. Everyone has seen King Arthur."

"You're quite mistaken, Miss Mellicent. I arrived only this morning."

She turned her sharp glare on Breunor. "Do you know anything about this artist Scullion?"

"He's telling the truth. He has never seen King Arthur. He came over from the lodge this morning."

The substitute lady-in-waiting was about to break into rage, being defied. Blueflow spoke quietly. "Miss Mellicent, your queen has been sitting beautifully for a full hour. Posing isn't easy. We might ask if she'd like a drink. Perhaps someone—"

He glanced at Breunor and the friendly guide motioned to one of the attendants. At once a cup of wine was brought to the queen. With a thank-you she accepted and drank. Then other courtesies were extended. The artist was pleased to accept a cup of water.

Refreshed, he turned to Mellicent and the others closed around him in a mood of natural friendliness. "As to my going ahead in the king's absence, there may be a way. Listen closely, please. There is a sort of miraculous method that only a few artists know how to use."

"Do it," Mellicent said.

"I will try, but only on certain conditions. Our Mr. Breunor who is kindly guiding me must be given command of everyone. The others must obey him and there must be no mistake. You, Miss Mellicent, must cooperate. And all of those around you. If you agree, I will try."

"Do it," Mellicent repeated.

# IV

The scene was changed and Blueflow was ready to start the lefthand side of the panel. The queen's chair had been moved close. She understood that she must be blindfolded to help her concentrate.

Three screens larger than doors had been brought from another part of the balcony. They were placed to stand upright in triangular arrangement, to enclose the artist and the subject at work.

At the start, Breunor and Mellicent were detained for a moment beside the queen and the artist inside the enclosure. It was Blueflow's wish that they listen while he explained his method. The crowd was closed out.

"As you know," Blueflow said, "I tested our Queen Guinevere moments ago with a few questions. She has proved to me that she is able to close her eyes and see a clear mental picture of his majesty King Arthur."

"What is that supposed to prove?" Mellicent asked. Breunor gave her a sign that said, "Hush and listen."

Blueflow continued, "Am I quite right, your highness? Can you see the king clearly in your mind."

Her reply was, "Of course. It's easy."

"Good. That's the whole secret of the miracle-art that I'm about to undertake. This means that your mind is able to hold the clear picture that I want to paint on this panel. Do you understand?"

"I understand."

"All right. We are now blindfolding you to help your concentration, and at once you will begin seeing his image. Your mental picture will enter my mind and guide my art. We are now almost ready. The crowd is outside these screens and will be kept silent. Miss Mellicent and Master Breunor are going out to join them. Now they have gone. You and I are alone within this triangle so that no one can see what I'm painting. Are you ready?"

"Ready."

"As you look at his majesty in your mind I want you to notice the shape of his forehead. Straight? Slanted? Wide? Narrow? You are not to answer me in words. My mind is taking the image from your mind. Your mental images guide my hand. And now I am painting."

"You are painting!" the queen repeated. "I don't know how you can do it. And I can't see through the blindfold, but I believe you, Mr. Artist. *My mind is telling you what to paint.*"

"Your highness, you are understanding perfectly. Keep your mind working. We won't have to talk. You keep watching your visions closely and my hand will keep working."

"And no one is watching us? No one?"

"No one."

The work went on quietly. Blueflow breathed slowly with a feeling of gratefulness. He spoke only an occasional word of guidance ... "Eyebrows ... cheekbones ... flesh colors ... shadows under the brows ... highlights on the bridge of the nose ..." The details were coming through to him faster than he could speak. Now he was catching the color areas on the face, a design that surely matched the lines of a helmet that had been worn in the sun ... on and on ... the upward tilt of one shoulder adjusted to the weight of the armor ...

Faster than human speech could have described the numberless details, the picture kept coming through. She was breathing slowly, almost as though she had gone into a trance ... a trance of visualizing the features she knew so well ...

Blueflow thought, would Mellicent suddenly appear around the corner of a screen and break the spell?. No, no such trouble. Breunor was in control, over there on the other side of the enclosure. All was well. The master artist worked on at lightning speed. Paint, paint! More images. More details. A profusion of colors from paints that were doubly alive from some of the magic the magician had once given them. Paint, paint! Keep catching the images that came through like a chain of fire. Shoulders, chest, form of the masterful body, sturdily armored; reflecting shafts of sunlight, shadows of the arms ... Almost finished? More to be done on the background, yes, but that could wait until the full resemblance had been captured. Almost finished? He heard a sigh of the queen's breathing.

At last, break the spell. "Your highness, you may remove the blindfold and see the painting."

"Thank you, Mr. Artist." She removed the blindfold. As if awakening, she saw the painting. Spontaneously she called her joy to the artist. "He's beautiful! He's handsome! So natural!" She jumped up as if to embrace the picture.

"Don't touch, please! It's wet! It will smear!"

Suddenly something changed her manner. She was stepping back from the painting. She touched her hands to her lips, her eyes went wide. She cried out as if in pain.

Mellicent and Breunor must have heard her cry and thought she was hurt. They dashed in, looked, and stood stunned by what they saw. Mellicent's arms flew out in shock. "*Oh, no—NO!*" And Breunor called in a tight, coughing voice. "*What happened?*" Again, Mellicent's shriek. "*That's not King Arthur, that's Sir Lancelot! Your artist has gone wild! This is tragic!*"

The queen was shocked. Artist Blueflow couldn't possibly understand what had gone wrong. It seemed as though something was crushing her. He caught her terrified words. She was moaning, "How did I do it? I was supposed to think of the king. But I slipped. How did my thoughts get mixed?"

Mellicent shouted, "Your artist did it! I'll have him executed! This is a high crime!"

"I did it!" the queen protested with weeping in her voice. "I—I—"

Mellicent cut in. "Not you! That mad painter! He's a criminal! This is blasphemy! Guards, guards, step up! Take this man."

Her uniformed guards came up, confused but trying to obey. At her order they batted down the screens and crowded in on Blueflow to seize him as their prisoner. Not understanding the situation in the slightest, Blueflow yielded. This must be a mistake. Whatever the matter was, let Mellicent and the guards play their game. But now her commands sounded dangerous.

"Crush him! Crush him! Smash the bones of his hands!"

The people were surging forward. What was the commotion all about? Suddenly they saw and were choked with surprise. Somehow an awful thing had happened. The new picture which the artist had added to the panel was not King Arthur, it was Sir Lancelot!

Sir Lancelot! The queen's favorite! What a terrible mistake! No one could understand. No one had time to think. The substitute lady-in-waiting was storming, calling wild orders to her guards. The tall Number One Guard, however, was slow to obey. He stood back while the other two seized Blueflow and pulled him over to the ledge. They placed his hands on the stone surface as Mellicent had ordered. She repeated, "You, Number One, I order you to crush his hands."

The tall guard had taken a battlehammer from inside his coat but he held back. He stared at Mellicent in disbelief. "If we break his fingers he will never paint again."

"I command you."

"I heard." He had moved a step closer.

"Strike!" Mellicent shrieked. "This artist is a criminal. Strike for the sake of the queen!"

The voice of the queen called, "No!" A single clearly spoken command. The tall Number One guard turned and bowed to her. He returned the weapon to his coat. The bewildered group surrounding the scene watched in awe. She was their beloved queen; whatever the situation, her words were sacred.

Now Breunor's voice shouted a surprising discovery. "Look! They're coming across the parade ground—some knights—and the king is with them!"

The queen's voice called, "His majesty! He's coming this way. He'll see. He won't understand!"

Breunor was on the alert. "Can we hide the second picture?"

For an instant Guinevere looked helpless. She covered her eyes with her hand. "Oh, what have I done? Why did I—"

Mellicent screamed at her. "You didn't do it! You didn't! It was that wild artist" She lurched forward, slipped and fell; she sank to the floor in a tantrum, beating her fists. Again Guinevere was controlled. She stood, hand upraised, and called a sharp order. "Mellicent, go! Go back! Go now! Someone help her!" Two friends nearby came to the rescue and led the distraught woman off toward a shadowed aisle.

Breunor was asking, "Shall I erase the second painting? Shall I tear off my shirt and mop off the paint?"

The queen's glance darted around. "Where is the artist?"

Blueflow stepped forward, gave a slight bow. "Your highness."

"Mr. Artist, do you understand what's happened? If my husband the king comes he'll see—he'll see—how shall I explain?"

Blueflow nodded. "Do you want me to remove the man's portrait? I have a wide brush. With your permission I'll brush away the entire left side of the panel." He went to work. The queen urged him to hurry. He worked at all possible speed, and the people around began to whisper in tones of relief. All of the second portrait was disappearing.

For a moment the pressure of time eased, for it appeared that the knights were riding on past. Maybe they would move on at a distance. Blueflow had heard that they were starting on a trip westward which the king had planned. But now the king turned to look back across toward the balcony scene and suddenly he came galloping straight toward the stairway. Two knights came with him. They stayed below to attend his horse. He marched to the stairway and ascended. When he reached the balcony there was only one portrait showing on the panel, and all was serene.


# V


The revered King Arthur stood before the crowd. Everyone bowed.

For a moment he was a proud statue. Motionless, taking in the quiet scene. Handsome in blue with a design of purple and gold across his chest. With fine dignity he lifted his plumed gold and blue cap in a gesture of greeting. Another deep bow from the crowd. They stood applauding. Guinevere, however, continued to bow. When she looked up, King Arthur was before her, arms open, to take her into his embrace.

She gestured toward the painting. The left side of the panel contained no figure, only a light gray smudge that might be a background for the new painting yet to be done. But on the right side was something wonderful: the life-size portrait of Queen Guinevere.

The king was deeply pleased.

He held an arm around her and together they gazed. The king's expression, as seen by the onlookers, was deep adoration, a prayer of devotion to his queen.

Guinevere said, "You are liking it. I see it in your eyes."

"Yes, my dear queen, and I will be doubly pleased if the artist can complete the portrait. But where is he?"

She gestured to Master Artist Blueflow. The artist bowed. He felt the king's gaze on him. The king offered a handshake that was more than the pressure of a strong hand. It was an entrance into Blueflow's heart of the spirit of a great and noble leader.

The king spoke to him in the tone of a friend. "We are grateful. I have heard about your skill from my own two top-ranking artists of Camelot, and also from our Merlin. They have given me the description of your remarkable ability to paint from memory. You know I wish I could take time to pose. But let me ask, Mr. Blueflow. During these minutes could you study my features—my expression—my clothes—my stature? Could it be done by you from memory during my absence? Or am I asking too much?"

Blueflow replied with a slight smile. "Your majesty, what you are asking me to observe I have now already observed and memorized. I am now prepared to start at once."

"Indeed?" The king studied him with admiration. "Sometime within a few days I will return, looking forward to seeing the completed double portrait."

His farewell embrace with the queen was prolonged, as though her heart compelled her to hold him, as though she could hardly let go. Then he gave the crowd a quick wave and bounded down the steps. He and his knights galloped away.

"At once" had been Blueflow's words to his majesty, and without hesitation the artist, with spirits lifted, started the new painting, with the warmth of the king's handshake giving tone to his work. The image in his mind was clear and strong.

At the completion of the portrait several of the spectators spoke words of praise. Were they becoming friendly to him, an itinerant artist? Blueflow wondered. He began packing his equipment and a good friend joined him, an old man with twinkling eyes and a long white beard.

"Do you think you've reached a happy ending?" Merlin asked. "How easily we may be self-deceived by the appearance of success. We must always be prepared for surprises. However—" momentarily changing his mood—"here come a couple of your admirers—those two corpulent fellows in the orange costumes. No deceit from them, I promise."

"I knew they were back of me, watching. I don't know who they are."

"They're the two most highly esteemed artists in Camelot. And I'd better warn you, they're a couple of clowns. I was afraid they might bother you with their jokes while you worked, but you evidently had them hypnotized."

The two orange-clad ones introduced themselves and extended congratulations. One asked, "How do you paint the whole picture out of your head?"

The other said, "We've come over to examine your head. How can you look so normal?"

Again, "What we really want, Brother Blue, is to sign our own names to your paintings, as though they are ours."

"When the king pays us, we'll give you a slice."

"And take you out to a banquet."

Blueflow laughed. "Keep talking. We artists like to be rescued from starvation." He relaxed, listening to their banter.

As they departed they called back. "Save some time for us. We want to take lessons." "Don't run away, but keep out of trouble."

Keep out of trouble? There it was again, a hint of something puzzling, similar to Merlin's remark. Just now, all that Blueflow wanted was to take a long walk away from this balcony. Walk where? Down the long slope away from the castle, across the meadows, back to the lodge where this long day had begun.

"Could I carry some of your luggage?" Merlin asked, joining him. But no, the artist never thought of needing help. Just now his brain was still spinning with images.

"Everything we see along the way," Blueflow confessed, "turns into faces waiting to be painted. These flowers look up at me like a garden of Guineveres. And those tree trunks resemble the one you call Lancelot, loaded down with armor. Or if with branches, they're kings reaching out as if to embrace their beloved queen."

Merlin added to the game, guessing that the plants with prickly spines might recall someone named Mellicent.

"Mellicent," Blueflow laughed. "I had almost forgotten. I hope she doesn't come back with more commands."

Apparently no such thought was in Merlin's mind. The queen had stilled her shrieking voice. But there was a real threat for Blueflow to look out for: the portrait he had painted that had to be erased.

Deep in the night this thought would break in on Blueflow's sleep through a strange circumstance.

# VI

Deep in the night the owner of the lodge tapped on Blueflow's door. "Sorry to awaken you, Mr. Artist, but someone is asking to see you. A friend named Breunor."

As Blueflow knew, Breunor was one of those who had volunteered to keep watch over the painting through the night. Now here he was, standing breathless on the lodge porch in the moonlight.

"Forgive my disturbance, Mr. Blueflow, but something very mystifying has happened to your double portrait."

"Has someone damaged it?"

"No one has touched it. Only the moonlight touched it. It changed."

"Possibly some slight change in the color effects?"

"A complete change in one of the faces," Breunor said. "Several of us were watching as the moonlight began, and—you must believe me—as the moon rose, the king's face melted away. It faded out and changed to the face of Lancelot, the queen's lover—just as you had painted it originally from the mental transfer."

"Unbelievable! There was nothing in my paints to account for this kind of thing. I'm trying to comprehend. Is this part of Camelot? Some mysteries are beyond my understanding." As he read Breunor's countenance he realized that no one should doubt this friend's honesty. "Is the change continuing? And no signs of the king's face visible? Of course I'll be blamed."

"Come back to the castle with me. You'll see for yourself."

They made the trip over the moonlit landscape.

As they approached the castle the moonlight over the scene was beginning to fade. Near the area of the east balcony Blueflow could see shadowy evidences of a crowd. No doubt many persons had watched through the night.

"We'll keep away from that mob," Breunor said. "For you it will be safer. Some of them may be angry over the way your painting has been changed by the moonlight."

"I want to see it for myself," said Blueflow.

"You will. I know a way. Follow me."

Instead of ascending the stairs from the parade ground to the balcony, he led Blueflow into a dark passage, through some heaps of storage in the understructure. He told Blueflow to follow closely through the darkness and feel his way. "There's a secret room up ahead. Here, we're coming into it. Catch sight of that vertical, narrow slice of sky, up, to your left. It's a slip in the architecture. It will be our window. No one sees it from above, but we'll have an upward view. See? A glimpse of the moon. And some of the people in front of your painting. Now, move your head slightly. Can you see it? Do you see how the moonlight has changed your painting?"

Blueflow concentrated his gaze. The night view could be made out. Yes, there it was. "The queen is just the same, but there's no king. What I see is the person I made from her mind, the one you call Sir Lancelot. It has come back!"

"Now you know why the night viewers are amazed—and some of them angry."

Blueflow's eyes took in the surrounding crowd and soon he discovered the queen herself. "Queen Guinevere. Over there to the left. She's acting sick. Does she dread what she sees? The very portrait that came out of her memory!" Blueflow studied the whole puzzling situation. "I don't see Miss Mellicent."

"Mellicent has been sent back to her own town. Now it's the queen's regular staff. That's the real lady-in-waiting trying to lead her away. But look, Blueflow, isn't something new happening to the painting?"

They watched in silence for several minutes. The crowd began to talk with excitement. "Look, look! The moonlight overhead is fading. The white light of dawn is changing the sky—and Sir Lancelot is fading out. His armor is growing dim. Now the lines of the king are coming back!"

Breunor whispered, "A miracle. Right before our eyes!"

Voices were sounding in astonishment. "*King Arthur—returning! His face—the blue of his shoulders—his strong hands—he's returning! The whole portrait! Daylight is bringing him back!*"

The lady-in-waiting was leading the queen forward to see, and everyone could hear her outcries of excitement.

Several minutes later the night crowd realized that the picture had come back to its daytime normality. Finally, eased in their minds, they began to depart. Some were quoting what they had heard the queen say before she left. *This was the picture that his majesty must see when he returns!*

When would he come?

It was certain that the rumors of this magical happening would race through the castle and spread out across the land almost at the speed of lightning. And with what emotional overtones! Even as Blueflow and Breunor listened to the conversations that echoed down to them they realized that some incriminating words were being spoken. Breunor whispered, "You're about to get an earful of danger."

"I'm hearing it. Someone is saying that I'm to blame. They're calling me a trickster. Listen!"

The strongest voice declared, "It was a deliberate act of evil . . . Dastardly mischief . . . It could shatter the peace of Camelot. If it happens again tonight when the moon rises we shouldn't hesitate. We'll hunt that artist down."

"Where did he come from?"

"And where did he go? Didn't he walk down the slope toward the lodge after he finished? We needn't wait for the king's return . . ."

The voices moved out of hearing but Blueflow and Breunor had caught the sound of action.

Blueflow wasn't accustomed to being wrong in his judgments;

however, now he began to ask, had he made a mistake, coming to this land? He should have packed up his luggage and hiked back into the forest as soon as his work was done. Breunor tried to counsel him, but one fact was obvious: he musn't return to the lodge.

"You must stay here, Blueflow, until the air is clear. I'll bring food and water. And a blanket. Before the danger widens I'll go to the lodge and pick up your luggage. I'll go now."

# VII

The magic effect of the moonlight on the portraits each night would soon be known across the land. Of course the moon was an hour later each night but that didn't keep the crowds from coming. It was believed that Sir Lancelot himself, who was stationed with some other knights nearly half a day's ride away, had not only heard; but had come in disguise, on the second night and strolled along the balcony at the back of the groups of onlookers; that he had now seen himself and the queen pictured together enjoying the blessings of a moonlight rendezvous.

Of course everyone was curious to know when King Arthur himself would return and see.

Blueflow, secluded in the understructure hideaway, listened hourly to the passing conversations above. Not all pleasant. Occasionally those hard-voiced accusers could be heard repeating their rumour that the artist must be totally evil, and that his trickery would cause a moral earthquake.

By midmorning of the new day Blueflow saw that the skies were growing dark. Now he heard soft steps approaching and knew that Breunor was returning.

"Big storm coming, Mr. Blueflow. I may have a chance to get you away, out of danger."

The rain came down in blinding torrents, and Blueflow, covered in the blanket from the top of his head to his knees, was led by Breunor up the slope of the balcony, past the guard and out over a narrow walk that led across toward the edge of the forest. Here was a knoll, lost in clouds and rain, thickly covered with trees.

"There, Mr. Blueflow. Catch your breath. Get close under these branches out of the storm, have some food and drink, and I'll give you the news from the lodge."

"If I had only brought my luggage, especially the paints and brushes—"

"They're all right here, almost within reach. I went for them the other day, before those three or four went down to the lodge to look for you. The lodge keeper was on our side, and the searchers never learned anything. They believe you've headed out to the northeast through the forest, in case—"

"In case of what?"

"In case our king, when he comes back and sees the painting switching by night, wants to try you in court. Don't mind my gloomy talk. Go ahead and eat. You must be starved."

"Thanks for food, and for hiding me out. I've taken in hours of overhead conversations, daytimes and nights. Am I safe here until the storm passes? If I accidentally fall asleep, who will be first to find me here?"

Breunor gave him some sort of answer, but it was lost in the roar of the rain.

# VIII

Blueflow slept on a cushion of damp leaves for two days. He awakened to the sounds of men laughing and joking. He blinked his eyes at the sight of two corpulent fellows in orange costumes. Where had he seen these orange clowns before? At first he thought they were having a sword fight with paint brushes—no they were engaged in some sort of game which involved their slapping at each other with wet paint.

They saw that he had awakened. Good. Just in time to see the finish of a contest. The game was not complicated, once you understood.

"See the idea, Mr. Blueflow? The storm tossed us this branch full of leaves. We've hung it up by a cord—"

"And given it a few hundred twists so that it hangs here spinning—"

"So it's a game of speed—a contest—to paint the leaves whirling by—"

"To see how many we can paint with your brushes—"

"*My brushes?*" Blueflow was waking up. He came closer to watch.

"Don't worry, Mr. Blueflow, we're using our own paint. Mine's the orange, his the blue."

"The idea is to slap paint on the leaves with lightning strokes. When the whirl stops, we'll count to see who wins."

"If he loses I'll push his face into the leaves. And paint his eyebrows orange."

"If I win, I'll paint him up with a blue mustache and a blue beard."

Blueflow walked over toward them. "*My brushes?* Where did you find my brushes?"

"Breunor brought all of your equipment up here. It's all hidden there under that fan-shaped bush at the foot of the big tree."

"When?" Blueflow asked. "When did you see him?"

"Two days ago following the big storm. He assigned us to watch over you. It was easy. You've been asleep for two days."

"Trust us, Mr. Blueflow. We're going to keep you out of harm until you have your appointment."

"What appointment?"

"With King Arthur. He returned a couple of days ago and he wants to see you."

Blueflow backed away to give the two orange-clad clowns space to go on with their game, slapping paint at the leaves and accidentally smearing a few strokes on each other's faces.

When the battle wore itself out, the two artists settled down to give Blueflow a few of the details that he wanted to hear. Especially about the king and his first hours after coming back and seeing the painting. Suddenly, to Blueflow's surprise, the two buffoons talked like a couple of sensitive, serious artists.

The king had planned his return, they explained, for two afternoons ago, and the event was to be his viewing of the double portrait, accompanied by his queen. The rain that had gusted in before noon suddenly ended by midafternoon. The two, accompanied by her lady-in-waiting and a few others, walked down the balcony promenade in the golden afternoon sunlight that came through in dramatic brilliance following the rains. Guards had protected the painting with screens throughout the storm. Sunlighted afternoon clouds heightened the color effects as the screens were being removed. King Arthur and Queen Guinevere held each other in close embrace for many minutes. They loved the painting. Later there was a dinner party.

But of course there was another drama yet to come, the one of the appearance of moonlight that would play its magic. It occurred late in the night, the unannounced but fully expected visit of the king to the painted panels. Were many people waiting there to watch from a distance? Curiously, not the expected crowd. Public courtesy to his majesty was evident. He appeared, accompanied by four knights; he sauntered along the way within fifteen or twenty feet of the painting, a few errant clouds intruded on the view; then came a well illuminated moment. The work of art was before his eyes; the queen and her lover together. The king asked no questions of those walking with him. However, it was known that he made a point of returning just before the coming of daylight to see the mysterious changing of the picture back to normal. "As far as we know he made no comments."

"Thank you," Blueflow said when the two Camelot artists had finished their description. "Perhaps he is saving his comments for me. Did you mention there is an appointment in store for me? . . . Will the two of you kindly visit me in prison?"

# IX

Late that night it was Merlin who led Blueflow to the scene of the portraits. His brief words were, "I wish you luck, brave Mr. Blueflow." He conducted the quiet artist to the row of chairs where King Arthur was sitting, watching the moonlight version of Blueflow's art.

One of the knights sitting beside his majesty, rose and moved aside, so that Blueflow could take his seat. The king's eyes turned from the painted panel to the artist. His expression was not unfriendly.

"Mr. Artist," he began in a low voice, "you may be surprised to learn that I am planning to build permanent seats on this part of the balcony, so that people may enjoy this art in comfort."

He paused and watched the affect of his words upon Blueflow. The artist could not read the King's expression and was unsure what to say. The King continued.

"I was surprised to learn about this painting of Sir Lancelot. I felt sure that neither of my two court artists would have painted it."

Blueflow's throat was dry with nerves, but he gulped and said. "I did it."

King Arthur nodded. "That is the information which others have given me. However, Master Merlin tells me that you didn't know what you were doing."

"That is true."

"Are you in the habit of not knowing what you are doing?"

"I knew what I was doing, sire, but I did not realise my mistake."

The king nodded again and turned his eyes back to the portrait. "Had you seen Sir Lancelot before this painting?"

"No, I have never seen him. I attempted to work from mental images, not realising—" Blueflow lapsed into silence.

The king had folded his arms, and it was hard to guess what he was thinking. His eyes were half closed. Then, more alertly, he began to watch the panel. The moonlight from overhead was fading and dawn was starting to transform the painting. The king watched in silent fascination.

Presently he returned to the unfinished conversation. "So you have never seen him. The portrait is quite a good likeness. If it continues to reappear by moonlight many people will come to see it, naturally. It will remind all of us that strange things can happen here at Camelot."

He lapsed into silence for a while, and then turned his eyes fully on Blueflow.

"You have done me a service, Master Artist, for which I thank you. I do not need to go into detail, but let me say that a king needs to always be alert. I shall encourage all visitors to come and see this portrait so that all may marvel at your art, and at the same time consider the world about them, and their part in it. Your talent is being greatly admired. My queen and I thank you deeply for the daylight glory of our portrait."

Blueflow looked into the king's eyes, where he saw a growing spirit overcoming a deeper sadness. The king smiled.

"I have a further idea. You must attune your mind to the mental images, as you call them, of this whole castle. I want you to paint a huge mural, capturing the entire city, bringing it alive. And," he added, as his eyes turned again to the portrait of himself and his wife, now gleaming in the morning sun, "I want it to be a true reflection of this castle, and all who are in it."

Blueflow did not know what to say, but bowed an acceptance to the King. After a while he realised that the audience was at an end, and he was ushered away. The king sat in silence, drinking in the portrait of himself with Guinevere, and dreaming a thousand dreams.

# X

Over the next few weeks Blueflow laboured hard over the mural, using Merlin's enchanted paints. He worked with the two court artists, but while they painted the background and the buildings, it was Blueflow who looked into the hearts and minds of the people who came to watch his work, and captured them forever.

And if you come today, to Camelot, you may be guided from the castle to a nearby knoll. There you will stand among the trees to look back at the fantastic architecture against the sky. And there you will discover, near at hand, a magnificent mural on a wide panel built between two trees, which reflects that same scene. But in that mural are all the citizens of Camelot, and if you stay to watch the mural as the moon rises, you will look into the hearts of the citizens and see what they really desire.

There, among the swirls of blue and gray, stands King Arthur, strong of feature, radiating greatness of spirit. About him his knights, courtiers and citizens go about their business. Each night, Arthur comes and watches the mural, and the people know he is watching them. And there are those who fear for the thoughts that are in their hearts. The pattern of the future is set.

# THE BROTHERHOOD OF BRITAIN
## by Keith Taylor

*This novella, which was specially written for the anthology, is an early episode in the life of Felimid the Bard who featured in "Buried Silver" in* The Pendragon Chronicles. *Taylor has now written five Felimid novels, though the events in this story predate those. Keith Taylor, an Australian fantasy writer, considers the events leading up to the historic battle of Badon. In his Felimid stories, Taylor, who is a learned enthusiast of Celtic history, blends the historical reality of the fifth-century Celtic-Saxon world, with the magical world of Celtic myth. The background to this story is as real as Dark Age history allows us to conjecture.*

*Taylor has, posed an interesting idea in having a Roman family descended from Lucius Artorius Castus, an historical figure who was Prefect of the Sixth Legion Victrix stationed at York in the second century. From him, Taylor surmises, three branches of descendants have emerged. One of these was the Artorius of legend. Another, more closely linked with the Artorius of history, appears here.*

# I

Because magic was in Felimid's heart-marrow, he did not expire of fear in the place where he found himself.

A kind of shining blue dusk surrounded it, so that air and sky seemed the same as the glassy water. Although the tall tor crowning the island was immutably real, it rose at the core of a foreign, eldritch world. Rome, the Church and Time had all conspired to eradicate it. All three had failed.

Elder Britain survived, here among the marshes.

A chariot road twisted around the tor through hazel, alder and bramble. Yelling like maniacs, half-naked men drove along it behind teams of galloping horses, their feet braced hard between wheels that bounced and sprang in the air at every stride, the spokes a whirling blur. Gilded and jewelled, the chariots passed in flashes of light. A white stag with silver-grey hoofs and antlers watched from on high.

Beside the racecourse, Gwyn ap Nudd's court feasted. The light, soft rain did not trouble them. Big rangy warriors in bright trousers laughed and boasted as they drank from golden cups. People of many callings sat at the various tables, with poets, Druids and magicians closest to Gwyn and his lady. All revelled freely, shouting, grinning, eating, quarreling and placing bets.

Each table was covered from end to end with delectable food. Herbed trout swam in their juices next to salmon cooked in cream and honey. Venison filled the air with its savour. Swans in their feathers with painted beaks looked almost alive, except that they steamed slightly. Baskets filled with bread abounded. Pigs basted and gleaming, to be eaten tonight and live again on the morrow, became a source of bloody contention in the meantime over who should have the cuts of most prestige. Dishes of curd and butter fought for the last bits of space with cheese, pears, apples and nuts. There was barley ale by the vat to drink, honey liquor, red and yellow wine poured in constant streams by naked cup-bearers, both youths and maidens.

Rumour said that guests from outside should not taste any of this if they wished to leave before the world ended. Felimid didn't worry. It was too late for him if that were true. Besides, he suspected that Gwyn did not intend to let him leave in any case, and at nineteen he was seldom inclined to worry about anything. These folk were extravagantly friendly now. But the

Island of Apples was a place where dark things could happen as well as good.

Morgan, the prince's lady, leaned towards Felimid and cried, "I am telling you Clust will win this race! Son of Fal, will you bet?"

Words were Felimid's craft. They blossomed in his mind as he looked at her. *The lifting of pride in her smooth brows, the ray of love-making in both her royal eyes, a dimple of sport in both her cheeks, in which there came and went flashes of fast purple.* She combined dark hair and blue eyes with the clearest, fairest skin Felimid recalled seeing—and powers of sorcery, it was said, to equal or surpass her husband's.

"Clust? He does well, yes. But Rhodri will come home before him. A song to your beauty on that!"

"A mere song?" Morgan looked at him scornfully. "A real bard would give that in any case."

"My songs are not mere," Felimid answered, unabashed. "Besides, lady, I have nothing else."

"You have your sword and harp."

"They are not mine. They are treasures of my race."

"Our race, bard. Ours. Don in Britain or Danu in Erin, she is the same goddess. Decide quickly! They will finish the race while you vacillate!"

She was playing with him, and he knew it, and still it stung to have her denigrate his nerve. But pride was a small thing now. Winning a bet with her (if he could do it) mattered gigantically because it might be his one chance of ever leaving this place. They could make mistakes too. The reckless, violent, feverish, excitable, drunken air they breathed promised it.

"Rhodri to win! I perform a service of your choice if he doesn't." Not the best phrasing, but he was drunk and the words were said now. "Against your promise that I leave at dawn, unhindered."

Morgan's queenly eyes widened. "My lord decides that."

Felimid bent forward. Low and controlled—for Gwyn ap Nudd heard things when one least expected it—the bard said, "Queen Morgan, it's told, can change his decisions. Bet?"

Morgan smiled gleefully. "Our guest, it is a bet."

The third and last circuit of the race was well advanced now. A man could see nothing for the wild, ancient growth around the tor. Prominent among it were the apple trees for which this island was named, untended for ages and weighted with trailing mistletoe. Felimid thanked Macha that he had watched chariot races at home and had an enthusiastic eye for beasts and drivers. Yet Morgan knew these better than he.

Here they came, Clust in the lead! Felimid's heart withered inside him. Morgan whooped like a hoyden girl.

They rushed down the stretch. Clust ran nimbly along the chariot pole between his matched dun horses, swinging his whip over their backs. Another team pressed close behind him—and it was not Rhodri's. The unmistakeable white-maned blacks lay in lowly third place.

"Clust!" Morgan shrieked. "Come on, Clust!"

Her husband bellowed, "Rhodri! You can do it still!"

Rhodri was his cousin. Loyalty, not judgement, made him say it, for no driver could pass two chariots now before the finish. It was fifty paces off.

Clust's flying wheels bounded a full yard off the ground. The left one shattered as it came down. He had been dancing back along the pole as it happened. His chariot's body tilted, bounced, turned end over end, and was kindling in a moment. Clust fell and dragged with it. The driver behind him swerved, reacting like wildfire, not caring where he went so long as it wasn't into the wreck. His team crashed through briars and plunged down towards the marsh.

Rhodri, tall and auburn-haired, his tattooed arms strong on the reins, drew his flying team wide of the smash and came home unchallenged. Hauling his blacks to a halt, he ran back to where Clust lay wrapped around a hawthorn bush, his shoulder, arm and ribs broken, an ash spoke impaling his belly. He died as Rhodri picked him up.

The winner threw back his head and screamed in grief. He carried the smaller man, holding him like a slain brother. Keening began among the feasters. Gwyn rose from his couch and covered it with his crimson-fringed cloak. Others dropped their garments atop his. The couch was a many-coloured bier by the time Rhodri reached it. Shaking, he laid Clust down and straightened his limbs. One thing—death—was as real in Gwyn ap Nudd's realm as in the daylight world.

Morgan led the wailing. Her husband gave his royal couch to Clust's shattered body, and scattered the bets he had won around the bier in tribute. The feast became a wake. All drank to the charioteer, lying there with a filled cup in his hand, and sang his praises. Rhodri was loudest in describing his arch-rival's virtues.

"Sure-handed horseman, bravest in battle, you would rush

against the spears without a shield to cover you. Never did you fail in driving your lord to the fight, never did you fail to bring him safely out.

"You were the darling of women, Clust the Nimble; you were the darling of swift-flying horses. Now the chariots of Britain lack a master, the fiery men of the wine-fed domain have tears at their eyelids.

"Sorrow is ours that we are parted from you, Clust. Finely your sword became you as you drove your slender horses, with your hounds all around you. Your honour-price was a multitude of cattle, and you worth every calf. Sorrow is ours, sorrow now freights each tree on the Island of Apples. Delight that you lived among us, woe that you died in our lifetime!"

Felimid the stranger among them, saved by Clust's mishap, paid his tribute last. He could not be niggard with feeling; tears ran down his face as he considered the price of his freedom. Yet he could not be other than glad that he had won.

If he did go free; if he had won.

The banquet turned wild to the point of madness after that. Women tore their flesh with distracted nails and danced between clashing swords. Gwyn's buffoons capered before Clust in shrouds and death-masks, with jugglers to follow as his stiffening face began to grin. His cup was emptied fifty times on the grass and refilled as often. One did not stint a man because he was dead.

"You are a most lucky gambler, Felimid mac Fal," Morgan said to him. "More so than Clust, poor lad."

"I'm sorry for him," Felimid answered. It was no lie. "Yet we all must die. He went feeling triumphant, with his blood hot. Let me go that same way—some years from now."

"A wise wish." She took his hand. "Come quickly if you want Morgan to pay her debt; dawn approaches. There is a boat among the willows that will take you to land by itself. You need not row. You must not row! You would soon be lost in the marshes if you tried. And I have other advice you will do well to follow. Never look back at this island. Never look behind you in the boat. Never look back at the boat after you leave it. The least glance will cause you to be caught and fetched back here."

"The lady Morgan is just."

"Don't praise me. You have done that with your harp."

"Not half to the height you deserve, lady."

She did not dispute him. "One day, perhaps, you will become able to play for me as I deserve. Our bards in the Island of Apples could teach you. Here is a fortress against time and mortality, where the years drift by unheeded, and your Danann blood may find a fitting home. Why you wish to leave is more than I know. Why, Felimid mac Fal?"

"A promise binds me," he muttered. "I have three years' exile to endure, and then I must take this harp and sword back to Erin where they belong."

"I grant you one chance to change your mind." Rich with implication, her voice now coaxed, and her beauty made a man think thoughts best kept to himself. "You may think back to this realm with longing after a year. Or much less! The world has grown shabby and mean since our day."

"Because you left it, surely." Felimid knew he must refuse. Yet Morgan's voice and the twilit glamour around Ynys Afallon bemused him until he could not remember why. He hunted for a courteous way to say no.

"Great Queen. You offer the joys of Tir-Tairn-Gire. Yet for Danann blood there is one other fitting home, and that the one that bred me—Erin, where magic still flourishes in the daytime. I promised to return. A bard may not take back his word. Now—no doubt I am a fool—but I must go."

Morgan's expression turned mocking. "You are, Felimid mac Fal! Yes, and a greater fool than you know! Can you imagine my lord Gwyn had you brought here for your company? A callow excuse for a bard like you? No. His wish is to have the harp and sword *here*. They would be safer than in your hands!"

"Maybe, lady." Felimid grew angry. "Yet they are the trust of my clan, not of King Gwyn ap Nudd. My grandfather gave them to me when I went into exile, and he's not callow, nor can any bard of yours compare with him."

"That you demean our court is what I should have expected!"

"That you insult a parting guest is not queenly. Now, since I've won our bet, I claim the right to go."

"Nothing hinders you," Morgan said freezingly. "I have told you the way to take. Go back to the world, Felimid mac Fal. The world of fowlers and fishers in the marsh who struggle for existence and suffer fever. The world conquered by Rome, that now battles against the Saxons and loses. Find your way home. See your grandfather grow feeble with age and lose his bardic powers. I wish you joy of all that!"

She dismissed him with a contemptuous gesture. Felimid bowed with all the grace and address he could summon, striving to put a jaunty impertinence into it.

"Your realm prosper, Great Queen!"

Yet even as he left her, it crossed his mind that all this was too easy. If the king's motives were as Morgan stated, he would not just let the sword of Ogma and the harp of Cairbre glide out of his domain. The thought made Felimid walk faster, down to the osiers and reeds of the shore, where the white shape of a water-fairy sped away from him, diving amid ripples. The stars had grown pale.

The promised boat lay there. Felimid entered it, moving forward to the high, curving post of the prow, and was not astonished when it began to move without rowers or sail. He remembered Morgan's warning never to look back, though he had not anticipated how strong the temptation would be. Teasing hints of strange, fascinating or ominous things appeared at the edges of his vision; a wading giant, a tree that changed into a man, his own fetch stalking him. Twice he nearly turned his head. After the second time, he realised that he glimpsed too many wonders, even for this enchanted marsh. They were illusions sent to provoke him. By Morgan herself, or her lord?

He closed his eyes, but that was worse. The terrors his own mind showed him teemed like ants in a broken nest. Each fish that splashed was a monster rising from the mud, each bird that called, a fatal banshee. It could not have been long before he opened his eyes again, though it seemed like a year.

Felimid embraced the stem-post and watched silken ripples around the prow. His neck ached from staring straight ahead. He became convinced this cursed boat was taking him around the marsh in circles, until he must defy Morgan's stricture. When it grounded at last on a shore of sedges and dark poplar, he could not believe it.

He stepped out on the wet ground.

Gwyn ap Nudd stood waiting, five yards off.

Auburn-haired like his cousin, big-bellied and fat but muscled like a bull under the corpulence, he made a figure of godlike power. He chuckled at Felimid through a vast pair of sweeping moustaches, and it was not friendly laughter. He carried a shield and axe.

"It's bad manners to run from a banquet with never a farewell to your host," he rebuked. "In Arthur's day we removed heads for smaller offences."

Very coolly, with anger blazing inside him, Felimid hung the harp Golden Singer on a tree. His eyes measured the distance between him and the king. He estimated that he could draw his sword in time.

"Have you come for mine?"

"Perhaps."

"Then take it if you can! You have that shield, but then you are wide enough for two men and should move only half as fast! Maybe I can wound you three times while you hurt me once. Do you wish to find out?"

"Before the goddess, you sound aggrieved! Am I not the one to complain?"

"Are you so? A guest is a guest. In good faith I came to your realm. Then I discovered that you did not plan to let me leave. That's a prisoner, not a guest."

"Then, if you are my prisoner, you must come back with me."

Felimid laughed wildly. He ripped out his sword in a blue-white flash. "King Gwyn ap Nudd, take me back!"

Thirty inches of slender grooved steel hissed in the morning air. The king barely moved his shield, and never shifted his feet at all. Felimid's edge scraped across the wrought metal surface. The king's axe flashed at his ribs.

He dropped almost flat to the ground, breaking his fall with the palm of one hand as the axe passed over him. He hurled himself upright again with a violent thrust of his right arm. Darting to the attack, he wasted three feints and two business strokes on the king's spiral-adorned shield. Gwyn chopped almost playfully at his thigh.

Felimid cut down at the axe's handle. The sword he carried could draw blood from the wind. Gwyn should have been left with a foot of wood in his hand. Instead, one little chip the size of a fingernail flew away, and the sword's edge stuck fast in the notch it had made. Gwyn turned his axe sideways at the last instant, so that Felimid was struck with the flat.

The blow knocked him down. Winded, paralysed for a few seconds, he kept hold of the sword and tried to tug it free, but it remained stuck in the axe-handle. Magic, beaten by magic! He who breathed it!

Gwyn went to one knee beside him and pressed him hard to the oozing earth with his long shield. He raised the axe. Trying to hold back his arm was like trying to hold back a rockslide. The hilt of Kincaid was pulled inexorably from Felimid's grip.

"Not bad," Gwyn said, "for a boy. But you are dealing with a warrior who fought against the legions. Care to come back now?"

"Take me back," Felimid gasped, "and I will raise such trouble as even you have not seen!"

"Oh, youngster. You have no idea what I've seen."

"The harp of Cairbre can alter the seasons. I'll summon winter unending to the Island of Apples. I'll play the sorrow strain so that your ladies and chiefs weep at feasts, the laughter strain so that they chuckle at a grave-side, the sleep strain so that they doze when you most need them wakeful! I'll satirise you and your kindred. What I am saying, king, is that you would do well to let me depart."

The pressure of the shield increased just enough to remind Felimid which of them was in a stronger position to threaten.

"Or kill you here," Gwyn said pensively.

"Or kill me here."

"Hmm." Gwyn did not lower the axe. "There may be a third choice. If you dislike our company so much, we won't insist on yours. A bard's word binds him like a hostage-chain. Are you willing to perform a service for me?"

Felimid began to see—or imagine he did.

"If you let me rise and give me back my sword I will hear you out."

Gwyn ap Nudd shook his head. "Just a pup, wet behind the ears. But maybe you were bred from Ogma's kennel after all."

He lifted his shield and leaned it against a willow. Felimid rose, dripping murky water. Wordlessly, he held out his hand. Gwyn pulled Kincaid free with one tug and gave it back with a flourish.

"Now, lord, you might tell me what you want."

## II

The Britons called this land simply the Summer Country. It enjoyed more warm, bright-blue days in that season than most other parts of the island, and this was one of them, even at the beginning of May. Felimid walked with small chirring grasshoppers flying around him. They landed on his tunic and sprang away again, he taking no notice. He felt dazed, like a man just roused from a weird wild dream.

Except that he had not been sleeping. He knew that too well. In ways he had been more vividly awake than he felt now.

Skylark and lapwing flew above him, calling. Cattle grazed in the fields, their hides still smelling of the Beltaine smoke, and a man ploughed his field nearby behind a team of horses. Felimid trudged onward, hot and thirsty, making for the road that led to Camlodd.

He had come a long way, walking fast. His harp gave him the right to cross pasture and field so long as he did it with care. Now Felimid was within sight of the road, tired, stained with sweat and dust, and angry with his recent luck.

*Cairbre and Ogma! Since I was nine I have taken all care to stay indoors at Beltaine and Samhain. I did it this year too. I know what uncanny beings you can meet on those nights. Didn't I wait, even, till an hour after sunrise before I left that fisherman's hut? And what happened to me? Gwyn's servitors were waiting around the third bend with an invitation to guest with their lord!*

*If I had known who they were—*

That was regret wasted, to be sure. Even if Felimid had known, he could not have refused to go with them, because of the geas he had carried from birth. When he was invited to be someone's guest, the geas compelled him to accept. It didn't matter who the person was. He wondered if Gwyn ap Nudd had known that and made deliberate use of it—but then that scarcely mattered either. He was committed to carry Gwyn's message, and was now within sight of Camlodd.

Worse, he had a tricky and rather foul condition to fulfill— without compromising his honour, somehow—or else return to the Island of Apples, from which he had thought he'd escaped.

*Can things be worse?*

In this lugubrious mood he came to the road. It carried a busy traffic. Four hundred men and their horses required a lot in the way of supplies and equipment. The striking thing, though, was how much of this need seemed to be met piecemeal, by poor common people who had walked longer distances than the bard. He saw a girl pass by with a flock of honking geese, and a kilted hunter carrying a slain hart. A cart filled with fresh rushes came next.

"Good-day," he greeted the farmer who drove it.

"Good-day," the man replied, with a curious look at Felimid's garments. Gwyn ap Nudd had given them to the bard. They were intended to replace those muddied in the fight at the marsh's edge. He wore a yellow cloak of light cool fabric, patterned all over with brown and orange interlocking spirals, and a linen tunic embroidered with grass-green silk at the sleeves and border.

"Good-day," the farmer repeated. "What happened to your horse?"

"What makes you think I had one to begin with?"

"Why, you aren't poor, and it zhows. Then, you walk like a horseman . . . I'll bet you are one of those who rode as soon as he toddled. Biggest reason of all, you are taking a zord to Camlodd, and only horse-warriors gather there."

"Shrewdly reasoned. Well, I have no horse. I'd rather not say how that comes to be. And it happens that I'm less of a fighting man than a herald and messenger."

"Ahhh," the farmer said, as though greatly enlightened. He scratched himself under his cowhide tunic. "You wouldn't be bringing word from zome king to tha Count Artorius?"

"You are right there, too."

The farmer puzzled over that for a moment. "Cornoul?"

"No. I came from north of here. Besides lacking a horse, I made a great wide sweep that brought me to the road this half league south of the fort, and my feet are a mortal torment."

He didn't care how blatantly he hinted.

The farmer chortled. "Tha most clumsy messenger breathing, you must be. Well, climb up. I'll take you to tha fort."

"Thanks," Felimid said fervently. In a moment he was perched atop the rushes. "My name is Felimid mac Fal."

"A Scot,* eh?"

"It's true. I have distant kin settled in these parts, and a bard is a bard in Erin or Britain. Not that there's any proper place for a bard to be now, except here. You know Camlodd well?"

"Been coming for years. Evryg's my name, from tha Dun of the Ztarlings. We're not rich there, but what we can give, tha Brotherhood will have. They are tha boys who fight to keep our roofs over our heads. God strengthen their arms!"

"Indeed."

"Wish every king in tha island had that much sense," the farmer grumbled. "Wi' tha bloody zea-wolves massing under tha best leader they've found since Hengist, you would think we could ztand together. Is your king ready to help?"

"He's ready. I cannot tell you how many men he is sending, you understand. Count Artorius must know first."

"I didn't ask, now, did I? But it's my belief tha Count 'ud rather

* In Felimid's time the Irish were described as Scots, meaning tribute-takers.

have more zupplies to feed and clothe tha men he's got. Much chance of your king sending zome?"

"I doubt it."

The farmer did not seem amazed.

Camlodd rose in front of them now, a high broad hill commanding the country. Four great ridged earthworks enclosed the crest, three very old, weathered away to grassy humps with shallow dips between. The innermost had been rebuilt. A long high roof thatched with straw shone in the afternoon sun. It looked like gold. The noise of busy forges drifted down to their ears.

A squadron of riders advanced in extended line, far out in the open country. Their helmets and mail glittered. Felimid watched them divide in two troops, wheel, retreat and advance in perfect order. Then the lances came down, a running blaze of sunlight on steel, and Felimid saw a full charge. Earth vibrated under the drumming hoofs.

"Cairbre and Ogma! They run at their foes like *that*?"

"Aye," Evryg said proudly, "and their foes do not stop for a second look."

"Hmm. Ever ridden a horse in a fight, Evryg?"

"Na. When would I? Even this cart's borrowed."

The bard had thought so. Small wonder this man and others like him were impressed, but what they had just seen had to be display. Men couldn't charge like that with lances on horseback, not and hit solid targets. They would be driven straight back over their horses' tails by the impact. Striking with sword or mace from the saddle was just as foolish. The moment a man put any real power into his blows, he would fall like an autumn leaf.

Those charges did *look* fearful, though. Maybe the Saxons knew no better than to break and run before them. By repute they were no horsemen either.

He considered the tales he had heard about Camlodd. Men talked of a fortress that was Britain's last glory, held by a leader who rode the horses of the sun and struck like the thunder god. They declared he stood twenty feet tall, with golden hair and a bronze body; that he was Arthur Pendragon himself, come back from west of the sunset to fight for his island again; that his sword grew from his fist so that he could never relinquish it even in sleep, until the last Saxon in Britain had perished.

Thus far the yarns and the talk. Felimid knew what they were worth, none better. He had met kinsmen of this Count Artorius's, though, men who did not strike him as easily impressed. They swore by the Count. Lately, in Caer Lleon, he had met closer relatives of the leader. He was real after all.

"How does a man join the Brotherhood, now?"

"Thinking of it?" Evryg asked. "Yes, every lad in Britain thinks of it. Some manage; you just have to be worthy.

"I'll tell you. A neighbour of ours has a cowherd, just a bald old man with dung on his feet, and this cowherd had an only zon who always craved to be one of tha Brotherhood. Boy by tha name of Tor. He practiced with wooden weapons and he ztole rides on horses, no matter how his father tried to beat tha foolishness out of him. Know where that boy is now? Riding in young Cynon's troop bezide a couple of king's zons, that's where, and accounted a credit."

"Cairbre and Ogma! I can picture his father's pride."

"Oh, aye. Taulks as though he helped him get there from tha first. Reckon he believes it by now, and Tor doesn't remind him. But that's tha Brotherhood. It's got all kinds in it. You will zee. There hasn't been anything like it zince the legions went."

They had climbed through shadows of oak and ash to the hill-crest while Evryg talked. A causeway led across the outer earthworks, while a timber bridge spanned the innermost ditch, steep-sided and ten feet deep, with outward-pointing stakes at the bottom. Within that rose a high rampart faced with unmortared stone, and atop it a log stockade, enclosing some eighteen acres of ground.

A big double gate stood open to receive them, with a timber watch-tower rising above it. Six men guarded the gate. Their arms were shields and six-foot spears. Out through that gateway burst a racket to make a feeble man flinch, unceasing.

"Hullo, Orel!" Evryg shouted. "Rushes and a few hides, here, and my neighbour's boys are zomewhere behind me with carts of fuel. Reckon you can always do with it. And here is a king's messenger I picked up on the road. Lost his horse, so he tells me."

Felimid jumped down from the small wicker-sided cart. "Well, no, I did not quite say that. I said I didn't have a horse. And the name of the king who sent me here to Camlodd is no less than Gwyn ap Nudd."

The gate-guards shouted with laughter.

"One way to get a ride," the one called Orel remarked. "Evryg! Don't you know that some bards will say anything, and not just bards? There's probably drink and a spare cloak stuffed in that bag instead of an instrument."

"He didn't tell me—" Evryg began.

"You have it wrong," Felimid said distinctly. "I'm a bard indeed, and this is my harp. Despite your bad manners, you may come and hear her tonight."

"That's doubtful, friend." Another guard, with rust-red hair and an ear that had been badly lacerated at one time, explained the situation through his chuckles. "We won't be leaving Camlodd, and even though you are a bard you probably won't be allowed to enter. This isn't a royal hall, as maybe you are thinking. It's a fortress where men muster for war, and we are doing that now, urgent and needful. We don't need more bards. We need soldiers, food, drink, armour and weapons."

"And willing women," a third contributed.

"And willing women. Not men who pretend to be emissaries from a cursed phantom!"

"Phantom, you would be saying?" Felimid echoed. "He appeared solid as a mountain when I met him, driving his chariot across the field where I lay sleeping." Gwyn had instructed him to tell this lie, saying that as he valued his life he should not admit to a sojourn in the Island of Apples. "He endowed me with these clothes, too, as the payment for taking his message. Fellows! I ask you! Do they look like any stuff we know?"

"Oh, you're rich, that's plain. I would we were! But it's in my mind that you made up this tale to explain the loss of your horse and other gear. It's humiliating to be robbed." Orel nodded, satisfied with this explanation. "Who did it?"

"Do we care?" the redhead asked. "Half the Summer Country is crowding up this road. We haven't time to waste."

"We have trouble with spies and traitors," Orel said explicitly. "The five-acre kings there are who hope to grab the rulership of Britain while better men die on Saxon spears are many. And they all have bards eating at their cost. You take my meaning, now? You could be one of theirs for all we know."

"I take your meaning," Felimid said, "and I take no offence." Serious, thoughtful, he faced them in the gateway. "I fancy I can satisfy you to let me enter. Your lords can decide about this business of Gwyn ap Nudd. What if someone in Camlodd vouches for me?"

"That might help," Orel said. "Who knows you here?"

"The Falcos of Cumbria, maybe. I guested with them in the lake country a year ago, and rode beside them after cattle some Gododdin had lifted. There are Falcos living near the Wall, too, and in Caer Lluel. I know Calidius Artorius Falco of the city council. If any of them are in Camlodd, they ought to remember me. And I cannot believe they would be absent now."

"That's right." The redhead looked relieved. "Their good word would be enough, Orel. Kinsmen of the Count, himself—"

"Distant kinsmen." Orel cut him short. "Mad as Picts, the whole lot. A couple of dozen did come down to kill Saxons, though, and if you know them, it'll save worry."

"I know them, surely, and they know me. If the leader's name is Terence, you will see a meeting of friends that should convince you."

Orel rubbed at his black-bearded chin. "No, it isn't Terence. I seem to recall his name is Crispus."

"Then he's not known to me," Felimid said. "Probably some of the others will be."

"All right, you may see them. Just remember that the last man we caught spying here drowned in a latrine."

"You say so?" Felimid looked at him with interest. "Yes. The splashes of dung are still on you."

The guards roared. Orel showed his teeth. "Take him along, Lip. This one is a walking miracle, for he has more mouth than you."

The soldier called Lip had a large amount of it, certainly. His big loose mouth sagged like a hound's. He said, "I have not seen these Falcos. Where are they?"

"Do you walk around asleep? Over by the western rampart. Their horses are mostly black. Just hand the bard over to a troop leader if you find he's told lies. Then come directly back here. And I don't mean by way of the baggage train."

"Aye, aye. Come on, bard."

With a parting word to the farmer, Felimid stepped into Camlodd, a crowded place seething with preparations for war. It smelled of cooking, horses, leather, iron, charcoal, middens and manure heaps. Close inside the ramparts he saw tents and brushwood shelters of the tribal auxiliaries who had answered the Count of Britain's summons, bringing their own light ponies. Towards the centre of the fortress lay long barrack-buildings of a kind he had never seen before, hurriedly raised and roughly thatched.

"They look new," he said.

"Since last autumn," Lip answered. "Never had so many men in Camlodd before. *Diawch*! We never had the whole Brotherhood gathered here before, come to that, and with levies from all the kingdoms coming and going besides, the place is crazy."

Felimid could see, but there was order in the madness. The barrack-buildings stood in a straight row, three of them, with a well and cooking area outside. To the west lay stables and an exercise ground, with other barrack-houses on the far side. South of the exercise ground lay two low barns, and between them, at the very centre of the fortified hilltop, the great high-roofed hall Felimid had seen from the road.

"That's where the Count is?" he guessed.

"That's where the Count's lady is, and his children, and special guests like Bishop Dubricius. The Count could be anywhere around here. Look, no offence, bard, but you are not with me to sightsee. I'm taking you to the Falcos, and I've got to lead you right across Camlodd to do it. Why in black Hell did they have to make their lines in the west?"

Felimid asked no more questions. He'd gathered that they could arouse suspicion. Lip was a surly, taciturn fellow anyhow, nor did he seem clever. The bard followed him in silence and used his eyes.

South of the hall and barns they passed through an area set aside for auxiliaries and other levies to camp. It wasn't nearly big enough for present needs. The Falcos and others from more distant parts had to make their lines beside the rampart as Orel said. Their dark horses, descended from the cavalry mounts of former times and tethered in neat rows, made them easy to find, for which mercy Lip expressed relief.

"Hey, lord!" he said as they approached. "I've a man here who reckons he is a friend of yours."

"A friend of mine?" The man who turned to look was Felimid's own age. "He's not from my parts dressed like that! No, I've never seen you before. Who are you?"

"Felimid mac Fal. Terence Artorius Falco knew me a year ago, in the lake country. We were friends."

"Terence? We're first cousins." Crispus Falco looked more closely. "That accent, and the harp. You wouldn't be the smooth-faced bard from Erin he talked about and advised me to avoid like sickness?"

"He's the one, Crispus!" A lake country youth put down the belt he was mending and joined them. "Hey, Felimid! It's Ronan! You mind that ride to the Long Hills after our cows?"

Even Lip had to be satisfied after that. He departed with warnings that the bard would have to see one of the squadron captains, still surly. Felimid assured him that he could not meet one quickly enough, and after that the Count of Britain. The Falcos laughed loudly.

"You don't want much!" Crispus said. "We're his kinsmen, and he stopped here once for a few words—and to inspect our camp. Pleasant he was, but Son of the Mother, Felimid, he's Count of Britain, and he has the greatest Saxon advance since the Vortigern's time to contend with!"

"That I understand. I've been in the City of Legions and heard all about it there. You have met him, then. What's he like? He, himself, not the yarns men tell."

"Gods! It's hard to say. To look at? He's nothing much, shorter and broader than me, with brown hair and a plain face, and sometimes a bit clumsy. Afoot," he added. "I've seen him ride. Man, he rides like a god! He handles a lance like a willow wand and hits his mark sure as raindrops fall, but none of that matters much. This Brotherhood has a spirit in it such as I've never met, and that matters. It comes from him. They would storm Annw* itself with sticks if he asked it. Yes, and I'd be with them, so."

"I believe it. It's unwise to be talking of the Otherworld so lightly, though, and I'm a man who knows; I met Gwyn ap Nudd lately, and he charged me to bring a message here. That is why I have to see Count Artorius, soon."

"Gwyn ap Nudd? What would *he* be wanting with you?"

"I dared not ask. It's my belief he wanted a mortal messenger who was a bard, yet not the hanger-on of any particular king. He provided me these garments but forgot to provide a horse, which is why they are stained from walking. I fancy he's too used to travelling by magic. He didn't think at all that mortals have their limits. Ronan, I'll just clean this finery if you can lend me a tunic or kilt."

"A tunic or kilt," Ronan repeated derisively. "You effete son of Erin, you are with lake country men here. You must take trousers and like it."

"Yes, I know you lack refinement, so trousers will do."

"Refined or not, you are mighty lucky we could identify you," Crispus said. "These southrons are edgy. They face mighty numbers, to hear them tell it, and they have traitors as a deerhound has fleas."

"True for you, and I know your word saved me a hard time. It wasn't just luck, though. The minute I thought about it, I knew that Falcos would join in the fighting, and was ready to bet some

* Hades.

of you would be in Camlodd already. I'm only astonished that Terence is missing."

"We threw dice," Crispus explained succinctly, "and he lost."

"Could you not both come?"

"That shows you don't know the north! Someone has to command the Wall patrols, or the Tattooed People would be across with nobody getting so much as a warning. No, Terence won't be here, and how he hated it! Nor will anybody else. This band of ours was all that could come."

The gesture with which Crispus indicated his men showed a blazing pride. Despite his Roman name and his kinship with the Count of Britain, Crispus looked like any barbarian cattle-lifter, as much Sarmatian as Roman and more Celtic than either; a foal from the same stable as his cousin Terence. Most of his band were young, like him. The oldest man there—and he was that by a good ten years—remained on the right side of forty. His features were somewhat foreign; broad head, wide cheekbones and a sort of oblique tilt to the eye-sockets. Some of the others had those characteristics as well, though not to so marked a degree.

"The Count understands," he grunted. "*He* knows how it is in the north. He's fought there. I witness, those were battles!"

"He's away," Ronan said. "Laochal, you could chant this in cadence."

Laochal's grey eyebrows bristled. "A better song it would make than some. It's fine for you to talk of how great the Horse Lord is. The world knows it now. My oath on the sword, I knew it then! He wasn't the Count of Britain in those days, but Dux, and he hadn't even been that for long. His Brotherhood numbered fewer than a hundred men. Nor were they mounted and mailed as they are now. The kings laughed at them. Huh! Nobody was laughing when that two years' campaign was over! Least of all the Picts."

"It's the Saxons' turn now." Crispus tossed his weapon high and caught it adroitly. "It won't take two years, either. We're here this time."

"That is an almighty relief to hear." Deep and ironic, a tool for command, the voice made Crispus jump. The man who had approached unnoticed was six feet tall, erect as a holly tree, with long powerful arms and huge hands. His dark beard jutted straight out from his chin. He wore a tunic of tanned deerskin with copper studs at the neck.

For a moment Felimid thought this must be the Count of Britain. Then he recalled Crispus's description and knew that he couldn't be. But surely he wasn't a nobody, either.

The bearded man came forward with the late afternoon sun shining tawnily on him. His tunic looked like brass, his skin like terra cotta. He surveyed the wild-haired young northerners in their trousers and bright wool tunics, and sighed patiently.

"Don't trouble to stand," he said. "A squadron captain of the Brotherhood doesn't deserve it."

That brought them to their feet, dropping whatever they had been doing. Felimid felt glad he and Crispus had already been standing. It spared him an awkward choice between appearing servile or offensive.

"Ulfius," the stranger said, "captain of the Hawk Squadron. You're Crispus Falco. Where is the bard who came in this day and asked for you?"

"I'm he," Felimid said. "Felimid mac Fal, of the Corco Baiscinn people in Erin. My grandfather is Chief Bard of the whole country."

"That'll be enough of your background. To be truthful, I'd rather not hear your genealogy back to the Goddess. Nor am I musical. Now. You came to Camlodd as the herald of King Gwyn ap Nudd, to speak with the Count of Britain?"

"I did."

"That's a big claim." Ulfius sat down on a saddle. "I had better warn you that unless you convince me, you will never get closer to Count Artorius than you are now; and I reckon Gwyn to be the same as any other children's goblin."

Felimid looked past the captain to the man who had followed him into the Falcos' lines. This one was no fighter, or not with weapons of metal. Lean and very dark, with a narrow but handsome face built on a foundation of precise bones, he wore a blue ankle-long tunic. Some of the dye had come off in the warmth of the day to stain his perspiring throat. He seemed to belong in Camlodd about as much as a nun or a rowboat.

"That is an error, captain," he said. His voice had a droning buzz at the edges, like a wasp trapped in a jar. It plucked at the nerves. "Gwyn ap Nudd was king of the Ordovices when Arthur Pendragon fought Caesar. Now he guards Arthur's grave . . . and all the things to which that grave is a gate, the inheritance of Elder Britain. He's not immortal, quite, but his realm lies outside time, and Arthur's sister Morgan rules beside him. No fighting man or magician is his equal."

"Not even your master?" Ulfius asked.

The man in blue answered smoothly, "I cannot take it upon myself to compare them."

"Captain," Felimid said gently, for that seemed to be the right title, "who's this cautious fellow?"

Ulfius's eyes gleamed as he answered. "It's right that you should know. You see, Felimid mac Fal, you are not the only one in Camlodd to come in a famous name, no. This is Clydno, a magician, a Druid, the pupil and the emissary of no other than—Myrddin."

Smiling like a wolf, he waited to see the effect of that revelation.

# III

"Myrddin?"

Felimid had heard that name in a dozen places, from Dalriada down to Caer Lleon.

"Yes, Myrddin." The captain was enjoying himself. "All the legends are joining us. Archdruid of Britain in Arthur's time, so he claims, killed at Mona by the legions, and transmigrated since then into the shapes of a fish, a wild boar, a tree and much else, including a dragon. Now he's a man again. And Clydno has proof that he's indeed from the master he names. What proof do you have?"

"I'll be short," Felimid said. He repeated his tale about meeting Gwyn ap Nudd while sleeping in a field, and finished with, "He bade me come here. He commanded my service and told me say to the Count of Britain that the powers of Elder Britain favour him. He said . . . other things more specific. Those are for no ears but the Count's."

Ulfius waited. When Felimid said no more, and it became plain that he would not, the captain rose and kicked the saddle across a cooking-trench.

"The ten plagues of Egypt light on you! Those half-wits at the gate sent me hither for this? Clydno! Did you hear something significant that I did not?"

"Silliness only, captain," Clydno replied. "My advice is to flog this so-called bard out of the fortress and tell him to leave the Summer Country."

"That is your advice, is it?" Felimid said. "The very best you can give? Imagine, now. A Druid and magician, skilled in reading omens, endowed with the piercing sight, surely able to know when a man has encountered the other-worldly; all this I hoped

you were, Clydno. Yet you cannot even see that these clothes I
wear were spun on no mortal looms. Either you are less than
you pretend, or you have reasons for wishing to see me depart.
I wonder which."

"Wonder as you travel," Ulfius said briefly. "Walk out of
Camlodd before sunset, lad. I cannot abide liars."

"Wait." Facing the angry captain, Felimid nerved himself to do
a thing he had never done before. "You don't understand. The
spirit and power of Britain is with Count Artorius, for that he
defends it. It has a message to send through me. Will you consider
taking me to him, if I work a marvel no fraud could do? Here and
now, captain, here and now."

"I admire your gall," Ulfius said, far from admiringly. "Perhaps
I will let you try, but I'm warning you—it'll have to be better than
pulling live frogs from your ears."

"Nothing of that sort," the bard said gravely. He seated
himself, and drew Golden Singer from her leather case with
solemn fingers. The strings glimmered like lines of light.

"See now the harp of Cairbre, who carries more centuries than
I have years, yet is younger than morning. In ancient Erin the
seasons came and went to the sound of her music, in the days of
the Tuatha De Danann and the bard Cairbre. Gentle, powerful,
splendid is she, the one darling of wisdom. So."

His fingers touched the golden strings. He breathed the air of
Camlodd and sensed the earth under him, drenched in blood long
ago when men of fiery courage had died here. He ran his palm
over the smoothly curving frame of black oak that had grown
in other soil. The wood had a silken sheen polished there by the
hands of countless generations.

There in the May evening, he moved his own hands. Music
rippled like flowing water. Warmth and richness grew out of it,
and the earth heated in response. Plants burst out of the earth
in a few breaths. Buttercups spangled the ground, and trefoils
bloomed in the horses' hoof-prints everywhere. Grass came to
seed. Hotter, thicker air settled over Camlodd, the air of full
summer, and a booming like thunder made it tremble.

Ulfius stood as though transformed to wood.

Crispus was goggle-eyed and helplessly mute.

Felimid made new melodies. He harped mists and ripening
fruit, the dirge of a million leaves turning yellow and brown,
the pride of belling stags as their antlers clashed in rivalry, the
patter of falling hazel nuts in profusion. Again, all over Camlodd,
it happened. Small apples that had just ripened untimely, now

wrinkled and fell. Grass thinned on the ground. The air grew sharp in men's lungs.

"Enough," Ulfius said hoarsely. "*Enough*!"

"Wait," Felimid said.

Now his harping was bright, clear and brittle, ringing like swords of ice. Gusts of frigid wind slashed across the hilltop and flurries of snowflakes, unbelievably, danced around barracks and hall. The sky darkened in a way that was not the fall of night. No birds sang.

"Shall I bring back the spring?"

"In God's name, yes!"

"Kill him, Ulfius!" Clydno raged. "The spring will return of itself, then!"

Felimid said softly, "Can you be sure?"

Sure or not, Ulfius left his long cavalry sword where it was. Felimid bent his head over the harp again. The music he created became vivid, wakeful and urgent. Bushes budded green and bees hummed in their hives, when a little before they had huddled in torpor. Swallows chased insects in the twilight air. May again was May.

"I haven't come here to make idle mischief, with magic or without it," Felimid said into the silence. "Far rather would I not have done that, for reasons Clydno can tell you. I did it because I have a message for Count Artorius that must be given, and you were about to send me packing. I'll repeat it to him naked and unarmed with my hands tied behind my back if you require it. So that it's soon."

He no longer seemed like a chance, unbearded roamer. It was as though the hundred generations of bardic ancestors he had stood behind him, lending him their accomplished power.

"I'll tell the Count," Ulfius said. "Listen, though; I cannot promise when, or even if, he will receive you. His biggest enemy is coming to force the doors of Britain, he holds council tonight with such men as King Melwas and Bishop Dubricius, and tomorrow won't bring him a respite. He's wary of magicians and their words at the best of times."

"I'm told Myrddin gained his confidence."

"Myrddin saved his family once, and helped him found the Brotherhood by leading him to buried treasure. Riches may not help you enter Heaven, but by God they're useful when it comes to paying for armour and horses!"

"You are saying that Myrddin is another matter."

"Wholly another matter, imbecile," Clydno said in burning anger.

Felimid paid him no attention. Ulfius gave the wizard a warning glance but did not address him. To Felimid he said, gruffly, "Don't meddle with Myrddin, or even his pupils. Believe me, I'll urge Artorius to see you, but if he won't—that finishes it."

"Captain, you will live to wish you had destroyed him and his harp," Clydno prophesied.

"If we miss dinner we will wish we had been in time. I'm not attending this night council on an empty stomach."

With a curt farewell to Felimid and Crispus, who had not recovered speech as yet, the captain left them.

Felimid held Golden Singer as though for solace. Horses neighed restlessly in distant stables. Where crickets had sung in the earth before he had changed spring to summer and made winter follow in less than an hour, now there was silence. The Falcos were looking at him as though he had become a demon.

Fighting a sudden deep melancholy, he said, "I am thinking that Ulfius was right about the perils of missing dinner. Maybe with full bellies you will all look less like Conall when he saw the giant pick up his own severed head. Come on, be cheerful; you can boast of me to the Brotherhood! It's not news to you, surely, that bards can enchant?"

Exhorted in that way, they breathed again, and all began talking at once. But it needed a couple of hours and some drinking of ale before they recovered their old manner.


# IV


The fire-trench in the Falcos' lines burned low. Much food had been eaten, and folk attracted by the news of Felimid's magic had come around to meet him, bringing meat and drink. He had swallowed his share and harped and sung, telling funny stories like *Bricriu's Feast*, with a view to dispelling any aura of the awesome. He did not care to be seen so.

Two of the Brotherhood squatted near him. One, to Felimid's surprise, had turned out to be the very cowherd's son of whom Evryg had spoken; the former "boy by the name of Tor," so hungry to fight for Britain. Big and broad, with large knuckly labourer's hands, he looked strong enough to crush a boulder in his hug. His countenance was pleasant, bony and freckled, with outsized ears jutting through his mouse-coloured hair. He spoke with a thick farm dialect still. There were scars on his thighs. Cavalry rider's scars.

Tor was clean-shaven, like his city comrade Marcus. The latter affected Roman manners and Roman military lore, now and then lifting a brow at the Falcos' taken-for-granted conviction that they too were Romans. A yellow-haired woman had appeared, too, and introduced herself as "Vera, from the baggage train."

"Felimid!" a merry saddler bawled through the jackdaw din. "Felimid, give us a song of Arthur!"

Others echoed him. Vera leaned forward so that the dimming fire painted her sensual face. "Yes, Felimid of Erin. Will you do that? Unless you do not know the story of Arthur."

"I've roved through Britain these two years! How should I not? For the glory of Britain, then, the delight of her women, the undoing of all who invade her, and most of all to the honour of her Brotherhood, a song of Arthur."

Wild and archaic was the music he made then, as befitted a tale out of Britain's last great days, of her last High King. The words were his own. He had reworked and polished them more than once, in cities and in chieftains' halls.

> "When Arthur Pendragon was lord of the Britons,
>     Trees blossomed like foam in the Isles of Grey Rain;
> Now those rough northern crags lie sea-weathered
>     and barren
> Until Arthur Pendragon shall come back again.

> "The island of Britain had great kings before him,
>     Manogan, and Bran, and invincible Lud,
> But while Arthur ruled in his vigour and glory,
>     His time was the flower as theirs was the bud.

> "No foreign invader dared look towards Britain,
>     A woman could walk decked in gold and be safe,
> Men planted their crops and were sure of the harvest
>     And never a hostage in shackles did chafe."

Men nodded solemnly at that, and Vera sat with her arms clasped around her bent knees, intent. The baggage train woman looked strangely like a little girl listening to a favourite story in that moment. Felimid grinned at her and continued.

"The pillars of London were red bronze and silver,
   The roofs could be seen in their splendour from Gaul,
And great Bran's buried head looking eastward forever
   Held Britain inviolate, proof against all."

Faces looked longingly back towards the past, then, a past that
was secure as well as splendid, faces of saddler, surgeon, bishop's
priest and bawd. Tor sighed deeply, and even Marcus looked
nostalgic for a moment.

"When Rome conquered Gaul with so mighty a slaughter
   That each fighting man of whole tribes lost a hand
The Pendragon stretched out his arm to the vanquished
   And lodged them in Britain as guests of the land.

"Then Caesar's strong legions came sailing to Britain;
   They sought to subdue her for aiding their foes,
But Arthur's swift chariots drove like a storm-wind
   And twice threw them back as the ebbing tide goes."

He sang then of Guinevere, the queen who remained a legend
after centuries, no less than her husband. Her beauty had never
been equalled, except by her wit and her sorrow. Foster-daughter
of a giant, she had tricked him in order to save Arthur's life when
he came seeking her in marriage. Wedded, she was faithful to
the High King even when he appalled all Britain by disinterring
the Head of Bran from its burial place in London. His double
victory over Caesar had inflamed his pride and eagerness for
glory. His own strength was enough to defend the island, he
proclaimed, and he would not share the credit of it with a dead
man's incorruptible head.

Nothing was the same for Arthur Pendragon after that, even
though he enjoyed three men's lifetimes and nine men's prowess.
When he raided the Otherworld in his ship Prydwen, barely seven
of his companions survived to return with him, losses that could
never be renewed. Brooding, sorrow-stricken, he became like a
stranger to his queen, and on the night that he killed their son
Amr in a fit of black fury, she turned against him. Then indeed
the end became sure.

Arthur lived to see Rome invade Britain again, this time with
success, and to regret in age the arrogance of his youth. Traitor
tribes turned against him. Guinevere and his one surviving son
made war on him. His sister Morgan, who had always been

treacherous, ironically came to his aid with her husband Gwyn. They carried him away from his last battle, mortally wounded. Despite all Morgan's healing efforts, he died, and there had never been a High King of Britain since.

> "His sepulchre lies in the Island of Apples,
>     Where Gwyn ap Nudd guards it with all of his might,
> And Morgan conceals it by baffling enchantment
>     Until Arthur returns from the dark to the light."

The final words echoed for Felimid, and made him wonder. No man raised as he had been raised held death in terror, or believed it to be anything but a gate between worlds. Then might Arthur truly come back? Most men in Britain thought so. Surely he, Felimid, had particular cause to know that Gwyn, Morgan and the Island of Apples were real.

A hush followed the end of the song. Vera, the baggage train woman, bit her lip. Tor swallowed, as though feeling awkward because his emotions were stirred.

"Aye," he said. "Tha Pendragon 'ull return. This Camlodd here was his fortress, in tha long ago, before tha legions destroyed it. Zome reckon he lies buried underneath this very hill."

"This very hill," Marcus echoed. "And others say he's buried in the Island of Apples, as the bard just sang, and others still make his grave on the crest of Yr Widdfa.* It's everywhere."

"I have had it pointed out to me in the Long Hills north of the Wall," Felimid admitted. "By Terence your own cousin, Crispus."

"Don't bring Terence into it; argue against Tor by yourself! It's true enough, he can't lie in all those places, but that does not make it a laughing matter. All Britain wants to claim him because he's the hero of all Britain. It's right that he should be."

"I wouldn't argue with that," Marcus said, shrugging. "None knows the truth anyhow, unless it's Myrddin, or that sour black goat of an envoy he has sent here."

"Sour black goat," Felimid repeated. "They are the apt words for him, so. Can it be true that he's Myrddin's emissary, as he says?"

"True as zunrise," Tor said positively. "He's been with the Count in tha hall. They aczept him there, and they 'ud detect an

* Mount Snowdon

impostor. Between me and God, you'd be mad to claim falsely
that you were here in Myrddin's name. He'd wither you with
lightning from an 'undred miles away."

"Myrddin truly has returned, then?"

"Bacchus! Who knows?" Marcus said. "Once he was helpful
to our clan, then he vanished for years, came back, was reported
dead, and appeared again. He's everywhere and nowhere, like
the Pendragon's grave. Ask this Clydno, if you trust him. He may
know."

"You said *our* clan." Felimid seized upon that with interest.
"You are Artorian too?"

"I have the honour, yes. Marcus Artorius Castus from Ratae. I
thought you knew. I'm distant cousin to Crispus and his kin—but
the Falcos you plainly do know. The Count belongs to the Spanish
branch."

"Spanish? Why are they called that, now?"

"They descend from the Emperor Magnus Maximus, the only
descendants of his that survive, so far as anybody knows. He was
Spanish."

"Tha Count has his zord," Tor offered. "It was kept in Gaul
a long time. Aye, and Myrddin prophezied when it was brought
back that young Lucius Artorius would be tha one to destroy tha
Zackzons with it."

"Myrddin prophesied nothing!" Marcus scoffed. "The Count's
wife brought him the imperial blade for a wedding gift! The last
Gaulish consul was her father, and—"

"Who toald you that?" Tor demanded hotly. "I know who
brought tha zord to Britain! A zoldier, that's who, a plain Gaulish
zoldier travelling alone, and what is more it happened before tha
Count had ztarted shaving! He didn't marry tha Lady Questa
until years after."

"Who told *you* that, the cows?"

"Cows can sometimes be smarter than city men," a Gwynedd
voice said from beyond the firelight. "Tor is right. That prophecy
was made! Most men reckoned it meant the Count's first cousin
Flavius, a brave lad, but he and his men went to green graves
when the damned heathen savages killed them."

"Anderida," the yellow-haired woman said. She spoke the
word like a curse.

"Anderida," the Gwynedd man confirmed. "For what was
done there, I will never meet a Saxon, to the end of my life,
but I take off his head. And my curses go after them all to their
sure lodging in Hell."

"I'm a stranger in this country," Felimid said. "What happened at Anderida? Bloody killing?"

"You might say so!" The woman was shocked. "I thought all the world had heard of Anderida!"

"Alas, no."

Marcus looked across at Tor. "Do you want to tell him?"

"Not I."

"I will do it, then," the Gwynedd voice said sombrely. "Listen, stranger. It's a bitter story. You hear any number of songs about it, but the gist is this. Anderida is a very old shore fortress with a forest behind it, far to the east. The Count's cousin had been fighting the Saxons there. He did well, he and his men. A number of British folk, men, women and children, had been driven from their homes. The Saxons pursued them. Flavius and his troop held off the pursuit until the people could take refuge in Anderida. By the skin of their teeth, he and his men got in too, but then they were in a trap. The Saxon chief Aelle was not minded to let them out again. He stormed the place and butchered them all. Right down to the youngest child."

"Mother Danu," Felimid said softly. "And the Saxons are massing now, I have heard, under a leader by the name of Aelle."

"The same one," Marcus said laconically.

"Fifteen years, it has been," Tor expanded, "but tha Count doesn't forget. A kinsman is a kinsman. And that particular one was most dear to him."

"Yes." Marcus looked into the fire-trench, possibly seeking words there. He found them. "Knowing him, though, he's set on keeping the same thing from happening again, even more than revenge. What his cousin did at Anderida was just what the Count would have done—except that he wouldn't have lost." Marcus added defensively, "I haven't said this because he is family; all Britain knows it."

"It's what drew me here, so. I have more and more desire to see this Count Artorius. Doesn't he leave yonder hall, or is he maybe invisible, with a mantle of shadows to wear?"

"He's buried to the shoulders in reports, emissaries, bishops and agents," Marcus said dryly. "He's planning a campaign. It's not won by charges and red slashing alone, as you bards make it appear, but you may well see him tomorrow. His lady and children too."

Felimid hoped so. Time was growing short. It occurred to him then that all those present, from Vera to the Falcos, probably

believed that he was going to fight beside them in the coming
struggle. He hadn't said that he would not. Passionate as they
were on the matter, if the question arose, there was sure to be
trouble for a certain bard.

Felimid was almost glad when the spectre interrupted.

# V

Its wail thickened the blood and wrung spasms from the limbs.
Descending over the Falcos' tethered horses with a second
bubbling cry, it sent them mad in an instant. Felimid saw it, a
twisting shape outlined in its own rotten glow, with a face like
half-melted wax and dead holes for eyes. It whirled into the air
as a dry leaf goes.

The horses stampeded. Felimid jumped for the baggage train
woman and rolled aside with her, hugging the harp between their
bodies. A hoof came down on his thigh. He never felt it until later.
Thrusting the harp into her arms, he jumped to his feet, waved his
arms in the face of a charging brute and screamed louder than the
spectre. The horse reared in front of him. Felimid slipped aside
from the hoofs, seized and twisted a handful of coarse mane
and sprang astride. Then he was riding a maddened creature
bareback, gripping with all the power of his thighs.

The hideous wraith came down on them again. Its cry went
into the ears like driven needles. Others beside Felimid had swung
onto horse's backs, with the quickness in emergency of men who
live with raids and forays. Their kinsmen threw ropes and bridles,
which they caught adroitly and then went chasing the rest of their
mounts.

Felimid had too many troubles to aid them. The spectre
fluttered around him, shrieking wildly. His horse, insane, crashed
into a rubbing-post and made it vibrate from top to bottom.
Felimid barely snatched his leg out of the way in time, slipping
off the dark nag's back in doing it. The spectre settled over the
horse and impelled it forward to stamp him lifeless.

Felimid's hand went to his shoulder. With a violent jerk he
pulled off his cloak. He cast it so that it wrapped blindingly
around the horse's head. Then he was throwing bardic fluency
and bardic scorn at the thing before him, knowing it for a being
of air and so more subject to the power of words than even flesh
and blood.

"Begone, you groaning bag of unsavoury conduct, ghost of a wounded, ailing, belly-diseased goat! Go from this gathering of brave and cheerful spirited men, you who do not belong among them, you who have no place where honour and judgement are found. I name your master, he who sent you, Clydno the furtive worker of harm. Begone, you exhalation of dungheaps!"

He ranted, throwing all he knew or could surmise of its nature in among the curses to add to their potency, even while he wrestled to bring the horse under control. The spectre lifted from its back and drifted away, as though purpose and intention had left it. Felimid never stopped cursing until it vanished from sight.

Vera came running with a halter to slip around the horse's neck, the harp still clutched under her arm. Felimid spoke soothing words to the beast as he led it back to the picket-row and hobbled its feet. They didn't calm it much, perhaps because it could sense he felt like red murder.

Vera knew the priorities of harpers. She gave him Golden Singer and held the case for him while he looked over the instrument for the smallest scratch or any broken string. Her hair was tousled and dirt smeared her forehead.

"She's all right," Felimid said at last. He meant the harp. "My gratitude to you for keeping her. I won't forget it. She might have been smashed to bits."

"You whirled me out of the way there. I might have been trampled flat."

She was handsome, Vera, with as splendid a body as Felimid had ever seen, and he wanted to take her in his arms that instant and whirl her away indeed—somewhere private for loving. And why not? There wasn't much he could do about the Falcos' horses. He was lucky to be alive.

But he knew that was a lie. There were things he could do. He rode as well as any Falco, and stood in arm's reach of a useful nag. Sighing, he flung a saddle on the horse, then loosed its feet from the hobbles.

Catching and bringing back those horses was a test of diplomacy even more than herding skill. Camlodd was filled with fighting men, none taking kindly to other men's mounts stampeding through their camps. The bard invented a good many stories at short notice that evening. Who would credit the explanation of a screaming wraith? Riding, placating, he brought back five animals in a line at last, and found that while others had returned sooner than he, only Laochal had recovered as many.

"You did your share," the grey-browed man owned. "These

southrons, though—a few tried to kill Sirus over by the great stables behind the practice ground! He was wounded when I got to him. If the turds hadn't wanted some fun kicking him before they slew, I'd have been too late, but as it is I slashed one in the arm and they all bolted. All of them! Ran from one!"

"They really were trying to murder?" Crispus was enraged.

"Trying! They may ha' succeeded! Whether he lives or dies, Crispus, you have to tell the Count we want these assassins found and hung. Those stables are right in between the Brotherhood's barrack-houses."

"What does that have to do with it? Laochal, you think those footpads were of the *Brotherhood*?"

"No," Laochal said, but he thought it over first. "The Brotherhood doesn't kill by stealth. And Brotherhood men would not have run. Who'd want to kill Sirus, though?"

Felimid remembered Sirus. Youthful even in this company, fair-skinned, quick with a joke, trying to raise a moustache and not succeeding very well, yet a good fighter, he wasn't the sort one murdered. Not even to rob. He possessed little.

Felimid slammed his hands against the rubbing-post. "May they rot! May they die in bad ways and the Cauldron of Rebirth reject them!"

"I'm in agreement there," Laochal said, dryly, "but why are you so hot in your curses? It's not as though Sirus is well known to you."

"He's a Falco. More than that, it's in my mind that this was a plan. The spectre, the horses running away so that we all had to scatter after them—and how, when they were on tethers? Did every one just break its rope and go?"

"You are saying that someone sneaked in and untied them?"

"Under the eyes of two dozen men like you? Before I'll believe that, I'll believe magic loosened those tethers, as I'm sure magic sent the spectre."

They listened and murmured uneasily, doubtful.

"Why?" Crispus said at last. "Why should someone go to so much trouble to do us a bad turn?"

"I'm not sure why, but I am sure who. We know of but one magician in Camlodd. Clydno, whose innocence is so neatly proven by his being in the great hall at a night council this minute."

"And who urged Ulfius to kill you," Crispus said slowly. "About ten of us heard him."

"You did. It won't condemn this slippery Clydno. He can

declare that he said it only in a furious moment, and it meant nothing. I couldn't show otherwise. It *was* a furious moment."

"It'll take some hard proof," grey Laochal agreed dourly. "Talking of spectres would only make them laugh the rafters down. The curs who tried to make wolf meat of Sirus were no phantoms, though, and I marked one of them. Find a fresh wound in someone's arm. That's where to start."

"No," Crispus said. "That's the second thing. The first is to learn how Sirus does. The magician can wait."

"That is a true word." Felimid looked drolly at the Falco leader. "The magician can wait. I reckon the—what do Romans call it, the duty officer?—will not wait, though, to come around and ask why your horses misbehaved over half of Camlodd. As Laochal says, he won't think much of a tale of phantoms. If you'd see Sirus first, and have some time to make your story right, go now."

The northern youth had an ugly wound in the neck, but he looked like surviving. The surgeon did not promise it, yet he was cautiously hopeful. Looking at the shape in the rough bed, by the yellow light of a lamp, Felimid wished that Laochal had managed to strike deeper. An idea began to sprout in his mind, also. It did not flower until the early morning, while he lay half asleep. When it did, he sat up. Sharply.

"Cairbre and Ogma!"

"What?" grumbled Crispus, from a nearby bedroll.

"Nothing. Sorry for waking you."

The bard's mind spun. That spectre had tried to kill him outright, with a horse for instrument, there was no question. Three murderers had tried to kill young Sirus shortly after. In form and build he was quite like the bard. *Sirus might well have been attacked because the killers had mistaken him for their real quarry in the dark.*

# VI

Over a morning meal of bacon and rye bread, the bard told Crispus of his suspicions. Crispus cursed in loathing and fury, echoed by his other kinsmen—all but Laochal. Laochal fingered the grip of his sword in silence.

"Do not go killing him yet," Felimid warned, seeing the gesture. "I may be wrong. If I am right, though, he's desperate to prevent my talking to Artorius, and that means he will try again."

"Murder a bard?" Laochal growled. "What if he succeeds?"

"Then you will know who did it, won't you? Just remember that if you kill him here, for any reason, the Count will punish you. He will send you from Camlodd and forbid you to share in the fighting. Not the slayer alone, but all of you."

"Even that will not stop us if Sirus dies," Crispus said. "Or if you do. I'll cut Clydno to pieces, by the gods!"

"I'll do it better," Laochal said.

Blood loyalty, blood revenge. Although it had its uses, it was better eschewed in Camlodd. And better, far better, to expose Clydno than murder him.

"Not unless I die," Felimid said again, "and I don't intend to. I'm going to the baggage train, now, for a word with Vera."

"Vera?" Laochal said, puzzled, while Crispus grinned and Ronan gave a whistle. They remembered the name.

"The yellow-haired woman."

"That bawd? There are girls in Camlodd that you could have for nothing."

"Outsiders like me. This one is part of Camlodd, part of the Brotherhood, almost, and must know all that happens. Also, I have seldom seen a finer body."

"I was wondering if you would mention that."

"Why should I not? I'm no monk to deny that I notice such things, and I have eyes. Now, if a message should come from the hall, you will know where to find me."

The heavy baggage carts lay drawn up in a double row. A blacksmith was seeing the anvil and bellows for his field forge loaded into a particularly sturdy cart, while at the far end of the area strapping, bold-eyed women worked over tubs, washing tunics and trews by the mountainous pile. Vera sweated among them, in a short-sleeved woollen bodice and a skirt kilted above her knees. The rich yellow hair was piled atop her head. One tress had come loose and hung down on her neck.

"Leave drudging for a while, Vera."

She looked at him. "You say so? Listen. We whore, but we work too. I made that rule and I will not break it. Satan's backside, bard, I had to fight the fiercest girls in this camp to get it established!" She indicated the washing. "I'll be done here in an hour. Mind, for those who are not in the Brotherhood, I charge three times as much."

"Well worth it," Felimid said, eating her with his eyes. "No wonder every proper man in Britain is hungry to join. Yet I'm not here for that, and I do not have an hour. If you care about the Brotherhood, Vera, you will talk with me in private. It's about that trouble we had last night."

"Ah?" She looked at him assessingly, a woman who had heard all the stories men tell, and made up her mind quickly. "I'll hear you, then. Come with me to that second store-house from the left."

The building was long and high, with great stands of rough shelving running from end to end inside, stacked with every sort of gear a fighting force requires. Vera bounced headlong into a lower bay piled with yellowing sheepskins.

"Down by here with me, and tell!"

Felimid sat, hitching his sword-belt around for comfort. "I'm after needing your help to keep my throat uncut. Last night's spook was no chance or accident."

Swiftly, he told her, and Vera listened with an intent frown, understanding as swiftly.

"Someone doesn't like my presence in Camlodd," he finished. "The man who has shown it most openly is that narrow-faced Clydno. Maybe he sees me as a rival. Maybe it's someone else entirely. Now you know Camlodd and its people better than I. Whom would you choose?"

She pursed her lips. Surely she was aware that her breasts surged half out of her bodice. She answered his question seriously, though, with no flirting.

"Nobody in the Brotherhood! Hundreds of them, I know, but a traitor there is as likely as a feathered fish. Neither would a traitor there use magic or phantoms to murder you. Nobody in the baggage train. I know them all. The light auxiliaries are mostly strangers, and far more likely. But for sorcery . . . no man in this whole place save Clydno. And of course you."

"And of course me."

"Why come to me for help, now? Why trust me? You might have gone to Ulfius or the tribune Cai."

"It was Ulfius who recommended you, in a way. A jewel of a woman. Those were his words. He said you have sometimes taken a spear in your own hands to help fight off thieves who would loot the baggage train. He said you have tended hurt men and comforted dying ones like an angel."

"He said all that? It doesn't sound like Ulfius to me. Now if he'd assured you that I am the best lay in Camlodd—"

"He said all that," Felimid assured her. "Best lay in Camlodd he did not say, and it's not much of a distinction, so why should he? There are no women to compete but the other baggage train girls, a few milkmaids and visitors—and the Count's wife Questa, to be sure."

"You want to be friends with me? You want my help? Then do not talk loosely of her."

"It wasn't my intention. But why? Because she is the Count of Britain's wife? Or because you like her?"

"I don't care one of these greasy sheepskins whose wife she is! When Bronwen had the sweating fever that nearly killed her, Questa took her into her own chamber. Now Bronwen is no friend of mine. She's a trouble-making cat I have had to teach lessons, but that doesn't matter. The lady would have done the same for any of us."

"A woman of heart," he agreed. "She's from Gaul, yes?"

"Was. Her father was a king over there until his realm fell to the savages. These were Franks, I think. She escaped to Britain, her breasts not even grown then, and the story is that Artorius was taken with her from the first, but had a hard time winning her. I wouldn't know. Stories aren't to be trusted . . . how did we shift to this subject? We were talking of who might want to kill you."

He told her what had happened to Sirus. "Three men did it. Laochal wounded one in the arm—laid it open, as he reckons. But old soldiers boast about the wounds they inflict as young boys boast about the women they've tumbled, and not necessarily with truth."

"Hmm." Her eyes laughed at him. "You are not an old soldier, or quite a young boy. Do you lie?"

"Often. Vera, I fancy these men may be part of some kind of treachery to Artorius, even if it's only as hirelings. Will you help me find them? The baggage train must hear everything that happens outside the hall."

"We hear a good deal of what goes on there, too! But why should you need my help? When you can make summer, autumn and winter in the same hour—"

The wonder in her voice was pleasant to hear. Sadly, Felimid had less than a heartbeat in which to enjoy it. The door banged wide. Feet trampled in the straw, someone laughed, an ugly sound, and someone else slammed the door shut behind them, with ramming and pounding noises to follow. A voice thick with bloodlust said, "There they are!"

Vera sat sharply upright. Three men were advancing upon them. Hard leather caps covered their skulls, scarves had been wrapped around their lower faces, and they wore undyed wool leggings. They carried swords, short broad weapons heavy enough to split bone, easy to conceal under cloaks.

"Welcome," Felimid said, his blood surging. "You lads made a mistake last night and mean to be correcting it now, ha?"

It did not puzzle them or cause them to hesitate because they barely heard it, much less thought about it. Brutish men at the best of times, they had come through the door with their brains crimson, pleasantly anticipating a double slaying, primed for it, wanting it. They rushed like boars.

"Vera, get through there and away!"

He pointed to the bottom shelf of the stand. Not waiting to see whether she did it, he moved to meet the three, knees bent a little, moving his feet in smooth, flat-footed circles. Three to one they might be. At least none of them was Gwyn ap Nudd, and none of them bore a shield.

Felimid warded a blow from one and almost skimmed around him, dancer-light, so that the other pair got in each other's way as they turned to follow him. Another slash from the first man was turned by Kincaid's shining edge. The assassin's sword, of steel not much better than plain iron, was deeply nicked. Felimid spun Kincaid over and struck with a drawing cut.

The assassin felt a tug at his side. Looking down, he saw his own flesh bared where the unclean tunic had been slashed. A moment later, blood welled out, and then followed pain, biting like an adder.

Felimid turned against the other two. Their eyes glinted above the scarves. Both were big men, nearly as large as Tor. Their weapons, held high, slanted back behind their shoulders. One cut fiercely at the bard's head while the other struck at his left hip. The blows came together, well timed.

Felimid bent his knees further and quickly, taking his head down, then straightened his left leg so that he moved to the right, staying low as he did so. It was graceful, fluent and just a fraction late. One killer missed his hip, but the other gashed his scalp through the thick brown hair and made his head resound. The bard dropped, rolled and came to a halt against one of the posts supporting the stand of shelves. Red gore covered one side of his face.

The murderers rushed him once more. Sure of their victim now, they forgot to act in concert. One dashed ahead of his mate with his butcher's sword held low. Felimid drew up one knee as though flinching, to gain purchase on the floor with that foot. Then he lunged hard.

Kincaid, a longer, slimmer sword with a far sharper point, went straight through the man's belly, to grate against his spine before sliding out of his back. His eyes widened in astonishment, then seemed to look inward. Felimid saw it clearly. Reaching out with his right hand, he snatched the man's weapon before he began to collapse.

It wasn't quick or quiet. The assassin fell kicking, thrashing about in his comrades' way, giving high breathy squeals. Felimid drew Kincaid from his body and backed clear of the shelves, holding a blade in each hand now.

The first man he had cut regained his feet. Holding the deep slash closed with one hand, he advanced, purpose and hate in the way he gripped his sword. Worse, much, much worse, he had a shield. No, two. They were wooden rounds, unfinished, neither covered not rimmed, but equipped with grips. He threw the second one to his mate, who grabbed it eagerly.

"I'll have your tripes out—and spread them, bard," he said. "Spread them bloody, see you?"

"Aye!" snarled the other, the one without wounds, over their comrade's dying howls. "And then the woman, too."

"She's gone, you fools," Felimid said. He retreated before them. "You cannot get out of Camlodd now, no matter what you do, so drop your weapons and hope for mercy. You might gain it if you tell who paid you!"

They answered him with foulness and renewed their attack. Felimid withdrew down the long aisle, cursing the lack of space between the massive shelves. Bounding onto the nearest one before the killers could stop him, he rolled over a pile of sacking, across the shelf and down to the floor again, dislodging stacks of carved wooden saddle-trees which showered down, clattering. Now he was near the big door. Cairbre and Ogma! It was shut still, and not only shut but jammed shut, wedged fast! That must have been the pounding he heard just after the murderers burst in.

Then Vera could not have escaped from the store after all.

No help would come.

He glanced desperately from side to side. Two blades were not much use against two men with blades *and* shields. He feinted, slashed, moved aside and ran back down the long aisle, swifter than a deer. As he went he shot looks about him for anything on the shelves that might help. Where had the wounded man found those accursed shield-rounds? If he could get one, he'd make these curs hop!

The killer with the wound in his side faltered. Groaning, he went down to his knees. His mate spared him a glance and a malediction before leaving him. Full of renewed confidence with a shield on his arm, he rushed against the bard.

Felimid ceased backing. Testing his man with a quick repertoire of strokes, both left and right-handed, Felimid learned at once that this rogue handled his shield competently, and that he was in dire trouble.

Their swords clashed together with jarring force. Felimid strove to send a thrust over or under that inconvenient shield. The assassin did not like it. Slashing and chopping with the edge was all the swordplay he knew, therefore those thrusts made him worry.

He moved his shield constantly to save himself from the glinting point. Felimid struck at the killer's head, and the shield rose like a moon to frustrate his blow. He reached under the shield's edge with the shorter blade, and nearly lost fingers as the killer parried, for their swords had no cross-guards.

While moving back he thrust very low with Kincaid, at a downward angle. The slim blade grated on a shinbone, to pass through the calf muscle like an awl through a turnip. The murderer lurched, hopped, and managed to stand on the skewered leg. The bard crowded him swiftly, keeping him off balance.

The killer with the wounded side rose from the floor and charged, roaring. In a wild upsurge of strength he slammed straight into Felimid behind the flat circle of his shield, knocking him down. His mate roared triumphantly. Looming above the bard, they raised their crude weapons.

Then various things happened at once.

A thunderbolt landed on one man's head in the shape of a tight bundle of long wooden stakes, driving him to the floor. In the same instant, Felimid slipped his point upward past the other's shield, into his armpit and on into the shoulder-joint, spoiling his cut. A bale of heavy tent-cloth followed the stakes from somewhere near the roof, to land across the same man's back.

The bard rolled to his feet. Groaning and cursing, the fallen thug heaved the tent-cloth aside and struggled to rise. Felimid kicked the lower edge of his shield. The upper edge caught him under the chin and broke it, audibly. He fell backwards, his eyes rolling. Felimid tore the shield from that slackened arm and placed it on his own.

"You yield?" he demanded of the one foe left.

The robber whimpered on the dusty floor, among rushes and old wood-shavings. He clutched his ruined shoulder with one hand and his side with the other.

"Mercy," he croaked. "Mercy, your honour."

"Mercy?" Vera climbed down from the topmost shelf of the huge stand, gripping the upright post with her knees. "Listen to it! Mercy! You tag-end of a devil's litter, you had it for us, didn't you? And wetting yourself now that you're beaten! Kill him, Felimid, and end his cries, for they sicken me."

"I will not. He's the only one left who can speak." That was one reason, but Felimid knew he had not the will to slay a beaten man who blubbered like an infant, and that was his real reason. "I'm owing you thanks, Vera. They had me well trapped when you dropped half the store-house on their heads."

"All I could do! I tried to get out and bring help. Couldn't. These dirty slugs had jammed the door so tight shut that I couldn't budge it."

"I saw. You have but to name it if there's ever some good turn I can do you. Now let's make sure they are all harmless, or we will have them starting a fresh fight."

The man Felimid had run through was now lifeless. The apparent leader, he of the transfixed calf and broken jaw, tried to resist and had to be subdued. Once soundly tied with cord from the stores, he lost his senses and began snoring. They hobbled the last one's legs and lashed his wrists together, which brought further tears.

"You may weep," Felimid told him. "I'd rather my head belonged to someone else this minute. Vera, bring some friends from the baggage carts to collect these three darlings, if you please. I'll stay with them."

Vera insisted that he have his head treated first, even trying outright to drag him. He refused. Prying out the wedges his enemies had hammered into the door left him sick, dizzy and sweating. His thoughts were confused; his tongue felt numb. He hoped very greatly that it meant nothing. Head blows could be bad, he knew.

Men came running in a short while to carry away the murderers. They offered Felimid barley spirit while his head washed, cleaned and stitched, and he swigged it freely, with no thought of keeping a clear head if the Count of Britain were to summon him.

The Count, of course, did.

# VII

"I'm looking for the bard."

Hearing those words, Felimid lifted his bandaged head without joy. Ulfius, maybe? But the speaker was unknown to him, a younger man than Ulfius, with coarse black hair that stuck up like a crest and ugly, mismatched features. When he saw Felimid, he shut his mouth at once with a snap.

"You! Are *you* he?"

"I am he."

"What happened to you?"

"Some hired dogs tried to murder him, Brewnor!" Vera said with heat. "And me because I was with him! Well, he says they were hired; I do not know. We have two of them fast, though, and the third one died. He's a bonny fighter, this bard!"

"Wait!" Brewnor said. "I'm stumbling after you. Let him tell it. Tell it slowly," he added, "and leave nothing out, for a favour. I want to be clear."

Felimid told the story. The single killer who retained the power of speech had his presence of mind back by now, and interrupted to claim that the whole thing had been no more than a brawl over Vera, provoked by her. The rascal with the broken jaw made emphatic if wordless noises of confirmation.

"Brewnor, can you believe that?" Vera asked. "I have a temper, but do I stir up wanton trouble or cheat men—or encourage hogs like these, for that matter?"

"Never to my knowledge," the man called Brewnor admitted. "Listen, both of you, this is too knotty an affair for me. The Count wants to speak with the bard. But he will waive that order if you are too hurt to move."

"No. I can walk or sit a horse. I wish—to see the Count as much as he wishes to see me. More."

"Then sit behind me."

"Wait, if you will." Felimid looked down at his garments with distaste. "I borrowed these *clothes* from the Falcos while I brushed and aired my own, and they were nothing splendid even before I fought in them and bled all over them like a butchered hog. I ask that you take me to the camp by the western rampart and let me change back."

"I cannot," Brewnor said. "I have been to the Falcos' lines once, and then here, where their leader told me I would find you, and it has all wasted time. The Count's word was *now*. Never fear, he does not judge by dress, and he has looked worse than you after many a fight."

Felimid argued in protest. Brewnor said wearily, "Listen. I do not do this for fun. The Count of Britain is more than pressed for time. He was barely persuaded to see you at all. I think you must come now, or miss your chance."

Vera burst out laughing at Felimid's look. "Now dear me! You waste your breath trying to convince this one that garb matters, Felimid. He's the most unkempt of all the troop leaders. He's noted for it."

Brewnor laughed with her. "It's true. Fine garb would not do much for a face like mine. Also, try taming an angry Saxon with your splendour and see where you land."

"But—Cairbre and Ogma!—the clothes are faerie garb. They could make the difference between my being believed, and not believed. And it is direly imperative for the Count's sake that he believe me."

"Go, Felimid," Vera said to him. "I'll get your clothes and bring them to you at the hall. I promise I'll be swift. Brewnor, allow him a moment to change in the foreroom; that cannot hurt."

"All right," Brewnor conceded, "if you are in time."

Felimid mounted Brewnor's big sorrel behind the ill-dressed troop leader. His head spun. Clenching his teeth, he clung to the high saddle-cantle and tightened his knees. Brewnor set off at a trot, which the bard found torturous, though pride would not let him protest.

Brewnor indicated the row of store-houses. "You must have thought your last hour had come, in there. Yon fellows were robbers of forest and mountain, I am thinking. The kind who wait to attack houses while the men are gone. Cutters of sleeping throats."

"What will happen to them?"

"Could you show the truth of what you say, they'd hang. Failing that, I daresay they'll be whipped out of Camlodd."

"Attacking a bard should be punished harder."

"The Count does not think so. He was raised in Roman ways."

"That is his loss," Felimid said. "It's the bards who sing the glory of his Brotherhood and lure men to join it. Have you been with the band long?"

"Three years. I was born in Lesser Britain* across the sea.

* Brittany

Enough bards out of Britain extolled the fight against the sea-wolves, but—not until Artorius came to our kingdom did I ever wish to be part of it, and I kept the desire. Once you see him you do not forget him."

"Why?"

They were passing the auxiliaries' lines now. These were the light tribal riders, with small quick horses and pads for saddles, knife thrust to the Brotherhood's hammer blow.

"He's Artorius," Brewnor said simply. "It cannot be explained. I might say that he's a great fighter, with the craft and sense that wins battles. I might say more. He's our leader, and yet one of us. I've never heard of his taking so much as a mouthful of food ahead of hungry men back from patrol, or having a wound dressed out of his rightful turn." He shook his head. "I might talk all day and still not show you the truth of him. You will meet him soon."

Brewnor turned his horse's head to the left and passed by the end of a great barn. The hall door was close, and the exercise ground almost as near, in plain view down a stretch of open earth. Sounds of neighing horses and clashing weapons rolled through that passage.

"Lamorak showing his prowess again," Brewnor grunted. He said it disparagingly.

"Who is Lamorak?"

"A comrade of Artorius's from the early days. Long before my time, aye. He came over from Gaul with the Lady Questa when her father's kingdom fell, and stayed here some years. Then he went back to Gaul. Believe me, I heard enough of his doings while I was growing up. You couldn't avoid it. He was our neighbour, and not a comfortable sort to have."

"Raiding and warfare?"

"We'd better go to the hall."

Brewnor had a word with the doorkeeper while Felimid watched the conflict on the practice field. It seemed to be one mounted troop against another, with single combats now and then. The noise split the sky.

"By the standing stones!" Brewnor swore. "After our hurrying here, Artorius is too busy to see you at once, and Vera hasn't arrived either! Let's just take a closer look at the mock fight, then."

"I'd like to see."

Brewnor urged his horse closer to the practice ground. "Raiding and warfare, yes," he said, taking up the discussion where he had left it. "He started by trying to overthrow the Franks, and he was always scheming to involve the princes of Lesser Britain. Sometimes he succeeded. An uncle of mine died that way. When Frankish power proved too much, he took his fighters south and made a kingdom of his own, jammed in between the Franks, the Goths and Lesser Britain." All of these tribes and places were only names to the bard. "How long it'll exist is anybody's guess."

"Then why is he here in Britain now, if he has what he wants in Gaul, and its state is so precarious?"

"The Count needs him. Old loyalties, maybe."

Brewnor sounded dubious.

"You do not like him."

"His warriors are welcome. And he dowered us with two shiploads of supplies that were even more welcome." Brewnor drew rein by the practice field. "Ha! It's Cynon's troop he has challenged! Good, they will beat him!"

The battle was not much less fierce than the real thing for being fought with wooden swords and maces. Blows pounded and crashed in a constant thunder. The big brutes of horses with their leather head—and chest-armour, ridden by men in chiming mail shirts, made it seem like a brawl of giants.

Then Felimid began to observe details. He reckoned their saddles laughable. Why, even old women could not fall out of those! And could they really be some sort of iron triangles attached to the saddles' heavy frames, in which the riders were bracing their feet? He glanced down. They were. Brewnor used them too, as he would have noticed before, but for his paining head.

Men who needed such aids would have been derided throughout Erin!

"That's Lamorak!" Brewnor shouted, betraying himself again. He pointed excitedly to a man in the thick of the conflict. Felimid saw a harsh, fork-bearded face under a shining helmet, a lifted arm roped with muscle, and a plunging grey horse. Swinging his wooden mace, he knocked a man of the Brotherhood into the dust and engaged two more.

"Showing off," Brewnor growled. "In Gaul there may be need for that. Here we fight Saxons, and they don't ride. He'd be practicing with lances if he wished to help. All he wishes is to prove that his men are better than ours."

"Their horses are like yours."

"The same breed. Gothic chargers. They are the only steeds with the strength and weight we need. Sa-ha! Look there among the crowd. Not the horsemen, those watchers there in bright cloaks, guarding the woman and children."

"I see her. Ah! She'd be the Lady Questa, Artorius's wife?"

"Aye."

She was distinctly pretty. Although short, she carried herself erect with gracious pride. Gilt combs glittered in her shining dark brown hair. She turned to the youth beside her with a laugh, so that her profile was towards the bard. He saw a short but high-bridged nose, rounded cheek curving to a pointed chin, and a lustrous dark eye. Pretty, yes, and perhaps more, for all that she must be thirty-five.

She set her hand on the youth's arm. He resembled her so much that he had to be her son, though all of six feet tall. His sister, a girl with chestnut hair, lifted a boy of ten to give him a better look at the combat, and nearly fell under his sturdy weight. Their brother took him and raised him shoulder-high.

"Where will they go when the Brotherhood departs to fight?" Felimid asked.

"The older boy, Flavius, goes with his father. The others will return to the City of Legions and wait—no easy task, though it's long familiar to Questa."

"Flavius." Felimid looked at the tall lad again. "Named for the Count's cousin who died at Anderida?"

"You know about that? Aye, named for him. I have always heard Artorius held him mighty dear. We'll bring Aelle to account for it this spring. For that, and much else."

Felimid looked again at the ardent brawl on the parade field. The big horses threw up clods thick as rain with their iron-shod feet, and broken bits of oak swords flew as freely. Shields boomed. Men with bloody faces and limbs came off the ground.

Questa, he saw, watched Lamorak with an intent, lambent gaze. No wonder. If he had come with her from Gaul when her father's kingdom fell he must be a strong link with her past. Having spent years trying to win it back from the savages who toppled it gave him a claim on her gratitude and favour, too.

"Vera's late with her errand," Brewnor said abruptly. "We'd best go back. It won't do to have the Count call you and you not be there."

"No, there she is now!"

She ran towards them, her conspicuous hair adrift, holding a bundle.

"Felimid! Here are your duds. Into the foreroom, now, and

dress, and I hope you will tell me every word that passed between you and Count Artorius when you come out."

# VIII

Unlike Brewnor, Felimid revelled in fine clothing and would go to great lengths to obtain it. Two years of wandering exile had often forced him to travel looking more like Brewnor than like himself, but as he had said, the garb Gwyn ap Nudd had given him meant more than a good appearance. In the foreroom of the hall he donned it, wondered how long he must wait, and reviewed in his mind the message of Arthur Pendragon's timeless henchman.

The inner door opened. Two warriors of the Brotherhood stood waiting, and one said briskly, "The Count of Britain grants you an audience."

Count of Britain! An ancient Roman title which, if one thought about it, Artorius had revived and bestowed upon himself. Roman in nurture, Roman in thought, Roman in ideals. All men described him so. And Felimid's bardic powers fled from him when he so much as set foot on a Roman highway.

*How can I convince him?*

Felimid walked into the long hall of Camlodd.

Except for the warriors, who remained by the door, there were just three men in the whole draughty place. As someone had said, this was no royal hall. The walls themselves were low, and the high thatched roof with its bare rafters held too much empty space when no throng of men occupied the tables.

The Count of Britain sat in a chair against the northern wall. Another man in a red tunic sat at his right. At his left, standing, was someone Felimid recognised.

Clydno.

He approached the three with his blood seething. If Clydno was present, it must mean that Artorius trusted him. Cairbre and Ogma, Felimid had asked that no others be here, and it was no help to reflect that his position for asking was feeble, his claimed status as the emissary of Elder Britain unbelievable in the daylight! It must be unbelievable at any time where Romans were concerned.

Count Artorius looked at him with a level grey gaze that assessed. It held candour rather than calculation. That was

Felimid's first and strongest impression, that he faced an honest man, the sort whose simplicity springs not from shallow wits, but from strength of spirit. The square blunt-featured face, powerful shoulders and broad chest were those of a soldier. A sheathed cavalry sword lay on the table before him.

"Felimid mac Fal?" Artorius indicated the bench on Felimid's side of the table. "You'd better be seated. Camlodd's hospitality has not been kind to you. I'm told it happened this morning."

"True, lord. The men who did it swear it was a common brawl in anger, but I think not. They came masked and too well prepared. It's my belief they were hired to make sure I never spoke with you."

"If that's true, brother, their blood money was on them," said the man at Artorius's right. He resembled the Count, though redder, more fleshy and a few years his senior. "Gold coins, no less."

"One doesn't obtain those just anywhere," the Count said. It was doubtless what all of them were thinking. "Felimid mac Fal, this is my brother Caius Artorius, Tribune of the Brotherhood. Clydno, the emissary of the Archdruid Myrddin, you have met before. I am Lucius Artorius Hispanicus, son of Calvinus Artorius, and Count of Britain." He added a bit grimly, "For my sins. You now know who we are. I am less than clear as to who you are. You had better tell me, but you may want to strengthen yourself with wine first."

"No, lord. I drank enough while my head was being stitched. Some of that water and bread would suit me well."

Artorius pushed the platter and jug across to him without a word. Felimid ripped the tough rye bread with his teeth and chewed it gratefully, washing it down with the clear water. Few things had ever tasted better to him. He felt strength and presence of mind come back. Although his head still hurt like fire, he could endure and even dismiss it.

"Who am I?" he said then. "At home in Erin, lord, I am the grandson of the island's Chief Bard, Fergus, and a bard of the third rank in my own right; pupil of the great Suibni; descendant of Cairbre the harp-master and the battle-champion Ogma. Here in Britain I am still a bard, but an exile for three years. Not for law-breaking; it's a story which goes back to my parents' youth and is too long entirely for the Count of Britain's concern at this time."

"Agreed."

Felimid took the dry interjection in his stride. "I came to

Camlodd because King Gwyn ap Nudd, who guards Arthur Pendragon's grave and the gates of Elder Britain, did send me. He gave me these garments I wear. They are not ordinary, lord. It can be seen."

They fitted to perfection though they had neither seam nor stitches. The weave was impossibly even, the dyes other-wordly. Artorius had never seen the like of them even upon kings, and he had argued the advantages of concerted action to far too many.

"Mortal sorcery could have made them," he said. "I've seen what mere mortal sorcery can do. Talking of that, it was perhaps impudent of you to bring three seasons to this fortress, unasked."

"True for you, lord. It was. Yet my choices lay between doing that and being thrown out of Camlodd. I may wish yet that I had chosen to be thrown out. Disturbing the round of the earth can bring her anger upon a man, and none does that lightly."

"But lightly he may offend the Count of Britain?" Caius said. "Your tongue led you astray there."

"Lord," Clydno expostulated, "how much more time will you waste with this crack-brained boy? He's produced nothing yet but idle words and bragging."

"I've offered the truth," Felimid said. "Lord, I've no wish to quarrel with this magician in your presence, but it's truth also that there is bad blood between us. I do not trust him."

Felimid wanted to declare that Clydno had paid the robbers to dismember him. The accusation was ready and leaping on the end of his tongue. Barely in time, he reconsidered and held it back. Artorius was giving him a hearing. If he went too far he would lose the man.

"I know something of this," Artorius said. "It's why I commanded that others say nothing for a time while I listened to you. Remember, Clydno?"

"Your pardon, lord," the magician said thickly. "Yet Myrddin my master—"

"—might not care to have me listen to any words but yours? True. He might not. But it's his own fault if I do. He's been silent where Artorians are concerned for enough years now. I promise to hear you fully, Clydno—when this lad has finished. And you may observe that he's ill."

"Lord—"

"Perhaps you should wait outside if you cannot stomach it."

"No, lord." Clydno subsided, red and almost choking. "I'll remain, by your leave. This I should hear."

Felimid did not agree. But since Artorius allowed it there was little he could do. He knew he walked on ice so thin it cracked at each step.

"It's time you delivered your message, with no more prequel. What has King Gwyn ap Nudd to say to me?"

"This, lord." Felimid drew a deep breath. "That you of all men living fight for Britain, with clear sight and a heart undivided by fears and follies. Because of this, the powers of Elder Britain stand with you against the Saxons, who are invaders and strangers to this sacred earth. Their gods of ice and storm and darkness will follow them in like a tide, unless they are halted, delayed, turned back—and in that tide the last shrines and lights of Britain might drown, the last cities be left deserted."

Artorius looked startled—and impressed, a little, for the first time. Felimid had no idea why. He continued, letting Gwyn ap Nudd's words come from his mouth as the faerie king had spoken them.

"When the Brotherhood meets the host of Aelle, Gwyn ap Nudd will be there. His chariots will drive against the sea-wolves and the terrors of Annwn will be unleashed against them. The wind in the trees will whisper their movements to you before the fight, and you will know them all. The rivers will rise, grumbling, to flood their homes and prevent their boats coming up the Thames, so that many will fail to join their Bretwalda in time.

"These advantages you will be needing. The kings of Britain who are supposed to aid you with war-men will prove false. None except two will keep their word."

Caius the tribune spoke for the first time since his rebuke to Felimid. "Huh! That last is a thing any man could know! Even a stranger to Britain, if he uses his ears. So two will support us? Then that's good news. It's one more than I expected. But it's not enough to fill me with confidence in the bard."

"Most true," Clydno said. "May I speak now, lord?"

"If you are no longer-winded than Cai."

The dark, narrow face looked scornfully at the bard. "The lord Cai is altogether right. This promise of aid from the Otherworld, from the very trees and rivers, comes second-hand also. My master Myrddin made the same promise through me, days before this upstart appeared. A bard's ears could hear it on the wind from far off. As for Gwyn ap Nudd's chariots and the demons of Annwn, I will believe it when I see them."

"Then you may have to believe it sooner than you looked for, man with the narrow head," Felimid said sweetly. "Let this stay between the four of us, if it pleases you, lord. King Gwyn vowed to me that on the third night after I came to Camlodd he would send a sign that this is all true. No man who stands on the rampart at sunset and watches the old outer rath will miss it. So said he."

"And what if some traitor with a bow is also there, hiding in the grass, waiting for a clear shot at the Count of Britain?" Cai asked.

"Search all the ditches, and the woods around the crest, just before the sun sets," Felimid offered. "Better still, let the Count of Britain not be there. Men he trusts can tell him what they saw. The guardian of Arthur's grave never said that the Count must be a witness."

"I'd not miss it," Artorius said. "Brother, you need not be concerned. I'll make sure I am safe. Is that the whole of your word, Felimid mac Fal?"

"Not quite the whole, lord." *I wish that it were*! "There is one thing more, and that I must say to yourself only, or not speak. When you hear it you will be glad that no others were near. My oath on it."

"Lord, this may not be!" Clydno burst out. "He has a sword—what if he should—"

"And I have a sword," Artorius answered impatiently, "and my brother and two warriors and a magician close at hand. How much safer must I be? Clydno, you are an old woman."

"And yet I have no need of a sword at present," Felimid said. "Maybe the lord Cai will honour me by looking after it?"

He unbuckled Kincaid and handed the sword across to Caius, who took it without comment.

"I'll hear it," Artorius said. "Just go as far as the door, if you will."

They obeyed, Cai looking puzzled and vaguely irked, Clydno as though he suffered an infestation of worms, to the bard's pleasure. Rather, it would have pleased him, had he words less chilling to impart.

"You look more troubled than I feel," Artorius told him, amiably enough. "Can it be that bad? You had best tell me."

"In Gwyn ap Nudd's own words, lord. He demanded that of me. He—prophesied a thing. *If Count Artorius of Britain goes to this battle, he will win, and win mightily. This although no kings but two shall assist him.*"

"One more than expected, as Cai said. Aye, I know who one of them will be. My foster-brother Melwas. Now tell me the rest.

There must be more. You look nearly heartsick, and nothing you have said yet justifies it."

"There is more." Felimid uttered it. "*But his flesh will lie cold and lifeless on the ground when it is over.*"

"Ssooo." Artorius loosed a soft outward breath. He said no more for a long time. His body loosened in the chair, and he thrust out his legs as though seeking freedom. His gaze remained on Felimid all the while.

"Did someone pay you to say this?"

The question was casual, almost, and the Count of Britain did not even sound angered. Yet Felimid felt his whole body react to it.

"None. And I would have satirised the man who tried." Blood crawled up hotly into Felimid's head and pounded there. The gash in his scalp felt ready to burst like a broom-pod. "I take nobody's pay to make a wreck of my host. I like to suppose Cu Roi himself could not threaten me into it. Now you are the Count of Britain with a war to fight. You are my host. But accuse me of such a thing again and I may satirise *you*."

"You frighten me." Artorius looked at him for a long moment more. At last he sighed. "I believe you. Did you never think, though, that someone might have sent this prophecy through you to make me lose heart? In hopes that I would? That you might be his tool?"

"I was giving thought to that each step of the way to Camlodd," Felimid said emphatically. "Almost I decided not to repeat it. Even as I sat here I had not made up my mind whether to tell you."

"And yet you did. Why?"

"It'll sound like flattery. It is not meant so. You do not seem the sort to be swayed or frightened by a prophecy, lord. I reckoned you would prefer knowing. Besides, it was not for me to decide whether you should hear. It concerned you. Had it come from some drunken soothsayer, I would not have given it thought or walked a yard with it. Yet the source makes it somewhat different from most."

"If you have not been fooled." Artorius grew pensive. "I have little time for prophecies, Felimid. Myrddin's were the only ones that ever impressed me. They came true. Yet even his—It has occurred to me that with his other, undoubted powers, he may have arranged for them to happen."

"I've heard much about Myrddin." Felimid asked a bold question. "Did you trust him, lord?"

"I will not answer that. It cannot be answered with a simple yes or no, anyhow. I'll say this. It always seemed to me that Myrddin was a far from common man."

"And Clydno?"

"Clydno is Myrddin's messenger. I'm satisfied of that."

There was a pause.

"If I believed completely," Artorius said, perhaps to the fates more than to Felimid, "if I knew I would die in this battle, it would mean nothing. I would still go. The wolf packs have gathered as never before. Myrddin has promised that the rivers will rise to delay the East and Middle Saxons, but even if none of them arrive, Aelle still has his own South Saxons, the Hastings, the Jutes of Kent and Westri, the Angles who are marching down the Icknield Way, and a slew of pirate chieftains from across the sea, hoping to gain kingdoms. This fight is the culmination of all the fights we have had," Artorius said, "and if they win they will divide Britain among themselves like a gralloched stag. It doesn't matter horse dung if the bogies and spirits are for me or against me."

"It may matter to your men," Felimid pointed out. "They believe in Myrddin as the Archdruid of Britain, most of them, even the Christians. They believe in Gwyn ap Nudd. Many believe the Count of Britain is Arthur Pendragon, returned or reborn."

Artorius smiled with a flash of genuine mirth. "I know. I always suspected Myrddin of spreading that one. Perhaps not, though. Men have said it of every strong leader or king to come along in this age. Gereint, Riothamus, Aurelian—even Vortigern in his day, Mithras save us! It's a long list. It will not end with me."

"What do you believe, lord?"

"About Arthur Pendragon? That he rebelled against Rome and murdered his son. That he wasn't much more than the overlord of a number of tribes, some of which betrayed him at their first opportunity, even to an outside power they might have seen would conquer them as surely as Arthur. And from that little acorn grew a huge spreading oak of legend."

"Then your opinion of Gwyn ap Nudd must be the same."

"Bard, I know too well there are spirits, and magicians, and superstitions as horrid as red bone! I know they resurge now that Rome's law is gone. It's the law and civilisation of Rome I keep as best I can. Against odds, for the dragons have returned, and it's said they were brought back by Myrddin. The Saxons, as you said, bring in their own savage demons. Now I'd rather see one town thriving, and one field sown in confidence of a harvest, than have all the power such beings can give."

"As would I," Felimid said, and let his words come leaping from the heart, across the gap between a young son of Erin and the last Count of Britain. "As would your men! Few of them know Rome, or care for Rome, as you do. They follow the banner of the Red Dragon, and you their war leader, not the eagles. Yet they fight as you fight. For Britain!

"Lord, Arthur Pendragon fought for Britain, in his day and by his lights. Gwyn ap Nudd with him. Their spirits now side with you, hold your battle as theirs too. Yes, powers of wood and torrent, all the wild spectres of the air, even the dead who remember what was!

"I came because King Gwyn ap Nudd commanded me. Lord, if I believed he meant to use me to betray brave men, and trap them in a pit, for robbers to despoil their homes and folk, I'd have refused him with contempt, no matter what he did. I'd not be in your fortress now.

"Whether I really met him—and since I have the bardic sight, I can't be fooled by glamour or illusion—wait two sunsets. Then you'll know."

Artorius was silent for a considerable time.

"Again I rather believe you," he said at last. "If you're not committed to eat with my cousins the Falcos, dine in this hall tonight. I wish to have you under my eye while we wait for your sign from Gwyn ap Nudd."


# IX


Dinner in the long hall was as rich as Camlodd could offer. Questa had done much to arrange it, and King Melwas of the Summer Country had sent wains of food and drink, including bright hangings for the walls. But brightest and most splendid was the great banner of Britain, the Red Dragon on its field of golden silk, that belonged to the Brotherhood.

It shimmered behind Artorius and his greatest guests. Questa sat beside him, next to Bishop Dubricius of Dyfed in his white and crimson vestments, a small man large in passion and faith. Melwas the Winged sat at the Count's right with Lamorak next to him—and then Clydno, looking to the bard like a dark carrion bird ready to pick corpses.

Melwas's queen, Liba, a sensuous tawny beauty, was a pleasure to watch. She flirted in a maternal kind of way with the Count's tall son—what was his name?—Flavius. The younger children sat further down the table. Two squadrons were absent from Camlodd, but the other three captains, Ulfius, Mag and Brychan, sat in their worn tunics as proudly as kings.

"Aelle has no chance!" Lamorak was saying. He was in high spirits, his men having beaten Cynon's troop. "With all his numbers, none! Barbarians on foot have never had a chance against mailed cavalry. You have shown that time and again here. Why, we showed it at Llongborth when we were all as young as Flavius yonder. Didn't we, Melwas?"

The king of the Summer Country laughed his agreement.

"Franks are much like these sea-wolves of yours," Lamorak went on. "Maybe even fiercer. They have the same weaknesses, though; they fight on foot, and they are boneheads all. A host of them came into my land once. With enough foresight to be well provisioned, I had nothing to do but hold the high ground and withstand their attacks. Within a few days the fools had nothing to eat, sickness and desertion were thinning their ranks, and we were healthy. Then we charged. Their spirit was gone; they broke before us. The survivors must be running yet."

"It's none so easy or quick with Saxons," Ulfius said. "They last. Nevertheless, by the close of the day it'll be with them as it was with your Franks, Lamorak. They haven't been able to stand against the Brotherhood once!"

The gathered horsemen cheered and shouted. Lamorak took this as encouragement to boast further, and louder, about his victories in Gaul. Seeing him thus, at closer range and without his helmet, Felimid thought to discern the effects of a long custom of ruthless arrogance in that visage. Once he must have been outstandingly handsome, but now there were sacks under the hawk eyes and broken veins in his cheeks. Felimid suspected a drunken looseness about the mouth, if the moustache and forked beard were removed to show it. Lamorak might still be made of iron, but the metal was rusting.

"After we settle Aelle, brother," he was saying, "you should take the Brotherhood across to Gaul! The port of Nantes dares not refuse any asking of mine. Your word could bring the princes of Lesser Britain together like that!" He snapped his fingers. "With them as allies and my realm for a base, we'd take northern Gaul in a year. By the time we died we'd have all of it to leave our children. The Emperor would fall on our necks and make us Consuls!"

Many of the younger, hotter spirits in the Brotherhood liked that. When their noisy approval stopped, Questa asked with a clarity that carried, "And what would become of Britain while Artorius made himself a consul in Gaul?"

"Ah, Britain," Lamorak said dismissively. "Britain will be safe for fifty years, once we have settled this upstart Aelle. Even safer for having her neighbour under one rule."

"Maybe," Artorius said. "It's the hope of us all. Gaul, though, will be no such easy prize as you make her while the Frankish king lives."

Lamorak snorted. "I thrive well enough despite all his efforts to crush me. When he dies, Artorius, when he dies, that savage kingdom of his will be split among his four sons, and I can tell you they will begin making war on each other at once. It'll be brother against brother until they are all gone; that is the Frankish way. Man, they will do half our work for us! I swear it! Their father cannot live forever."

"Neither can we."

Lamorak looked at his boyhood friend with disappointment and something like contempt. "What are your thoughts, Questa? It's your sire's kingdom, and you were always burning to regain it."

Questa flushed, and answered with a certain amount of anger. "That was long ago, Lamorak, nor was my father ever a king. The barbarians called him one. Did that make it so? *He* was consul, and his murderer has been made consul now, which shows what the Empire thinks of the matter—and how much honour is left in the title. Better, I think, to be content with your kingly rank. You won it by your own courage and strength, and what is greater, you rule it nobly." She pledged him in wine. "Your aid to us here we will never forget."

Cheering shook the rafters. Lamorak responded to the toast, but a baffled, thwarted look remained with him, for no matter how pleasantly, he had been refused. He did not seem accustomed to that at all.

Felimid reckoned him an idiot for asking in public. Perhaps he had hoped the Brotherhood would demand that Artorius lead them to Gaul and glory forthwith. He had miscalculated, if so. Now Clydno leaned towards him and spoke what seemed to be solace and caution in his ear.

Strange.

Lamorak answered him curtly, and Clydno spoke to the squadron captain on his other side thereafter, so belike there was nothing in it; a matter of Clydno poking his nose where it did not belong and having it snubbed.

The meal ended. Bishop Dubricius pronounced a blessing on all those present and preached a short sermon against the Saxons, urging the Brotherhood to destroy them, with never a hint that their conversion might one day be a thing to desire. Then the women left and the activities of men waiting to go to war began. Drinking was limited, because of the supplies, but the gossip and yarns and reminiscences flowed freely. Felimid told the ancient stories of voyages, monsters, love and elopement, until his fingers stung on the harp-strings, and in exchange he learned more about the Brotherhood in one night than he had in the two previous years.

"Are you having a good time, bard?" Ulfius inquired.

"I am having a good time," Felimid said. "But my head is aching again, and I think I will leave before long."

"What I have to tell you may make it ache more. You call to mind those robbers who accosted you and Vera? The ones you thought were paid?"

"Indeed. Would I forget? It's not every day I have such close calls, now."

"I suppose not. Well, there was a travelling horse-doctor in the fortress—no more than a quack, and I wouldn't have let him near our steeds if I were desperate, but he made a good thing out of the auxiliaries. He was killed in his booth, hacked to death, last night. It seems that is where the gold coins came from."

"The shocking, murderous fellows they were, then." Felimid's leaf-green eyes had seldom looked more innocent. "They robbed him? And then came for me and Vera hours later?"

"Either that or he paid them to slay you, acting as someone else's agent, and they slew him out of greed afterwards, which does not make them very clever. The one who can talk claims that the horse-doctor did pay them. He's trying to avoid a noose, which he will not do, but our trail ends now with the horse-doctor, whether or not there was someone else beyond."

*Indeed there was; Clydno!*

"This ends the matter, then? No more?"

"You sound disappointed," Ulfius said. "It's all unless you can think of more."

"Little enough, except, now that you remind me, one of those murderers should have had a new slash on his upper arm that I didn't put there, which he got while committing a different outrage the night before."

"Ah, that. Yes, Crispus Falco told me. The devils all had scars in plenty, and one just about answers your description of it, except that the fellow must have had it at least a month, not a single night."

*At least a month. Not possible, unless Clydno worked magic to heal it quickly, and have his paid killer in condition to murder me the next morning. Wait, though! From what Ulfius says, these poor brutish dupes do not even know Clydno was the source of their money. They have never spoken to him.*

*Maybe he healed the man without letting him see who was doing it. A blindfold's a simple safeguard. Och, I'll never be sure now, and I can prove nothing.*

"My thanks, captain," he said ironically. "I'll sleep well for knowing this."

Downcast at the news, he drew aside, brooding. Leaning against a pillar, he looked around the hall, and after some time it came to him that Lamorak was missing.

Felimid recalled the jarring sight of Clydno leaning across to whisper to the Gaulish warlord. His motives came down to little more than restlessness and unease; but he left the hall, prowling.

Moving with the softness of the earth-mother's breed, he listened, and heard a strong hectoring voice from the shadows. He knew it at once. Lamorak was making an effort to keep his tone low, but being wholly unused to any such necessity, he barely held it to a normal pitch.

Felimid could not distinguish any of the actual words being spoken. That aroused real suspicion in him. Lamorak didn't mumble, nor did he speak in hopelessly strange accents. If Felimid's ears were baffled, then something out of the common must be doing the baffling. Waiting in shadows, he willed himself to hear the voices, not as they had been distorted by a wizard's glamour, but as they were.

"Woman, you cannot mean it! You cannot have turned to milk and water in so few years."

"It has been more than a few."

Felimid left the solid earth. That second voice belonged to Questa. The figure Lamorak held by the shoulders was almost as tall as he, but glamour deceived sight almost as easily as hearing. Before Felimid's eyes, the illusion melted and formed again as a shorter, more rounded shape, but he scarcely took notice. He knew who she was.

Questa, talking to Lamorak in such clandestine circumstances, when she might do so in the open whenever she wished, implied

. . . trouble. The more so since Felimid knew of only one man
in Camlodd with the ability to cast such a glamour. Clydno the
magician, surely.

Wait. Clydno knew the bard could penetrate such glamour
with his trained senses. All men, not magicians only, knew it.
Clydno would not willingly take the risk. He wasn't a lunatic.
Rash, imperious Lamorak must have insisted—which meant
that, where Clydno was concerned, Lamorak was able to insist.

*Cairbre and Ogma, who will believe it?*

"You forget it all?" Lamorak's voice held anger and torment.
"My father served yours. He died when those stinking Franks
came to Soissons, and I helped you escape with the tears barely
dry on my face, bringing you to Britain— "

"Lucius and his cousin were also there."

"All right! Yet I loved you before he did. I urged the Britons
to avenge your father, not he. I fought and worked to become
great among them so that I could give the command myself.
You plotted with me, darling." Felimid had never heard the
word spoken with so much bitterness. "When we both saw
that Artorius would get there rather than me, because of his
ancestry, you turned to him, hoping to make him your tool. You
married him."

"It wasn't for that only, Lamorak."

"For that mostly, then! Else why did you turn to me when your
plans fell through? Your precious husband lacked the guts to seize
power, and did nothing even when old Governor Aurelian tossed
you into a nunnery for a year."

"Because my father had died and I felt betrayed—by Lucius
Artorius, by all the Britons, even my father and God, I suppose.
Because I knew you loved me greatly. Because I partly loved you,
then—and used you badly, yes, for which I am ashamed."

"I don't want your shame, girl. I want you. I love you yet. I
returned to Gaul for you, thinking I could break the Frankish grip
on Soissons. For you! Twice I came so close I could whiff the prize.
Three times I was wounded nearly to death, and the last time I had
to make my recovery in a filthy swamp as a hunted outlaw. Then
I carved out my own kingdom, with you always in mind, and not
even I could have achieved it else. Always, always I dreamed of
you beside me. I came here for you, not to risk my neck. I'll tell
you now that I don't care a sprinkling of dust whether Aelle or
Artorius wins this fight, or if the whole Brotherhood of Britain
dies in it."

"That is why you've lost me."

Questa's voice was sad, a terrible, vibrating sadness that struck deep into the listening bard. Yes, but Lamorak now appeared as more than a headstrong villain, too. Mad for her yet, he was, after all those years, and she said no. That could not bring him much joy.

"No!" If roaring in a whisper was possible, then Lamorak did it. "Before I lose you, Questa, I will tell Artorius to his face that you were my lover in the old days, and that the boy he thinks his son, the boy he named Flavius, is mine."

"You will tell him a lie, then," Questa answered fiercely. "Flavius is *his* son."

"The child of a little woman like you, and a man of no more than middle height like Artorius? It's true, he had tall uncles, but still—even you cannot be completely sure I never fathered him. I can count months as well as the next."

"Listen to me, Lamorak. Do what you threaten, and I will give you the lie before all, under oath, if it perjures my soul to hell. Don't force me to think it might be best if you were slain! You were my lover, if not my love. There was a time when I reckoned you my one friend in the world. Do not befoul that in trying to have me. You cannot have me."

"Words!" Lamorak snarled. "Whatever else happens, my men and I won't be taking part in the battle, Questa. I've my own kingdom to care for. I came for you."

There was a long pause.

"I'm sorry, Lamorak. You came for nothing, then."

Even Felimid, young and prone to enthusiasm, would have taken those words as final had he been in Lamorak's place.

Not the Gaul.

"I supposed you might lie," he said harshly. "I've a cure for that. Look here." He produced something that flashed vitreously as he exposed it. "The Cup of Truth they tell stories about. It breaks in three pieces when a lie is told over it, and becomes whole again when the truth is told. I can show every man in Camlodd, again and again, that it really has that virtue. How far will perjury take you then?"

So. Felimid knew he was not merely trying to frighten her. Clydno must have given him the cup, and Clydno in turn could only have obtained it from his master. The nature of Myrddin's interest in all this he could not fathom. He did not try.

Questa reached frantically for the shining thing. The Gaul caught her wrist with one hand, and held the cup far out of her reach. Felimid stared at it across the intervening distance. The glitter of it looked like glass, not metal—and it was inconvenient for all concerned, save Lamorak and Clydno.

The bard emerged from darkness like a pouncing otter. Springing, he seized the cup in both hands, twisted it out of Lamorak's astounded grip, and slammed it against the nearest wall. It remained whole. The glitter he had thought was glass was jewel-work on a metal chalice, and he had no time for a second attempt to destroy it. Seizing Questa by the hand, he ran with her into the darkness.

Behind them, Lamorak wasted time groping for the cup, which he must have believed fallen to the ground, until he realised his mistake. Then he trampled after Felimid and Questa, growling, sword out, but they had vanished. He bellowed like a barghest. Barely retaining the sense to ram his sword back into its sheath, he raged back and forth, hating to accept the need to tell Clydno of this ludicrous bungle.

The frustrated passion so hot in his heart then was not love.

# X

In daylight, wearing her own appearance, Questa listened to clear plangent music. She had every right to ask the bard to play for her. They could be together and talk with none to question. Because they had no warping illusions to hide the words they spoke, they could not discuss what had happened save in most oblique ways. The bard for one saw little need to speak of it at all.

Questa felt differently. She said in a murmur, "Why?"

"I dislike Clydno, lady," Felimid answered in a normal tone. "I suppose all Camlodd knows it. I suspect him of setting on the men who attacked me—but here in the Count of Britain's fortress I will make no quarrel with him."

"You do that now, by talking of your suspicions," she said. "Guilty or innocent, he will hate you for accusing him, and what more likely to start a quarrel?"

"But if guilty, knowing he's suspected, he will be less likely to try again," Felimid said. "Especially as he now has nothing to gain thereby. Count Artorius has the message I brought."

In one way it was sufficient explanation. In another way it explained very little.

Lower yet, Questa said, "Why help me?"

*. . . sound of the calm wave on the beach, pure shadowing tree
of true music, voice of the swan over shining streams . . .*

A direct answer, a direct mention of last's night's events, he
could not give. Yet an answer there was, and it came to his mind
as his fingers drew soft wandering music from Golden Singer.

"Lady, I have a mother. Now when she was young, maybe too
young, she married. A couple of years later she was discontented,
and in that state of mind she met my father. And he met her. They
ran away together.

"The husband followed, set on revenge. They could not go
to my tribe for refuge, as that might have meant war. Now my
father, although young, was a pirate chieftain who had raided
Gaul, Spain, and Britain. He had fighting men on his own ship
and did not need to appeal for protection. He killed the husband
in a fight. Then my mother, repentant and stricken, left him and
asked for refuge in a nunnery. I was born there.

"My father knew where she was. He loved her, though, too
much to drag her away with him when she did not wish it."
Questa made a small grimace. Felimid caught her eye and gave
a perfunctory nod. "Yes, lady, just so. Well. The husband's clan
also knew, or had learned, and came down on the nunnery raging
to destroy the faithless wife and her baby. Myself."

"One can see they failed with you. But—your mother?"

"My father had been watching for such an event. His crew took
my mother and me to safety in his ship, the *Osprey*. My father
stayed behind to ensure our escape, which he did, though it took
red battle. Sadly, he died in the doing. I never knew him."

"I'm sorry. It's a terrible story."

"Terrible enough, yes, but my father was no innocent."

"He didn't leave you," Questa said. "He died defending your
mother and you."

"Yes, lady, I know, and I'd not have you think I am gnashing
my teeth over it." Felimid smiled a bit. "I was almighty young
when I last felt that way."

Questa smiled too. "What are you now? I asked why, and
perhaps you have told me. Thank you, my friend. I do wonder
why you are here in Britain rather than at home where you
seemingly would rather be."

"The old trouble arose again. There'd have been a feud if I had
not agreed to go into exile for three years, so I said my farewells
and left. Two years are gone."

"More likely you were sentenced as a thief," said a voice at his
elbow, hissing with ire and horror.

"You forget yourself, magician," Questa said reprovingly, with a sparkle of mischief somewhere behind it. Her attendant women drew closer, loving the whiff of scandal. "This young man is my husband's guest."

"Not by my advice, *lady*," Clydno said. "I desire words with him concerning an—urgent matter—if you will allow him to depart."

"Maybe I had better," Felimid said cheerfully. "We can walk on the rampart and see the outer rath where Gwyn ap Nudd's sending will appear. That ought to be pleasant. Lady, if you permit . . ."

"I do. Master Clydno seems to find it an urgent matter indeed. Come back afterwards, if you like, bard. Your harp makes sweet music."

"If you like," Clydno mimicked viciously, once they were safely out of general earshot on the windy rampart. "If you like! The insolent whore!"

"Best we settle something at the beginning, Clydno," Felimid said. "More words like that and I heave you into the ditch down there. I'll try to drop you clear of the sharpened stakes, but I make no promise. Also, you will not learn what you so greatly want to know."

"*What did you do with the cup?*"

"I'll bargain with you. Tell me what your master plans for the Brotherhood and Artorius are, and why, and then I will tell you—truly—what I have done with the cup, which plainly you are desperate to regain. My oath as a bard."

"I can find it. You forget I am a magician, boy. The cup is magical. I can find it no matter where in Camlodd you hid it. I ask because time is lacking."

"Come. I took it so that you might not use it against Artorius's lady. Am I likely to hand it back to you?"

"It won't be so used!" Clydno bent forward, teeth bared almost in supplication, the wind pressing his blue robe in folds against him. "I can give you sureties which even you will believe. Even without them, I'll never again let that fool Lamorak within touching distance of such a treasure, or use it on his behalf."

"I believe that, indeed." Very pensive, very reasonable Felimid looked, as though half persuaded.

"Then we're agreed?" Clydno absolutely quivered.

"Very well. Answer my question, Clydno, and we have a bargain. My oath as a bard."

Clydno lowered his voice to a whisper. "You have said it.

You have asked it. Well, it's soon told, boy. My master seeks to bring back the times before Rome. Long has he aided the last Roman authorities against the Saxons, because he does not wish the sea-wolves to conquer us; but with Aelle dead and his host broken, that threat will be ended. The Archdruid has no place for a Count of Britain then. The time will come for a Pendragon, a new High King. No doubt my master has long been grooming some prince of the ancient blood for that place. But Artorius would stand in his way. He must win this fight, yes; but then he must die. There."

"There," Felimid echoed. "That is all of it, then? That little; that mean?"

"It's greater than you can comprehend. Now, the cup!"

"Yes. I did swear to tell you what I have done with it and where you may find it. I can't break such an oath."

Clydno nodded avidly. Felimid savoured the moment, remembering the murder attempt. He held Clydno's gaze.

"I hacked it apart with my sword," he said deliberately, "in many more pieces than three, and threw them in an armourer's furnace."

"What?" Clydno seized Felimid's arm. His fingers trembled. "That is not amusing, boy!"

"Call me boy all you wish. Just notice that I am not laughing, Clydno. You've heard the truth."

"No!"

"Yes. I knew you would find the thing no matter where I hid it. You did not have to tell me. I suppose I could have contrived some way to use it against you and Lamorak, but none that did not carry too much risk to Questa. Therefore I destroyed it."

Clydno tottered, pressing white knuckles to his temples. His eyes bulged. "Do you know what you have done?"

"Made you far too afraid to go back to your master, I hope. Oh, it tore my heart to smash the cup. It was unique, and so beautiful. But there was too much danger in it. What you have told me of your plotting just convinces me I did well."

"Well?" Clydno looked white and sick. He appeared to drag himself back by main force from the brink of utter collapse. "My master will turn me out of the Druid order to wander without purpose, if I am lucky. Lucky! Ahh!" Grinding his teeth, he drew himself upright. "From this day you have made of me a most cruel and unrelenting enemy, Fal's son."

"It's an honour," Felimid said briefly. "You should not have tried to have me killed. Now I would depart Camlodd in a quick hurry and in secret, were I you. It's in my mind that the place is unfortunate for you."

# XI

The sun hung low. Dark shadow already filled the ancient ditches around Camlodd, though ruddy light lay on the banks and the stone-faced inner rampart. Felimid watched from the wooden tower above the gate, his heart pounding wildly. Beside him stood Artorius, with his tall first-born Flavius on the other side.

Questa had decided not to see, because of Christian scruples about such a heathen matter. Felimid supposed the bishop had been talking to her. He wasn't sorry, really, because the watchtower seemed too small as it was, with not enough air. Men crowded the rampart below, but Artorius was taking his men's advice not to expose himself. Felimid approved that caution, especially now that he knew what the Druid order in Britain was after.

He hadn't spoken of it to Artorius yet. Maybe later, if the sign eventuated and he won sufficient standing to be taken seriously.

"Easy, Felimid," Artorius said. "I've told you. I'll not hold you culpable if nothing occurs. I believe you honest."

"If nothing occurs," the bard answered, "it might be a relief, lord. I'm as tight as my own harp-strings because I am sure something will!"

Artorius laughed. "It's like a vigil before battle to you. Do not wear yourself out."

They were all three silent, then.

The sun touched the earth's rim.

A battle-cry to freeze the heart rang around Camlodd. Rumbling, jolting chariot-wheels sounded, where none had been heard in five hundred years. Not since the legions had taken this place with sword and spear, and then ploughed up the hill-crest.

Three chariots appeared, each with a stark naked white-skinned driver, racing headlong around the outer rath. All else about them was red. Blood-red horses with red eyes; red severed heads dangling in clusters from the chariot bodies like grisly fruit; red harness; red tunics and mantles on the warriors standing behind the drivers; red shields, red limbs and faces, red eyes and teeth; red tracks of fire behind the wheels in the grass, fading slowly.

The first of these terrible men wielded a flail made of five red-hot chains. They hummed in the air as he swung them, more lightly than ever could any mortal man. The second brandished a spear with a great nine-barbed head that could rip out a man's insides, and it wailed as though thirsty. The last, and the hugest, bore a beaked war-hammer as red as the other weapons. They guffawed as they drove, their naked feet braced on the chariot floors, and called towards the ramparts of Camlodd.

"LOOK, MEN OF BRITAIN. WE BRING GREAT NEWS. FEARSOME ARE THE HORSES WE DRIVE, FEARSOME OUR WEAPONS. CUTTING OFF OF LIVES, SATISFACTION OF CROWS, NOISE OF KILLING, MULTITUDES OF SHARPENED BLADES. THROUGH ANCIENT ENCHANTMENT YOUR ENEMIES ARE DESTROYED. BROKEN SHIELDS AND LANCES AFTER SUNSET. VICTORY TO THE ISLAND OF THE MIGHTY!"

Bishop Dubricius was praying loudly. Some members of the Brotherhood crossed themselves. In the square wooden tower, Count Artorius of Britain did the same, but for him the gesture invoked Mithras Unconquered, as it had for many long before the Christians adopted it. His son stood rigid against the temptation to take a backward step.

*The red men*, Felimid thought. *The harbingers of great war and slaughter. The three who travelled before King Conaire Mor on the road to Da Derga's hostel, the night that his doom overcame him. Indeed and truly, they make an omen none can reject.*

Shouting, they made a full circuit of Camlodd and returned to the gate, where they vanished from mortal sight. When men of the Brotherhood went out to investigate, bearing torches, they found no tracks of wheels or signs of scorching by fire.

"Come back in, brothers," Artorius called, his voice steady. "Our visitors do not seem to have cared to enter and sup with us. They did not even tell us a thing we don't already know."

"Father!" Flavius cried. "Look there!"

"What? Lord of Light!"

A black mist was burgeoning from the soil of Camlodd, seeming to spread outward from the central hall. Heavy, blinding, it covered the whole fortress and spilled through the gate in thick tendrils, though elsewhere it remained within the stockade.

Artorius turned furiously upon the bard. "Is this another sign?"

"Lord, I do not think it is from Gwyn— " Felimid began.

The thunder of heavy horses galloping drowned out his words. Surging through the gate like a wave, they trampled those in their path without mercy, and forced the men on the outer rath to jump for their lives, into the ancient ditches. Then they were gone.

"That was Lamorak!" Flavius said, stunned. He had admired the man from over the sea. "Lamorak, with his entire troop!"

"And that's not all!" Artorius sprang for the narrow ladder leading down from the tower. "He carried a woman with him on his saddle-bow, who called for help, and I'm sure it was your mother, Flavius!"

The last words came up muffled from the darkness. Felimid and Flavius looked at each other for a startled instant, then jumped to follow. They hoped it was not true. But Artorius would have known Questa even through a veil of Druid's mist.

It proved true. Lamorak had abducted her. The mist had covered the act for long enough, straight on the heels of Gwyn ap Nudd's sign, and none but Clydno could have raised that mist; his last act of spite against the Count of Britain.

No. This treachery was more than mere spite, Felimid saw, galloping through the dark behind Artorius and his foster-brother Melwas. It was aimed at ensuring Artorius's death. When it became common tidings that the Count of Britain's wife had been stolen from his own fortress, he'd be a laughing-stock, and men do not follow or support a laughing-stock. Coming just before his greatest battle, it might cost him the assistance even of Melwas.

If Questa wasn't recovered . . .

They ravened through the night, an entire squadron on the trail of Lamorak's forty riders, making for the sea that surely was Lamorak's goal. Patrols spread out across the country, looking for their tracks, finding nothing. Felimid listened to the wind that spoke to him, blowing from the south and the sea, but from it he received no news.

Before dawn a weary, hard-riding patrol came to Artorius with news to hearten and enrage at once. News to surprise, above all. Felimid, sore in the saddle and running with sweat, could not believe it.

"Lamorak did not go south, sir. He swung around Camlodd and made for the marshes, where none of us would expect him to go. We have a squadron on his trail and one keeping order in the fort, but what he hopes to achieve none of us know."

"The marshes?" Artorius repeated. "He must be mad! He can't get through them, and his ships that would take him safe back to Gaul lie south of here."

"Yes, sir."

"You're sure of this?"

"Certain sure, sir."

"All right." Artorius turned to Melwas. "Brother, will you take one troop and ride on to the sea? Hold those ships where they are. Take their crews ashore and don't let them move! Lamorak may have some notion of getting word to them so that they can come around through Sabra to take him home. It must not happen."

"It won't, brother. And you?"

"I am turning around. I go back to Camlodd for fresh horses, and then on to the marshes. What Lamorak thinks he's about I do not know, but unless he and his men are assumed into Heaven at a moment's notice, we have them trapped."

"The marshes are Gwyn ap Nudd's country," Felimid said, with turmoil in his heart . . . and a wild rising hope. "Listen, lord, what if he cannot be trusted after all? Suppose Lamorak is going there by Clydno's advice, and this is some scheme to lure you there and make you a captive when Britain needs you?"

"With a squadron of the Brotherhood behind me, I'd raid Annwn itself," Artorius said harshly, "and with Questa taken from me, don't talk to me of captives! We ride."

They did ride. For generations after, men talked of that ride by the Count of Britain and his men, to the rescue of the lady Questa. The story changed, of course; it was told that King Melwas of the Summer Country was the traitor who carried off Artorius's wife, not the friend who helped him, and for good measure he, not Gwyn ap Nudd, became the supernatural otherworldly ruler.

None of this would have astonished the bard. That night and that day, though, he thought of little but staying with Artorius and his raging horsemen, hard on the trail of the Gauls. Once in a while he looked at the Count of Britain and thought with a certain dark amusement that the rectitude and control of Rome was nowhere to be seen in him now. Lucius Artorius Hispanicus had reverted to his blood and his times, a primitive leader at the head of an angry war-band, chasing a personal foe.

They rode like a storm, without stopping even to change horses, leaping astride their remounts at the gallop and turning their exhausted beasts loose to go where they would. Field and pasture saw them thunder past, going over low fences like a torrent, until the edges of the haunted marshes glittered before them and they saw Lamorak and his soldiers.

"They are ours," Artorius said exultantly, and rode forward.

Lamorak came forth before his band as well, Questa gripped tightly on his saddlebow, his sword shining bare.

"Enough, Artorius," he shouted. "Come closer, and I throw Questa's head under your hoofs."

The Count of Britain stopped. There must have been things, many things, he yearned to say, was bursting to say; threats, insults, orders to attack and wipe these betrayers out of existence. Instead he managed, in a dispassionate voice:

"What do you want?"

"My own ships on the coast north of here. Peace to depart freely, with Questa, for she's mine by right."

"Or else you will kill her."

Not a word passed between Artorius and Questa, but only a look. Felimid saw it. So did Lamorak, and it gave the lie to his claim more than all the speeches on earth, for there was trust and faith in it. Pain and bitter anger filled his face.

"Or I'll kill her."

Whether he meant it, whether he even knew himself, did not matter. Artorius would not take the risk, and he cared less than nothing for his pride, his reputation or even the coming battle by comparison. Felimid saw it all, laid out before him, and he saw an answer that no other man there could produce.

Walking his horse to the head of the band, he said urgently to the Count, "Let me talk to him, lord. I believe I can do something here."

"You don't have your harp here. What can you do?"

"Lord, there's no time to talk! Will you trust me?"

"When you do not even trust your precious Gwyn ap Nudd any more?" Artorius's face was like granite. "Listen; go to him as my herald. Tell him I will send him home with honour if he releases Questa, but no more. No trying to be a hero. This matter is between Lamorak, Questa and me. You understand?"

"Indeed."

Felimid dropped his sword and rode forward until he looked into Lamorak's bloodshot eyes. Almost he felt sorry for the abductor. Then he looked at Questa, gripped hard against the big man's mailed breast, and felt less sorry.

"The Count of Britain offers you free passage home, lord," said, "provided you free the lady Questa now."

Lamorak sneered. "The Count of Britain might have saved his breath! Questa is my woman, and once we're in Gaul she will realise it. He can't threaten me. He wouldn't dare take the risk that I'll behead her as I promised. In that he's wise."

"You may be right. I'd say that shows he loves her more than you do, lord. This then is your unalterable will?"

"Yes, milksop, so get back to him."

Felimid felt hot, eager satisfaction. A yard away from Lamorak, he raised his voice and yelled like a war-cry, "Gwyn ap Nudd, I bring a guest to you! Here is one to take the place of Felimid mac Fal! One worthy, a king, a champion! Lamorak of Galice!"

The warm spring air quivered around them. Sedge and willow altered their semblance to stranger herbs, and the day became a shining blue twilight, soft and cool. From a nearby pool burst a being seven feet tall, with webbed feet and a tendrilled face. It dragged Lamorak from his horse like a child, while Felimid seized Questa and hauled her astride his own mount, nearly falling with the effort.

Lamorak's troop spurred to interfere. The waterside plants twined and plaited around their horses' feet, holding them still despite all their terrified struggles. Felimid wheeled his horse and rode back to the squadron with the lady of Britain.

She clung to him with both hands. Felimid did not have to carry her all the way; Artorius was upon them with his red cloak blowing before the bard's horse could run five yards. He caught Questa in one arm, and although older than the bard he did not sway dangerously in the saddle as her full weight came upon him, but received her as though he had been created for the purpose.

"Questa!"

The blue Otherworld was no longer there. But a voice out of the marshes, that seemed to come from sky, earth and water at once cried, "Go free, Felimid mac Fal. You have met my terms."

Artorius paid no heed. He rode with Questa the long way back to Camlodd, and paid heed to nothing else. But Ulfius drew close to the bard, and riding almost knee to knee with him, he demanded, "Just what terms were those?"

"Ah. There was something I did not mention."

"I've guessed that much."

"There was a condition Gwyn ap Nudd made when he let me depart the Island of Apples as his herald. I had to return, and remain, unless I could bring him another man of worthy rank in my place."

"God! And just what would you have done if Lamorak had not deserved it?"

"Tried to trap Clydno, I suppose, and if that failed . . . I'd have come back myself."

"Yes," Ulfius said at last. "I suppose you would." After a while he said, "We'll be seeing the last of you, then."

"Not just yet." Felimid looked over his horse's ears towards Camlodd. "I have decided to ride to the battle with Crispus and his kin."

# Epilogue

A sunset like a dragon's breath filled all the western sky. Across the hillside stretched the vast ancient figure of a running horse, cut out of the turf to expose the white chalk below, kept clean and distinct down the long centuries. Beneath it, in the valley called White Horse Vale, hidden by the purple shadows of dusk, a thousand Saxon corpses lay scattered for a mile; corpses and moaning, pain-racked wounded.

Weary to death, Felimid rode his small nimble horse back up the hill, wiping his sword on the rags of his tunic. Crispus and Laochal rode beside him, with the others straggling behind, down into the darkness where the Saxons had broken.

Indeed, the Count of Britain had won, and won mightily. Aelle the Saxon lay dead, and his hearth-companions had died around his standard, scorning to desert their lord. The red men from Annwn had returned in their chariots, crashing through Angle fighters, the first of them whirling that awful flail of chains, the others their own weapons. Felimid had glimpsed other beings; a black boar on whose hide no weapon would bite, ripping men wherever it went; spirits of a thousand trees, marching down a slope to dismay a horde of Kentish spearmen; Gwyn ap Nudd himself, huge and awesome; a dragon, red as the men from Annwn, red as the spilled blood, spreading its glowing wings above the battle.

Yet at last the day had been won by none of these. The Saxons had stood fast despite all the terrors of Elder Britain, but broken in the end before the timed charges of the Brotherhood, the ranked lances that drove through flesh and bone to shouts of "Britain! Artorius!" The barbarian spearmen had died under shod hoofs, stabbing as they perished, and mailed riders fell in their turn with the name of their leader in their mouths.

They had won. Without support from any kings but two, the Brotherhood had shattered the greatest Saxon war-host ever seen in the island, and left it as wreckage. Every word of Gwyn's prophecy had come true, every word. Each of his promises had been kept. Therefore Felimid rode for the crest where sunlight still lingered, his heart and stomach like stones within him, empty of hope that Count Artorius had survived.

The bard's horse staggered. He dismounted and led it, seeing no reason why it should suffer. No longer was there any need to hasten.

A score of the Brotherhood waited on the crest. Crusted and stickied with gore, filthy, reeking, surrounded by a purgatory of keening flies, they looked nothing like heroes in any of the ancient tales. Ulfius lay propped against a stone, cursing between his teeth, his right leg transfixed by a Saxon spear. Men Felimid did not know stood beside him, and others formed a knot around someone on the ground.

"Count Artorius," Felimid said, forcing the name from his tongue. "Does he live?"

"He lives," a man said, coming forward to bar Felimid's way in a manner that forbade any debate, "but if he had choice he might rather be dead. For God's love, let him be."

"He lives?" Felimid echoed foolishly. Then the other words reached his mind. "What? Is he crippled or blind?"

"No, damn you! It's young Flavius. The sea-wolves killed him. Now ask me no more."

Flavius.

*He will win mightily, but his flesh will lie cold and lifeless on the earth.*

Not his body, but his flesh; his son.

Felimid didn't approach. If Questa could not be there, none but the Count's own Brotherhood had the right to be around him. Oh, great, powerful, unrelenting gods . . .

Night covered the hilltop. Camp-fires began to twinkle and a hundred kinds of work had to be done. Felimid did his share in a kind of empty exhaustion, while thoughts moved slowly in the battered places of his mind. One came back and back with the persistence of a dark moth.

What would Questa do when she heard?

He didn't know. Perhaps, though, she might find comfort in talking to the one man breathing natural air who knew the truth, and did not judge, and would not repeat it.

The night wore on. He thought about it. He talked with his comrades, barely hearing much of what was said, catching a few strange looks. At one time Crispus asked, "Where will you be going after these mighty events, Felimid?"

His mouth answered for him, and he knew then that he had decided hours before.

"Caer Lleon, Crispus. The City of Legions."

# JOHN, THE KNIGHT OF THE LION

## from the *Medieval Stories* of Professor Schück

*In* The Pendragon Chronicles *I reprinted the story "The Lady of the Fountain" from* The Mabinogion. *The story is one of the oldest in the Arthurian canon and one of the most popular. Over the centuries generations of minstrels and poets have recounted the story, adding to it their own embellishments. To show the extent to which that same story can develop into another, I've selected the following. Although it began its life as "The Lady of the Fountain", it was picked up several generations later by Chrétien de Troyes, and then some years after him by an anonymous Norwegian balladeer, possibly one Brother Robert, who translated several Arthurian sagas around the year 1226. The original Norwegian version of this story is now, I gather, lost, but its translation into Swedish survives. This had happened at the request of the Norwegian queen Euphemia around the year 1303. It was that version that was saved by Professor H. Schück, an authority on Swedish history and literature, for his volume of* Medieval Stories. *That was in turn translated into English by W.F. Harvey, Professor of English Literature at the University of Malta. A much more international pedigree would be hard to find. Whilst you will find some similarities between the stories, they are sufficiently different to make it worthwhile reprinting this interesting example here.*

Many a long year ago there reigned a mighty king in England whose name was Arthur. He was the finest warrior of his time, and kings' sons, dukes, earls, and counts came from far and wide to his court to gain instruction in courtesy and the practices of chivalry; but only the bravest were received, and these formed themselves into a league which, under the title of the Knights of the Round Table, became feared and famous throughout the whole world. A knight of the Round Table never shrank from any adventure however daring it might be, and had always to be prepared to take the field for the protection of the weak and persecuted. He had to be brave, generous, faithful and high-minded, and show tact and delicacy of feeling in his behaviour, and for these reasons membership of the Knights of the Round Table was regarded as the highest honour that a knight could attain.

Once upon a time King Arthur held his court at Caerleon, and the noblest knights in that country had foregathered there. The day began with a magnificent tournament, and at night the king gave a banquet in his castle, where the knights, who had now doffed their armour, led the dance with the fair ladies whom King Arthur's queen Guenevere had brought together. During the dancing the king sat on his throne, watching the dancers and listening to the songs which were sung as an accompaniment, but suddenly he was seized with an unaccountable sleepiness and had to withdraw to his chamber, where he was followed by his queen and a few attendants. His knights accompanied them, and remained outside the door, and soon they got into conversation about the adventures they had severally met with. There sat Segramore, Gavan, Kalegrevanz, John, and many knights far-renowned for bravery; but there was also with them a knight named Kay who was disliked by the rest for his sharp tongue and his spitefulness.

At length Kalegrevanz related an adventure with which he had recently met. He told it without any embellishments or any attempt to make it appear that his own share in it was more glorious than it actually was. When he had finished there arose a murmur among the rest, and the general opinion was that

Kalegrevanz had only reaped shame and infamy in the incident he had related. Kay naturally pronounced this opinion more strongly and pitilessly than the others.

The queen, who was attracted to the spot by the murmuring, inquired what they were talking about, and when Kay in a few scoffing words had hinted at the thing, she upbraided him for his discourteous way of speaking, and went on to say:—

"It almost seems to me, my dear Kay, as if it were an absolute necessity for you to speak ill of your friends. It is well they never pay you back in your own coin, for you have, I doubt not, some weak points, and would possibly not come off quite so well in the verdict of ungentle tongues. In any case, it is better not to turn others to ridicule, but to treat all with modesty and friendliness. Let me now hear the adventure of which Knight Kalegrevanz was speaking."

"I will not wrangle with Kay," said the latter. "Whatever I say he turns into ridicule against me, and, with my gracious queen's permission, I would much rather keep silence about the matter."

"Do not trouble yourself about Kay's revilings," answered the queen, "but tell us your adventure. I know you to be a noble knight, and am convinced that you have no cause to blush for any deed you have done."

"Although I should prefer not to speak of this matter again, yet I will comply with your wish and tell my adventure once more. I beg only that you will put the best construction on it."

"A short time ago," he began, "I clad myself in full armour and rode out from Karidol. On taking a turning to the right, I came to a narrow bridlepath which led me to a dark and dense grove, and after riding a whole day without halting, towards evening I perceived a strong castle surrounded by broad ramparts and approached by a drawbridge. On this bridge I met the lord of the castle, who had just returned home from hunting, and was still carrying a falcon on his hand. He greeted me in a friendly manner and said:—

"'I was fortunate to meet you. Pray alight from your horse and rest the night at my house. We will do all we can to make you comfortable.'

"I thanked him and sprang off my horse, and followed him into the hall, and there he again bade me welcome. Then he went to a table wrought of melted bell-metal, grasped the hammer that lay on the table and struck it in such a way that there was a sound like thunder all over the house. At this summons the knights and squires who were up in the tower hurried down at once to the drawbridge, welcomed me, and took my horse and led it to the stables. With them came the most lovely damsel I had ever beheld. She greeted me with modest dignity, took off my armour, and had some other raiment brought with which she arrayed me. The mantle she threw over me was of scarlet lined with ermine, and fastened round the neck by a clasp of gold set with precious stones. After this she conducted me to a grove where lilies and roses bloomed amid the trees, and there we enjoyed ourselves for some while, she and I alone, and gradually I utterly forgot all else in the world for her.

"I declared to her that my sole desire was to remain near her; but just as I was on the point of making my meaning plainer, the owner of the castle came and bade us come into supper, which was now ready. It was as exquisite as everything else in that hospitable castle, and the amiability of my host made the dishes on the table even more delicious. He asked me to promise that I would again claim his hospitality when I returned from my journey, and this promise I was naturally not loth to make, and then I was ushered into my chamber.

"At the dawn of day I arose, thanked the people of the house for their hospitality, took my horse and rode away. After riding for a while I met a whole herd of wild beasts, lions, buffaloes, bears and panthers, which were fighting with each other amid an awful din; but with these creatures I noticed a shepherd whose appearance was even more appalling. He was blacker than a negro and uglier than any human being I had ever beheld. His head was bigger than a horse's, his nose was as crooked as a ram's horn; his hair was, in stiffness and roughness, like the thorns on a briar-bush; his lips were blue, and his chin hung down over his chest. His face was as hairy as a bearskin rug; his beard bristly and matted; his back adorned with a hump; his feet had claws like a griffin's, and were flat and misshaped. His clothes consisted of two ox hides, and he held a sledge hammer in his hands; serpents and lizards were crawling over him. When he saw me he ran up a hillock, and stared at me like an idiot, without uttering a word. After looking at him for a while, hesitating what I should do, I said:—

"'What kind of being are you? Are you an evil spirit or what?'

"'I am what I am,' answered he, 'and no man has seen me better looking than I now appear to you.'

"'Well, and what is your calling?'

"'I tend the beasts which you see here.'

"'Your answer seems to me strange. I do not think you can be minding the beasts that are roaming about the woods here, and they do not appear to me to be tied up.'

"'They are as gentle as lambs. As soon as they hear my voice they come immediately; but should one of them prove refractory I merely seize him by the horns and throw him on the ground; then the others tremble, become tame, and run to me as if to plead for the froward ones. They obey me without a murmur, but I should not advise any one else to try the same thing, for it would not go well with him. But tell me, pray, what you yourself are.'

"'I am a knight who has ridden out in quest of adventures. Tell me, therefore, if you know of any difficult enterprise that I might perform and so win renown.'

"'Readily, if such be your pleasure. Not far from here there is a spring, the loveliest you could see. Yonder path leads to it, but I fear you will not return if you actually venture to approach the spring of which I am now going to tell you more. Rose bushes and trees rich in foliage hem it in, and they never lose their leaves even in winter. These trees extend their greenery so thickly over the spring that the rays of the sun can never reach it, and the water remains as chilly as ice. On a post hard by the spring there hangs a golden cup attached to a chain of such length that by means of it you can fetch water out of the well, and near the post there stands a chapel. Now, if you fill the cup with water from the spring, and throw it over the post a hurricane of such awful violence breaks out that all the beasts near—lions, bears, and birds tremble and flee before the rainfloods and hailstones that stream from the sky. Thunderbolts will whiz round you, and thunderclaps boom in your ears. If you escape unscathed you will be luckier than other knights that have ventured on the same quest.'

After uttering these words he bade me farewell, and I rode along the way he had showed me to the spring. After riding for some time, I saw the loveliest grove I had ever beheld, and in it I discovered the spring as the shepherd had said. It was entirely hidden by foliage, so much so that hardly a drop of rain could trickle through it. I also noticed the precious cup and the post which was of emerald set with rubies. On dismounting from my horse I filled the cup with water, and poured the contents over the post, but instantly I regretted my daring act, for suddenly the sky grew overcast, and certain violent gusts of wind came and shook the trees. Then the inky clouds belched forth a pattering shower of hail, and the lightning began to flash, so that I feared that I must needs perish. I swooned away and fell like a corpse to the ground, and had not our Lord been specially gracious to me, I should, in good sooth, have been killed by the trees that the wind broke and uprooted.

"After I had lain unconscious for some time, I began to recover my senses, and now I heard the nightingales singing and trilling as before, and lifting up my eyes I again saw the sun shining, and at the sight I forgot the peril through which I had lately passed. I arose to my feet, and observed the grove, which again seemed like a paradise, but I had scarcely recovered from my swoon before I saw a knight in full armour come galloping towards me. When I perceived that he was alone and none were in his company I rushed to my horse, mounted the saddle, and hurried to meet him, glad at having at length come across some one with whom I might measure my strength. The knight who approached me was in a terrible fury. He cried out to me:—

"Halt, you knave! For this you shall pay. Had you had grounds of complaint against me it would have been your duty to challenge me to single combat; but now you have insulted me out of sheer wantonness, and dearly you shall smart for it. You have destroyed a great part of my wood, and not even in my own castle can I rest in peace by reason of the hurricane which you, in your folly, have raised. I will give you something to remember this by, and that you won't forget in a hurry."

"After he had uttered this, he drove at me with his spear, but I caught the blow with my shield; however, I could not long contend against him, for his horse was as swift as a hind and his blows rained thick. Finally, my lance broke on meeting his helmet, and with a single blow he hurled me, there and then, off my horse. Then he took my charger from me, and rode right away without bestowing a glance at me. I have never yet come across a knight so stalwart.

"I lay for a long time on the ground utterly bewildered at my overthrow, but when I perceived that day and night were at odds, I got up, mangled in all my limbs, and approached the spring. I was now without a horse, and did not know what to do. In a shamefaced way I wandered through the wood back to the castle where I had, on the previous evening, been received with such hospitality, and I now stood once more blushing before the master of the castle. He received me, however, with the same cordiality as before, and even the other inmates of the castle—the maidens, knights, and squires—treated me quite in the same way, and showed me no lack of respect, but, on the contrary, congratulated me on having got off so easily, for hitherto no one who had striven with Red Vadoin—such was the name of the knight at the spring—had escaped with his life.

"Such then is my adventure. I have added nothing to it which could redound to my honour, and I have concealed nothing which might lessen the shame of my defeat."

"By the saints," said John, "I am ill pleased with you, my kinsman, for not having told me this adventure before, but, by God's help, I will avenge you or lose my life."

"John," exclaimed Kay, in his usual irritating way, "vaunts his bravery overmuch, but it seems to me that he has fetched his courage from the winebowl that he so industriously emptied this evening. He will sing another song when he has slept over the matter, for I'll warrant he will dream such horrible dreams about Red Vadoin that, when morning comes, he will have lost all desire of venturing on a bout with such a redoubtable antagonist."

The queen then chided Kay for his malice, and said:—

"It almost seems as if your heart must have burst if you had forborne discharging your spleen; but shame on every evil tongue. We blush for you, and, as for you, sooner or later, this malice will occasion you misfortune."

"Noble queen," said John, "don't bandy words with Kay, for it is part of his nature to revile and flout, but when it comes to manly exploits he holds aloof. A gallant man is quick in action, but cautious in judging."

Kay was about to retort when the king, who had been disturbed by the wrangle, came out and asked what the brawl was about. The queen told him, in a few words, about Kalegrevanz's defeat, and ended by recommending his cause to the king. Then the king waxed mighty wroth, and swore a great oath that he would, within fourteen days, proceed with all his knights to the spring, and there avenge the insult which Red Vadoin had put on the Round Table.

When this was known all rejoiced at the thought of the adventures and frays that awaited them. John alone heard of this expedition with other feelings, for he had hoped to have avenged the wounded honour of his kinsman; so, in order to prevent the rest from robbing him of this opportunity, he resolved that very same night to betake himself immediately to the spring, without waiting for the others. He therefore hurried home to his squire, and bade him, straight-way saddle his charger. Then he strictly forbade his squire to reveal anything about his departure, especially before Kay, and, without wasting time in further talk, he mounted his steed and rode into the dark wood. Without other adventures than those Kalegrevanz had experienced in the course of his journey, he reached at length the wonderful spring, and there found everything as his friend had described.

He immediately grasped the drinking-cup, filled it with water, and dashed its contents over the post. That instant, just as Kalegrevanz had related, a furious hurricane, accompanied by thunderbolts and hailstones, arose, but John endured it without quaking. When the clouds dispersed and the sun again broke forth, he saw a knight dashing towards him at a furious pace. John was not loth to meet him, and they rushed at one another with such violence that their lances were splintered like glass, strong and heavy as they were. When Red Vadoin saw John sitting calmly in his saddle, he was beside himself with vexation, and shouted to him:—

"Never before has the shame befallen me that one who has met my lance has not been forthwith hurled to the ground; but you shall not escape me".

Then they drew their swords and dashed against each other again. Blow followed blow with such violence that fire glinted from their helmets when the strokes told, their shields were shivered, and their coats of mail hacked to pieces; but neither would yield to the other. At last John dealt Vadoin a blow which cleft his helmet and reached his head, so that a stream of blood gushed down over his armour. When Vadoin received that crushing blow he collected his remaining strength, turned his horse, and fled back to his castle, closely pursued by John.

When those that were in the castle perceived this unwonted spectacle they let down the drawbridge and opened the gates to admit Vadoin; but John pursued him over the bridge, and pressed in through the small outer door immediately after him. There was a portcullis over this, which was let down as Vadoin rode through, and John very narrowly being cut into pieces by the sharp iron of the gate. His horse was cloven in twain just behind the saddle, so that its hinder part fell outside the drawbridge, whilst the foremost part tumbled down in front of the portcullis. Even both John's spurs were cut off by the fall of the portcullis, and it was only by the gain of a second that the rider did not share his horse's fate. However, he fell down and Vadoin disappeared through the principal gateway, which was closed upon him at once, so that John now found himself shut in the little passage between the two gates. The situation he now found himself in was anything but agreeable. He was a prisoner in a strong castle, the master of which was his deadly enemy, and his valour could avail him little against the latter's numerous retainers. As he was vainly searching for the means of rescuing himself from this danger a maid came to him.

"Good knight," said she, "why tarry you still here? My master has just died of the wound you gave him; my mistress is beside herself with despair, and all the people in the castle are burning with eagerness to avenge his death; but know that, though you are hidden here, still you are not forgotten. They will be up on you directly."

"Ere they overcome me," he answered, "many lives will be lost, for they shall not take me captive without a struggle."

"Resistance against such superior force is of no avail, but you once stood by me, and so I will help you. Once I came wretched and abandoned to King Arthur's court, and it was you who took care of me. The courtesy and kindness you then showed me I will now try to requite."

With these words she pressed a golden ring into his hand and said:—

"The stone in this ring is from India, and the man who wears the ring and closes his hand becomes that moment invisible. Employ it to extricate yourself from your peril, but let me have it back afterwards."

"God reward you, noble maiden, for this gift. I shall never forget your goodness."

"Let us now flee at once from here. Shut your hand so as to become invisible, and follow me, and I will conduct you to a hiding-place where you can be concealed till I can free you altogether."

Then he followed her across the vast courtyard, where all was bustle and confusion, by reason of Vadoin's death to a little chamber, and there she showed him a bed on which he threw himself down and soon fell asleep, exhausted by all the struggles and hardships he had undergone.

Some hours afterwards the maid returned and brought him wine and food. John helped himself to the refreshments, and looked down through the window and saw how they were searching for him everywhere. Swords rattled and bows clanged as Vadoin's men rushed about to find the man who had slain their master.

First they hurried to the arch in which John had been shut, but they found to their astonishment that it was empty, though the locks were unbroken. John heard them talking among themselves and exhorting each other to make further search, "for," said they, "unless he is a bird and has wings he cannot have cleared the wall". Then they at once began to make a fresh search, and poked about in all the nooks and crannies in the castle. They even went into the room John was in, and almost touched him, but not a trace could they find of the vanished knight.

While they were engaged in searching, the body of the deceased lord of the castle was carried across the courtyard, accompanied by a crowd of women and squires uttering lamentations. At the head of them walked the dead lord's widow, a tall and beautiful woman, whose countenance, however, was disfigured by grief. She wept and lamented aloud, and, when her glance happened to fall on the bier, she shrieked wildly and fell to the ground in a swoon. As soon as those about her had restored her to consciousness, a messenger was dispatched for priests and monks to say masses for the soul of the dead man, and then they all went in procession to the castle chapel, where the bier was laid on the ground, and the priests began to intone the service.

John had, without being perceived, contrived to mingle with the funeral party and entered the chapel with them; but, as he drew near the body, its wounds began to bleed afresh, and then every one was aware that the slayer was somewhere near the slain. The knights began therefore to search afresh, and the châtelaine burst out sobbing again.

"There is sorcery at work here," said she, "for the murderer is in the midst of us without our being able to see him. Alas, my God, I shall never be able to bear the sorrow of not even looking on him who wrought me such great affliction! He would never have slain my noble husband if he had not employed treachery, for no braver knight was ever born. No one dared to await his onset, much less engage him in battle, and even this man would have failed to win the fight had he not had recourse to sorcery."

With weeping and wailing they carried the body to the grave and buried it. Then masses were sung for his soul, and at last all departed; but when the burial was over the maid who had succoured John—her name was Luneta—went to the chamber in which she had hidden the knight, and to which he had withdrawn himself.

"Noble knight," said she, "you heard yourself how they were searching for you everywhere. Now, give thanks to God that they failed to find you."

"For my rescue I have, methinks, to thank God in the first place, and you too for having shown me such kindness. You have saved my life, and this service might be deemed sufficient, but I have still a boon to crave of you, and that is that I may see just once the noble lady who owns this castle."

"I will readily satisfy you in this request. You have only to cast a glance through this window to see what you desire. She is sitting in mourning weeds in the midst of the other dames."

When John looked at her, he found her again lamenting in their presence the hard lot that had befallen her, and marked how her gestures betrayed deeper and deeper despair, so that at last she swooned away again for grief. John's first impulse was to go up to her and crave her pardon and seek to console her, knowing that he himself was the cause of her despair, but Luneta held him back.

"Now you must obey me and not stir from your place here. Should any one see you here, then your fate is sealed, for no one will show you mercy. Keep quiet where you are, and where you can observe without danger the course of events. I shall meanwhile tell you all that it is important for you to know, and my only fear is that my lady, or one of her attendants, may grow suspicious at my absence, and suspect that I am with you."

After she had said this she left the knight alone to his reflections. He now began to consider his position more calmly. He determined not to steal secretly from the castle without having revealed to some one that it was he who had defeated Red Vadoin, for he stood in fear of Kay's jeers if he was not in a position to prove that Vadoin had fallen by his sword and not by another's. On the other hand, his life would be in danger if any one discovered him in the castle.

Whilst engaged in these thoughts he again cast his eyes at the poor châtelaine who was now slowly recovering from her swoon, and when he saw her beauty he sighed and thought to himself:—

"Would to God you were mine. Could I but gain your love I would willingly renounce all the honours in the world; but that can never come to pass, for I have done her so much wrong that she can never forgive me. I have slain him whom she loved best in this world, and she has every reason to hate me. Loving her is sheer madness, and I well know she would rather see me dead; but, nevertheless, I have heard a certain man who knew human nature assert that women's feelings often change, and perhaps even her hate may be turned to love. All things rest in God's hands, and He has power even over her heart. Possibly He may induce her to grant me pardon and love."

While he was thus musing, the lovely châtelaine arose and went, accompanied by her dames, into the castle. John gazed at her for a long time, and acknowledged to himself that it was not merely fear of Kay's gibes that kept him in the castle, but also love for Red Vadoin's widow. He knew he would rather die than flee from where she was.

After a while Luneta came back to him, and on perceiving his sadness she asked him what had occasioned it.

"When you come here," replied John, "I forget my sorrows altogether and wax as merry as of yore. Let us therefore not speak of them."

"Open your heart to me if there is aught that makes you sad. Possibly I may be of some help to you."

"Well, then, know that it is love for your mistress that makes me so downcast: I cannot live without her."

"I guessed that already, and will, to the best of my ability, advance your cause; but first you must ride away from the castle, where your life is every moment in jeopardy."

"In this respect I cannot obey you. I will not steal away from the castle secretly, but ride hence so that every one may see me."

"Do what seems good to you. I shall watch over your safety as well as I can, and now I am going to my mistress to endeavour to question her heart. I shall not tarry long ere I return to tell you what my impressions are."

Then she went to the châtelaine, whose name was Laudine, and, after falling on her knees before her and saluting her, she said:—

"Noble lady, try and calm your bitter grief, and think of this: he whom you are now weeping for can never come back".

"Alas," answered Laudine, "I know full well I can never have him again, though I loved him with all my soul. Nothing remains to me but to weep till I die of weeping."

"Rather than that should be I hope that God may bestow on you another husband who shall be as good a knight as him you have lost. Even you yourself ought to admit that that would be best for you."

"You ought to blush to talk like that. *His* peer is not to be found in the whole world."

"Oh, yes," replied Luneta, "I know one who quite equals him. Please god he may be your husband."

"Now I really ought to be angry with you for saying that; the like of it I have never heard."

But Luneta held her ground bravely and proceeded to say:—

"My noble lady, there is still another thing to be thought of, and that is, if King Arthur with all his troops and knights were to come here to lay your lands waste, who is there to defend them against him? Out of all your people I cannot find a knight capable of performing such a deed. They could not do it in a body even if they were to enlist us women to help them. No doubt they could ride to the spring, but as for protecting it, that they could not; so listen to my advice, and try and find some knight capable of protecting your land and yourself. Take him for your consort, and hold him dear, for both you and your country will be the gainers by it."

Laudine acknowledged to herself that Luneta not only spoke wisely, but to the point; yet she was not of a mind to let herself be persuaded quite so readily, but pretended to get very angry, and cried:—

"Go your way, you silly wench. I do not fully understand your meaning; some hidden purpose lies, methinks, behind your words. Never will I follow your advice."

"Say not so, for I venture to prophesy that, in the end, you will do what I have said."

After saying this Luneta got up and departed, but Laudine sat where she was, engrossed in her thoughts.

"What knight can that be," thought she, "that Luneta alluded to? A brave and famous man must he be, forsooth."

Her curiosity was now aroused, and she could no longer restrain it, so she summoned Luneta again into her presence for the purpose of questioning her. The artful girl came and repeated her previous conversation.

"Away with dull care," she exclaimed. "What boots it your longing after one who is departed never to return? It is absurd, you know, to shorten your life in that way; besides, you are mistaken if you think that chivalry and honour died in this world with Red Vadoin. Marry, no; brave as he was, there are many braver knights than he to be found."

"Name me one, then," cried Laudine, "and if you can prove you have spoken the truth, I am ready to listen to you."

"That I will," answered Luneta, "but you must first promise me not to be angry if I happen to name one whom, perhaps, you have cause to hate."

Luneta, after she had extorted a solemn promise from Laudine, went on to say:—

"As we are now sitting quite by ourselves, with no one to hear us, I will gladly reply to your question, and only hope you will bestow your love on the knight I am now going to tell you of; but first answer me one question. If two knights fight together, which do you deem the superior—he who is slain, or the one that slew the other?"

"Luneta, I think I suspect what you are driving at. With cunning words you are seeking to lead me astray."

"That I cannot admit. What I am saying is simply the truth, and that is that the knight who slew Vadoin was braver and stronger than he."

"You are mad to talk in the way you do. Never again let me hear any hint at such a thing, or you will forfeit my friendship for ever. How can you imagine I could bring myself to love the man who slew my husband?"

But Luneta was not a girl to be easily frightened by a few angry words. She remained, and began her speech once more, but with greater caution, and thus, little by little, Laudine began to repent of her impetuosity. What seemed to her at first an all but mad idea now appeared, at any rate after what the artful Luneta had said, something worth considering. She turned to the zealous girl and said:—

"Pardon me the words that escaped me ere my wrath subsided, and tell me more of this knight who seems to have grown so dear to you. I would know of what lineage he is, and if he be my equal in birth."

"You need harbour no misgivings on that score. A knight more courteous or of gentler birth cannot be found than he."

"Tell me the name of the man whom you vaunt so highly."

"His name has often sounded in your ears, for he is known everywhere where knightly sports are prized. He is called John."

"True it is that I have often heard speak of him," cried Laudine, "and his bravery is not unknown to me, for no finer knight than John, King John's son, is to be found if you search the wide world over. Where is he, for I would fain speak with him?"

Luneta began to laugh at her eagerness, and when she found she had gained a complete victory, she could not refrain from making some little fun of her mistress. Then, assuming a serious countenance, she said the knight was a long distance off from them, and it would take him five days to reach the castle; but when she noticed from the lady's dejected mien that the time seemed to her to be too long, she added:—

"A bird could not fly quicker, so long is the journey; but I have a squire who is a fleeter messenger than the rest. Him I will send to the knight, and try if the latter can come in three days hence—quicker than that I do not think it could be done. Meanwhile we will assemble all your knights and squires, and ask them the question if there be one among them who would dare take it upon himself to defend your land and castle against

King Arthur when he comes hither; and I tell you for certain beforehand that not a single one would venture to take upon himself so hazardous a task. If such be the case, then no one will wonder at your choosing for yourself a consort that can defend your kingdom, especially when he is so renowned a warrior as John, King John's son. This must not appear to be your own proposal, but ask the advice of your friends and kinsmen, and let them propose this expedient."

Laudine found this plan excellent, and, on the date fixed, she summoned her council; but, ere that, Luneta went to John to impart to him the intelligence which he was awaiting so impatiently. After greeting him, she said:—

"Now you can be happy, for everything has come about as you have wished. Soon, perhaps, the woman you love will be yours."

Then she gave him a detailed description of the conversation between Laudine and herself, and depicted the gradual awakening of her mistress' heart on being told that it was John, the famous Knight of the Round Table, who had defeated Red Vadoin; but she refrained from telling him that her lady had fully pardoned him, and was ready to take him for her husband, for that was a sudden shock which she wished to spare him as yet.

After Luneta had in this wise restored heart and interest in life to the knight, she had a bath prepared for him, brought out some precious raiment—a cloak, jerkin, and baldric—in which she attired him, in place of the damaged armour he had worn in the fight with Red Vadoin; and she herself combed his hair and made him so trim that she herself thought, when she had put the finishing touches on, that she had never seen a more handsome or stately knight.

Then she went to Laudine and said:—

"The squire I sent after John has now returned. He has fulfilled his commission, and the knight is now here only awaiting your behests".

"Send him to me at once," said the châtelaine, "but take particular heed that none in the castle see him. For the present this must be a secret between us three."

Luneta did as her mistress bade her, and went to John; but even at the very last she could not refrain from teasing the love-sick knight.

"My lady," said she, "now knows that you are hiding here in the castle, and she is very angry with me for having deceived her so long; but I hope you will put me right with her again, and regain me her favour. You are to go to her now. Entertain no fears, but should things go awry and she take you captive, resign yourself submissively to that fate."

"Alas," replied John, "you know as well as I do that there is no one whose prisoner I would rather be than hers. For good or evil I yield myself up to her."

"I do not think," said Luneta laughing, "that this captivity is likely to bring any disgrace on you. But let us go at once."

They betook themselves forthwith to Laudine's room without being noticed by any one, and when the lady of the castle saw John's manly figure before her, she was so struck by his beauty that it was long before she was able to speak; even John was disconcerted at this interview, and did not quite know how to begin his speech. Luneta, on perceiving their embarrassment, could not repress a smile, and, turning to John, said:—

"Noble knight, why are you so faint-hearted as not to venture on a yea or a nay? I presume you did not come here to be silent. Take heart and approach my mistress. I can now tell you to your face that she has granted you full pardon for Red Vadoin's death, that it was she herself who summoned you to tell you this, and that no one can be more welcome to her than you."

When John heard this he fell on his knee before the lovely châtelaine and said:—

"Noble lady, I came here to give myself to you—for weal or woe: my life is in your hands".

"I shall do you no hurt," answered Laudine. "I have already forgiven you everything."

"I know, unfortunately, that I have caused you a great sorrow, but I am ready to make all the reparation in my power. I will hold all my life at your service."

"You acknowledge, then, that you did me sore wrong when you killed my husband."

"Judge for yourself. He assailed me with all his might, and I am not used to brook defeat. I had no choice between killing or being killed, and every man defends his own life."

"You are right, and I cannot refuse you my pardon. I pardon you willingly, for all that I have heard of you is good. Sit here by my side, and tell me how it came about that you conceived such a passion for me as to love me beyond all other women."

"Can you ask that? As soon as I gazed on your beauty I felt that my life depended on your returning my love."

Laudine listened to his words with pleasure, but interrupted him after a while by asking this question:—

"Tell me now on your honour as a knight if, in the event of King Arthur coming here to lay waste my land, would you venture to do battle with him in my defence?"

"That I swear to you on my honour as a knight."

When Laudine received this promise she plighted him her troth, and both swore that nothing but death should part them. Then they proceeded together to the hall, where all Laudine's knights and squires were assembled for the conference to which she had summoned them; and when they saw John they said among themselves that they had never beheld a more majestic knight.

"Just such another man we want for our lord. Our mistress should take him for her husband, and that would be as great an honour to her as if she got the imperial crown in Rome."

Laudine bade them all be seated, and after they had sat down, the chamberlain called for silence and said:—

"You know full well how great a loss we have lately suffered through the death of our lord Red Vadoin, and just now we are more than ever in need of a leader, for King Arthur has now armed himself to attack us with shield and sword in order to conquer our kingdom. He will be here within fourteen days, and then our future fate will hang in the balance. It seems to me necessary, on that account, that our lady should marry again and choose herself a husband who could protect her kingdom. No one shall be able to censure her for such a step, and we therefore hope that she will, for our sakes, agree to take it, though, possibly, out of love for Vadoin, she be reluctant to comply with our wish."

All agreed with this speech, and they besought her, on their knees, to choose a consort fit to direct the helm of her state and maintain its ancient renown. But the châtelaine feigned that this request was highly objectionable to her, and made them beseech her for a long time before she would say yes, but, nevertheless, she finally suffered herself to be prevailed on by their necessities, and said:—

"As this matter is of such grave importance to you I will sacrifice my personal feelings to the common weal. This knight whom you here see" (pointing to John) "has long desired me for his spouse. He is both wise and courteous, in birth my peer, being a king's son, and pre-eminent in valour and might in war. I surrender to you the choice of my husband, and ask you, therefore, if you will accept him for your lord."

When they had all expressed their consent in a loud voice, she went on to say:—

"Since this marriage is thus decreed, it seems to me foolish to long delay that which must some time or other take place, and my will, therefore, is that this wedding be celebrated at once".

All the knights waxed marvellously glad thereat, and thanked her warmly for having met their wishes with such exceeding readiness, and the marriage was at once celebrated with mirth and merriment. Minstrels from all directions flocked together to exhibit their skill, and returned home laden with rich gifts, and extolling the generosity of the bridegroom. Squires and maidens threaded the dance with each other, and the dance-songs chimed merrily in the vast banqueting-hall, but, outside, the more veteran knights contended in a grand tournament, and the clash of their arms was heard far and wide. John was now radiantly happy; he had gained for himself a kingdom and a bride, and the dead man was already forgotten. The new bridegroom was loved and honoured by all, and he marked that they greatly preferred him for their leader to Red Vadoin.

But the marriage mirth was soon to be troubled by the din of war. King Arthur had not forgotten to avenge the insult put on Kalegrevanz, but summoned all his knights, and marched to the land whose lord was now John. They reached the spring on Mid-summer-day, and there encamped. At the council which was opened at once, Kay was the first to speak; and, in accordance with his usual practice, he began to slander the absent John.

"I wonder," said he, "where John can now be lurking, seeing he came not hither with the rest of us. When the wine had mounted to his head he bragged valiantly, and swore that he would alone avenge his kinsman, contentious that we should leave him this honour; but it comes to pass that his courage seems to have vanished after he had considered the matter more closely. Well, yes, a man in his cups says much that he cannot afterwards perform, and this proves the truth of the saying, 'Big in words, little in deeds'."

"If John is not here," Gavian answered him, "there is some cause for his absence. Who knows what may have happened to him. After he rode from Caerleon much may have occurred to hinder him from reaching here; but one thing I *do* know is that John would never have spoken ill of a man absent, and so unable to defend himself; and we all know well enough that never yet has John kept aloof from a perilous venture out of fear."

"I will not bandy words with you," replied Kay, "but the truth of my words is sure to be established, and I venture, moreover, to assert that he fled from the palace like one distraught."

This wrangle ended, King Arthur approached the spring, took

the cup, filled it with water, and poured the contents over the post. At once a pelting shower of rain came down, as on the previous occasion, followed by thunder and lightning. As soon as John perceived this from the castle, he put on his armour, and leapt on the best courser Red Vadoin had, and dug his spurs into its flanks, and galloped at full speed towards the well. When Kay caught sight of the strange knight he went into the king's presence and eagerly sought his permission to break the first lance with the defender of the spring, and as King Arthur did not refuse him this favour he hurriedly donned his armour and rode against John. The latter recognised his adversary at once, and his heart was filled with joy at having at length found an opportunity of punishing the man who had so long disparaged and flouted him. He grasped his lance with a lusty grip, and struck it into Kay's breast with such force that both horse and knight rolled over, and each wallowed in the mire. Kay experienced no sympathy as he lay there helpless and beaten.

"God help you," said they all. "You, who used to gibe at every one else, have now got a lesson that you will not forget. Lie where you are, a laughing-stock to all."

He got on his feet at last in a shamefaced sort of way, but he did not dare to return to the camp and expose himself to the jeers of the rest. John took no further notice of him, but led his horse by the bridle, and rode with it to the tent without any one recognising him. When he reached it he exclaimed:—

"Although, by the law of battle, this horse belongs to me, yet I will not carry it off, for I do not wish to appropriate to myself anything that belongs to King Arthur or his knights, so take the steed, and treat him well, while I pursue my journey."

When King Arthur heard this he said:—

"Who are you who speak such words as these? I do not remember having seen your badge before."

"My lord," replied the unknown knight, "perhaps you will know when I tell you my name. I am called John."

Great was the rejoicing now, and all hastened to bid John welcome. After they had partly got over their surprise, King Arthur bade him explain the mystery, and tell what had taken place since the night he quitted Caerleon. John then recounted all his adventures, the victory over Vadoin, whereby he gained a kingdom and a wife, and ended by inviting King Arthur and all his suite to his castle. The king expressed his thanks, and John rode home to inform his wife that the dreaded enemy was now coming as a welcome guest, and had promised to stay in their castle for eight days. When Laudine heard this news she rejoiced exceedingly, and at once gave orders for receiving the king in the most sumptuous fashion.

On the following morning King Arthur sallied forth from his camp, and was greeted first by a troop of knights and squires, who came out to meet him with drums and music. When these saw the king they alighted from their horses, and bade him, in their mistress' name, welcome to the castle. Immediately afterwards he was met by another company composed of minstrels and musicians, who played their instruments in his honour. The castle itself was adorned with precious cloth of gold and costly stuffs which swayed from every nook and corner, even the walls were hung with mats of various colours. The mistress of the castle, followed by a bodyguard of knights, met the strangers at the drawbridge, in order to accompany them to their quarters, and soon her retinue mingled with King Arthur's.

The eight days were taken up with chivalrous exercises, hunting, and sport, and when they were over King Arthur resolved to take his departure. He had John summoned secretly to his presence, and ordered him to come with him, and even his kinsman Gavian advised him to accompany them.

"It ill-beseems you," said he, "to lie idle henceforward in this castle and let all the honour you have won fade away; neither is it honourable to your bride. As a knight it is your bounden duty to fare from court to court where joust and tournament are held, and break a lance in her honour. And is it not far more noble to hazard life and lands in her honour than to lie at home like a woman? You shall never lack a trusty comrade-in-arms, for in sunshine and in rain I will follow you, so that only death shall part us. Do not think I say this because I grudge you and your spouse the happiness you enjoy in mutual love, or that I would lure you to forget her, but that both she and you may gain the highest renown by following my counsel and again setting out in quest of adventures."

John, who was rent between his wish to stay with Laudine and his desire to resume the life to which the knights of the Round Table were accustomed, answered that he would follow his comrades-in-arms, provided his wife gave her consent thereto. He went to her at once and said:—

"I venture to approach you with a petition. You are my wife, and as such it is within your rights to grant or refuse it. Let me once more for a season go forth in quest of adventures, for I am loth to hear it said that I laid aside all chivalrous exercises on the very day I won myself a bride."

His wife could not rightly understand his wishing to abandon her so soon, but she gave in to his wish, and granted him leave to go.

"But," she added, "I give you this permission only on one condition—you must return before the lapse of a year; if not you will have lost my love for ever, and I should then look on you as a recreant knight."

When John heard these strong words he grew exceedingly rueful, and sighed:—

"God forbid that I should not come back to you as speedily as I can, but none can provide against accidents, and mayhap sickness or captivity may hinder me from returning within the year".

"Harbour no fears of dangers such as those," answered she, placing a ring on his finger. "So long as you wear this ring and think of me sickness shall not reach you, nor shall any man take you captive; but guard it well, for it is a miraculous ring which I can bestow only on him who is dearest to me of all the world. Now God be with you."

John thanked her with many kisses for this precious gift and then they parted. John rode with King Arthur's company, pleased at finding himself once more among his brethren-in-arms, but at the same time melancholy, for his heart still tarried with the fair lady of the castle whom he had been constrained to give up.

Gavian and he soon parted from the others, and set out in quest of adventures.

In every tournament that was held they took their part and always came off conquerors, and, consequently, there was but one universal, unanimous opinion, and that was that no braver knights were to be found elsewhere. But, as time went on, months slipped away without John, in his eagerness for the fray, paying any heed to them, and soon the year was gone without his having remembered his promise. At the beginning of the new year King Arthur called all his knights together to a meeting, and thither went John and Gavian, who received much praise for the feats they had recently accomplished; but whilst they were sitting at the Round Table they saw a maiden come riding up to them. On reaching their tent she alighted from her horse, divested herself of her mantle, and courteously stepped into the presence of the assembled knights. John recognised her as one of his wife's maids, and then remembered with dismay his promise. The damsel greeted King Arthur and said:—

"My mistress has sent me to you to give you and all your knights her greeting; but for John I have a special message. I declare him, in my lady's name, to be a liar and a recreant knight that has broken the word he gave a woman. Despite his promise, he has not returned to her within the year, and so she declares through me that he has forfeited her love, and she will never more look with favour on him. The ring she gave him at parting she now demands back, for he is no longer worthy of wearing that symbol of her troth."

While she was speaking John sat mute and motionless without replying, and it seemed as if her words had deprived him of his senses; but the damsel hurriedly walked up to him, pulled the ring off his finger without his even making an effort to resist her.

"Blush, false knight!" exclaimed she, "and never dare show yourself among men of gentle breeding or where manly deeds are done. May you be dead to all as you are to my mistress. And now farewell, King Arthur. God shield you and your knights."

Then she rode away, but John remained as it were unconscious, only brooding over the shame that had befallen him. At length he rushed wildly from the table, and ran off without uttering a word. Madness instantly clouded his brain so that he tore his clothes to pieces, and he scourged himself with thorns and twigs. People tried to stop him and lead him back, but he ran away and sped towards the woods, and so all traces of him were soon lost. After running for a good while he saw a man hunting in the wood, and assailed him, and snatched the bow and arrow from him, and disappeared before the hunter could recover from his amazement.

Without regaining the use of his reason, he lived for some time amid the woods and fells, where he wandered about without shelter or any sort of clothing wherewith to cover his nakedness. Thanks to the bow, he was not without food, for he brought down by his arrows the wild creatures of the wood. He ate his food raw, for he no longer understood the use of fire; he had no bread, and took no notice of the herbs in the wood.

One day, in the course of his wanderings, he came to a hut in the wood, where a poor hermit dwelt. When the hermit saw the naked and almost black man he became dreadfully frightened and thought the latter had come to rob him, so he called to him out of the window:—

"Of my own free will I will readily give you all I possess, but there is nothing here save water and coarse bread. I have nothing else to live upon. You may have that and welcome."

Through the little window-hole he handed him all the bread there was in the hut, and John sat down and ate up ravenously every bit, as if it had been the most dainty food. After he had finished he got up and ran again to the woods, but though he had long been weak in intellect, nevertheless he preserved a sense of gratitude. He carried to the hermit the first beast he shot, and laid it down before his cottage by way of repayment for the bréad the hermit had given him. The good hermit, who was touched by this silent gratitude, sold the animal and bought with the money meat and wine which, on the following day, when John returned, he handed to the latter through the window. This was repeated day after day, for John came daily to the hermit with some bird or beast he had shot, and the hermit boiled or baked the meat for him, as well as gave him bread and wine for the parts of the animals he had sold.

One day, as John lay sleeping under a lime tree in the wood, there came a bevy of ladies riding past him, to wit, a châtelaine of the name of Murina and three of her handmaids. On their remarking the queer black figure, one of the handmaids was moved by curiosity, and stepped off her palfrey to observe the strange object. His skin had become black through the savage nature of the life he had been leading, and his face was hidden by a long matted beard. Well, the more closely she scrutinised his features the more familiar they seemed to her to be, and at last she noticed a scar on his forehead, and then recognised the unhappy knight, for John had received this scar in a tourney that had been held in Murina's castle. She was seized with sorrow and amazement at seeing the ghastly state to which he had been reduced, and hurriedly remounted her horse and rode back to her mistress.

"My lady," cried she, "the man who lies there is the bravest knight that ever splintered a lance: it is John, King John's son. I cannot conceive what has happened to him, but it is clear that some great misfortune has overtaken him, and he has lost the use of his reason. God grant that he may be again the man he was when last I saw him, for, in good sooth, he would avenge all the wrongs that Arlan the earl has committed against you."

"If he would only remain there long enough for me to ride home," answered her mistress, "I think I have a remedy which will make him hale and hearty again. My godmother, the fairy Morgana, has given me a salve which possesses the marvellous virtue of being able to drive madness from the brain, and this salve I will blithely give him. After saying this the lady of the castle rode home as fast as she could, opened her coffer, and took from it a box which she delivered to the damsel who had first caught sight of John. She not only gave her the box of ointment but also a store

of rich garments with which John might array himself, as well as
two splendid coursers, one for her, and the other for the knight.
She then told her to ride back fast to the luckless wight to release
him from his misery.

The damsel, on returning to the lime tree, found John still
asleep, so she alighted from her horse, stepped up to him
cautiously, not without some trepidation, for she knew, of
course, that he had not the use of his reason. Then she rubbed
him with ointment from the crown of his head to the soles of
his feet, laid the raiment beside him, and concealed herself right
in the wood, so that he should not suspect, when he woke up, the
part she had played in his recovery. After a while the sun began
to shine through the leaves, and warmed the wonderful ointment,
and, as this penetrated his body, reason slowly returned to John.
Then he awoke and looked about him in amazement, without
any recollection of the long season during which he had been
wandering about the wood, like one bereft of his senses. He
was seized with shame at discovering his nakedness, and at once
hastened to don the handsome suit of raiment that lay beside him
on the grass. Directly he had done this he looked round to discover
some human being who might tell him where he was, and help
him to find his way out of the wood. When the damsel perceived
from her hiding-place that he was completely cured, she resolved
to conceal herself no longer, but walked towards him, without
letting him suspect that she had been there. When he saw her he
rejoiced exceedingly, and called out to her:-

"Noble damsel, tell me where I am, and help me out of here".

But when she affected not to notice him he repeated his request,
and begged her fervently not to abandon him. She stopped her
palfrey and asked him courteously what he wanted. He replied
that he could not tell her how miserable and forlorn he felt, and
ended his speech by asking her if she would lend him the horse she
was leading.

"I will let you have it willingly, provided you will bear me
company."

"Where do you live, then?"

"In a castle that lies not very far from here."

"With your leave I will gladly escort you. I know not how I shall
repay your kindness. Is there no service I can render you?"

"Perhaps there is," replied she. "Only follow me, and it will not
be long before I shall remind you of the offer you have made."

They rode away, and soon they reached Murina's castle, and
there the châtelaine met and received him with marks of deep

respect. She had a luxurious bath prepared for him, and her servants not only washed him, but clipped his long hair and shaved his matted beard. The châtelaine did all she could to make his stay at the castle as pleasant as possible, and all her dependents were only too ready to satisfy his lightest wishes. Thus the days passed by, and, little by little, he got back his health, his strength returned to him, and he began anew to long for the combat. He had not long to tarry ere such an opportunity came into his way.

I should mention that the châtelaine had an enemy named Arlan, the earl with whom she had a feud of long standing, and this fellow attacked her territory, laying it waste far and wide, even going so far as to burn the houses that lay immediately under the castle-hill. All the inmates of the castle donned their armour, knights and squires, and strove as to which of them should first be ready to confront the earl's people. John, who had now recovered his old lust of fighting, was the first to get his armour on, and galloped on his battle-steed out of the castle in advance of all the rest. The first knight he encountered was struck so violently by his spear that he fell to the ground never more to rise from it. Then John rode like a nettled lion into the very ranks of the foe, gripped with both his hands the hilt of his broad falchion, and hacked wildly about him so that his enemies fell round about him like corn before the sickle. The knights who were in his train were encouraged still further by his valour, and exhorted each other not to abandon so brave a leader. From the castle towers the châtelaine and her dames looked on the savage strife and recognised John's helmet in the midst of the hostile ranks. They marked how he hurled himself, like a hawk, down on his enemies and slew such as failed to yield themselves up at once. They thought they had never seen a braver knight before, and there was many a maiden who would fain have had such a warrior for her husband.

The enemy was just meditating flight when one of their bravest knights galloped up to John, and attacked him so valiantly that the tide of victory almost turned. With a single blow he cleft John's shield, and Murina's champion narrowly escaped being dangerously wounded; but he managed to snatch another shield from one of the enemy, and levelled his spear against the knight with such force that both horse and rider were overthrown. Then John waxed wroth and hacked away at the foe until his sword streamed with blood. Resistance was no longer to be thought of, and those who escaped his steel sought safety in flight. John, on perceiving this, put spurs into his horse and pursued them.

He observed Arlan, the earl, amid the ranks of the fugitives, recognising him by his arms, and then directed his onslaught against him, having sternly resolved not to let the earl escape, but to kill him or take him prisoner. The earl put his spurs into his jaded horse to try to escape, but both horse and rider were too much exhausted to get the start of John. At last he overtook the earl, and raised his sword over him, and as the latter was alone, his man having ridden away, he had no choice but to surrender.

"For God's sake," cried he, "leave me my life, and then you are welcome to hold my lands and castle as your own."

"It is possible that I may spare you; but it is not I who shall pronounce your doom, for I shall lead you to Lady Murina, and it rests with her to grant you mercy or withhold it."

Then John deprived him of his arms and carried him captive to the castle. When they came before the châtelaine, and John had delivered to her the captive earl, the latter fell on his knees before her and craved for mercy.

"I acknowledge," said he, "that I have wronged you, but I will offer you all the reparation that lies within my power, money and goods as much as you desire, and for what you suffer me to retain I will be your vassal."

When John had pleaded for the captive earl the Lady Murina agreed to pardon him for John's sake. The earl then rose up gladly and thanked his generous foe, but John advanced to the châtelaine, and asked her leave to go his way now the strife was over. Although she would have liked to keep him even longer with her, she said she could not hinder him from going, and thanked him with tears for the help he had afforded her.

John now rode from the castle the same way he had come. He was utterly alone, for his gloomy spirits caused him as much as possible to shun the society of his fellows. When he had journeyed a while he heard a terrible roaring in the thicket, and saw, on riding there, a serpent and a lion engaged in deadly strife with each other. The serpent had wound itself round the lion, and was holding it in such a tight embrace that it could not move. When John saw that the poor beast could not resist any longer, but would be choked, he was moved with compassion, jumped off his horse, and tied it up a good distance from the scene of combat, where the serpent's venom could not harm it. Then he held his shield in front of him and nimbly attacked the serpent. With the first blow he cut its head off, and the lion was then able to release itself from its adversary's fatal embrace. John next put himself on the defensive, thinking that the lion would now attack him, but when the lion saw the serpent lying dead, it walked up to John, laid itself at his feet, and tried to express its gratitude as best it could. John noticed a wound in the lion's neck—the result of the serpent's poisonous bite—and, in order to prevent the poison from spreading, he promptly cut off the flesh round the wound. It seemed as if the lion understood the service he had rendered it, for it made no resistance, but stretched its neck forward and glanced gratefully at its deliverer. When John rode away the lion followed him, and, showed, as well as an animal can express, that it meant to serve and follow him for the future; and so it did constantly. The lion followed him as faithfully as a dog, and this companionship caused him to be known everywhere by the name of the Knight of the Lion.

The faithful beast, determined to manifest its attachment in every way, ran before the rider into the wood, seized a buck, and hurried off to overtake him with it. The lion then laid down its prey in front of the horse, and when John did not stop, but pursued his journey, the lion would not delay to consume the animal, but ran along by the knight. When night came on, and John interrupted his ride, the lion seemed to understand that he was hungry, and rushed off at once amongst the trees to hunt for some game. It knocked over and killed the first stag it saw, threw it on its back, and hurried with it to John, who drew his hunting-knife and flayed the creature, giving the lion its entrails, liver, lungs and heart, and roasting the rest for himself. When he sat down to eat, the lion stretched itself at his feet, and refused to leave him. Even by night the faithful animal kept watch over his master when he laid himself down to sleep on his shield beside the camp fire.

When day dawned John rode on, and so they lived together for fourteen days, hunting and roaming about the wild wood, but on the evening of the fifteenth day they came to a spring, and when John saw it he recognised it as being the very same spring beside which he had done battle with Red Vadoin. All his sorrowful memories surged through his soul, shame and despair overwhelmed him once more with such violence that he fell to the ground unconscious. As he fell his sword slipped out of its sheath and wounded him in both shoulder and breast, so that blood poured forth from beneath his coat of mail. When the lion saw this it began to tremble with anxiety, and crept cautiously up to the fallen knight, grasped his sword with its teeth and carried it off some distance so that it should not further hurt him; then it laid itself at his feet and waited until he returned to life. On opening his eyes, John's first thought was of his broken promise to his wife, and then his despair began afresh.

"Why should I seek further to avoid my fate?" he sighed; "all my happiness in life is over, and sorrow alone is left to me. It is best, then, that I end my days. There is none to see me here, and I can kill myself without a soul knowing it. The only creature to mourn me would be this poor lion."

As he uttered these words he was standing near a chapel which had been built just beside the fountain. In this chapel there was a captive maid who, hearing his voice, interrupted her melancholy reflections and asked, in moving words, to have speech with him. John, much amazed, went to the chapel and asked who was in there.

"I am," answered the captive, "the most luckless being the sun shines upon."

"Do not say that," said John, "for my sorrow is many times greater than yours."

"You, indeed, are free, and your time is your own; you can ride whither you will; but I am sitting in captivity here on a false charge, and to-morrow they will burn me on a pyre."

"Tell me what they have charged you with, and why they have condemned you to such a painful death."

"Let God be my judge. If I be guilty may He never succour me in body or in soul. The chancellor and both his brothers accuse me of having betrayed my mistress, and on this false charge I am doomed to lose my life, unless I can find a knight willing to fight single-handed on behalf of my innocence against all my three slanderers."

"Then your misfortune is less than mine," said John, "for you can get help; but as for my grief, that no man can cure."

"Who do you suppose will be my champion? There are only two knights in the whole world in whom I dare hope. God grant I may find them."

"Let me hear who these are who would dare to fight against three knights at the same time."

"One is the knight Gavian and the other is John, King John's son. It is because of him that I am to die on the morrow."

"What is it you say?" shouted John. "It is because of him that you are accused? Well, then, know that he whom you are now addressing is John, King John's son, and by God's help I will set you free if it be that you are the girl who so generously helped me after I had slain Red Vadoin. You saved my life, and what you did for me then I will do for you now. But tell me what has happened since that luckless hour when I rode away from the castle."

"You remember that I helped you in your direst need, and you remember also that it was I who brought you and your lady together—and these things I do not regret. Afterwards you rode away with Knight Gavian, and the year went by without any tidings being heard of you. Then my mistress waxed wroth, and blamed me for having treacherously brought about this marriage. When the chancellor perceived that I had lost her favour, his old spite against me broke out; he began to slander me, and ended by charging me formally with treason towards my mistress. He bade me get a knight who would dare single-handed to vindicate my innocence against him and his two brothers; but if none would or could do this, the pyre awaited me. No one in the castle ventured to stand forth as my champion, and all in vain I made my supplication at other courts: not a soul would take up my cause. Then I rode to King Arthur at Caerleon, and inquired after Knight Gavian, but there I heard sad tidings. A knight had been there and carried the queen off by main force, and Gavian had been sent by the king to take vengeance on the ruffian, and bring back the stolen queen. I could find neither you nor Gavian, and I was forced, woe-begone as I was, to return hither. So, I am now sitting in captivity. To-day a priest prepared me for death, and to-morrow I must die, unless you will, of yourself, do battle single-handed with the three."

"Fear not," answered John, "to-morrow I shall come hither ere the judgment falls on you, and I will either save you or fall in the lists; but, whatever may happen, you must promise me that you will reveal my name to none: that must remain a secret 'twixt us twain."

"I would rather die than utter aught which you have bidden me keep secret; but, alas, they will perhaps kill you and then burn me."

"Say not so, for were they ten instead of three, I should vanquish them to-morrow. I shall now ride off to seek lodging for the night and bait for my horse, but do not fear my not appearing in the lists. God forbid that I should betray you, so, good-night, noble damsel, and rely on my word."

John remounted his horse and plunged into the wood, followed by his lion. Soon the trees began to grow less numerous, and he perceived a castle before him, the walls of which were strong and high, but the country round about was desolate and laid waste. Not a habitation appeared, and he failed to find even bait for his horse. Seeing this he rode straight to the castle, and when he reached it the drawbridge was lowered for him, and its lord and his men came out and received him with great courtesy. They asked him, however, to chain up the lion outside the gate, for they feared that it would otherwise do mischief, but John answered:—

"That I cannot do, for he and I have promised never to be parted, and I myself will answer for us both; but have no fear, the lion shall not do any one harm."

They answered that he might do what seemed best to him, and then they went into the castle, and there John was welcomed by the dames and damsels, who met him with torches, and lighted him into the banqueting-hall. There they took off his armour and gave him other raiment, and then ushered him into supper. John could not, however, help noticing that their merriment at table was occasioned more by politeness to him than by cheerfulness of mind; and when he heard his host heaving deep sighs, and saw him unable any longer to conceal his tears, John thought he ought to ask him the cause of his distress.

"Right gladly will I tell you," replied his host, "concerning the misfortune that has befallen me. Hard by there dwells a fierce giant of the name of Harpin, and he is moved by hatred towards me. He has laid waste my land; my manors and castles are burnt down, and now nothing remains to me of all my possessions save this castle, which has hitherto resisted his attacks, though he has come hither day after day. I had six sons—the bravest knights you could see—and this giant has succeeded in taking the whole six prisoners. Two of them he slew outside this castle. I witnessed the deed with my own eyes; and to-morrow he is coming back with two others to slay them in sight of us all. There is only one means of my escaping this, namely, the monster has demanded my only daughter, not to take her to wife himself, but to give her to the foulest and most scoundrelly scullion he has; and I would rather suffer death than an indignity such as this."

"It seems to me passing strange," said John, "that you have not informed King Arthur of this matter, for there are many at his court who would willingly help you, and do battle with this giant, however strong he be."

"I have done what I could and sought to find the brave Gavian, for my wife and he are sister and brother. However, as ill-luck would have it, he was not in Caerleon, but had ridden off in quest of the queen, who had been carried off. Had he been aware of what his sister has to suffer he would assuredly have been here long ere this."

"If I can do anything for you," said John, "you may count on me, and should the giant come here early to-morrow morning, ere I ride hence, I will do battle with him whatever the issue be, but I cannot tarry longer than daybreak, for I have promised to fight at midday on behalf of a captive maiden whose life depends on my being present, and that promise I must irrevocably keep."

The lord of the castle was beside himself with joy at this promise, and could not say enough to express his thanks; but, while he was talking, his wife and daughter came into the banqueting-hall, both with tear-stained faces, which they sought to conceal under their veils. On seeing them the lord of the castle cried out:-

"Now, dry your tears, for God has sent us this noble knight to assuage all our grief."

When they heard this, and learnt that John had promised to fight the fierce Harpin, they grew exceeding glad and fell on their knees before him in thanksgiving; and when the daughter lifted her veil John beheld the loveliest face he had ever looked upon. He hastened to raise them up, and said:-

"You ought not to go down on your knees before me, and you must put off your thanks until the morrow. What the issue of this fray will be, even supposing I can wait for it, no man can tell; but it is high time to sleep and recruit our strength for to-morrow's fight."

John, followed by his faithful lion, then proceeded to the bed-chamber assigned to him. Shortly before daybreak a priest knocked at his door and asked him if he would like to hear Mass. John expressed his thanks, clad himself hurriedly in his armour, and went down to the chapel to prepare himself by devotion and prayer for the perilous encounter which he would have to sustain that day. When Mass was over he went out into the courtyard to look for the giant. The sun had already risen, but not a glimpse of the giant was yet to be seen. After waiting a while, he turned to the lord of the castle and said:

"God knows how gladly I would stay with you, but my promise prevents me waiting any longer for your enemy; so, farewell, and may God retain you in His keeping".

He then took farewell of them at once, and as he was about to mount his horse the damsel fell on her knees before him, entreating him not to abandon them, and her parents offered him lands and gold if he would but stay, but he said:-

"God forbid that I should sell my service. Never let Gavian or any other valiant knight hear that you made me such an offer."

"Then stay for Blessed Mary's sake," entreated the damsel in tears. "Stay for your friend Gavian's sake, and forget not that my mother is his sister."

John knew not quite what to answer them. It cut him to the heart to see the young girl's tears, but he could not break the oath he had sworn to Luneta, and he knew he could never survive the grief and shame which would befal him if she were to suffer death through his broken promise. In his perplexity he turned to the damsel and said:-

"I leave this matter in God's hands, and, relying on His succour, I will bide yet awhile".

He had hardly uttered these words before he saw the giant rushing over the plain like a madman, and carrying on his shoulder a tremendous bar of steel, so heavy that ten men could hardly have managed to carry it. He had brought with him the two knights, both bound hand and foot. He had thrown each on a horse, and there they lay across the saddles, with their heads hanging down towards the ground. The horses themselves were wretched, half-starved jades, hardly able to go by themselves, and driven by a miserable dwarf, who lashed with his scourge not only them, but also the poor knights, whose clothes were torn to rags, and from whom blood was flowing in streams. When the giant reached the castle gate he lifted up his voice and ordered that the damsel should be given up to his scullion, otherwise they would have reason to repent it.

John then turned to the lord of the castle, who was bewailing his hard lot, and said:-

"I have never heard of such an outrage before, but, with God's help, we will hinder him from getting your daughter into his power".

Then he called for his horse and arms, the drawbridge was let down, and he galloped over the plain towards the astonished giant.

"Who are you?" cried the latter, as he saw the knight; "who dare fight against me? They are no real friends of yours who urge you to such a foolhardy act."

"I have not come here to waste time in bandying words," answered John. "Your threats do not alarm me, and you shall see I have no intention of running away from you."

Having said this he dug his spurs into the horse's sides and rushed towards the giant. The giant wore for armour a thick bear's hide, but that was pierced by John's lance so that the blood gushed out in a stream. But he troubled himself little or nothing about the wound, but seized hold of his iron bar and aimed a blow at John which shattered his shield into splinters. John waxed mightly wroth, and swore that the giant should pay dearly for this, whereupon he grasped his sword with both hands and gave the giant such a tremendous cut across the forehead that a piece of flesh, the size of an ordinary man's head, dropped off at the blow. Harpin shrieked with pain and rushed blindly at his enemy. His steel bar glanced so close to John that the knight reeled in his saddle and looked, for an instant, as if he was about to fall to the ground; but the lion, as soon as it perceived the peril in which John stood, rushed up and took his share in the sport. The faithful beast hurled himself on the giant, tore his bear's skin to tatters, dug his claws into the monster's body, and tore and rent it till the flesh and muscles flew about. The giant managed, after some few minutes, to extricate himself; but it was in vain that he tried to reach the lion with his iron bar. It was too unwiedly and the lion far too nimble. In spite of all his blows, it knew how to avoid them, and at last the giant, in aiming a crushing blow at this enemy that constantly eluded his efforts to reach him, directed his weapon with such force that the bar fastened itself into the ground and there stuck. John then rushed forward and buried his sword right in the monster's body. The fight was now finished, and the giant tottered to the ground a dead man.

The people in the castle, who had trembled as they watched the varying fortunes of the fray, now hurried out when they saw the giant fall. Their joy at their deliverance from the monster knew no bounds, and the lord of the castle said to John:-

"I do not know how I shall ever thank you enough for delivering us all. Unfortunately, I know I must not keep you longer with me, but I hope you will not be long before you come back, so that I may prove to you that you have helped no ungrateful man."

"Let us say nothing more on this score," replied John, "but only ask your sons to take the dwarf that was in the giant's retinue, and send him to Gavian as a gift from me."

"We will willingly do that," said they, "but if he asks us who has sent him, what are we to say?"

"Well, only say it was the Knight of the Lion, and that his friendship for Gavian induced him to fight this battle for his sister's sake; but naught further than this are you to tell him."

After saying this he waved his hand to them in farewell, and galloped at a furious pace to the enchanted spring.

The sun indicated that noon was already past when he reached the spot, and poor Luneta had already been brought from the chapel and conducted to the pyre. The fagots had been carried there, and only needed to be lighted, just as John came galloping up to order them to desist from their work. When the people saw the steel-clad knight galloping up at full speed they scampered away so as to escape the horse's hoofs, and a broad road was opened out between the rider and the pyre. John saw where Luneta lay. Her clothing consisted only of coarse linen, which hardly concealed her nakedness. When John arrived she had already made her confession and prepared herself for death. Around her stood a crowd of women lamenting and shedding tears. John shouted out that he had come to vindicate her innocence, and urged those who accused her to step forth and do battle with him, after which he approached the pyre, and sought to comfort her with some kindly words.

"My poor Luneta," said he, "tell me now who they are who have so shamefully belied you. I have come to vindicate you, and I shall compel them to withdraw their charges or else perish in the attempt."

"God requite you, noble knight, for having come," answered Luneta. "Had you been but a few minutes later, I had been undone; but now I hope my sorrow will be turned to joy. My accusers are standing here close by the pyre, but I know that God will grant you the victory, as surely as I am innocent."

When the chancellor and his two brothers heard her say this, they bade her hold her peace.

"Do not put any faith in what she says," cried they to John. "You are bereft of your senses if you mean to risk your life for such a liar. Be wise and ride away; and venture not to fight one against three."

"I am not going to run away for your big words," answered John. "It is true enough that I have no friends or kinsmen here; but I put my trust in God and my good sword, and I shall not blench from you, though I am one and you are three. You must either withdraw your words or else maintain them sword in hand."

"Since you refuse to follow good advice, then let your death be on your own head. But before the combat begins be good enough to order your lion to quit the lists."

"Should the lion attack you then you must strive to protect yourselves as well as you can."

"We will not fight against both of you; either tie up your lion or ride off. In any case we will not begin the fray."

John made a sign to the lion to go away, and the sagacious beast went off at once and lay down at a distance. John fastened his helmet tighter on his head, seized a lance, and the fray began.

The chancellor and his brothers immediately attacked the solitary knight with the greatest fury, but John carefully reserved his strength. When they rushed against him he avoided their attack by a clever movement, but they had hardly passed him before he turned his horse and made for the chancellor. He tilted against him with all his might, and caught him full in the chest with his lance, so that he was lifted out of his saddle and hurled to the ground, where he lay long in a swoon. When the brothers saw this they brought their horses close together, and rode against John. Dexterous as his movements were and doughty his blows, yet he found it difficult to defend himself against their furious attack, and, worse still, the chancellor, having recovered consciousness, and frantic at his overthrow, seized his arms and joined his brothers. There was now three of them again, and he felt that his strength was beginning to desert him in the unequal fight.

But the lion, when it saw the peril in which John stood, could no longer keep still; it rushed up and hurled itself on the chancellor, throwing him to the ground. With its powerful teeth the savage beast caught hold of the rings in his coat-of-mail, wrenched them apart one from another, and then dug its claws into his side, and butchered him instantly. John was now released from his most dangerous enemy, but the two others now attacked him the more fiercely, and he thought he had never before been so hard pressed. The lion, however, again came to his assistance by jumping up from the lacerated corpse of the chancellor, and rushing on both the brothers. They were not unprepared, but received the lion's onset so that it fell down before them sorely wounded. However, when John saw the faithful beast's fall, he was beside himself with rage, and fell on the two knights with such fury that they were constrained to give themselves up and declare themselves vanquished, in order to save their lives. But this did not avail them much, for when John pointed his sword at their breasts, and forced them to acknowledge that they had slandered poor Luneta out of nothing but malice, the multitude waxed so frantic that both her traducers were dragged to the pyre, instead of her, and there died the death they had devised for her.

Luneta's innocence was now established, and she descended from the pyre to thank her preserver, but, according to her promise, pretended that the knight was a stranger to her. No one else knew who he was, and not even his own wife suspected who the Knight of the Lion in reality was. She approached him, however, in a courteous manner, and invited him to accompany her to the castle to stay there until the lion's wounds should be healed. John bowed low in his saddle, and expressed his thanks without lifting his visor.

"God requite you for the honour you would show me, but I cannot enter any man's house, or find joy or gladness in life, until I have regained my wife's love which I forfeited through my own fault."

The châtelaine answered that she thought it strange for a woman not to love so brave a knight, and added that she did not suppose he had committed such a serious crime against his wife that it was beyond the reach of forgiveness.

"I must not reveal my crime: it is a secret between her and me."

"Tell me, noble knight," she went on to say, "is it only you two who are aware of the way in which you displeased your wife?"

"Only we two. If any third party could suspect it, it is you."

"Now I do not understand you any longer. Tell me, then, your name that I may have some clue to solving your riddle."

"People call me the Knight of the Lion. I possess no other name."

"The name itself sounds strange to me, and I have never heard the Knight of the Lion spoken of."

"The reason of that is not far to seek. I am no renowned knight whose name has been on every man's tongue. If I had more often joined in the fray or assisted at tournaments doubtless you would have heard the name of the Knight of the Lion mentioned."

"Again I ask you to come with me to my castle."

"No, noble lady; I will not go thither until I am reconciled with my wife."

"Good-bye, then, and may God grant you, in all fulness, your desire for forgiveness."

"May your prayer be heard, and," added he in a whisper, "may you yourself be not more implacable than you would have the wife of the Knight of the Lion to be."

Then he remounted his horse and proceeded to the wood. Luneta, who had now regained her mistress' favour, followed him a part of the way, partly to thank him, and partly to question him further. To her expression of thanks he merely answered:—

"Whatever may happen, I beg you not to betray my name".

"No one shall beguile it out of me."

"I have yet one petition to make to you. You have now regained your lady's heart, and you can talk with her as of yore. Keep me in your thoughts, and should you seem to have an opportunity of assuaging her anger against me, and effecting our reconciliation, do not utterly forget me."

· "I have no higher wish than that," answered Luneta, "and be assured that I shall have you always in my thoughts."

Then they parted, and John returned to his sick lion, which now could hardly stand on its legs from loss of blood. He jumped off his horse and entered the wood to collect leaves and moss, and after a while he came back with an armful and laid them together on the shield and made a soft couch for the wounded creature. At last he hoisted the shield up on the horse's back, and there lay the lion while John walked beside the litter. About nightfall they reached the castle which John visited the first time he went to the enchanted spring, and was there received by all the inmates of the castle with their wonted hospitality. He thankfully accepted the master's invitation to stay until the lion's wounds were healed, and for this he had not long to wait, as both the master and his daughter were skilled in leechcraft, and soon the lion regained his former strength. Then John took leave of his hosts, and went forth in quest of adventures, seeking thereby to blot out his transgressions.

One evening, after he had been riding the whole day long and was very tired, he came to a strong castle that was called Torture Castle; and when those who kept watch on its towers saw John, they cried out to him:—

"Go away. You have nothing to do here, where only a madman would seek shelter. Sorrow and despair alone make this their home. Hasten away from it as fast as you can."

"What do you mean?" answered John dumb-founded. "What have I done to you that you should receive me with such discourteous words?"

"Ride away at once. Evil will befal you if you venture to force yourself in."

At these words John grew angry, and rode right up to the gate, which he ordered the porter to open at once.

"I insist on entering," said he, "whatever fate be mine."

"Noble knight," answered the porter, "insist not on that. There is no honour to be won in this abode of woe. Ride away, and seek not to enter this castle."

As he was speaking a courteous old damsel came out and said:—

"Be not angry, noble sir, at these harsh words, and, believe me, that all they have said to you has been said in a kindly spirit. It is their wont to receive all strangers with snubs and rudeness so as to warn them against entering this castle, for they know that no one who has found shelter here has had cause to rejoice at it. Now I have said my customary say, so hearken to my counsel and pursue your journey."

"The night is now far spent, and I prefer this shelter, however bad it be, to all other."

"Do as you will, but should you go hence with your life, thank God and His inexhaustible mercy."

"May He requite you for this friendly counsel, but my curiosity has now been roused, and even if it should cost me my life, I shall still not swerve from my purpose."

He called again to the porter and ordered him to open, and this time the latter no longer refused to obey; the gate was opened, the drawbridge let down, and John, followed by his lion, rode into the courtyard, which was extensive and almost as big as a plain. In the middle of this was an enclosure made of poles and brambles, and in it he saw three hundred women engaged in spinning gold and weaving it into ribbons. Notwithstanding all the precious things that lay strewn around them, they all seemed to be in deep despair, and had scarcely a whole thread on their bodies; their clothes were torn and patched, their cheeks sunken, and their complexions sallow from hunger and neglect. When they saw John they all began to weep grievously and betray the deepest despair. When John had watched this ghastly spectacle for a while he grew heavy of heart, and rode back to the gate to get away from this abode of misery; but the porter went up to him and said:—

"I warned you beforehand, but you would not heed my advice, and now it is too late. A stranger may, I trow, gain admission herein, but no man who has once entered escapes."

"Good," answered John; "I am not thinking of slinking away, however inhospitable the place appears. But tell me, my friend, who these women are who sit here and spin, and who, methinks, are suffering such sore distress."

"You shall never get from me the key to the mystery. Find someone else to tell you what has happened."

John, fully convinced that he would learn nothing from the porter, turned his horse, and rode again into the great courtyard, and observed, in the enclosure itself, a little gate standing open. He dismounted from his horse, and after tying it up to a pole, went in, and, on approaching the unhappy women, said:—

"God be with you both old and young, and may He turn your sorrow into joy".

"O, may He grant your prayer," answered an aged woman. "I

believe you have come hither to learn who we are, and why we are tortured in this wise. Listen, then, to the story of our unhappy lot. Once upon a time there was a brave young king who ruled over the land whence we came. He was seldom at home, but journeyed into all countries in quest of adventures and to take part in tournaments and jousts. Once he came to this castle, and for that deed we are all paying the penalty now, and perhaps you, too, will have to suffer for his mad daring. Two fiends hold sway over this castle. Now, when our king had lain here a night, and was about to pursue his way on the morrow, these two fiends hindered him, and offered him the choice between fighting them both, or abandoning himself to their tender mercies. Our king was young—not quite twenty years old—and, brave as he was, he dared not engage the monsters in battle, so he had no choice but to yield himself captive. Then they put before him another choice, which was that they should either kill him or else, to regain his freedom, he was to send each of them a hundred and fifty damsels from the country wherein he was king; nor were they satisfied with that, but demanded that whenever one of them died he was to send another in her stead, so that the number should always be complete. This has been the state of things for many years past, and so it will continue until some one slays our tormentors and sets us free; but the man who can fight these fiends single-handed is not to be found, and so our sufferings will therefore, I believe, go on for ever. You yourself see how we are treated. We suffer hunger and thirst, and though we labour from morning till night, we do not get enough wages to sustain our bodies or clothe our nakedness; and we suffer not only from our own ill-fate, for often knights and squires come here to free us, but they have all, for our sakes, perished in the enterprise."

"Do not despair," replied John, "for I will release you if I can."

The night was now far spent, and John quitted the enclosure to find shelter for himself. Followed by his lion, he began strolling about the wide courtyard, and came at last to a building that was lighted up, and servants, hearing the tramp of the horse, came out and invited him to enter. They took his horse and led it to a stable, and ushered him into the hall. There he was received by an old knight and his daughter, who both bade him welcome. They all tried to serve him to the utmost of their power, but John could not be certain whether this hospitality was the outcome of kindness, or whether some mockery lay hidden under all the attention they were showing him. Meantime, however, he did not trouble to inquire about this, but betook himself, tired out as he was, to the bed-chamber that was assigned him, and soon fell asleep there. In the morning the old knight went up to him, and conducted him to a chapel where a priest said Mass for them. When this was over John wished to take leave of the old knight, but he laid hold of him saying:—

"Dear friend, you may not go so soon, for there is a certain custom in this house—to wit, that every stranger who finds shelter for the night must, ere he depart, fight with two devils, unless he submits to yielding himself their prisoner."

"That was a curious custom for you to introduce into your house, and one that reflects scant honour on your hospitality."

"*My* house," exclaimed the old knight; "you are mistaken, young man. I have no longer any voice in this house wherein I too am a prisoner, although I am treated less harshly than the rest. Do not believe that it was I who introduced this savage custom, which is as scandalous to me as it is to you. I have no dearer wish than that you may overcome the two monsters and free all the prisoners in this castle. If you succeed in performing this achievement I will gladly give you my only daughter for your wife."

"I thank you for your kindly promise, but your daughter is too good for a poor knight-errant whose sole possessions are his sword and steed. Reserve her rather for some powerful emperor. I have no desire for so rare a reward."

Whilst he was speaking the two devils came rushing into the courtyard, each of them having in his hand a mighty club studded with spikes and formed of the entire stem of a tree. Their heads and feet were bare, but the rest of their bodies was protected by a strong coat of mail, and, for further defence, each of them had a shield. When the lion saw these horrid creatures it began to tremble like an aspen leaf, arched its back, and lashed the ground with its tail: the poor beast was both angry and frightened at the same time. When the two devils saw the lion they said to John:—

"Drive your lion away, for we will have nothing to do with it".

"You seem frightened at the lion. I should be amused to see a fight between the lion and you two."

"Are you afraid to fight us by yourself that you must needs make use of that sort of help?"

"Do not imagine that. I am quite ready to shut the lion up if you will show me some place."

Then they showed him a place, and in it John shut up his lion, locked the door, and threw the key in the devils' faces to show them he was not afraid of them, and, immediately afterwards, vaulted into the saddle and rode against the two.

Before the fiends could put themselves into position to meet the knight's attack, John struck one of them with his spear and hurled him to the ground, so that he howled with agony; but the next minute the fiend was on his legs again, and now a hot fight began. Both their clubs whizzed all the time about John's ears, and blow succeeded blow with such rapidity that he could not ward them off himself, but was beaten about just as one beats a piece of meat. His shield broke into bits, and his helmet was dented just as if it had been made of leather. He cut about him with both hands, but that was of little use, and he felt that he had never been in a worse plight, feeling his strength getting exhausted, and his blows more and more beside the mark. For a second he thought it best to give up such a hopeless fight and acknowledge himself worsted, but just then he received help that he little expected.

The lion had witnessed this combat from its cage, and grew more and more restless as John was more furiously beset. It looked everywhere for some means of getting out, but the cage was shut, and the bars resisted the lion's efforts; but suddenly it caught sight of a little hole in the flooring, and this the faithful beast began to widen, and after that scratched up a passage through the ground, by means of which it was able to crawl out. It had hardly got into the open air before it threw itself, with a wild rush, on one of John's adversaries, dashed him to the ground, and laid its terrible paws on his breast. Now John took fresh courage, and when his remaining adversary was torn from his clutches by the lion's unexpected assault, John took advantage of this to give him a terrible slash, so that his head was cleft smartly from his trunk. The other of the two devils then began to howl to John for mercy, promising him at the same time lands and gold, on condition that he released him from the ravening beast that had dug its claws into his breast; but John answered that as this devil had, to his knowledge, never shown mercy to others, he, therefore, was undeserving of human compassion, and so left him for the lion to work its will on. It was not many minutes before it had torn him to pieces.

All who dwelt in the castle now came running out to congratulate John on the victory he had gained, and the porters craved his forgiveness for having treated him on the previous evening in such a discourteous manner. The old knight, too, came and congratulated him, adding that John had now honestly won his daughter and all the treasures that were to be found in the castle.

"Your daughter, old man, can never be my bride, for I already love another, of whose affection I am trying to make myself worthy, and, as to the treasures in the castle, I will not touch them, for I do not fight for gold. Keep them, then, and give them as a dowry to your daughter. But I desire you to set free all unhappy women that are held captive here, and send them back to their own country."

Although the old man could not conceal his disappointment at not getting the brave Knight of the Lion for his son-in-law, he, nevertheless, lost no time in carrying out his behest, and the poor women now approached with tears to thank their saviour. After he had given them seemly clothing they went merrily past him out of the castle in which they had spent so many melancholy years. After seeing them depart he vaulted into the saddle, waved farewell with his hand to the people of the castle, and rode away.

He then returned to King Arthur's court, where he was received with uncommon joy, inasmuch as they had given up all hope of seeing him again in the flesh; but his good friend Gavian, who had just succeeded in conducting back to the court King Arthur's stolen queen, rejoiced above the rest. To his astonishment he found that the mysterious Knight of the Lion, who had so nobly helped his sister, was none other than John, his good friend and brother-in-arms. Side by side they did many a doughty deed, but still John could not win back his joyousness of old days, for the thought of Laudine's cold indifference incessantly grieved him sorely.

At last he could bear the agony no longer, but resolved to go to her and crave her forgiveness. If she refused it he felt that he no longer had the strength to live. So early one morning, ere the sun was up, he started on his journey, without telling any one, and with no other company than that of his trusty lion. On reaching the enchanted spring he seized the cup once more, and poured the water in it over the post, and, as happened before, a raging hurricane broke forth, lightning flashes darted round him, and peals of thunder rattled.

When the people in the castle heard the roaring of the thunder and saw how the gusts of wind shook the battlements and towers, all trembled and bewailed aloud that the castle had been built on such a dangerous spot. It seemed to them a sorry fate to have to suffer insult because they could no longer protect the spring, or, failing that, be exposed to the violence of thunder, lightning and storm; for now that Red Vadoin was dead and John had gone away, there was no longer any one powerful enough to overcome all the knights errant who had a mind to mock them.

Then Luneta said to her mistress:—

"Again some fellow has ventured to insult us, and it looks as if we must forfeit the honour we held for so many years of being guardians of the enchanted spring. It seems to me absolutely necessary for us to try to find some knight with the will and the courage to protect our land against such miscreants. It cuts me to the heart to think that this fellow may go his way unmolested because there is no one in our castle to punish his arrogance."

"Well, Luneta, as you are always rich in resources, you must hit on some expedient to help us out of our troubles, for I myself am at my wits' end to think of anything."

"You know I would do all in my power for you, but what can a poor girl like me do? You have such a number of clever counsellors. Ask them what their advice is; and, to tell the truth, I dare not venture to suggest any expedient, for, supposing it did not turn out according to your wishes, you would hold me responsible for it, and perhaps I should again forfeit your favour."

"Alas!" replied Laudine, "my counsellors are of no more avail than my knights, and they certainly cannot help me. My sole hope is centred in you."

"Very well, then, I have one piece of counsel to offer you. You remember the Knight of the Lion, who overcame single-handed the chancellor and both brothers. Before that he had slain the terrible giant Harpin, and a braver knight is not to be found. If we could but gain him for our champion, then our troubles would be over; but, as you remember, he refused to enter this castle until he had made his peace with his wife. Our fate, therefore, depends on this reconciliation being effected."

"My dear Luneta, make haste at once to find where this knight is and bring him hither. If he comes I promise to do all in my power to reconcile him and his wife."

"Before I go I want you to promise me solemnly that you will not be angry with me for what I am about to do on your behalf, be the issue what it may."

When Laudine said she would readily take the oath that Luneta demanded, the damsel produced a reliquary and a Mass-book, and bade her mistress swear on them, first, that she would never hold Luneta responsible if things went contrary to her wishes; secondly, that she should reconcile the Knight of the Lion and his wife, and make the latter forgive the knight all his marital transgressions. When Luneta had exacted the oath, she could not repress a furtive smile, and, in order that her mistress should not perceive it, she commanded her horse to be brought round immediately, vaulted into the saddle, and rode to the spring, and there met the Knight of the Lion, who greeted her blithely. It did not take her long to tell him what had occurred at the castle, and let him into the secret of the new ruse she had employed to overcome the châtelaine's pride. When John wished to thank her for the trusty help she had given him, she interrupted his thanks by saying:—

"Let us not delay this reconciliation, but mount your steed and make for the castle".

"Does not my wife know who I really am?"

"Not a soul suspects that John and the Knight of the Lion are one and the same person."

When they reached the castle John went up to his wife and greeted her courteously. His visor was lowered over his face so that she could not recognise him, whereupon she welcomed him heartily; but Luneta said:—

"Now, my lady, the time has come for you to show what you can do. You promised to procure him his wife's pardon, and you alone can do that."

"Noble knight," said Laudine, "be seated here beside me and tell me your story, and I will do all I can, in accordance with my oath, to soften your wife's hard heart."

"There is no good whatever in hiding the truth any longer from you," interrupted Luneta. "That hard-hearted creature is yourself, and the Knight of the Lion is your lawful husband John, the son of John, who has now suffered quite enough for his forgetfulness. All you have to do now is to keep your promise, and render him back the love you promised, and the pardon which you alone can grant."

When the haughty dame heard this she first fell into a violent rage with the artful Luneta for having fooled her in this manner, but, ere long, she felt grateful to her trusty friend for having constrained her to pronounce the words of pardon which had hung upon her lips, but had hitherto been kept back by pride. She thereupon offered John her hand, drew him to her bosom, saying that she would now grant him full pardon by reason of her oath, and with this pardon ends the story of John, the Knight of the Lion, who went forth no more in quest of adventures, but stayed in his castle, content with his spouse's love, without any desire to gain any other honour whatsoever.

# MORTE D'UN MARCHEANT
## by Maxey Brooke

*Time for another light interlude. In* The Pendragon
Chronicles *I reprinted a story revealing Merlin's
talents as a detective—"Morte d'Alain" by Maxey
Brooke. I knew of one other Merlin story by
Brooke, which I listed in the appendix. When
I corresponded with Brooke I discovered that
he had written three more Merlin stories, but
had not sought to have them published. I'm
delighted to be able to present one of them
for you now. Brooke (1913– ) was, for many
years, a petro-chemist. Now retired he is a
part-time water consultant, and edits a technical
newsletter* The Water Drop.

"'Tis not as it was in the old days" said I to myself. But on saying, I
must needs smile. For I remembered hearing my father growl those
same words one day in the smithy while beating out a head piece
for some knight's steed.

"Had the Good Lord intended," he went on, "horses to
have armor, He would have given them skins of iron. In the
old days knights knew how to joust without injuring their
mounts."

And my grandsire, the fletcher, muttered them once.

"In the old days an arrow was the length of my forearm. Now
the archers want them longer and longer. One day a bow will be
as long as a man's body."

No doubt his grandsire spoke also the same words. And e'en *his* grandsire.

But times must change. No longer could a master magician and one helper meet the demands of a growing court. My master Merlin and I were no longer adequate. We must needs have a full dozen apprentices. And busy, too, they were kept mixing the unguents and ointments and all the things for better living that are a magician's business.

I had but come from the workroom wherein the apprentices were distilling essence of lavender and other flowers so valued by the ladies of the court. Indeed, I too was experimenting with attar of roses according to a formula my master Merlin had brought to England from his youthful travels in Persia.

But now perfumes must wait. 'Twas May-day morn and I had other and more important duties to perform.

I hied me to the battlement. Far away I could see a procession wending toward Camelot. The merchants, richly dressed, each riding a donkey. Each accompanied by pack-animals and body guards. The merchants coming up from London Town to pay tribute to our King Arthur for protecting them from the marauding Danes and Scots and Welchmen.

Long I stood there watching the sun glint off buckles of gold and cloth of scarlet. Ten of them, there were, rich, and fat, and comfortable. 'Twas a far easier life than that of a magician.

When they at last came nigh the castle gate, I took me away to my quarters for I knew that soon my services would be required.

Nor was I wrong. Ere long a page appeared.

"Sir, you are wanted in the great courtyard."

"Thank you."

I enjoyed being called "sir" as only one who has been base born can. I had since gathered together that which was required of me. I took a last look at my preparations of attar and proceeded toward the great courtyard slowly as befits a magician, e'en though he has but recently achieved the rank of journey-man.

In the great courtyard was a stately array. Our King Arthur was seated on a high throne, overlooking all. Beside him, a step down and a steep back was my master, Merlin. Arrayed at a still lower level were certain of the Knights of the Roundtable. Sir Kay, the Chamberlain and others concerned. Behind them all was a row of men-at-arms, swords at ready, bucklers agleam. Across the court were the merchants, their clothes well nigh of stuff as fine as the King's. Serfs had set up pavilions for them and they sat there, fat and satisfied on cushions of down.

Betwixt the two, the soft merchants and the hard warriors of the court, was a plain table with a chair so placed that from it one could see both groups. 'Twas my place. I walked to the chair, turned my back on the merchants and bowed full deep to my Liege, the King. The King ran his hand through his great red beard, amused at my disdain, and rumbled,

"Are you ready, my good Aleric?"

"Ready, Sire."

"Then begin."

I raised my forefinger. Two servingmen leapt forward to help the first merchant to his feet. He waddled across the courtyard to kneel before our King, puffing and blowing. There was a smile behind King Arthur's beard as he bade him arise.

"Sire, I am known as Carder of Mulberry Row. I represent the threescore, six, and ten of the Wool Merchants Guild. Our yearly tribute is one gold pound for each member. One-tenth I bring you in fine gold. For the rest, one-hundred ells of woollen cloth, half of it bleached and half dyed in all the known colors but purple.

"In addition, my Guild prays that you will accept as a gift, a fine woollen cloak, trimmed in ermine, and dyed with Tyrian purple."

As he spoke those words, he ceased to appear as a fat figure from out of a comedy and became the staunch representative of British trade whose service was full as important as that of her army.

Our King nodded his head gravely,

"Your gift, good Carder," he said, "is accepted with pleasure and we will wear it in fond recollection of your Guild. Your tribute we would accept without reckoning were it not for the Guild-rules. You may proceed, Aleric."

Servingmen placed a small chest and many bolts of cloth upon my table. The gold I weighed and tested for purity in the manner of Archimedes. The woollen-stuff I measured with a staff marked off from the length of the King's arm.

At last I cast up my figures on the abacus and recorded them on parchment. This last the merchants looked upon, some with interest, some with disdain, for the abacus was but newly brought to England from Italy and was unfamiliar to them. And many took not kindly to new inventions. I bowed to the King.

"The gold is in full measure, Sire, and the cloth a half an ell over."

"'Tis well," he answered, "and be assured the Guild will not suffer for its generosity."

The fat Carder returned to his down cushion with obvious pleasure and was replaced with the representative of the wheat Merchants Guild.

And so till mid-afternoon they came, one after another. And for each I cast a reckoning and recorded it on parchment to be taken back to the Guild-hall in token that the tribute had been fairly paid. Now and again would I find an error, but none were grave save those in the Wine Merchants Guild. Here each goldpiece was light by half a barleycorn and each firkin short by half a gill.

When I announced these results, the wine merchant, Preston by name, made some slighting remark about incompetent clerks. At this, the King turned toward my master.

"How say you, good Merlin?"

"Master Aleric is neither incompetent nor a clerk. He has a fine mind and is aided by the best instruments in all England."

"Then 'tis sorcery," exclaimed Preston, "the quantities were correct when I left London-town."

"Nor sorcery either, unless aided by men."

The King looked at me.

"You will record the weights and measurements as you found them."

"Nay!" cried Preston, "'Twould but anger the Guild. See, I will make up the difference from my own purse."

"Not so." said the King sternly, we will report to the Guild that which we received from the Guild. If 'twere an honest error, we trust them to make good the difference. If dishonest, we trust them to punish him who was dishonest.

"But Sire, we need not trouble the Guild . . ."

"Silence, merchant!" roared King Arthur, "Return to your place that we may be on with the next accounting."

When, at last, the accounting was finished, the King had regained his humor.

"Thank you, good merchants. You will be our guests at tonight's feast. On the morrow, Master Aleric will give you your receipts with our seal. Until then, we bid you good-day."

We all arose whilst the King and his officers retired. I gathered my instruments and papers and retired to my quarters. The instruments I put in their keeping-place and the accounts in a cabinet. I then resumed my experiments with the attar until a page announced the evening meal.

As a rule, my master Merlin and I took our sup in his

quarters that we might discuss philosophy and the sciences. Many and wonderful were the things he taught me of his youth in Alexandria. But on special occasions, we dined in the great hall that we might entertain the King and his guests with our small tricks.

So 'twas that my master and I presented ourselves, attired in full magician's regalia before our King. Merlin, as befitted his position, sat at the round table with the knights of the realm. I sat at the lower, smaller table with the merchants. Indeed, I headed it.

I have oft remarked on the feats of trencher and beaker performed by the knights of the round table. But tonight they were as monks on a fast day compared with the merchants from London-town. Ne'er have I seen such quantities of meat and ale consumed by so few.

After, there were songs of derring-do by sweet voiced minstrels and juggling by a troupe of traveling dwarfs.

For myself, I entertained with cords. Starting with two cords the length of my forearm, I knotted them together. Running my hand the length of the cords I caused the knot to disappear, leaving only one cord. This I did again and again with variations until I had a ball of cord as large as my head. The ball, I placed in a sack, tapped with my wand, and turned the sack inside out to show that it had disappeared.

Sweet was the applause to my ears. Sweeter, even, since I had learned the secret of the false knot from a Gypsy and had taught it to my master, Merlin.

But if my small tricks entertained, Merlin set them mouth agape as he produced eggs from such unseeming places as the ear of the court jester. Each egg he placed under a basket and when the last egg was under, he tapped the basket with wand. But when he lifted the basket, there were no eggs, but rather a flock of baby chicks which ran chirping in all directions.

Thus ended the evening.

Though the knights and merchants went to their quarters to bed, Merlin and I climbed to the highest battlements. On such clear nights, 'twas our wont to study the stars. Merlin had learned astronomy from the magi and many and wonderful were the things he taught me of their journeys through the sky. Tonight there was no moon and the stars seemed low enough to touch. We recorded our observations and Merlin questioned me to test my knowledge of the constellations and bright stars. 'Twas well past midnight when we went indoors.

I wished my master a good morrow at his door and proceeded

to mine own quarters. Later I realized that my door had been ajar, but at the time my mind was still in the stars and I entered thinking naught of it.

I was well within the room before I knew that was not well. And as I realized that I smelled the odor of a taper just extinguished, something hard and heavy descended upon my head.

Once again I saw the constellations but this time not from the battlements. I floated among them, bathed in their cold fire. Now and again I would approach the shining platter of the earth and each time it would try and pull me to it. But each time I would fly away among the bright lights that were the stars. At last I approached the earth too closely. I could no longer resist its pull and down and down I fell, ears over teakettle. As I neared the castle, I closed my eyes awaiting the crash as I encountered Mother Earth.

No crash came. I opened my eyes to the dull dawn fingering through my casements. Some evil fellow had cast sand under my eyelids. A blacksmith was working busily within my skull and my mouth tasted as the nesting place of some unsanitary bird. I was laying on the floor of my quarters.

I pulled myself to my feet, noting stupidly that cabinets and drawers had been ransacked. Parchment and broken apparatus littered the floor. Holding to the wall, I made my way out of the apartment, down the hall, and beat with clumsy fists on my master Merlin's door. Ere he opened it, I had sunk to my knees.

"Aleric, my son, what . . ."

The bow-cord which was stretched between my temples suddenly parted and I knew no more.

When next I opened my eyes, I was on Merlin's own couch. A cool napkin was on my head. It was full daylight but I had not the will to arise.

Anon the door opened and my master entered, his face grave. When he saw I was again awake, he smiled.

"Ah . . . I see it takes more than an alembic to dent a British skull."

I tried to smile back but the muscles of my face would not permit.

"I know not what happened, sir, but . . ."

"Do not bother yourself. I took on myself the privilege of examining your quarters, Methinks I know what occured."

"What, then?"

"One of the merchants, desiring not to pay tribute, destroyed the records and your abacus. You must have surprised him ere he finished."

"'Twas the wine merchant, Preston!" I cried.

"Nay. Any but him. He is but a petty pilferer. Who did this deed must needs be bold."

"Who, then?"

"That we shall soon know. I have advised our Sire, King Arthur, of the happenings. E'en now, he issues an order to assemble the merchants in the courtyard. Feel you like attending?"

"The wild assess of Tartary could not hold me. Let us away."

Once again I entered the courtyard, leaning heavily on Merlin's arm despite my brave words. We were in full magician's regalia. But instead of my conical hat, my head was swathed with bandages until I looked like an Eastern potentate.

The merchants were assembled at their pavilions, strangely silent in contrast with yesterday. Merlin and I took our stations at the foot of the dais. A solitary trumpet sounded and our Liege Lord, King Arthur, entered the court, strode toward the dias, mounted, and seated himself. The officers of the court followed and found their places. The chamberlain thumped a table with his mace, unnecessarily, because the court was clothed in silence. Our King arose, looked over the merchants for a long minute and said.

"A crime has been committed in our castle. That is intolerable. The criminal must be punished."

"One of you merchants, having eaten our bread and drunk our ale has seen fit to assault one of our advisors and destroy certain records.

"Mayhap one of you kept back a part of our tribute and destroyed those records that your guilt would not be learned of.

"One of you is guilty. Attend our faithful magician."

Our King seated himself and my master Merlin advanced to the center of the area separating the court from the merchants. He turned and bowed to King Arthur.

"Sire, in the night, some varlet entered Master Aleric's quarters during his absence. While there, he destroyed the Royal Standards, divers mathematical tools, and the records of yesterday's transactions. He tampered with valuable experiments and on Aleric's return, smote him such a blow on the head that it well nigh clove his skull."

His Majesty's face darkened. He glared at the merchants.

"Standards can be replaced; tools can be repaired; records can be retallied; experiments can be redone; and battered heads will heal. But when a trust is broken it is gone beyond recall. The honor of the Merchants Guilds has been tarnished and will forever remain besmirched."

He paused full a dozen heartbeats and looked directly at each merchant in turn.

"Some of the stain can be removed if he who performed this vile deed will step forward. He will be permitted to leave the castle unharmed, e'en though he be forever barred from the Guild."

Long minutes he waited for the merchants answer. When none was forthcoming, he crashed his great fist down on the arm of his chair and thundered

"So be it!"

He turned to his magician.

"Master Merlin, mark me the culprit!"

"Aye, Sire."

He clapped his hands.

"Ho, Theodore! Ho, Humphrys!"

Two lads, wearing the jerkins of apprentice magicians rushed into the courtyard from a sally-port. The large one bearing a small tray, the small one bearing a large tray. The contents of both were hidden beneath napkins.

'Twas the first time since Merlin found me in the cock-ring, I had not assisted him. Jealousy battled with pride briefly, but my head hurt overmuch to sustain either.

Merlin slowly raised his hands, palms up, until they were shoulder-high. The merchants glanced at each other nervously, struggled to their feet, and stood in a ragged line.

"I must, perforce, use the blackest magic of Ancient Egypt to uncover this foul deed." His deep voice rolled across the courtyard causing shudders among all but our King and I. "The black cat has ever been the symbol of such magic. And I shall cause a black cat to choose the one who has forfeited his soul to the devil."

He plucked the napkin from the larger tray. Thereon reposed a cage in which a black cat sat, spitting spitefully.

"But lest the innocent should suffer, I have that which will protect the pure in heart."

He uncovered the smaller tray revealing an instrument like unto a baby's rattler.

"This sprinkler holds water that was blessed by the good Saint Columbine, himself. It will protect those not tainted with evil."

Merlin picked up the sprinkler and strode to the line of merchants. He paused before each, studying him intently, then dashed a spray of water on him.

This done, he returned to the center of the court.

"You are now all protected, except him who battered Master Aleric."

He waited a long moment. The tension was well nigh unbearable.

"Humphrys, release the beast."

The cat hurtled from the cage with a squall. But once out, she regained her dignity, sat a while, and washed a forefoot.

She looked at the line of merchants as though seeing them for the first time, arose, and started toward them with quiet dignity. Her dignity decreased as she approached them. Until at last she flung herself upon the fat belly of one called Porter, of the silver merchants' Guild.

As she clawed her way to his shoulder and sat thereon licking his face, Porter made no move to displace her. He began quaking like a great mound of jelly; his face, turning green under its natural red, took on a most peculiar hue. His eyes lost their focus and his mouth worked but issued no sound.

I thought he would swoon. But instead he dropped heavily to his knees, held his hands out to Merlin and said huskily

"Take it away . . . Please . . . Take it away."

Merlin walked slowly toward him, lifted the cat from his shoulder and held her cradled in his arms.

"You destroyed the records." It was a statement, not a question.

"Aye." Porter could not take his eyes from the cat.

"For what reason?"

"I substituted *nikelsilber* for the silver bars."

I was not familiar with the term *nikelsilber*. And from the slight narrowing of Master Merlin's eyes, I knew him to find it a new word. But he merely turned his back on the merchants, handed the cat to Humphrys, bowed silently to the King, and departed the courtyard. I fell in behind him as did the two aprentices.

Not often have I the stomach to watch a punishment, but this one I did. Porter was led into a small court. His right arm was laid on a oaken block where a hooded villein severed it with one blow of a sharp axe. Against the block was a brazier of glowing coals. A man of courage could plunge his arm into them to staunch the bleeding.

But Porter was not a man of courage. He merely stood there staring at the bleeding stump until he fainted. I could watch no longer.

*     *     *

That night, on the battlements, I could not put my mind on the stars. At last I could stand it no longer.

"Sir, I know ere now that such things are not magic, but follow the laws of nature. But which law used you this morn with the black cat?"

"The cat? Ah, yes. The sprinkler I used was divided. One side contained water, the other an infusion of catnip. The cat merely lept upon him whom I sprinkled with the infusion."

I sighed. Merlin made mysteries so simple.

Carefully I sighted Venus with the astrolobe, assuring myself that she was following the epicyclical course plotted by Ptolomy. But something kept nagging in the back of my mind. Venus . . . Ptolomy . . . Egypt . . . black magic . . . cats . . . Porter. Suddenly I had it.

"But sir, how did you know on whom to sprinkle the catnip?"

A smile tugged briefly at the corner of Merlin's mouth.

"The most obvious things are the best hidden. So long have you worked with attar that you are unaware that both you and your quarters reek of it. And one who so thoroughly wrecked your apartment could not help but get some attar upon him. I simply sprinkled catnip on the merchant who smelled like a rose."

# SIR LANVAL
## by A. R. Hope Moncrieff

*Ascott Robert Hope Moncrieff (1846–1927)—
what a wonderful name—was better known
under his alias Ascott R. Hope, which he used
on dozens of boys' books from 1865 to his death.
Moncrieff was an Edinburgh schoolmaster, who
turned to full-time writing in 1868. Apart from
his boys' fiction he was an expert on American
history. He was also entranced by medieval
legend and romance. He brought the fruits of
those studies together in a volume* Romance and
Legend of Chivalry (1913) *which contained both
a study of the development of medieval romance
and a collection of legends which Moncrieff had
revised for publication. The story of Sir Lanval
came from the twelfth century lays of Marie
de France, where he seems to have been the
prototype of Sir Lancelot.*

At King Arthur's court was a knight of foreign birth, by name Sir
Lanval, who, even among that famed brotherhood of the Round
Table, excelled in knightly graces and virtues. Sir Lancelot, Sir
Percival, Sir Gawayne, the bravest of his companions in battle and
the wisest in council, knew well the worth of this stranger, and
were proud to call him friend; and, when his name was spoken,
the bitter Sir Kay himself forbore to sneer. By the poor, as well
as by his own attendants, he was much beloved, for his kindness
and generosity were unbounded, and he gave freely to all in need,
so that his purse would have been always empty but for the rich

253

rewards which the king was wont to bestow on those who served him faithfully.

Thus all went well with him till Arthur wedded the false and fair Guinevere. Henceforth Lanval had one enemy at the court, and that an all-powerful one. Once the new queen had loved this knight, but when she found her love unreturned, it changed to bitter hatred, and she set her mind on working his ruin.

It is an old tale, how the greatest heroes have shown themselves weak to the wiles of a woman. The noble Arthur too easily listened to and too blindly confided in his unworthy wife. She soon took occasion to poison his mind by false charges against Lanval, so that the king began to look coldly on his good knight; nor was it long before Lanval felt the ill effects of this disfavour. When, after a successful war, distribution was made of honours and rewards, he alone found himself passed over, though none had less deserved to be thus slighted.

Right well knew he to whom he owed such neglect, but he was too loyal to let any word pass his lips that might assail the name of his master's queen. Patiently he bore himself under the king's displeasure, and made no complaint of the troubles which soon came upon him. His liberality had always kept him poor, and now that the just recompense of his services was withheld, he found himself falling into arrant want. No longer could he indulge his disposition by feeding the hungry and clothing the naked. It began to be a question with him how he might maintain himself and his household.

He lodged in the house of a burgher, who, now that he was without money, seemed to grudge him entertainment. Pride drove him to conceal his poverty, and he was fain to keep his chamber day and night. He could no more appear at tournaments in gallant array; his friends ceased to invite him to feasts; he could not even go to church for want of decent clothes. One by one, he had parted with his servants, his chargers, his equipments, till at last there was nothing left him but an old baggage horse, a torn saddle, and a rusty bridle. For three days he had not tasted meat or drink. Having come to this, he saw nothing for it but to leave the court of Arthur, and seek his fortune elsewhere.

So one day, while his brother knights were holding high festival at the castle, he mounted his sorry steed, and rode forth in such a plight that the people he met hooted and laughed as he urged on the stumbling beast, dreading to be seen by any who had known him in the days of his prosperity. Having thus stealthily left the town, he hid himself in the nearest wood, then rode through it till he came to a rich plain, across which ran a clear sparkling river. Here the unfortunate knight dismounted, to let his horse feed at will, and, wrapping himself in his tattered cloak, lay down beneath the wide branches of an oak that overshadowed the stream.

But now, when he would have given himself up to his sorrowful thoughts, he raised his eyes for a moment from the ground, and was aware of two damsels advancing towards him on the shady bank. As they drew near, and he stood up to salute them, he saw that they were strangely fair and richly attired. The one bore a gold basin, the other a silk napkin, with which they came to Lanval and offered to serve him, saying:

"Speed thee, Sir Knight! Our lady greets thee, and prays thee, if it be thy will, to speak with her."

"Lead me whither ye please," answered Lanval courteously. "Whichever way ye go, there I gladly follow, for never saw I fairer damsels."

"Nay, but you have yet to see our mistress," said they, smiling, and forthwith led him to a blooming meadow, where was set a magnificent pavilion covered with rich hangings and ornaments of gold and dazzling jewels, such as no queen on earth could call her own.

Within, all was alike costly and bright, but Sir Lanval had eyes only for the mistress of the place, a lady pure as the lilies of May and sweet as the roses of June, with hair shining like threads of gold, and eyes of enchanting radiance. At the first glance this marvellous beauty made all charms he had ever beheld or dreamed of seem as naught. And when she rose to give him friendly welcome, the knight felt that his heart had already gone into slavery after his eyes; he could love no other woman in the world, now that he had once seen this image of perfect loveliness.

"Gentle sir," she began in tones that thrilled him with delight, "think not that you are a stranger to me. I have long seen your worth, and now I have sent for you to ask if you may deem me worthy of your love."

"Oh, lady, command me in all things!" faltered the knight, scarce able to believe his senses. "What more might man hope than to serve such a peerless dame? But I am poor—friendless—despised."

"I know all," said the lady. "But so you will freely and truly give me your heart, I can make you richer than any emperor, for I have wealth at will, and nothing shall be wanting to him who is my knight."

For answer, Sir Lanval could only throw himself speechless at her feet. Need she ask if he loved her? She gave him her hand and made him sit down by her side, all ragged and rusty as he was; then short time served for his misery to be lost in a happiness too great for words.

The two damsels now appeared, covering a table with exquisite viands, of which neither the half-starved knight nor his fair hostess cared to eat. Long and lovingly they held converse together, and the hours flew by like minutes. Fain would Lanval have lingered in that charmed spot for ever, if the lady herself had not bid him return to Arthur's court, where she promised he should have means of putting to shame all who had scorned him.

At parting she gave him noble gifts—a suit of white armour such as the most cunning smith might have been proud to claim for his handiwork; a curiously worked purse which, she told him, he would always find full of gold, let him spend as he pleased; and, best of all, the assurance that he should see her again.

"One thing only I require of you," was her last word, "that you take heed not to boast of my love. Call me when and where you please, so it be in some secret place, and I will come; but you must never speak of me to mortal ears, on pain of seeing me no more on earth."

Sir Lanval kissed her hand, and vowed by his knighthood that her wishes should be obeyed. Then they took tender leave, promising each other that it was not for long.

Without, a gallant white charger was awaiting the knight, and bore him like the wind to his lodging in the town. There sumptuous furniture and apparel now abounded where he had left bareness and signs of poverty. At the door he was met by a retinue of servants, well provided with new liveries and everything needful for a wealthy household. Astonished, he perceived that he had to do with a queen of fairyland. And when he opened her purse, he found that it verily held an endless supply of gold. The more he took out, the less it ever seemed to be empty.

Lanval rejoiced that he was now able to place no stint on his open-handedness. He hastened to search out all who might be in want or distress, and abundantly relieved them. He feasted the poor; he gave alms to pilgrims; he ransomed prisoners; he became the bountiful patron of minstrels; he heaped rich gifts on his friends and rewards on his followers. Once more his name was everywhere spoken with gratitude and affection, and he held his head high among his fellows at the court. The white armour that had been given him was enchanted against every weapon; so, mounted on his matchless courser, he still overthrew all comers in tourney or battle. But his greatest joy was in seeing his fairy princess; for as often as he repaired to a solitary spot, and called upon her, she would appear, to bestow on him a wealth of bright glances and sweet words that could have made the most wretched of men forget his woes.

One alone grudged the young knight's good fortune. This was the queen, who had brought him to such a point of poverty that he might be fain to sue humbly for her favour. She was sore at heart to see him more and more generous and beloved; and she cast about for new means of venting her ill will upon him.

On the feast of St. John the knights and ladies had gathered to sport and dance in a meadow, whither came also the queen with her maidens. And when she saw that Sir Lanval joined not in the diversions of the others but walked apart, thinking ever of his mistress, she turned aside to him and spoke scornfully, saying that he was not fit to be in the king's service, since he loved no woman, and no woman found him worthy of her love. At this the knight's pride took fire; forgetting the command that had been laid upon him, as well as the reverence due to the queen, he cried:

"Nay, madam; for know that I am beloved by the most beautiful lady in the world!"

"Who dares speak to my face of one more fair than me?" exclaimed the queen with kindling eyes.

"Aye, the least of her maidens is fairer than you," answered Lanval hotly; but, as he spoke, his spotless white armour turned black as coal, and he remembered with dismay how the fairy had bid him tell of her to no mortal ears.

And these words filled up the cup of Guinevere's hatred. Furiously she broke away from him and hurried to her chamber, where she shut herself, weeping for shame and rage, till Arthur returned from hunting; then she presented herself before him with red eyes and dishevelled hair, making loud complaint of the insult she had received that day, and demanding that a heavy punishment should be dealt out to the presumptuous knight who had so set at naught his duty and her charms. And other false and shameful things she laid to his charge, trying to provoke her husband's utmost vengeance. Nor was Arthur unmoved by the dishonour done to his queen. Wrathfully he bid four of his sergeants seek out Sir Lanval, and bring him to answer for what he had said.

Little did Lanval heed this displeasure; a heavier misfortune had fallen upon him, beside which the king's displeasure seemed but a light matter. When Guinevere left him, what would he not have given to recall his rash words? But nothing had he now to give. No sooner had he disobeyed the commands of his mistress than all her gifts melted away like snow. His magic purse was empty; he found his lodging bare as before; his servants had disappeared. He hurried to the wood where they had been wont to meet, and loudly and often called upon the fairy, but only the echoes mocked him. She came not; the charm was broken, and his love was lost for ever.

Bitterly he reproached himself and cursed his folly, but little could this avail him now. Beating his breast and tearing his hair, he fell on the ground as in a swoon, and thus Arthur's officers found him.

"Thou traitor," said the king, when Lanval was brought bound into his presence, "how hast thou stained thy loyalty! What boasts be these that thy mistress is fairer than my queen? Speak and justify thyself, if thou wouldst not be hanged like a thief."

But Sir Lanval's eye quailed not, as he bent before the king and spoke: "My lord, so have I said, and what I have said is true, though I should die for it."

"Now, falsely hast thou spoken, and sorely shalt rue it!" vowed the king, and named twelve lords who should be sworn to sit in judgment on the accused knight.

All were sorry for him, and the noblest champions of the Round Table came forward to offer themselves as sureties that he should appear before the court on the day of trial. But Lanval heeded little what might now be his fate. If he could no longer live in the love of his lady, he could at least expiate his fault by death for her sake.

The day came, and the judges assembled. Some few of them, wishing to make court to the queen, were for condemning the poor knight forthwith; but the most part, knowing her falseness, thought it pity that such a brave man should thus be lost, and were willing to find cause for acquitting him, or at least for changing his sentence from death to banishment. And one of the oldest of the lords spoke thus, careless of Guinevere's frowns.

"Sir Lanval is arraigned because he has boasted his lady to be fairer than the queen. It is right that we have knowledge of the crime, and, therefore, let him be required to bring this lady here that so we may judge whether or no he has spoken truth."

To this all readily agreed; but Sir Lanval shook his head, knowing that he could not call his lady there, or even speak her name; and men murmured that he must die the death.

But as the judges still deliberated, there came to the castle two damsels robed in rich samite, and riding upon royally caparisoned

mules. Dismounting before the king, they let him know how a
great princess was approaching, who desired him to receive her.
Arthur declared that their mistress should have all courteous
entertainment, ordering certain of his knights to attend upon the
damsels. Then he bid the trial proceed, for the queen was urgent
to have that proud traitor condemned without more ado.

The lords were at last about to give sentence when a great cry
was heard without, announcing the arrival of the mistress of the
two damsels. Clad in a wondrous robe of silver sheen, over which
was a purple mantle bordered with ermine, and crowned with a
circlet of gold and gems, she rode upon a milk-white steed, the
housings of which were worth an earldom. On her wrist sat a
falcon that marked her high birth, and behind her ran two gallant
greyhounds of the purest breed. All in the town, old and young,
gentle and simple, had come forth to see her pass, and now, as
she entered the hall of the castle, the whole assembly rose to do
her honour. Every eye could not but gaze upon her, for such a
wonder of beauty and loveliness had never before been seen in
Arthur's land. And well Sir Lanval knew her.

"O lady, I forget all my troubles since I have seen thee once
again!" he cried, stretching his hands towards her; but she
answered him not a word, and passed proudly on to where
the king waited to greet her. Then she mounted the dais on
which sat Guinevere among her maidens, whose beauty grew
pale before hers, as the moon and stars before the sun. Standing
beside the queen and throwing off her mantle, this marvellous
stranger turned herself to address the judges.

"Sirs, ye do wrong to this good knight, and may well see that
he is unjustly accused. I loved him; he hath called me; I am here.
Judge for yourselves which of us two be the fairer."

With one voice all exclaimed that she was fairer than any lady
upon earth. It was in vain for Guinevere to frown and weep; the
king himself exclaimed that she was no peer of this unknown
dame. Lanval had but spoken the truth.

So amidst loud acclamations the knight was justified and let
go free. But little recked he, since his love, taking leave of none
present, after throwing one scornful glance upon the false queen,
had strode from the dais and was already remounting her steed at
the gate of the castle, without a word or a look for him.

"Oh, have pity on me!" he cried in vain. "Why give me my life
when, without thee, it were more bitter than death?"

Still she answered him not, nor so much as turned her head, but
rode away with her attendant damsels. Sir Lanval's horse stood

by the castle gate. In despair he leaped upon its back and spurred wildly after her, none staying him.

By field and forest he followed her, ever crying piteously and beseeching her to speak to him if it were but one word. But in silence she rode swiftly on, till she reached the river bank on which they had first met. There she dismounted and plunged into the deep and rapid stream. The knight, all in mail as he was, did the same, stretching out his arms and trying to seize and hold her. Deeper and deeper she made her way into the water, and on he pressed after her, though the current was strong, and he had much ado to keep his footing. Still deaf to his entreaties, she disappeared below the surface; whereon Lanval, throwing himself forward with a last effort to snatch at her shining robe, was carried away, sank, lost sight and hearing, and gave himself up for dead.

But as the waters closed round his helpless form the lady turned and caught him and bore him with her. And when he came to himself he was lying on a flowery bank, his love bending over him, while, with a radiant smile, she told him that he was forgiven, and that they never more should be parted.

Never again was Sir Lanval seen by mortal eyes. But men tell how, with his bride, he dwells for ever in fairyland. His gallant steed—so the story goes—has ever since roamed riderless through the country. Often has it been seen by peasants and travellers, but it will suffer itself to be approached by none. Every year, on the day when it lost its master, it still comes to the river bank and stands long, neighing loudly and tearing up the ground with its hoofs by the place where Sir Lanval disappeared.

# THE TRUE STORY OF GUENEVER

## by Elizabeth Stuart Phelps

*Both "Blueflow", and "Sir Lanval" considered the faithlessness of Arthur's wife Guinevere. What was the real nature of this lady? Elizabeth Stuart Phelps (1844–1911) used Arthurian imagery as an allegory to consider the plight of women who are victims of themselves. The story is not typically Arthurian, and is one not recognised within the standard Arthurian bibliographies. Miss Phelps, later Mrs. Ward, was a middle-class American writer, social reformer and advocate of women's rights. Although virtually now forgotten, she became famous early in her career with* The Gates Ajar *(1868), a story set in a beautiful afterlife, which brought much solace to thousands of Civil War widows. The following story is reprinted from her collection,* Sealed Orders *(1879).*

In all the wide, dead, old world of story, there is to me no wraith more piteously pursuant than the wraith of Guenever. No other voice has in it the ring of sweet harmonies so intricately bejangled; no other face turns to us eyes of such luminous entreaty from slow descents of despair; no other figure, majestic though in ruins, carries through every strained muscle and tense nerve and full artery so magnetic a consciousness of the deeps of its deserved humiliation and the height of its lost privilege. One pauses as

261

before an awful problem, before the nature of this miserable
lady. A nature wrought, it is plain, of the finer tissues, since it not
only won but returned the love of the blameless king. One follows
her young years with bated breath. We see a delicate, high-strung,
impulsive creature, a trifle mismated to a faultless unimpulsive
man. We shudder to discover in her, before she discovers it for
or in herself, that having given herself to Arthur, she yet has not
given all; that there arises now another self, an existence hitherto
unknown, unsuspected,—a character groping, unstable, unable,
a wandering wind, a mist of darkness, a chaos, over which Arthur
has no empire, of which he has no comprehension, and of which
she—whether of Nature or of training who shall judge?—has
long since discrowned herself the Queen. Guenever is unbalanced,
crude, primeval woman. She must be at once passionately wooed
and peremptorily ruled; and in wooing or in ruling there must be
no despondencies or declines. There are no soundings to be found
in her capacities of loving, as long as the mariner cares to go on
striking for them. At his peril let him hold his plummet lightly or
weary of the sweet toil taken in the measure of it; at his peril, and
at hers.

To Arthur love is a state, not a process; an atmosphere, not
a study; an assurance, not a hope; a fact, not an ideal. He is
serene, reflective, a statesman. The Queen is intense, illeducated,
idle. Undreamed of by the one, unsuspected by the other, they
grew apart. Ungoverned, how shall Guenever govern herself?
Misinterpreted, value herself? Far upon the sunlit moor, a speck
against the pure horizon, Launcelot rides,—silent, subtle, swift,
a Fate rides ever . . .

Poor Guenever! After all, poor Guenever! Song and story, life
and death are so cruel to a woman. To Launcelot, repentant, is
given in later life the best thing left upon earth for a penitent
man—a spotless son. To Launcelot is reserved the aureola of
that blessed fatherhood from which sprang the finder of the Holy
Grail, "pure in thought and word and deed." To Guenever is
given the convent and solitary expiation; to Guenever disgrace,
exile, and despair. Prone upon the convent floor, our fancy leaves
her, kissing Arthur's kingly and forgiving, but departing feet,
half dead for joy because he bids her hope that in some other
world—in which she has not sinned—those spotless feet may
yet return to her, her true and stronger soul return to him; but
neither in this world—never in this. Poor soul! Erring, weak,
unclean; but for that, and that, and that, poor soul! poor soul!
I can never bear to leave her there upon the convent floor. I rebel

against the story. I am sure the half of it was never told us. It must be that Arthur went back some autumn day and brought her gravely home. It *must* be that penitence and patience and acquired purity shall sometime win the respect and confidence of men, as they receive the respect and confidence of God. It must be that at some distant but approaching day *something* of the tenderness of divine stainlessness shall creep into the instinct of human imperfection, and a repentant sinner become to human estimates an object sorrowful, appalling, but appealing, sacred, and sweet.

Who can capture the where, the how, the wherefore of a train of fancy? Was it because I thought of Guenever that I heard the story? Or because I heard the story that I thought of Guenever? My washwoman told it, coming in that bitter day at twilight and sitting by the open fire, as I had bidden her, for rest and warmth. What should *she* know of the Bulfinch and Ellis and Tennyson and Dunlop; that had fallen from my lap upon the cricket at her feet, that she should sit, with hands across her draggled knees, and tell me such a story? Or were Dunlop and the rest untouched upon the library shelves till after she had told it? Whether the legend drew me to the fact, or the fact impelled me to the legend? Indeed, why should I know? It is enough that I heard the story. She told it in her way. I, for lack of her fine, realistic manner, must tell it in my own.

Queen Guenever had the toothache. Few people can look pretty with the toothache. The cheeks of royalty itself will swell, and princely eyelids redden, and queenly lips assume contours as unaesthetic as the kitchen-maids', beneath affliction so plebeian. But Guenever looked pretty.

She abandoned herself to misery, to begin with, in such a royal fashion. And, by the way, we may notice that in nothing does blood "tell" more sharply than in the endurance of suffering. There is a vague monotony in the processes of wearing pleasure. Happy people are very much alike. In the great republic of joy we find tremendous and humiliating levels. When we lift our heads to bear the great crown of pain, all the "points" of the soul begin to make themselves manifest at once.

Guenever yielded herself to this vulgar agony with a beautiful protest. She had protested, indeed, all winter, for that tooth had ached all winter; had never even told her husband of it till yesterday. She had flung herself upon the little crocheted cricket by the sitting-room fire, with her slender, tightly-sleeved arm upon the chintz-covered rocking-chair, and her erect, firm head upon her arm. Into the palm of the other hand the offending cheek crept, like a bird into its nest; with a caressing, nestling movement, as if that tiny hand of hers were the only object in the world to which Guenever did not scorn to say how sorry she was for herself. The color of her cheeks was high but fine. Her eyes—Guenever, as we all know, had brown eyes, more soft than dark—were as dry as they were iridescent. Other women might cry for the toothache! All the curves of the exhausted attitude she had chosen, had in them the bewitching defiance of a hard surrender to a power stronger than herself, with which certain women meet every alien influence, from a needle-prick to a heartbreak. She wore a white apron and a white ribbon against a dress of a soft dark brown color; and the chintz of the happy chair, whose stiff old elbows held her beautiful outline, was of black and gold, with birds of paradise in the pattern. There was a stove, with little sliding doors, in Guenever's sitting-room. Arthur thought it did not use so very much more wood to open the doors, and was far healthier. Secretly he liked to see Guenever in the bird-of-paradise chair, with the moody firelight upon her; but he had never said so—it was not Arthur's "way." Launcelot, now, for instance had said something to that effect several times.

Launcelot, as all scholars of romantic fiction know, was the young bricklayer to whom Arthur and Guenever had rented the spare room when the hard times came on,—a good-natured, inoffensive lodger as one could ask for, and quite an addition, now and then, before the little sliding doors of the open stove, on a sober evening, when she and Arthur were dull, as Guenever had said. To tell the truth, Arthur was often dull of late, what with being out of work so much, and the foot he lamed with a rusty nail. King Arthur, it is unnecessary to add, was a master carpenter.

King Arthur came limping in that evening, and found the beautiful, protesting, yielding figure in the black and golden chair. The Queen did not turn as he came in. One gets so used to one's husband! And the heavy, uneven step he left upon the floor jarred upon her aching nerves. Launcelot, when he had come, about an hour since, to inquire how she was, had bounded down the stairs as merrily as a school-boy, as lightly as a hare; and turned his knightly feet a-tip-toe as he crossed the room to say how sorry he felt for her; to stand beside her in the moody light, to gaze intently down upon her, then to ask why Arthur was not yet at home; to wonder were she lonely; to say he liked the ribbon at her throat; to say he liked a hundred things; to say it quite unmanned him when he saw her suffer; to start as if he would say more to her, and turn as if he would have touched her, and fly as if he dared not, and out into the contending, mad March night. For the wind blew that night! To the last night of her life Queen Guenever will not forget the way it blew!

"Take some Drops," said Arthur. What a tiresome manner Arthur had of putting things! Some Drops, indeed! There was nothing Guenever wanted to take. She wanted, in fact, to *be* taken; to be caught and gathered to her husband's safe, broad breast; to be held againt his faithful heart; to be fondled and crooned over and cuddled. She would have her aching head imprisoned in his healthy hands. And if he should think to kiss the agonizing cheek, as *she* would kiss a woman's cheek if she loved her and she had the toothache? But Arthur never thought! Men were so dull at things. Only women knew how to take care of one another. Only women knew the infinite fine languages of love. A man was tender when he thought of it, in a blunt, broad way.

There might be men—One judged somewhat from voices; and a tender voice—Heaven forgive her! Though he spoke with the tongues of all angels, and the music of all spheres, and the tenderness of all loves, what was any man's mortal voice to her—a queen, the wife of Arthur, blameless king of men?

The wife of Arthur started from the old chair whereon the birds of paradise seemed in the uneven firelight to be fluttering to and fro. The color on her cheeks had deepened painfully, and she lifted her crowned head with a haughty motion towards her husband's face.

"I'm sure I'd try the Drops," repeated Arthur.

"I'll have it out!" snapped Guenever. "I don't believe a word of its being neuralgia. I'll have them all out, despite him!"

Guenever referred to the court dentist.

"I'll have them out and make a fright of myself once for all, and go mumbling round. I doubt if anybody would find it made any difference to anybody how anybody looked."

It cannot be denied that there was a certain remote vagueness in this remark. King Arthur, who was of a metaphysical temperament, sighed. He was sorry for the Queen—so sorry that he went and set the supper-table, to save her from the draughts that lurked even in the royal pantry that mad March night. He loved the Queen—so much that he would have been a happy man to sit in the bird-of-paradise rocking-chair and kiss that aching, sweet cheek of hers till supper-time to-morrow, if that would help her. But he supposed, if she had the toothache, she wouldn't want to be touched. He knew he shouldn't. So, not knowing what else to do, he just limped royally about and got the supper, like a dear old dull king as he was.

If Queen Guenever appreciated this little kingly attention, who can say? She yielded herself with a heavy sigh once more to the arms of the chintz rocking-chair, and ached in silence. Her face throbbed in time to the pulses of the wind. What a wind it was! It seemed to come from immense and awful distances, gathering slow forces as it fled, but fleeing with a compressed, rebellious roar, like quick blood chained within the tissues of a mighty artery, beating to and fro as it rushed to fill the heart of the black and lawless night.

It throbbed so resoundingly against the palace windows that the steps of Launcelot, blending with it, did not strike the Queen's ears till he stood beside her, in the firelight. Arthur, setting the supper-table, had heard the knightly knock, and bidden their friend and lodger enter (as King Arthur bade him always) with radiant, guileless eyes.

Sir Launcelot had a little bottle in his hand. He had been to the druggist's. There was a druggist to the king just around the corner from the palace.

"It's laudanum," said Launcelot. "I got it for your tooth. I wish you'd try it. I couldn't bear to see you suffer."

"I'm half afraid to have Guenever take laudanum," said Arthur, coming up. "It takes such a mite of anything to influence my wife. The doctor says it is her nerves. I know he wouldn't give her laudanum when her arm was hurt. But it's just as good in you, Sir Launcelot."

Guenever thought it very good in him. She lifted her flushed and throbbing face to tell him so; but, in point of fact, she told him nothing. For something in Sir Launcelot's eyes, the wife of Arthur could not speak.

She motioned him to put the bottle on the shelf, and signified by a slight gesture peculiar to herself—a little motion of the shoulders, as tender as it was imperious—her will that he should leave her.

Now Launcelot, we see, was plainly sorry for Guenever. Was it then a flitting tenderer than sorrow that she had seen within his knightly eyes? Only Guenever will ever know; for Arthur, on his knees upon the crocheted cricket before the palace fire, was toasting graham bread.

Guenever, on her knees before the rocking-chair, sat very still. Her soft brown eyes, wide open, almost touched the cool, smooth chintz where the birds of paradise were flying on a pall-black sky. It seemed to her strained vision, sitting so, that the birds flew from her as she looked at them, and vanished; and that the black sky alone was left. The eyes that watched the golden birds departing were fair and still, like the eyes of children just awake. It was a child's mouth, as innocent and fair, that Guenever lifted just that minute suddenly to Arthur, with a quick, unqueenly, appealing smile.

"Kiss me, dear?" said Guenever, somewhat disconnectedly.

"Why, yes!" said Arthur.

He wasn't able to follow the train of thought exactly. It was never clear to him why Guenever should want to be kissed precisely in the *middle* of a slice of toast. And the graham bread was burned. But he kissed the Queen, and they had supper; and he eat the burnt slice himself, and said nothing about it. That, too, was one of Arthur's "ways."

"Only," said Guenever, as the King contentedly finished the last black crust, "I wish the wind would stop."

"What's the trouble with the wind?" asked Arthur. "I thought it was well enough."

"It must be well enough," said the Queen, and she shook her little white fist at the window. "It *shall* be well enough!"

For the pulse of the wind ran wildly against the palace as Guenever was speaking, and throbbed and bounded and beat, as if the heart of the March night would break.

All this was long, long, long ago. How long Guenever can never tell. Days, weeks, months,—few or many swift, or slow—of that she cannot answer. Passion takes no count of time; peril marks no hours or minutes; wrong makes its own calendar; and misery has solar systems peculiar to itself. It seemed to her years, it seemed to her days, according to her tossed, tormented mood.

It is in the nature of all passionate and uncontrolled emotion to prey upon and weaken the forces of reflective power, as much as it is in the nature of controlled emotion to strengthen them. Guenever found in herself a marked instance of this law. It seemed to her sometimes that she knew as little of her own story as she did of that of any erring soul at the world's width from her. It seemed to her that her very memory had yielded in the living of it, like the memory of a person in whose brain insidious disease had begun to fasten itself. So subtle and so sure had been the disease which gnawed at the Queen's heart, that she discovered with a helpless terror—not unlike that one might feel in whom a cancerous process had been long and undetected working—that her whole nature was lowering its tone in sympathy with her special weakness. She seemed suddenly to have become, or to feel herself become, a poisoned thing.

We may wonder, does not the sense of guilt—not the sensitiveness to, but the *sense* of guilt—come often as a sharp and sudden experience? Queen Guenever, at least, felt stunned by it. Distinctly, as if it and she were alone in the universe, she could mark the awful moment when it came to her. Vivid as a blood-red rocket shot against her stormy sky, that moment whirred and glared before her.

It was a fierce and windy night, like that in which she had the toothache, when she and the King had eaten such a happy supper of burnt toast (for *hers* was burnt, too, although she wouldn't have said so for the world, since the King had got so tired and warm about it). How happy they had been that night! Sir Launcelot did not come again after supper, dimly feeling, despite the laudanum, that the Queen had dismissed him for the evening. She and Arthur had the evening to themselves. It was the first evening they had been alone together for a long time. Arthur sat in the chintz rocking-chair. He held her in his lap. He comforted her poor cheek with his huge, warm hand. His shining, kingly eyes looked down on her like stars from Heaven. He said:—

"If it wasn't for your tooth, little woman, how happy we would be."

And Guenever had laughed and said: "What's a toothache? I'm content, if you are." And then they laughed together, and the golden birds upon the old chair had seemed to flit and sing before her; and brighter and sweeter, as they watched her, glimmered Arthur's guileless eyes.

The stars were fallen now; the heavens were black; the birds of paradise had flown; the wind was abroad mightily and cold; there was snow upon the ground; and she and Launcelot were fleeing through it and weeping as they fled.

Guenever at least, was weeping. All the confusion of the miserable states and processes which had led her to this hour had cleared away, murky clouds from a lurid sky. Suddenly, by a revelation awful as some that might shock a soul upon the day of doom, she knew that she was no longer a bewildered or a pitiable, but an evil creature.

A gossip in the street, an old neighbor who used to borrow eggs of her, had spoken in her hearing, as she and Launcelot passed swiftly through the dark, unrecognized, at the corner of the Palace Court, and had said:—

"Guenever has fled with Launcelot. The Queen has left the King. All the world will know it by to-morrow."

These words fell upon the Queen's ear distinctly. They tolled after her through the bitter air. She fled a few steps, and stopped.

"Launcelot!" she cried, "what have we done? Why are we here? Let me go home! Oh! what have I done?"

She threw out her arms with that tender, imperious gesture of hers—more imperious than tender now—which Launcelot knew so well.

Strange! Oh! strange and horrible! How came it to be thus with her? How came she to be alone with Launcelot in the blinding night? *The Queen fled from the King? Guenever false to Arthur?*

Guenever, pausing in the cruel storm, looked backward at her footsteps in the falling snow. Her look was fixed and frightened as a child's. Her memory seemed to her like snow of all that must have led her to this hour.

She knew not what had brought her hither, nor the way by which she came. She was a creature awakened from a moral catalepsy. With the blessed impulse of the Prodigal, old as Earth's error, sweet as Heaven's forgiveness, she turned and cried: "I repent! I repent! I will go home to my husband, before it is too late!"

"It is too late!" said a bitter voice beside her. "It is too late already for repentance, Guenever."

Was it Launcelot who spoke, or the deadly wind that shrieked in passing her? Guenever could never say. A sickening terror took possession of her. She felt her very heart grow cold, as she stood and watched her foot-prints, on which the snow was falling wild and fast.

It was a desolate spot in which she and Launcelot stood. They had left the safe, sweet signs of holy human lives and loves behind them. They were quite alone. A wide and windy moor stretched from them to a forest, on which a horror of great darkness seemed to hang. Behind them, in the deserted distance, gleamed the palace lights. Within these the Queen saw, or fancied that she saw, the shadow of the King, moving sadly to and fro, against the drawn curtain, from behind which the birds of paradise had fled forever.

From palace to wilderness her footsteps lay black in the falling snow. As she gazed, the increasing storm drifted, and here and there they blurred and whitened over and were lost to sight.

So she, too, would whiten over her erring way. Man was not more merciless than Nature.

"I will retrace them all!" cried Guenever.

"You can never retrace the first of them," said again bitterly beside her Launcelot or the deathly wind. "Man is more merciless than Nature. There is no way back for you to the palace steps. In all the kingdom, there is no soul to bid you welcome, should you dare return. The Queen can never come to her throne again."

"I seek no throne!" wailed Guenever. "I ask for no crown! All I want is to go back and to be clean. I'll crawl on my knees to the palace, if I may be clean."

But again said sneeringly to her that voice, which was either of Launcelot or of the wind:—

"Too late! too late! too late! You can never be clean! You can never be clean!"

"Launcelot," said Guenever, rallying sharply and making, as it seemed, a mighty effort to collect control over the emotion which was mastering her, "Launcelot, there is some mistake about this. I never meant to do wrong. I never said I would leave the King. There is some mistake. Perhaps I have been dreaming or have been ill. Let me go home at once to the King!"

"There is no mistake," said once more the voice, which seemed neither of Launcelot nor of the wind, but yet akin to both; "and you are not dreaming and you can never return to the King. The thing that is done is done. Sorrow and longing are dead to help you. Agony and repentance are feeble friends. Neither man nor Nature can wash away a stain."

"God is more merciful!" cried Guenever, in the tense, shrill voice of agony, stung beyond endurance. It seemed to her that nature could bear no more. It seemed to her that she had never before this moment received so much as an intellectual perception of the guiltiness of guilt. Now mind and heart, soul and body throbbed with the throes of it. She quivered, she struggled, she rebelled with the accumulated fervors and horrors of years of innocence. But it seemed to her as if the soil of sin eat into her like caustic, before whose effects the most compassionate or skillful surgeon is powerless. She writhed with her recoil from it. She shrank from it with terror proportioned to her sense of helplessness and stain.

"They who are only afflicted know nothing of misery!" moaned Guenever. "There *is* no misery but guilt!"

She flung herself down in the storm upon the snow.

"God loves!" cried Guenever. "Christ died! I *will* be clean!"

It seemed then suddenly to the kneeling woman, that He whose body and blood were broken for tempted souls appeared to seek her out across the desolated moor. The Man whose stainless lips were first to touch the cup of the Holy Grael, which all poor souls should after Him go seeking up and down upon the earth, stood in the pure white snow, and, smiling, spoke to her.

"*Though your sins,*" he said, "*are scarlet, they shall be white.*"

He pointed, as he spoke, across the distance; past the safe, sweet homes of men and women, toward the palace gates. It seemed to Guenever that he spoke again and said:—

"Return!"

"Through those black footsteps?" sobbed the Queen.

But when she looked again, behold! each black and bitter trace was gone. Smooth across them all, fair, pure, still, reposed the stainless snow. She could not find them, though she would. They were blotted out by Nature, as they were forgiven of God. Alas! alas! if man were but half as compassionate or kind. If Arthur—

She groveled on the ground where the sacred Feet had stood, which now were vanished from her. Wretched woman that she was! Who should deliver her from this bondage to her life's great holy love? If Arthur would but open the door for her in the fair distance, where the palace windows shone; if he would take a single step toward her where she kneeled within the wilderness; if he would but loiter toward her where that Other had run swiftly, and speak one word of quiet to her where He had sung her songs of joy! But the palace door was shut. The King took no step toward the wilderness. The King was mute as death and cold as his own white soul. On Arthur's throne was never more a place for Guenever.

Guenever, in the desert, stretched her arms out blindly across the blotted footprints to the palace lights.

Oh! Arthur. Oh! Arthur, Arthur, *Arthur.* . . .

"Why, Pussy!" said Arthur. "What's the matter?"

However unqueenly, Pussy was one of the royal pet names.

"My little woman! Guenever! My darling! Why do you call me so?"

Why did she call him indeed? Why call for anything? Why ask or need or long? In his great arms he held her. To his true breast he folded her. Safe in his love he sheltered her. From heaven the stars of his eyes looked down on her. As those may look who wake in heaven, whose anguished soul had thought to wake in hell, looked Guenever. She was his honored wife. There was no Launcelot, no wilderness. The soul which the King had crowned with his royal love was clean, was clean, was clean!

She hid her scarlet face upon his honest heart and seemed to mutter something about "dreams." It was all that she could say. There are dreams that are epochs in life.

"But it wasn't a dream, you see," said Arthur. "We've had a scare over you, Guenever. You took the laudanum, after all."

"Launcelot's laudanum! Indeed, no! I took the drops, as I told you, Arthur."

"The bottles stood together on the shelf, and you made the blunder," said Arthur anxiously. "We think you must have taken a tremendous dose. I've sent Launcelot for the Doctor. And Nabby Jones, she was in to borrow eggs, and she said a little camphire would be good for you. She just went home to get it. But I've been frightened about you, Guenever," said Arthur. Arthur spoke in his own grave and repressed manner. But he was very pale. His lips, as the Queen crept, sobbing, up to touch them, trembled.

"Well, well," he said, "we won't talk about it now." Guenever did not want to talk. She wished Nabby Jones would stay away, with her camphire. She wished Launcelot would never come. Upon her husband's heart she lay. Within her husband's eyes the safe, home fire-light shone. Across the old chintz chair the birds of paradise were fluttering like birds gone wild with joy.

Without, the wind had lulled, the storm had ceased, and through the crevices in the windows had sifted tiny drifts of cool, clean snow.

And this, know all men henceforth by these presents, is the true story of Guenever the Queen.

# SIR BORLAYS AND THE DARK KNIGHT
## by Anthony Armstrong

*This is the first of two humorous Arthurian spoofs. I was delighted to encounter this story in the December 1933 issue of* The Strand Magazine. *To my knowledge it is not listed in any Arthurian bibliography. Anthony Armstrong was the pen name of George Anthony Armstrong Willis (1897–1976), a prolific writer of humorous stories and sketches, as well as historical and crime novels. He began writing for* Punch *in 1924, and produced his last book,* One Jump Ahead *in 1972. He has rapidly been forgotten, though some of you may recall the film* The Man Who Haunted Himself *(1970), starring Roger Moore, which was adapted from Armstrong's novel* The Strange Case of Mr. Pelham *(1957).*

Christmas afternoon long ago, in the days when knighthood was in flower and chivalry was so rampant that a girl could hardly go for a quiet country walk without being forcibly rescued from something or someone, a certain Sir Borloys, a minor segment of King Arthur's Round Table, was riding in full armour through a wood. He was young, he was passably good-looking, *but*—unfortunately Sir Borloys was stout. Worse still, and in spite of trying everything for it—except less food and more exercise—he was daily growing stouter.

This steady increase of bulk so early in life worried Sir Borloys considerably, because he rather fancied himself with the ladies of the Court. When first he joined up he had, as his friend, Sir Perivale, put it, "practically had to keep them off with a club, dear boy," but this last year—just when he had decided that after all it was not fair to the sex to remain single any longer—he had begun to detect them laughing covertly at his shadow on the arras, or watching him with unflattering interest at the tenth course of the weekly banquet, or talking in audible undertones about the strain on certain equatorial plates of his armour. In short, whenever he now showed signs of forming an intimacy with any one of them, view matrimony, they just didn't, as Sir Perivale put it, "seem to respond, old boy." If his figure went on increasing at this rate, thought Sir Borloys, moodily, not only would he fail to secure any sort of wife at all, but he would even have to get a bigger and stronger charger.

In between pondering on his increasing girth Sir Borloys peered anxiously about him into the snow-covered and tangled under-growth. It was getting dusk, he had long ago finished all the sandwiches in the haversack-safe attached to his armour, and his thoughts dwelt anxiously on the roast turkey and plum-pudding which in a couple of hours time would be being carried round and round the Round Table. Yet he was far from home and he had not done his good deed for the day, which, as it was Christmas, ought really to be an extra special one. He was still hoping to see a youth struggling with a band of robbers, or an old woman struggling with a heavy load of sticks, or, better still, a damsel in distress. It was just the season for damsels in distress, and the wood he was in, being reported to be strictly preserved by a local Ogre, was, as Sir Perivale had told him only the day before, "simply crawling with 'em, dear boy."

Sir Borloys had at last been forced to the conclusion that all the Ogres of the neighbourhood were keeping Christmas at home and that he had better ride back to Court as soon as possible and hope to get in on a spare drumstick, when a young man came suddenly running out of the wood.

"Ha!" cried Sir Borloys. Lowering the visor of his great helm, he at once put himself in a fighting attitude ready to repel the pursuing robbers, while his horse, who knew what this sort of thing meant, braced its legs to stand all shocks and dropped into a doze till the affair should have blown over.

"Oh, Sir Knight, I crave thy assistance," cried the youth, dropping on one knee in the snow.

"And shalt have't. Art frighted? Think not on't," responded

Sir Borloys, nobly. His answer, a difficult one at the best of times, sounded, owing to his lowered visor, like water-hammer in a faulty pipe. It startled the young man considerably, and for a moment he even appeared to consider running back into the wood.

"Well, where are they?" asked Sir Borloys, after a minute's tense wait.

"Who, Sir Knight?"

"The robbers, you fool," snapped Sir Borloys in muffled tones, struggling with his visor, which was an old model and apt at times to shut down completely.

"There aren't any. I only want help for a rescue." He became more communicative. "There's a castle near by and a girl . . ."

"A damsel," corrected the knight, sternly, who had by now got his face tolerably clear of his armour plate.

"A damsel shut up in it . . ."

"Incarcerated."

"Incar—just as you say. Against her will . . ."

"In distress!"

"And there's a wicked knight called the Dark Knight who keeps her . . ."

"When you say 'keeps her,'" again interrupted Sir Borloys, severely, "you mean 'keeps her in durance vile.' Anyway, who is she?"

"My sister, Sir Knight. And I pray you, win her freedom for me!"

Sir Borloys, glancing at the young man, saw that he was handsome and reflected that the least a rescued damsel could do in those days was to offer to marry her preserver. "Ay, that will I right speedily," he cried. He thrust two fingers into his helm, twirled his moustache gallantly and became quite colloquial. "Nice-looking kid?" he queried, with assumed casualness.

"As fair as a May morn. Nay, fairer."

"Make it a June morn then."

"Thou hast said 't, Sir Knight. July even, if you like."

"July it is. And she is as good as rescued," replied Sir Borloys, decisively. He drew his sword, and shouting, "For chivalry! For chivalry!" set spurs to his horse and galloped headlong into the wood.

One minute later he returned with a great air of nonchalance.

"Wood's looking very beautiful this evening. Lovely for a trot round! Snow effect on the boughs terribly attractive! Hrmha! By the way, I don't think you told me *exactly* where the castle was."

"I'll show you. You see, I'd have rescued her myself, only it's a job for two. My sister's name is Yseult," he began, as they set off, "and she is imprisoned in a tall tower."

"Will she let down her hair for me to climb up?" asked Sir Borloys, a stickler for old customs and the Spirit of Romance.

The young man looked at him. "No," he said, briefly.

The Knight sighed. It seemed that in these modern times neither the Spirit of Romance nor maidens' hair could stand any little strain.

"There's a long ladder," the youth resumed, "by the Castle toolshed at the back, and two of us could put it up. Then I could go up while you—er—guarded the bottom. In case the Dark Knight comes upon us."

"You wouldn't prefer me to carry the damsel down?" Sir Borloys was not afraid of Dark Knights, but he did rather fancy himself carrying this good-looking young man's sister in his arms.

The youth glanced again at Sir Borloys and thought the ladder would never stand it. But he didn't put it quite like that. He said politely that his sister might be a little nervous of being carried down ladders by strange knights, besides, it would be presumptuous for a young chap like himself to take the post of honour at the foot.

SIR BORLOYS ruminated a moment, appeared to think of something important, and asked:—

"Have you any sandwiches or anything?"

"Only a few biscuits for the night."

"That's considerate of you," said the Knight, and took them.

They soon reached the castle, a forbidding mass of masonry with one tall tower.

"Any watch-dogs?" whispered Sir Borloys, finishing the last biscuit and still feeling just as hungry, for he took a good bit of filling these days.

"No. Nothing except a dragon."

"A dragon?" Sir Borloys looked a little startled. He thought the young man might have mentioned that before. Not that a dragon or two made any difference to a Knight of the Round Table, but still one just liked to know.

"It's all right. He's quite a tame dragon."

"Quite *tame*?"

"Absolutely. Only kept to scare off wandering minstrels and tramps and so on."

"Hm!" said Sir Borloys, getting slowly off his horse and tying it to a tree.

"Come and get the ladder," continued the young man.

"This is all very well," grumbled the Knight, "but I'm not used to conducting rescues in this underhand way. I shall go and challenge the Dark Knight to single combat. And when I've worsted him . . ."

"Can't we get the ladder up first? I mean, supposing he worsts *you*, my sister will still be up there."

Sir Borloys agreed reluctantly. The Spirit of Romance was indeed, as Sir Perivale had said only last week, "passing right out, dear boy."

Leaning a heavy ladder up against a tower in the frosty dusk of a Christmas evening, with only a young man to help one, is a tricky business at the best of times. If one is in full armour and one's visor keeps shutting down completely when one most wants to see, it is darn difficult. And if a large and lumbering dragon suddenly materialises from nowhere and starts snuffing noisily round one's heels for overlooked biscuit crumbs just when one has got the thing balanced precariously upright, it begins to feel, as Sir Perivale would have put it, "like a bally circus turn, old fellow."

"He doesn't bite," panted the young man.

"I dare say not," rejoined Sir Borloys, "but his breath is so fiery. It's heating up my back-plate." He kicked out petulantly at the dragon and landed it a good wipe in the starboard slats.

"Woo-*oof*!" went the dragon in surprised tones, and retiring a short distance sat down in the snow to meditate on the strange thing that had happened, thus giving the Knight and his helper a chance to get the ladder up against the tower.

"Goof-woof-woof," began the dragon suddenly, having decided it was all a game. It advanced once more with a playful rush which almost bowled Sir Borloys over into a snowdrift.

"Here! Sorcerer's curses on the thing!" snapped the Knight. His first impulse was to reach for his sword, then as he surveyed the dragon's vast though friendly bulk he changed his mind, smiled nervously, and said, "Good Dragon, then!"

"Galumph!" remarked the dragon, as who should say, "Same to you." It suddenly let out a blast of playful flame and sat up and begged, an action which Sir Borloys misinterpreted. His backward start of apprehension shook his visor down again and once more cut him off from communication with the outside world.

He levered it up at last, just in time to hear a stern voice say, "*Pongo!* Kennel!" and to see the dragon creeping off shame-facedly with as much of its tail between its legs as it could get. Facing him, clad in black armour, was the menacing figure of the Dark Knight. Of the youth there was now no trace, except a bush still quivering at the forest's edge as if at the passage of some rapidly moving body.

"Well, where's the beard and sack of toys?" asked the new-comer, chattily. "Or have you come about the pipes?"

"Ha!" retorted Sir Borloys, fiercely—his usual exclamation when preparing for battle—and swiftly put himself in a state of defence at every point.

But the Dark Knight, an elderly man with a humorous twist to his visored bassinet, was apparently quite unconventional.

"So much better to have a *tame* dragon, isn't it?" he began, chattily. "I mean, it always gives one warning and yet, not being fierce, it doesn't run the risk of getting killed by visitors. And quite house-trained—even castle-trained, to be precise. Good idea, don't you think?"

Sir Borloys was nonplussed. In answer to his "Ha!" the fellow should have retorted, "Have at thee!" or something, and then had at him. Perhaps he hadn't heard.

"Ha!" he repeated more suddenly, and added involuntarily a second later, "Merlin's bane on this visor!"

"Wing-nut thread's worn, I should think," suggested the Dark Knight, affably. Sir Borloys decided that this was absolutely all wrong. They should have each been on guard five minutes ago, and instead of that here they were still chatting about house-dragons and armour defects. And the annoying thing was that the Dark Knight was right: it was a worn thread.

He tightened the wing-nut warily and then cried, "Have at thee! For King Arthur!"

"We can't have at each other properly here," objected the other. "Not even for King Arthur. Close of play will be declared as soon as we've begun, owing to the failing light. Come round to the hard-combat-court at the back, where I've got everything ready and . . ."

"Foul imprisoner of helpless . . ."

"What shall it be?" asked the other, beginning to lead the way. "Tournament knock-out? Or three rounds Mortal Combat on points? Poisoned weapons and magic barred, of course."

Sir Borloys here lost his grip of things altogether. He had never before had an adventure so strange as this, not even when he had tried to rescue a damsel from a magician's cavern and had unexpectedly found himself for the best part of a day figuring as a double-headed lemur. Like a man in a dream he allowed himself to be conducted round to the back of the castle.

Here squires were already holding torches round an open space and an elderly magician was waiting with a large bell in his hand. There were also, Sir Borloys noted at once, servants with trays of refreshments.

"This is Magus. He's a Qualified Umpire. Or we'll fight without, if you prefer it. But Magus is absolutely unbiased and knows Jousting Rules backwards. Magus. Meet Sir——?"

"Borloys."

"Sir Borloys. Of King Arthur's Court, Magus, I feel certain? He has the Arthurian gift of gratuitous interference. We were just going to have a short combat."

At the word "combat" Sir Borloys began to find himself again.

"Out, dastard!" he cried in a ringing voice, and following it up with a mighty roar of "On guard!" he leapt into the open space—and a moment later heard the Dark Knight saying, kindly: "You really must let my man fix that wing-nut for you."

Sir Borloys gave an echoing "Nay!" like a war-horse, and hastily propped the visor open with a small spanner from his armour repair pocket. Then shouting. "An Arthur! An Arthur!" he rushed upon his foe.

The fight was a bloodthirsty one and, worse still for one of Sir Borloys's stoutness, extremely fatiguing. Blows rang back and forth on helm and gorget, camail and bassinet, like a smith striking upon his anvil. Sparks flew. Spectators cheered and made excited bets. Some tough eggs at the back did quite a spot of barracking. Magus muttered powerful incantations into the recesses of his beard, and now and then rang his bell in order to caution one or other of the combatants for striking out of turn. The fight, however, appeared evenly contested, and little damage occurred, except on one occasion when Sir Borloys's visor nut failed again and he had to strike without aim for three turns. By the third he had got completely off his bearings and nearly decapitate a ringside onlooker. Magus, however, only told the man severely off for getting in the way and changed him into a scarlet tortoise till breakfast-time as a punishment. After which there was but little demand for ringside seats.

At the end of the third round Magus rang the bell twice and the Dark Knight walked to the side.

"Interval for refreshments," announced Magus, and Sir Borloys, who was about to accuse his opponent of weakening, beat him to the side by three seconds.

If the fight had been so far evenly contested the interval was entirely in Sir Borloy's favour. He only spoke twice, on each occasion to remark—with his mouth full—that the Dark Knight's chef was the best he had ever come across.

When at last every plate was empty, he replaced his helm, tightened up his vambraces and rerebraces, let out his mainbraces and prepared to resume battle. He felt more of a man now: indeed, he *was* more of a man. He shook his sword, skilfully changed a hiccup of repletion into a "Ha!" of aggression, and added, "Have at thee once more," to give verisimilitude.

They had only been battling a further five minutes when the Dark Knight appeared to have an idea. Instead of delivering his blow, he stopped again.

"I say, Sir Borloys?" he called. "One minute."

A muffled booming only resulted from the interior of Sir Borloys's armour, and the Dark Knight called again, accompanying his summons with a polite knock on his opponent's front breastplate.

Part of Sir Borloy's face appeared abruptly at the fanlight.

"What?" he panted, expectantly, hoping against hope that it might be the arrival of more refreshments.

"Just one question?"

"Well?" growled the other. Dash it all, a combat was a combat, not an opportunity for small talk. Refreshment, of course, was quite a different matter.

"I forgot to ask: what are you fighting me for?"

Though a trifle surprised, Sir Borloys knew the answer to this one.

"I am come to rescue a fair damsel in distress, cruelly immured by force in you tower," he cried, rapidly.

"Beautifully put!" said old Magus. "Charming! Charming!"

"Come again?" requested the Dark Knight, after a moment's polite thought.

Sir Borloys came again. "And when thou hast cried 'Quarter!' I shall bear her away to safety—and she will become my wife," he added. Remembering how good-looking the girl's brother had been, he already, such was the power of romance in those days, felt he was deeply in love with the fair Yseult. Moreover, did not King Arthur himself always encourage each unmarried Knight to provide a Home for a Rescued Girl?

"You will really marry her?" asked the Dark Knight.

"I will."

The other dropped his shield and sword and advanced with outstretched hand.

"My dear fellow," he cried. "Why didn't you say all this before? I didn't know you were just conducting a rescue. I thought you'd come to convert me to Christianity or Temperance, or something. You Knights of King Arthur are so—er—— " he tried to think of a word which meant "interfering", but didn't sound like it. "So chivalrous," he concluded.

"I don't quite understand," stammered Sir Borloys. "I came here to rescue a dam—— "

"Damsel in distress, cruelly immured—yes, yes, I've got that bit now. Well, I'll help you."

"Help me?"

"Yes, to rescue her. Come along!"

"But—— "

"And you'll stay to out Yuletide banquet afterwards, of course."

Sir Borloys understood this last part and brightened perceptibly. That chef was, as Sir Perivale would have said, "an absolute one-er, old boy."

Then he found that the Dark Knight, having dismissed the squires and sent the servants off on errands, was already leading the way round to the front of the castle, followed only by Magus and his bell.

"This is all wrong," began Sir Borloys. "I—— " The rest of his sentence once more devolved into an internal mumbling as the spanner holding his visor open slipped from its position.

"I really think," said the Dark Knight, as he helped him in friendly fashion, "you'd better give up this old-pattern helmet. It's not really efficient, you know. A bassinet's so much more useful—in many ways. Don't wriggle so; I can't fix it."

"Spanner's dropped down *inside*," complained Sir Borloys. "It tickles."

"We'll take off your inspection plate and get it out."

"Haven't got an inspection plate."

"Then you'll have to take off your armour. Where's your undressing spanner?"

"That's the one inside," pointed out Sir Borloys, briefly.

The Dark Knight laughed loudly. "That's good, isn't it, Magus?"

"Eh?"

"The spanner inside is the one he wants."

"What one? Inside what?"

"Oh, never mind. You'll see the joke later. A bit short on humour," he whispered to Sir Borloys. "Now come along to the rescue."

Sir Borloys soon found himself again at the tower, where the ladder still stood. This Dark Knight was too much for him altogether.

"I don't really see that you ought to be here at all," he began, petulantly.

"My dear fellow. You must have *someone* to hold the ladder for you. You're no light weight. By the way, you ought to take something for it."

Sir Borloys, who had got one foot on the ladder, took it off again in order to tell the Dark Knight what he *had* taken for it. He expended ten minutes on this before he turned reluctantly to the ladder again. It was his subject.

The Dark Knight yawned. "Quite, quite! But you haven't tried Magus's special dope, have you? The Magus Weight-Reducer for Portly Knights. Infallible!"

Sir Borloys once more took his foot off the rung.

"Infallible?"

"Yes. Reduced me two stone the first time. At least, the second time, to be precise. First time it only turned me apple-green. But that was because Magus had got it confused with some stuff he'd mixed up for an insolent servant."

"I'd like to hear more of this," began Sir Borloys, eagerly. "You see, my family magician said that my case was—— "

"What about this rescue?" interrupted the Dark Knight. "You can tell me all that afterwards, at the banquet."

"Oh—er—yes." He began to ascend ponderously. The ladder creaked and somewhere inside him the missing spanner rattled.

Half-way he called back: "Which is the room?" For the end of the ladder rested between two windows, and Sir Borloys, though he did not in the least mind bursting into a maiden's bedchamber in the name of chivalry, did not want to come unannounced upon the Seneschal or even the Head Parloure Mayde.

"On the left."

Sir Borloys continued. With some gruntings he at last crawled through the window. There was almost at once a maidenly cry of delight, and he reappeared with a figure muffled in a travelling cloak and carrying a considerable amount of hand luggage.

The ladder bent like a bow, and the Dark Knight watched apprehensively till the other, puffing and panting, reached the ground, whereupon he wrung his hand with enthusiasm.

"I congratulate you! A most daring rescue. All Christendom will ring with your fame. Minstrels will sing of how Sir Borloys broke into the Dark Knight's castle and rescued a fayre young damosel from durance vile and married her and——What's the matter?" he broke off, ominously.

For, now that she had finished busily checking over her luggage and had unwrapped herself, Sir Borloys was gazing for the first time on the face of the fayre young damosel he had rescued, and had sustained a certain shock. For, though probably still a damosel, she was not particularly fayre, nor was she particularly young. Momentarily Sir Borloys wondered whether he hadn't got the Dark Knight's lady herself, or even the Head Parloure Mayde. Apparently, however, he had not, for next minute she had flung her arms tightly round his neck and vibrated "My preserver!"

"Eh?" stammered Sir Borloys. Over her head he signalled frantically to the Dark Knight, "Is this the one?"

The Dark Knight signalled back grimly that it was.

"Ah," breathed the lady, coyly, into Sir Borloys's gorget, "I cannot resist your importunity, Sir Knight. Yes, in gratitude for your noble rescue I *will* consent to become your wife."

Sir Borloys by now didn't see eye to eye with her in this. He attempted a strategical retreat. "Here, I—what I mean is this isn't a real rescue, you know. I mean, I've only been, so to speak, employed to do it by your——Well, you see, it was like this: I was riding through a wood—— "

But before he could explain a servant came running up to the Dark Knight, who had tactfully moved some distance away.

"Oh, my lord, woe upon this Christmas Day! The Lady Yseult is gone from her chamber. Shall I rouse the men-at-arms in pursuit?"

"How now, varlet!" cried the Dark Knight, falling into such a furious rage that Sir Borloys had to come over and intervene. For the chap to pretend now to be angry on hearing of the disappearance of a lady he had himself helped to escape was really, he felt, carrying unconventionality too far. Besides, he had just had what Sir Perivale would have called "an absolute stroke of genius, old boy."

"I am overcome by your emotion, Sir Knight," he said, rapidly. "And we of Arthur's Court can be chivalrous to a foe. So—er—I give Yseult back to you." He tried to detach the lady, now clinging to him with all the tenacity of one who after many years has at last achieved a potential husband.

"What are you talking about?" snapped the Dark Knight, still angry. "That's not Yseult; that's the Lady Ygraine. Your wife to be," he added, pointedly. "The Lady Yseult is younger and—er"—he was about to say "better looking," but collected himself in time and substituted "more unruly. Indeed, she has been confined to her chamber by me because she has been trying to run away. Now, it seems, she's done it."

Sir Borloys was puzzled. Apparently the fair Yseult's brother had got her away while he was engaged in combat—or with the refreshments—and he'd got the wrong one. But exactly how it had happened he could not understand.

"Which was her chamber?" he asked at last.

"The one on the right of the ladder."

"But you pointed out the *left* window."

"You never told me which damsel you wanted. And I wouldn't presume to advise one of Arthur's knights on the subject of rescuing fayre young damsels."

"This isn't a fayre . . ." Helped by the Lady Ygraine's loving arms round his neck, he choked back the rest of the sentence. "What I mean is, I've rescued the wrong one. It's your fault that her expectations have been aroused." He drew himself up with a simple dignity that was only spoilt by the tinkle of the spanner falling a little further down inside. "As one of Arthur's knights, my advice to you is that the only chivalrous thing is to marry her yourself."

The Dark Knight laughed till a couple of lorications on his breastplate buckled outwards. Magus peered hopefully from one to the other. As his employer had said, he was short on humour. Even the Lady Ygraine smiled pityingly, and Sir Borloys began to feel that there was, as Sir Perivale might have said, "a snag in it somewhere, old boy."

There was.

"My dear Sir Borloys," the other managed to get out at last, "Ygraine is my *daughter*. So for that matter is Yseult."

"Your *daughters*?"

"Why not? Do you imagine I'd be so stupid as to keep strange damsels about the place with you knights so busy making the world pure?"

Sir Borloys said nothing. He was too occupied in trying to look dignified. Also, much to his disgust at such a serious moment, he was acutely conscious of a growing hunger on which the refreshments had barely made an impression. And after all this he could hardly stay on to the Yuletide banquet.

"It seems to me," continued the other, "that, since apparently your original intention was to become my son-in-law, and since it's entirely your fault that Yseult's run away, the only thing for you to do is to marry Ygraine."

"I shall do no such thing," said Sir Borloys, stiffly. With a sigh for the lost banquet, he began to plod through the snow to his horse, limping slightly because the spanner had now worked down inside his solleret. "And anyway it was her brother—your own son—who helped Yseult to get away." He felt inclined to add: "So there!" but realized that it was hardly in the best Arthurian tradition. He was glad, however, to see that the Dark Knight was definitely staggered by this revelation of his own offspring's treachery.

"Well. I can't force you," said the Dark Knight, getting his breath at last, "but remember, if you go away you won't get any of Magus's Weight-Reducer."

Sir Borloys hesitated. That was a point. If he didn't do something about his girth he'd have to get a new suit of armour.

"And there's the Banquet. We were thinking of having clear soup, ortolans, venisons, wild boar, tame boar, four veg., leveret pie, and cold roast swan. And, seeing that it's Christmas, turkey, of course, for the main dish."

Sir Borloys removed his helm in order to hear better. His emptiness became insistent. He half turned back. But still—Ygraine!

"Besides," concluded the Dark Knight, and his voice quivered with emotion, "this will all make a very funny story. If I were you I wouldn't like it to get round. You see, *Yseult has no brother.* The young man was, no doubt, what she calls 'her boy friend.'"

And at last he burst into uncontrollable laughter. "'Pon my soul, young Garaine deserves to get her. We'll drink their health to-night in the '06 mead . . . Her *brother*! Ha! Ha!"

Sir Borloys definitely did turn back; though as he afterwards put it, at that instant he suddenly fell deeply in love with Ygraine. "And what," he asked, "is there to follow? After the cold roast swan?"

"Sirloin of Unicorn, hashed cockatrice," the Dark Knight was beginning, when Magus burst into a loud cackle of laughter.

"I see the joke," he tittered. "Heh! Heh! Heh!"

The Dark Knight laughed again. He dug Magus in the ribs and began to explain it further. They liked to make the most of a jest in those days. "Her brother! *Garaine* said he was her *brother*!"

"Eh? What brother? I was laughing about that spanner that went inside. It was his undressing one . . . so he couldn't undress to get it out . . . Heh! Heh! . . . But who said who was whose brother? . . ."

# SIR AGRAVAINE
## by P.G. Wodehouse

*One might not at first associate P.G. Wode-
house with Arthurian fiction. But Wodehouse
(1881–1975)—whose brilliant wit gave us the
characters of Jeeves, Bertie Wooster, Lord
Emsworth and others—was so breathlessly
prolific that he would use anything as grist
to his literary mill if he turned his mind to
it. Sir Agravaine comes from his collection*
The Man Upstairs (1914). *Wodehouse tells
us these stories were written between 1909
and 1912 in a bedroom at the Hotel Earl in
Greenwich Village, New York, and were sold
to the American pulp magazines. I'm not sure
which one this surfaced in.*

Some time ago, when spending a delightful week-end at the ances-
tral castle of my dear old friend, the Duke of Weatherstonhope
(pronounced Wop), I came across an old black letter MS. It is on
this that the story which follows is based.

I have found it necessary to touch the thing up a little here and
there, for writers in those days were weak in construction. Their
idea of telling a story was to take a long breath and start droning
away without any stops or dialogue till the thing was over.

I have condensed the title. In the original it ran, "'How it came
about that ye good Knight Sir Agravaine ye Dolorous of ye Table
Round did fare forth to succor a damsel in distress and after divers
journeyings and perils by flood and by field did win her for his
bride and right happily did they twain live ever afterwards,' by
Ambrose ye monk."

It was a pretty snappy title for those times, but we have such a high standard in titles nowadays that I have felt compelled to omit a few yards of it.

We may now proceed to the story.

The great tournament was in full swing. All through the afternoon boiler-plated knights on mettlesome chargers had hurled themselves on each other's spears, to the vast contentment of all. Bright eyes shone; handkerchiefs fluttered; musical voices urged chosen champions to knock the cover off their brawny adversaries. The cheap seats had long since become hoarse with emotion. All round the arena rose the cries of itinerant merchants: "Iced malvoisie," "Score-cards; ye cannot tell the jousters without a score-card." All was revelry and excitement.

A hush fell on the throng. From either end of the arena a mounted knight in armour had entered.

The herald raised his hand.

"Ladeez'n gemmen! Battling Galahad and Agravaine the Dolorous. Galahad on my right, Agravaine on my left. Squires out of the ring. Time!"

A speculator among the crowd offered six to one on Galahad, but found no takers. Nor was the public's caution without reason.

A moment later the two men had met in a cloud of dust, and Agravaine, shooting over his horse's crupper, had fallen with a metallic clang.

He picked himself up, and limped slowly from the arena. He was not unused to this sort of thing. Indeed, nothing else had happened to him in his whole jousting career.

The truth was that Sir Agravaine the Dolorous was out of his element at King Arthur's court, and he knew it. It was this knowledge that had given him that settled air of melancholy from which he derived his title.

Until I came upon this black-letter MS. I had been under the impression, like, I presume, everybody else, that every Knight of the Round Table was a model of physical strength and beauty. Malory says nothing to suggest the contrary. Nor does Tennyson. But apparently there were exceptions, of whom Sir Agravaine the Dolorous must have been the chief.

There was, it seems, nothing to mitigate this unfortunate man's physical deficiencies. There is a place in the world for the strong, ugly man, and there is a place for the weak, handsome man. But to fall short both in features and in muscle is to stake your all on brain. And in the days of King Arthur you did not find the populace turning out to do homage to brain. It was a drug in the market. Agravaine was a good deal better equipped than his contemporaries with grey matter, but his height in his socks was but five feet four; and his muscles, though he had taken three correspondence courses in physical culture, remained distressingly flaccid. His eyes were pale and mild, his nose snub, and his chin receded sharply from his lower lip, as if Nature, designing him, had had to leave off in a hurry and finish the job anyhow. The upper teeth, protuding, completed the resemblance to a nervous rabbit.

Handicapped in this manner, it is no wonder that he should feel sad and lonely in King Arthur's court. At heart he ached for romance; but romance passed him by. The ladies of the court ignored his existence, while, as for those wandering damsels who came periodically to Camelot to complain of the behaviour of dragons, giants, and the like, and to ask permission of the king to take a knight back with them to fight their cause (just as, nowadays, one goes out and calls a policeman), he simply had no chance. The choice always fell on Lancelot or some other popular favourite.

The tournament was followed by a feast. In those brave days almost everything was followed by a feast. The scene was gay and animated. Fair ladies, brave knights, churls, varlets, squires, scurvy knaves, men-at-arms, malapert rogues—all were merry. All save Agravaine. He sat silent and moody. To the jests of Dagonet he turned a deaf ear. And when his neighbour, Sir Kay, arguing with Sir Percivale on current form, appealed to him to back up his statement that Sir Gawain, though a workman-like middle-weight, lacked the punch, he did not answer, though the subject was one on which he held strong views. He sat on, brooding.

As he sat there, a man-at-arms entered the hall.

"Your majesty," he cried, "a damsel in distress waits without."

There was a murmur of excitement and interest.

"Show her in," said the king, beaming.

The man-at-arms retired. Around the table the knights were struggling into an upright position in their seats and twirling their moustaches. Agravaine alone made no movement. He had been through this sort of thing so often. What were distressed damsels to him? His whole demeanour said, as plainly as if he had spoken the words, "What's the use?"

The crowd at the door parted, and through the opening came a figure at the sight of whom the expectant faces of the knights turned pale with consternation. For the new-comer was quite the plainest girl those stately halls had ever seen. Possibly the only plain girl they had ever seen, for no instance is recorded in our authorities of the existence at that period of any such.

The knights gazed at her blankly. Those were the grand old days of chivalry, when a thousand swords would leap from their scabbards to protect defenceless woman, if she were beautiful. The present seemed something in the nature of a special case, and nobody was quite certain as to the correct procedure.

An awkward silence was broken by the king.

"Er—yes?" he said.

The damsel halted.

"Your majesty," she cried, "I am in distress. I crave help!"

"Just so," said the king, uneasily, flashing an apprehensive glance at the rows of perturbed faces before him. "Just so. What—er—what is the exact nature of the—ah—trouble? Any assistance these gallant knights can render will, I am sure, be—ah—eagerly rendered."

He looked imploringly at the silent warriors. As a rule, this speech was the signal for roars of applause. But now there was not even a murmur.

"I may say enthusiastically," he added.

Not a sound.

"Precisely," said the king, ever tactful. "And now—you were saying?"

"I am Yvonne, the daughter of Earl Dorm of the Hills," said the damsel, "and my father has sent me to ask protection from a gallant knight against a fiery dragon that ravages the countryside."

"A dragon, gentlemen," said the king, aside. It was usually a safe draw. Nothing pleased the knight of that time more than a brisk bout with a dragon. But now the tempting word was received in silence.

"Fiery," said the king.

Some more silence.

The king had recourse to the direct appeal. "Sir Gawain, this Court would be greatly indebted to you if—"

Sir Gawain said he had strained a muscle at the last tournament.

"Sir Pelleas."

The king's voice was growing flat with consternation. The situation was unprecedented.

Sir Pelleas said he had an ingrowing toe-nail.

The king's eye rolled in anguish around the table. Suddenly it stopped. It brightened. His look of dismay changed to one of relief.

A knight had risen to his feet. It was Agravaine.

"Ah!" said the king, drawing a deep breath.

Sir Agravaine gulped. He was feeling more nervous than he had ever felt in his life. Never before had he risen to volunteer his services in a matter of this kind, and his state of mind was that of a small boy about to recite his first piece of poetry.

It was not only the consciousness that every eye, except one of Sir Balin's which had been closed in the tournament that afternoon, was upon him. What made him feel like a mild gentleman in a post-office who has asked the lady assistant if she will have time to attend to him soon and has caught her eye, was the fact that he thought he had observed the damsel Yvonne frown as he rose. He groaned in spirit. This damsel, he felt, wanted the proper goods or none at all. She might not be able to get Sir Lancelot or Sir Galahad; but she was not going to be satisfied with a half-portion.

The fact was that Sir Agravaine had fallen in love at first sight. The moment he had caught a glimpse of the damsel Yvonne, he loved her devotedly. To others she seemed plain and unattractive. To him she was a Queen of Beauty. He was amazed at the inexplicable attitude of the knights around him. He had expected them to rise in a body to clamour for the chance of assisting this radiant vision. He could hardly believe, even now, that he was positively the only starter.

"This is Sir Agravaine the Dolorous," said the king to the damsel. "Will you take him as your champion?"

Agravaine held his breath. But all was well. The damsel bowed.

"Then, Sir Agravaine," said the king, "perhaps you had better have your charger sent round at once. I imagine that the matter is pressing—time and—er—dragons wait for no man."

Ten minutes later Agravaine, still dazed, was jogging along to the hills, with the damsel by his side.

It was some time before either of them spoke. The damsel seemed preoccupied, and Agravaine's mind was a welter of confused thoughts, the most prominent of which and the one to which he kept returning being the startling reflection that he, who had pined for romance so long, had got it now in full measure.

A dragon! Fiery withal. Was he absolutely certain that he was capable of handling an argument with a fiery dragon? He would have given much for a little previous experience of this sort of thing. It was too late now, but he wished he had had the forethought to get Merlin to put up a magic prescription for him, rendering him immune to dragon-bites. But did dragons bite? Or did they whack at you with their tails? Or just blow fire?

There were a dozen such points that he would have liked to have settled before starting. It was silly to start out on a venture of this sort without special knowledge. He had half a mind to plead a forgotten engagement and go straight back.

Then he looked at the damsel, and his mind was made up. What did death matter if he could serve her?

He coughed. She came out of her reverie with a start.

"This dragon, now?" said Agravaine.

For a moment the damsel did not reply. "A fearsome worm, Sir Knight," she said at length. "It raveneth by day and by night. It breathes fire from its nostrils."

"Does it!" said Agravaine. "*Does* it! You couldn't give some idea what it looks like, what kind of *size* it is?"

"Its body is as thick as ten stout trees, and its head touches the clouds."

"Does it!" said Agravaine thoughtfully. "*Does it!*"

"Oh, Sir Knight, I pray you have a care."

"I will," said Agravaine. And he had seldom said anything more fervently. The future looked about as bad as it could be. Any hopes he may have entertained that this dragon might be comparatively small and inoffensive were dissipated. This was plainly no debilitated wreck of a dragon, its growth stunted by excessive fire-breathing. A body as thick as ten stout trees! He would not even have the melancholy satisfaction of giving the creature indigestion. For all the impression he was likely to make on that vast interior, he might as well be a salted almond.

As they were speaking, a dim mass on the skyline began to take shape.

"Behold!" said the damsel. "My father's castle." And presently they were riding across the drawbridge and through the great gate, which shut behind them with a clang.

As they dismounted a man came out through a door at the further end of the courtyard.

"Father," said Yvonne, "this is the gallant knight Sir Agravaine, who has come to——" it seemed to Agravaine that she hesitated for a moment.

"To tackle our dragon?" said the father. "Excellent. Come right in."

Earl Dorm of the Hills was a small, elderly man, with what Agravaine considered a distinctly furtive air about him. His eyes were too close together, and he was over-lavish with a weak, cunning smile. Even Agravaine, who was in the mood to like the whole family, if possible, for Yvonne's sake, could not help feeling that appearances were against this particular exhibit. He might have a heart of gold beneath the outward aspect of a confidence-trick expert whose hobby was dog-stealing, but there was no doubt that his exterior did not inspire a genial glow of confidence.

"Very good of you to come," said the earl.

"It's a pleasure," said Agravaine. "I have been hearing all about the dragon."

"A great scourge," agreed his host. "We must have a long talk about it after dinner."

It was the custom in those days in the stately homes of England for the whole strength of the company to take their meals together. The guests sat at the upper table, the ladies in a gallery above them, while the usual drove of men-at-arms, archers, malapert rogues, varlets, scurvy knaves, scullions, and plug-uglies, attached to all medieval households, squashed in near the door, wherever they could find room.

The retinue of Earl Dorm was not strong numerically—the household being, to judge from appearances, one that had seen better days; but it struck Agravaine that what it lacked in numbers it made up in toughness. Among all those at the bottom of the room there was not one whom it would have been agreeable to meet alone in a dark alley. Of all those foreheads not one achieved a height of more than one point nought four inches. A sinister collection, indeed, and one which, Agravaine felt, should have been capable of handling without his assistance any dragon that ever came into the world to stimulate the asbestos industry.

He was roused from his reflections by the voice of his host.

"I hope you are not tired after your journey, Sir Agravaine? My little girl did not bore you, I trust? We are very quiet folk here. Country mice. But we must try to make your visit interesting."

Agravaine felt that the dragon might be counted upon to do that. He said as much.

"Ah, yes the dragon," said Earl Dorm. "I was forgetting the dragon. I want to have a long talk with you about that dragon. Not now. Later on."

His eye caught Agravaine's, and he smiled that weak, cunning smile of his. And for the first time the knight was conscious of a curious feeling that all was not square and above-board in this castle. A conviction began to steal over him that in some way he was being played with, that some game was afoot which he did not understand, that—in a word—there was dirty work at the cross-roads.

There was a touch of mystery in the atmosphere which made him vaguely uneasy. When a fiery dragon is ravaging the country-side to such an extent that the C.Q.D. call has been sent out to the Round Table, a knight has a right to expect the monster to be the main theme of conversation. The tendency on his host's part was apparently to avoid touching on the subject at all. He was vague and elusive; and the one topic on which an honest man is not vague and elusive is that of fiery dragons. It was not right. It was as if one should 'phone for the police and engage them, on arrival, in a discussion on the day's football results.

A wave of distrust swept over Agravaine. He had heard stories of robber chiefs who lured strangers into their strongholds and then held them prisoners while the public nervously dodged their anxious friends who had formed subscription lists to make up the ransom. Could this be such a case? The man certainly had an evasive manner and a smile which would have justified any jury in returning a verdict without leaving the box. On the other hand, there was Yvonne. His reason revolted against the idea of that sweet girl being a party to any such conspiracy.

No, probably it was only the Earl's unfortunate manner. Perhaps he suffered from some muscular weakness of the face which made him smile like that.

Nevertheless, he certainly wished that he had not allowed himself to be deprived of his sword and armour. At the time it had seemed to him that the Earl's remark that the latter needed polishing and the former stropping betrayed only a kindly consideration for his guest's well-being. Now, it had the aspect of being part of a carefully-constructed plot.

On the other hand—here philosophy came to his rescue—if anybody did mean to start anything, his sword and armour might just as well not be there. Any one of those mammoth low-brows at the door could eat him, armour and all.

He resumed his meal, uneasy but resigned.

Dinner at Earl Dorm's was no lunch-counter scuffle. It started early and finished late. It was not till an advanced hour that Agravaine was conducted to his room.

The room which had been allotted to him was high up in the eastern tower. It was a nice room, but to one in Agravaine's state of supressed suspicion a trifle too solidly upholstered. The door was of the thickest oak, studded with iron nails. Iron bars formed a neat pattern across the only window.

Hardly had Agravaine observed these things when the door opened, and before him stood the damsel Yvonne, pale of face and panting for breath.

She leaned against the doorpost and gulped.

"Fly!" she whispered.

Reader, if you had come to spend the night in the lonely castle of a perfect stranger with a shifty eye and a rogues' gallery smile, and on retiring to your room had found the door kick-proof and the window barred, and if, immediately after your discovery of these phenomena, a white-faced young lady had plunged in upon you and urged you to immediate flight, wouldn't that jar you?

It jarred Agravaine.

"Eh?" he cried.

"Fly! Fly, Sir Knight."

Another footstep sounded in the passage. The damsel gave a startled look over her shoulder.

"And what's all this?"

Earl Dorm appeared in the dim-lit corridor. His voice had a nasty tinkle in it.

"Your—your daughter," said Agravaine, hurriedly, "was just telling me that breakfast would—"

The sentence remained unfinished. A sudden movement of the earl's hand, and the great door banged in his face. There came the sound of a bolt shooting into its socket. A key turned in the lock. He was trapped.

Outside, the earl had seized his daughter by the wrist and was administering a paternal cross-examination.

"What were you saying to him?"

Yvonne did not flinch.

"I was bidding him fly."

"If he wants to leave this castle," said the earl, grimly, "he'll have to."

"Father," said Yvonne, "I can't.".

"Can't what?"

"I can't."

His grip on her wrist tightened. From the other side of the door came the muffled sound of blows on the solid oak.

"Oh?" said Earl Dorm. "You can't, eh? Well, listen to me.

You've got to. Do you understand? I admit he might be better-
looking, but—"

"Father, I love him."

He released her wrist, and stared at her in the uncertain light.

"You love him!"

"Yes."

"Then what—? Why? Well, I never did understand women,"
he said at last, and stumped off down the passage.

While this cryptic conversation was in progress, Agravaine,
his worst apprehensions realized, was trying to batter down the
door. After a few moments, however, he realized the futility of
his efforts, and sat down on the bed to think.

At the risk of forfeiting the reader's respect, it must be admitted
that his first emotion was one of profound relief. If he was locked
up like this, it must mean that that dragon story was fictitious,
and that all danger was at an end of having to pit his inexperience
against a ravening monster who had spent a lifetime devouring
knights. He had never liked the prospect, though he had been
prepared to go through with it, and to feel that it was definitely
cancelled made up for a good deal.

His mind turned to his immediate future. What were they going
to do with him? On this point he felt tolerably comfortable. This
imprisonment could mean nothing more than that he would be
compelled to disgorge a ransom. This did not trouble him. He was
rich, and, now that the situation had been switched to a purely
business basis, he felt that he could handle it.

In any case, there was nothing to be gained by sitting up, so he
went to bed, like a good philosopher.

The sun was pouring through the barred window when he
was awoke by the entrance of a gigantic figure bearing food
and drink.

He recognized him as one of the scurvy knaves who had dined
at the bottom of the room the night before—a vast, beetle-browed
fellow with a squint, a mop of red hair, and a genius for silence.
To Agravaine's attempts to engage him in conversation he replied
only with grunts, and in a short time left the room, closing and
locking the door behind him.

He was succeeded at dusk by another of about the same size and
ugliness, and with even less conversational *élan*. This one did not
even grunt.

Small-talk, it seemed, was not an art cultivated in any great
measure by the lower orders in the employment of Earl Dorm.

The next day passed without incident. In the morning the

strabismic plug-ugly with the red hair brought him food and drink, while in the evening the non-grunter did the honours. It was a peaceful life, but tending towards monotony, and Agravaine was soon in the frame of mind which welcomes any break in the daily round.

He was fortunate enough to get it.

He had composed himself for sleep that night, and was just dropping comfortably off, when from the other side of the door he heard the sound of angry voices.

It was enough to arouse him. On the previous night silence had reigned. Evidently something out of the ordinary was taking place.

He listened intently and distinguished words.

"Who was it I did see thee coming down the road with?"

"Who was it thou didst see me coming down the road with?"

"Aye, who was it I did see thee coming down the road with?"

"Who dost thou think thou art?"

"Who do I think I am?"

"Aye, who dost thou think thou art?"

Agravaine could make nothing of it. As a matter of fact, he was hearing the first genuine cross-talk that had ever occurred in those dim, pre-music-hall days. In years to come dialogue on these lines was to be popular throughout the length and breadth of Great Britain. But till then it had been unknown.

The voices grew angrier. To an initiated listener it would have been plain that in a short while words would be found inadequate and the dagger, that medieval forerunner of the slap-stick brought into play. But to Agravaine, all inexperienced, it came as a surprise when suddenly with a muffled thud two bodies fell against the door. There was a scuffling noise, some groans, and then silence.

And then with amazement he heard the bolt shoot back and a key grate in the keyhole.

The door swung open. It was dark outside, but Agravaine could distinguish a female form, and, beyond, a shapeless mass which he took correctly to be the remains of the two plug-uglies.

"It is I, Yvonne," said a voice.

"What is it? What has been happening?"

"It was I. I set them against each other. They both loved one of the kitchen-maids. I made them jealous. I told Walt privily that she had favoured Dickon, and Dickon privily that she loved Walt. And now—"

She glanced at the shapeless heap, and shuddered. Agravaine nodded.

"No wedding-bells for her," he said, reverently.

"And I don't care. I did it to save you. But come! We are wasting time. Come! I will help you to escape."

A man who has been shut up for two days in a small room is seldom slow off the mark when a chance presents itself of taking exercise. Agravaine followed without a word, and together they crept down the staircase until they had reached the main hall. From somewhere in the distance came the rhythmic snores of scurvy knaves getting their eight hours.

Softly Yvonne unbolted a small door, and, passing through it, Agravaine found himself looking up at the stars, while the great walls of the castle towered above him.

"Good-bye," said Yvonne.

There was a pause. For the first time Agravaine found himself examining the exact position of affairs. After his sojourn in the guarded room, freedom looked very good to him. But freedom meant parting from Yvonne.

He looked at the sky and he looked at the castle walls, and he took a step back towards the door.

"I'm not so sure I want to go," he said.

"Oh, fly! Fly, Sir Knight!" she cried.

"You don't understand," said Agravaine. "I don't want to seem to be saying anything that might be interpreted as in the least derogatory to your father in any way whatever, but without prejudice, surely he is just a plain, ordinary brigand? I mean it's only a question of a ransom? And I don't in the least object—"

"No, no, no." Her voice trembled. "He would ask no ransom."

"Don't tell me he kidnaps people just as a hobby!"

"You don't understand. He—No, I cannot tell you. Fly!"

"What don't I understand?"

She was silent. Then she began to speak rapidly. "Very well. I will tell you. Listen. My father had six children, all daughters. We were poor. We had to stay buried in this out-of-the-way spot. We saw no one. It seemed impossible that any of us should ever marry. My father was in despair. Then he said, 'If we cannot get to town, the town must come to us.' So he sent my sister Yseult to Camelot to ask the king to let us have a knight to protect us against a giant with three heads. There was no giant, but she got the knight. It was Sir Sagramore. Perhaps you knew him?"

Agravaine nooded. He began to see daylight.

"My sister Yseult was very beautiful. After the first day Sir Sagramore forgot all about the giant, and seemed to want to do nothing else except have Yseult show him how to play cat's cradle. They were married two months later, and my father sent my sister Elaine to Camelot to ask for a knight to protect us against a wild unicorn."

"And who bit?" asked Agravaine, deeply interested.

"Sir Malibran of Devon. They were married within three weeks, and my father—I can't go on. You understand now."

"I understand the main idea," said Agravaine. "But in my case—"

"You were to marry me," said Yvonne. Her voice was quiet and cold, but she was quivering.

Agravaine was conscious of a dull, heavy weight pressing on his heart. He had known his love was hopeless, but even hopelessness is the better for being indefinite. He understood now.

"And you naturally want to get rid of me before it can happen," he said. "I don't wonder. I'm not vain . . . Well, I'll go. I knew I had no chance. Good-bye."

He turned. She stopped him with a sharp cry.

"What do you mean? You cannot wish to stay now? I am saving you."

"Saving me! I have loved you since the moment you entered the Hall at Camelot," said Agravaine.

She drew in her breath.

"You—you love *me!*"

They looked at each other in the starlight. She held out her hands.

"Agravaine!"

She drooped towards him, and he gathered her into his arms. For a novice, he did it uncommonly well.

It was about six months later that Agravaine, having ridden into the forest, called upon a Wise Man at his cell.

In those days almost anyone who was not a perfect bonehead could set up as a Wise Man and get away with it. All you had to do was to live in a forest and grow a white beard. This particular Wise Man, for a wonder, had a certain amount of rude sagacity. He listened carefully to what the knight had to say.

"It has puzzled me to such an extent," said Agravaine, "that I felt that I must consult a specialist. You see me. Take a good look at me. What do you think of my personal appearance? You needn't hesitate. It's worse than that. I am the ugliest man in England."

"Would you go as far as that?" said the Wise Man, politely.

"Farther. And everybody else thinks so. Everybody except my

wife. She tells me that I am a model of manly beauty. You know Lancelot? Well, she says I have Lancelot whipped to a custard. What do you make of that? And here's another thing. It is perfectly obvious to me that my wife is one of the most beautiful creatures in existence. I have seem them all, and I tell you that she stands alone. She is literally marooned in Class A, all by herself. Yet she insists that she is plain. What do you make of it?"

The Wise Man stroked his beard.

"My son," he said, "the matter is simple. True love takes no account of looks."

"No?" said Agravaine.

"You two are affinities. Therefore, to you the outward aspect is nothing. Put it like this. Love is a thingummybob who what-d'you-call-its."

"I'm beginning to see," said Agravaine.

"What I meant was this. Love is a wizard greater than Merlin. He plays odd tricks with the eyesight."

"Yes," said Agravaine.

"Or, put it another way. Love is a sculptor greater than Praxiteles. He takes an unsightly piece of clay and moulds it into a thing divine."

"I get you," said Agravaine.

The Wise Man began to warm to his work.

"Or shall we say——?"

"I think I must be going," said Agravaine. "I promised my wife I would be back early."

"We might put it——" began the Wise Man perseveringly.

"I understand," said Agravaine, hurriedly. "I quite see now. Good-bye."

The Wise Man sighed resignedly.

"Good-bye, Sir Knight," he said. "Good-bye. Pay at ye desk."

And Agravaine rode on his way marvelling.

# THE ROMANCE OF TRISTAN AND ISEULT
## by Hilaire Belloc

*As with Wodehouse, the name of Hilaire Belloc does not come immediately to mind when thinking of Arthurian fiction. In fact today, Belloc's name is sinking fast, although I'm sure some will remember his* Cautionary Tales for Children *(1907). Belloc (1870–1953), was another very prolific writer, turning his hand to a wide variety of subjects—politics, history, philosophy, travel—as well as fiction and verse. Belloc's "The Romance of Tristan and Iseult" was a fairly free translation of a French volume,* Le Roman de Tristan et Iseut *(1900) by Joseph Bédier. Bédier (1864–1938), was a Professor of French Medieval Language and Literature, and he had brought his volume together from a variety of medieval texts.*

*The primary text for the Tristan story comes from the lays of Marie de France, a half-sister of King Henry II, who introduced Tristan in the* Lai de Chevrefoil, *written sometime before 1175. She used as her sources various Breton legends and folktales which probably bore the same origins as the Arthurian tales. The Tristan story was further developed by Gottfried von Strassburg around the year 1200. It was this version that probably formed the basis of Richard Wagner's great opera* Tristan and Isolde *(1865).*

*There are such close parallels between the
tragic love of Tristan and Iseult and that between
Lancelot and Guinevere, that they may share a
common source. Whatever the true origin of this
legend, it is as relevant and as powerful today,
as it was to all those who listened enthralled to
the balladeers at the court of Henry II over eight
hundred years ago.*

# The Childhood of Tristan

## Part I

My lords, if you would hear a high tale of love and of death, here
is that of Tristan and Queen Iseult; how to their full joy, but to
their sorrow also, they loved each other, and how at last they died
of that love together upon one day; she by him and he by her.

Long ago, when Mark was King over Cornwall, Rivalen, King
of Lyonesse, heard that Mark's enemies waged war on him; so
he crossed the sea to bring him aid; and so faithfully did he
serve him with counsel and sword that Mark gave him his sister
Blanchefleur, whom King Rivalen loved most marvellously.

He wedded her in Tintagel Minster, but hardly was she wed
when the news came to him that his old enemy Duke Morgan had
fallen on Lyonesse and was wasting town and field. Then Rivalen
manned his ships in haste, and took Blanchefleur with him to his
far land; but she was with child. He landed below his castle of
Kanoël and gave the Queen in ward to his Marshal Rohalt, and
after that set off to wage his war.

Blanchefleur waited for him continually, but he did not come
home, till she learnt upon a day that Duke Morgan had killed him
in foul ambush. She did not weep: she made no cry or lamentation,
but her limbs failed her and grew weak, and her soul was filled
with a strong desire to be rid of the flesh, and though Rohalt tried
to soothe her she would not hear. Three days she awaited re-union
with her lord, and on the fourth she brought forth a son; and
taking him in her arms she said:

"Little son, I have longed a while to see you, and now I see you
the fairest thing ever a woman bore. In sadness came I hither, in

sadness did I bring forth, and in sadness has your first feast day gone. And as by sadness you came into the world, your name shall be called Tristan; that is the child of sadness."

After she had said these words she kissed him, and immediately when she had kissed him she died.

Rohalt, the keeper of faith, took the child, but already Duke Morgan's men besieged the Castle of Kanoël all round about. There is a wise saying: "Foolhardy was never hardy," and he was compelled to yield to Duke Morgan at his mercy: but for fear that Morgan might slay Rivalen's heir the Marshal hid him among his own sons.

When seven years were passed and the time had come to take the child from the women, Rohalt put Tristan under a good master, the Squire Gorvenal, and Gorvenal taught him in a few years the arts that go with barony. He taught him the use of lance and sword and 'scutcheon and bow, and how to cast stone quoits and to leap wide dykes also: and he taught him to hate every lie and felony and to keep his given word; and he taught him the various kinds of song and harp-playing, and the hunter's craft; and when the child rode among the young squires you would have said that he and his horse and his armour were all one thing. To see him so noble and so proud, broad in the shoulders, loyal, strong and right, all men glorified Rohalt in such a son. But Rohalt remembering Rivalen and Blanchefleur (of whose youth and grace all this was a resurrection) loved him indeed as a son, but in his heart revered him as his lord.

Now all his joy was snatched from him on a day when certain merchants of Norway, having lured Tristan to their ship, bore him off as a rich prize, though Tristan fought hard, as a young wolf struggles, caught in a gin. But it is a truth well proved, and every sailor knows it, that the sea will hardly bear a felon ship, and gives no aid to rapine. The sea rose and cast a dark storm round the ship and drove it eight days and eight nights at random, till the mariners caught through the mist a coast of awful cliffs and sea-ward rocks whereon the sea would have ground their hull to pieces: then they did penance, knowing that the anger of the sea came of the lad, whom they had stolen in an evil hour, and they vowed his deliverance and got ready a boat to put him, if it might be, ashore: then the wind and sea fell and the sky shone, and as the Norway ship grew small in the offing, a quiet tide cast Tristan and the boat upon a beach of sand.

Painfully he climbed the cliff and saw, beyond, a lonely rolling heath and a forest stretching out and endless. And he wept, remembering Gorvenal, his father, and the land of Lyonesse. Then the distant cry of a hunt, with horse and hound, came suddenly and lifted his heart, and a tall stag broke cover at the forest edge. The pack and the hunt streamed after it with a tumult of cries and winding horns, but just as the hounds were racing clustered at the haunch, the quarry turned to bay at a stone's throw from Tristan; a huntsman gave him the thrust, while all around the hunt had gathered and was winding the kill. But Tristan, seeing by the gesture of the huntsman that he made to cut the neck of the stag, cried out:

"My lord, what would you do? Is it fitting to cut up so noble a beast like any farm-yard hog? Is that the custom of this country?"

And the huntsman answered:

"Fair friend, what startles you? Why yes, first I take off the head of a stag, and then I cut it into four quarters and we carry it on our saddle bows to King Mark, our lord: So do we, and so since the days of the first huntsmen have done the Cornish men. If, however, you know of some nobler custom, teach it us: take this knife and we will learn it willingly."

Then Tristan kneeled and skinned the stag before he cut it up, and quartered it all in order leaving the crow-bone all whole, as is meet, and putting aside at the end the head, the haunch, the tongue and the great heart's vein; and the huntsmen and the kennel hinds stood over him with delight, and the Master Huntsman said:

"Friend, these are good ways. In what land learnt you them? Tell us your country and your name."

"Good lord, my name is Tristan, and I learnt these ways in my country of Lyonesse."

"Tristan," said the Master Huntsman, "God reward the father that brought you up so nobly; doubtless he is a baron, rich and strong."

Now Tristan knew both speech and silence, and he answered:

"No, lord; my father is a burgess. I left his home unbeknownst upon a ship that trafficked to a far place, for I wished to learn how men lived in foreign lands. But if you will accept me of the hunt I will follow you gladly and teach you other crafts of venery."

"Fair Tristan, I marvel there should be a land where a burgess's son can know what a knight's son knows not elsewhere, but come with us since you will it; and welcome: we will bring you to King Mark, our lord."

Tristan completed his task; to the dogs he gave the heart, the head, offal and ears; and he taught the hunt how the skinning and the ordering should be done. Then he thrust the pieces upon pikes and gave them to this huntsman and to that to carry, to one the snout to another the haunch to another the flank to another the chine; and he taught them how to ride by twos in rank according to the dignity of the pieces each might bear.

So they took the road and spoke together, till they came on a great castle and round it fields and orchards, and living waters and fish ponds and plough lands, and many ships were in its haven, for that castle stood above the sea. It was well fenced against all assault or engines of war, and its keep, which the giants had built long ago, was compact of great stones, like a chess board of vert and azure.

And when Tristan asked its name:

"Good liege," they said, "we call it Tintagel."

And Tristan cried:

"Tintagel! Blessed be thou of God, and blessed be they that dwell within thee."

(Therein, my lords, therein had Rivalen taken Blanchefleur to wife, though their son knew it not.)

When they came before the keep the horns brought the barons to the gates and King Mark himself. And when the Master Huntsman had told him all the story, and King Mark had marvelled at the good order of the cavalcade, and the cutting of the stag, and the high art of venery in all, yet most he wondered at the stranger boy, and still gazed at him, troubled and wondering whence came his tenderness, and his heart would answer him nothing; but, my lords, it was blood that spoke, and the love he had long since borne his sister Blanchefleur.

That evening, when the boards were cleared, a singer out of Wales, a master, came forward among the barons in Hall and sang a harper's song, and as this harper touched the strings of his harp, Tristan who sat at the King's feet, spoke thus to him:

"Oh master, that is the first of songs! The Bretons of old wove it once to chant the loves of Graëlent. And the melody is rare and rare are the words: master, your voice is subtle: harp us that well."

But when the Welshman had sung, he answered:

"Boy, what do you know of the craft of music? If the burgesses of Lyonesse teach their sons harp-play also, and rotes and viols too, rise, and take this harp and show your skill."

Then Tristan took the harp and sang so well that the barons softened as they heard, and King Mark marvelled at the harper from Lyonesse whither so long ago Rivalen had taken Blanchefleur away.

When the song ended, the King was silent a long space, but he said at last:

"Son, blessed be the master that taught thee, and blessed be thou of God: for God loves good singers. Their voices and the voice of the harp enter the souls of men and wake dear memories and cause them to forget many a mourning and many a sin. For our joy did you come to this roof, stay near us a long time, friend."

And Tristan answered:

"Very willingly will I serve you, sire, as your harper, your huntsman and your liege."

So did he, and for three years a mutual love grew up in their hearts. By day Tristan followed King Mark at pleas and in saddle; by night he slept in the royal room with the councillors and the peers, and if the King was sad he would harp to him to soothe his care. The barons also cherished him, and (as you shall learn) Dinas of Lidan, the seneschal, beyond all others. And more tenderly than the barons and than Dinas the King loved him. But Tristan could not forget, or Rohalt his father, or his master Gorvenal, or the land of Lyonesse.

My lords, a teller that would please, should not stretch his tale too long, and truly this tale is so various and so high that it needs no straining. Then let me shortly tell how Rohalt himself, after long wandering by sea and land, came into Cornwall, and found Tristan, and showing the King the carbuncle that once was Blanchefleur's, said:

"King Mark, here is your nephew Tristan, son of your sister Blanchefleur and of King Rivalen. Duke Morgan holds his land most wrongfully; it is time such land came back to its lord."

And Tristan (in a word) when his uncle had armed him knight, crossed the sea, and was hailed of his father's vassals, and killed Rivalen's slayer and was re-seized of his land.

Then remembering how King Mark could no longer live in joy without him, he summoned his council and his barons and said this:

"Lords of the Lyonesse, I have retaken this place and I have avenged King Rivalen by the help of God and of you. But two men Rohalt and King Mark of Cornwall nourished me, an orphan, and a wandering boy. So should I call them also fathers. Now a free man has two things thoroughly his own, his body and his land. To Rohalt then, here, I will release my land. Do you hold it, father, and your son shall hold it after you. But my body I give up to King Mark. I will leave this country, dear though it be, and in Cornwall I will serve King Mark as my lord. Such is my judgment, but you, my lords of Lyonesse, are my lieges, and owe me counsel; if then, some one of you will counsel me another thing let him rise and speak."

But all the barons praised him, though they wept; and taking with him Gorvenal only, Tristan set sail for King Mark's land.

# The Morholt out of Ireland

When Tristan came back to that land, King Mark and all his Barony were mourning; for the King of Ireland had manned a fleet to ravage Cornwall, should King Mark refuse, as he had refused these fifteen years, to pay a tribute his fathers had paid. Now that year this King had sent to Tintagel, to carry his summons, a giant knight; the Morholt, whose sister he had wed, and whom no man had yet been able to overcome: so King Mark had summoned all the barons of his land to Council, by letters sealed.

On the day assigned, when the barons were gathered in hall, and when the King had taken his throne, the Morholt said these things:

"King Mark, hear for the last time the summons of the King of Ireland, my lord. He arraigns you to pay at last that which you have owed so long, and because you have refused it too long already he bids you give over to me this day three hundred youths and three hundred maidens drawn by lot from among the Cornish folk. But if so be that any would prove by trial of combat that the King of Ireland receives this tribute without right, I will take up his wager. Which among you, my Cornish lords, will fight to redeem this land?"

The barons glanced at each other but all were silent.

Then Tristan knelt at the feet of King Mark and said:

"Lord King, by your leave I will do battle."

And in vain would King Mark have turned him from his purpose, thinking, how could even valour save so young a knight? But he threw down his gage to the Morholt, and the Morholt took up the gage.

On the appointed day he had himself clad for a great feat of
arms in a hauberk and in a steel helm, and he entered a boat and
drew to the islet of St. Samson's, where the knights were to fight
each to each alone. Now the Morholt had hoisted to his mast a
sail of rich purple, and coming fast to land, he moored his boat
on the shore. But Tristan pushed off his own boat adrift with his
feet, and said:

"One of us only will go hence alive. One boat will serve."

And each rousing the other to the fray they passed into
the isle.

No man saw the sharp combat; but thrice the salt sea-breeze
had wafted or seemed to waft a cry of fury to the land, when
at last towards the hour of noon the purple sail showed far off;
the Irish boat appeared from the island shore, and there rose a
clamour of "the Morholt!" When suddenly, as the boat grew
larger on the sight and topped a wave, they saw that Tristan
stood on the prow holding a sword in his hand. He leapt ashore,
and as the mothers kissed the steel upon his feet he cried to the
Morholt's men:

"My lords of Ireland, the Morholt fought well. See here, my
sword is broken and a splinter of it stands fast in his head. Take
you that steel, my lords; it is the tribute of Cornwall."

Then he went up to Tintagel and as he went the people he
had freed waved green boughs, and rich cloths were hung at the
windows. But when Tristan reached the castle with joy, songs
and joy-bells sounding about him, he drooped in the arms of King
Mark, for the blood ran from his wounds.

The Morholt's men, they landed in Ireland quite cast down. For
when ever he came back into Whitehaven the Morholt had been
wont to take joy in the sight of his clan upon the shore, of the
Queen his sister, and of his niece Iseult the Fair. Tenderly had
they cherished him of old, and had he taken some wound, they
healed him, for they were skilled in balms and potions. But now
their magic was vain, for he lay dead and the splinter of the foreign
brand yet stood in his skull till Iseult plucked it out and shut it in
a chest.

From that day Iseult the Fair knew and hated the name of
Tristan of Lyonesse.

But over in Tintagel Tristan languished, for there trickled a
poisonous blood from his wound. The doctors found that the
Morholt had thrust into him a poisoned barb, and as their
potions and their theriac could never heal him they left him in
God's hands. So hateful a stench came from his wound that all

his dearest friends fled him, all save King Mark, Gorvenal and Dinas of Lidan. They always could stay near his couch because their love overcame their abhorrence. At last Tristan had himself carried into a boat apart on the shore; and lying facing the sea he awaited death, for he thought: "I must die; but it is good to see the sun and my heart is still high. I would like to try the sea that brings all chances . . . I would have the sea bear me far off alone, to what land no matter, so that it heal me of my wound."

He begged so long that King Mark accepted his desire. He bore him into a boat with neither sail nor oar, and Tristan wished that his harp only should be placed beside him: for sails he could not lift, nor oar ply, nor sword wield; and as a seaman on some long voyage casts to the sea a beloved companion dead, so Gorvenal pushed out to sea that boat where his dear son lay; and the sea drew him away.

For seven days and seven nights the sea so drew him; at times to charm his grief, he harped; and when at last the sea brought him near a shore where fishermen had left their port that night to fish far out, they heard as they rowed a sweet and strong and living tune that ran above the sea, and feathering their oars they listened immovable.

In the first whiteness of the dawn they saw the boat at large: she went at random and nothing seemed to live in her except the voice of the harp. But as they neared, the air grew weaker and died; and when they hailed her Tristan's hands had fallen lifeless on the strings though they still trembled. The fishermen took him in and bore him back to port, to their lady who was merciful and perhaps would heal him.

It was that same port of Whitehaven where the Morholt lay, and their lady was Iseult the Fair.

She alone, being skilled in philtres, could save Tristan, but she alone wished him dead. When Tristan knew himself again (for her art restored him) he knew himself to be in the land of peril. But he was yet strong to hold his own and found good crafty words. He told a tale of how he was a seer that had taken passage on a merchant ship and sailed to Spain to learn the art of reading all the stars,—of how pirates had boarded the ship and of how, though wounded, he had fled into that boat. He was believed, nor did any of the Morholt's men know his face again, so hardly had the poison used it. But when, after forty days, Iseult of the Golden Hair had all but healed him, when already his limbs had recovered and the grace of youth returned, he knew that he must escape, and he fled and after many dangers he came again before Mark the King.

# The Quest of the Lady with the Hair of Gold

My lords, there were in the court of King Mark four barons the basest of men, who hated Tristan with a hard hate, for his greatness and for the tender love the King bore him. And well I know their names: Andret, Guenelon, Gondoïne and Denoalen. They knew that the King had intent to grow old childless and to leave his land to Tristan; and their envy swelled and by lies they angered the chief men of Cornwall against Tristan. They said:

"There have been too many marvels in this man's life. It was marvels enough that he beat the Morholt, but by what sorcery did he try the sea alone at the point of death, or which of us, my lords, could voyage without mast or sail? They say that warlocks can. It was sure a warlock feat, and that is a warlock harp of his pours poison daily into the King's heart. See how he has bent that heart by power and chain of sorcery! He will be king yet, my lords, and you will hold your lands of a wizard."

They brought over the greater part of the barons and these pressed King Mark to take to wife some King's daughter who should give him an heir, or else they threatened to return each man into his keep and wage him war. But the King turned against them and swore in his heart that so long as his dear nephew lived no king's daughter should come to his bed. Then in his turn did Tristan (in his shame to be thought to serve for hire) threaten that if the King did not yield to his barons, he would himself go over sea to serve some great king. At this, King Mark made a term with his barons and gave them forty days to hear his decision.

On the appointed day he waited alone in his chamber and sadly mused: "Where shall I find a king's daughter so fair and yet so distant that I may feign to wish her my wife?"

Just then by his window that looked upon the sea two building swallows came in quarrelling together. Then, startled, they flew out, but had let fall from their beaks a woman's hair, long and fine, and shining like a beam of light.

King Mark took it, and called his barons and Tristan and said:

"To please you, lords, I will take a wife; but you must seek her whom I have chosen."

"Fair lord, we wish it all," they said," and who may she be?"

"Why," said he, "she whose hair this is; nor will I take another."

"And whence, lord King, comes this Hair of Gold; who brought it and from what land?"

"It comes, my lords, from the Lady with the Hair of Gold, the swallows brought it me. They know from what country it came."

Then the barons saw themselves mocked and cheated, and they turned with sneers to Tristan, for they thought him to have counselled the trick. But Tristan, when he had looked on the Hair of Gold, remembered Iseult the Fair and smiled and said this:

"King Mark, can you not see that the doubts of these lords shame me? You have designed in vain. I will go seek the Lady with the Hair of Gold. The search is perilous: never the less, my uncle, I would once more put my body and my life into peril for you; and that your barons may know I love you loyally, I take this oath, to die on the adventure or to bring back to this castle of Tintagel the Queen with that fair hair."

He fitted out a great ship and loaded it with corn and wine, with honey and all manner of good things; he manned it with Gorvenal and a hundred young knights of high birth, chosen among the bravest, and he clothed them in coats of home-spun and in hair cloth so that they seemed merchants only: but under the deck he hid rich cloth of gold and scarlet as for a great king's messengers.

When the ship had taken the sea the helmsman asked him:

"Lord, to what land shall I steer?"

"Sir," said he, "steer for Ireland, straight for Whitehaven harbour."

At first Tristan made believe to the men of Whitehaven that his friends were merchants of England come peacefully to barter; but as these strange merchants passed the day in the useless games of draughts and chess, and seemed to know dice better than the bargain price of corn, Tristan feared discovery and knew not how to pursue his quest.

Now it chanced once upon the break of day that he heard a cry so terrible that one would have called it a demon's cry; nor had he ever heard a brute bellow in such wise, so awful and strange it seemed. He called a woman who passed by the harbour, and said:

"Tell me, lady, whence comes that voice I have heard, and hide me nothing."

"My lord," said she, "I will tell you truly. It is the roar of a dragon the most terrible and dauntless upon earth. Daily it leaves its den and stands at one of the gates of the city: Nor can any come out or go in till a maiden has been given up to it; and when it has her in its claws it devours her."

"Lady," said Tristan, "make no mock of me, but tell me straight: Can a man born of woman kill this thing?"

"Fair sir, and gentle," she said, "I cannot say; but this is sure: Twenty knights and tried have run the venture, because the King of Ireland has published it that he will give his daughter, Iseult the Fair, to whomsoever shall kill the beast; but it has devoured them all."

Tristan left the woman and returning to his ship armed himself in secret, and it was a fine sight to see so noble a charger and so good a knight come out from such a merchant-hull: but the haven was empty of folk, for the dawn had barely broken and none saw him as he rode to the gate. And hardly had he passed it, when he met suddenly five men at full gallop flying towards the town. Tristan seized one by his hair, as he passed, and dragged him over his mount's crupper and held him fast:

"God save you, my lord," said he, "and whence does the dragon come?" And when the other had shown him by what road, he let him go.

As the monster neared, he showed the head of a bear and red eyes like coals of fire and hairy tufted ears; lion's claws, a serpent's tail, and a griffin's body.

Tristan charged his horse at him so strongly that, though the beast's mane stood with fright yet he drove at the dragon: his lance struck its scales and shivered. Then Tristan drew his sword and struck at the dragon's head, but he did not so much as cut the hide. The beast felt the blow: with its claws he dragged at the shield and broke it from the arm; then, his breast unshielded, Tristan used the sword again and struck so strongly that the air rang all round about: but in vain, for he could not wound and meanwhile the dragon vomited from his nostrils two streams of loathsome flames, and Tristan's helm blackened like a cinder and his horse stumbled and fell down and died; but Tristan standing on his feet thrust his sword right into the beast's jaws, and split its heart in two.

Then he cut out the tongue and put it into his hose, but as the poison came against his flesh the hero fainted and fell in the high grass that bordered the marsh around.

Now the man he had stopped in flight was the Seneschal of Ireland and he desired Iseult the Fair: and though he was a coward, he had dared so far as to return with his companions secretly, and he found the dragon dead; so he cut off its head and bore it to the King, and claimed the great reward.

The King could credit his prowess but hardly, yet wished justice done and summoned his vassals to court, so that there, before the Barony assembled, the seneschal should furnish proof of his victory won.

When Iseult the Fair heard that she was to be given to this coward first she laughed long, and then she wailed. But on the morrow, doubting some trick, she took with her Perinis her squire and Brangien her maid, and all three rode unbeknownst towards the dragon's lair: and Iseult saw such a trail on the road as made her wonder—for the hoofs that made it had never been shod in her land. Then she came on the dragon, headless, and a dead horse beside him: nor was the horse harnessed in the fashion of Ireland. Some foreign man had slain the beast, but they knew not whether he still lived or no.

They sought him long, Iseult and Perinis and Brangien together, till at last Brangien saw the helm glittering in the marshy grass: and Tristan still breathed. Perinis put him on his horse and bore him secretly to the women's rooms. There Iseult told her mother the tale and left the hero with her, and as the Queen unharnessed him, the dragon's tongue fell from his boot of steel. Then, the Queen of Ireland revived him by the virtue of an herb and said:

"Stranger, I know you for the true slayer of the dragon: but our seneschal, a felon, cut off its head and claims my daughter Iseult for his wage; will you be ready two days hence to give him the lie in battle?"

"Queen," said he, "the time is short, but you, I think, can cure me in two days. Upon the dragon I conquered Iseult, and on the seneschal perhaps I shall reconquer her."

Then the Queen brewed him strong brews, and on the morrow Iseult the Fair got him ready a bath and anointed him with a balm her mother had conjured, and as he looked at her he thought, "So I have found the Queen of the Hair of Gold," and he smiled as he thought it. But Iseult, noting it, thought, "Why does he smile, or what have I neglected of the things due to a guest? He smiles to think I have forgotten to burnish his armour."

She went and drew the sword from its rich sheath, but when she saw the splinter gone and the gap in the edge she thought of the Morholt's head. She balanced a moment in doubt, then she went to where she kept the steel she had found in the skull and she put it to the sword, and it fitted so that the join was hardly seen.

She ran to where Tristan lay wounded, and with the sword above him she cried:

"You are that Tristan of the Lyonesse, who killed the Morholt, my mother's brother, and now you shall die in your turn."

Tristan strained to ward the blow, but he was too weak; his wit, however, stood firm in spite of evil and he said:

"So be it, let me die: but to save yourself long memories, listen awhile. King's daughter, my life is not only in your power but is yours of right. My life is yours because you have twice returned it me. Once, long ago: for I was the wounded harper whom you healed of the poison of the Morholt's shaft. Nor repent the healing: were not these wounds had in fair fight? Did I kill the Morholt by treason? Had he not defied me and was I not held to the defence of my body? And now this second time also you have saved me. It was for you I fought the beast . . .

"But let us leave these things. I would but show you how my life is your own. Then if you kill me of right for the glory of it, you may ponder for long years, praising yourself that you killed a wounded guest who had wagered his life in your gaining."

Iseult replied: "I hear strange words. Why should he that killed the Morholt seek me also, his niece? Doubtless because the Morholt came for a tribute of maidens from Cornwall, so you came to boast returning that you had brought back the maiden who was nearest to him, to Cornwall, a slave."

"King's daughter," said Tristan, "No . . . One day two swallows flew, and flew to Tintagel and bore one hair out of all your hairs of gold, and I thought they brought me good will and peace, so I came to find you over-seas. See here, amid the threads of gold upon my coat your hair is sown: the threads are tarnished, but your bright hair still shines."

Iseult put down the sword and taking up the Coat of Arms she saw upon it the Hair of Gold and was silent a long space, till she kissed him on the lips to prove peace, and she put rich garments over him.

On the day of the barons' assembly, Tristan sent Perinis privily to his ship to summon his companions that they should come to court adorned as befitted the envoys of a great king.

One by one the hundred knights passed into the hall where all the barons of Ireland stood, they entered in silence and sat all in rank together: on their scarlet and purple the gems gleamed.

When the King had taken his throne, the seneschal arose to prove by witness and by arms that he had slain the dragon and that so Iseult was won. Then Iseult bowed to her father and said:

"King, I have here a man who challenges your seneschal for lies and felony. Promise that you will pardon this man all his past deeds, who stands to prove that he and none other slew the dragon, and grant him forgiveness and your peace."

The King said, "I grant it." But Iseult said, "Father, first give me the kiss of peace and forgiveness, as a sign that you will give him the same."

Then she found Tristan and led him before the Barony. And as he came the hundred knights rose all together, and crossed their arms upon their breasts and bowed, so the Irish knew that he was their lord.

But among the Irish many knew him again and cried, "Tristan of Lyonesse that slew the Morholt!" They drew their swords and clamoured for death. But Iseult cried: "King, kiss this man upon the lips as your oath was," and the King kissed him, and the clamour fell.

Then Tristan showed the dragon's tongue and offered the seneschal battle, but the seneschal looked at his face and dared not.

Then Tristan said:

"My lords, you have said it, and it is truth: I killed the Morholt. But I crossed the sea to offer you a good blood-fine, to ransom that deed and get me quit of it.

"I put my body in peril of death and rid you of the beast and have so conquered Iseult the Fair, and having conquered her I will bear her away on my ship.

"But that these lands of Cornwall and Ireland may know no more hatred, but love only, learn that King Mark, my lord, will marry her. Here stand a hundred knights of high name, who all will swear with an oath upon the relics of the holy saints, that King Mark sends you by their embassy offer of peace and of brotherhood and goodwill; and that he would by your courtesy hold Iseult as his honoured wife, and that he would have all the men of Cornwall serve her as their Queen."

When the lords of Ireland heard this they acclaimed it, and the King also was content.

Then, since that treaty and alliance was to be made, the King her father took Iseult by the hand and asked of Tristan that he should take an oath; to wit that he would lead her loyally to his lord, and Tristan took that oath and swore it before the knights and the Barony of Ireland assembled. Then the King put Iseult's right hand into Tristan's right hand, and Tristan held it for a space in token of seizin for the King of Cornwall.

So, for the love of King Mark, did Tristan conquer the Queen of the Hair of Gold.

# The Philtre

When the day of Iseult's livery to the Lords of Cornwall drew near, her mother gathered herbs and flowers and roots and steeped them in wine, and brewed a potion of might, and having done so, said apart to Brangien:

"Child, it is yours to go with Iseult to King Mark's country, for you love her with a faithful love. Take then this pitcher and remember well my words. Hide it so that no eye shall see nor no lip go near it: but when the wedding night has come and that moment in which the wedded are left alone, pour this essenced wine into a cup and offer it to King Mark and to Iseult his queen. Oh! Take all care, my child, that they alone shall taste this brew. For this is its power: they who drink of it together love each other with their every single sense and with their every thought, forever, in life and in death."

And Brangien promised the Queen that she would do her bidding.

On the bark that bore her to Tintagel Iseult the Fair was weeping as she remembered her own land, and mourning swelled her heart, and she said, "Who am I that I should leave you to follow unknown men, my mother and my land? Accursed be the sea that bears me, for rather would I lie dead on the earth where I was born than live out there, beyond . . ."

One day when the wind had fallen and the sails hung slack Tristan dropped anchor by an Island and the hundred knights of Cornwall and the sailors, weary of the sea, landed all. Iseult alone remained aboard and a little serving maid, when Tristan came near the Queen to calm her sorrow. The sun was hot above them and they were athirst and, as they called, the little maid looked about for drink for them and found that pitcher which the mother of Iseult had given into Brangien's keeping. And when she came on it, the child cried, "I have found you wine!" Now she had found not wine—but Passion and Joy most sharp, and Anguish without end, and Death.

The Queen drank deep of that draught and gave it to Tristan and he drank also long and emptied it all.

Brangien came in upon them; she saw them gazing at each other in silence as though ravished and apart; she saw before them the pitcher standing there; she snatched it up and cast it into the shuddering sea and cried aloud: "Cursed be the day I was born and cursed the day that first I trod this deck. Iseult, my friend, and Tristan, you, you have drunk death together."

And once more the bark ran free for Tintagel. But it seemed to Tristan as though an ardent briar, sharp-thorned but with flower most sweet smelling, drave roots into his blood and laced the lovely body of Iseult all round about it and bound it to his own and to his every thought and desire. And he thought, "Felons, that charged me with coveting King Mark's land, I have come lower by far, for it is not his land I covet. Fair uncle, who loved me orphaned ere ever you knew in me the blood of your sister Blanchefleur, you that wept as you bore me to that boat alone, why did you not drive out the boy that was to betray you? Ah! What thought was that! Iseult is yours and I am but your vassal; Iseult is yours and I am your son; Iseult is yours and may not love me."

But Iseult loved him, though she would have hated. She could not hate, for a tenderness more sharp than hatred tore her.

And Brangien watched them in anguish, suffering more cruelly because she alone knew the depth of evil done.

Two days she watched them, seeing them refuse all food or comfort and seeking each other as blind men seek, wretched apart and together more wretched still, for then they trembled each for the first avowal.

On the third day, as Tristan neared the tent on deck where Iseult sat, she saw him coming and she said to him, very humbly, "Come in, my lord."

"Queen," said Tristan, "why do you call me lord? Am I not your liege and vassal, to revere and serve and cherish you as my lady and Queen?"

But Iseult answered, "No, you know that you are my lord and my master, and I your slave. Ah, why did I not sharpen those wounds of the wounded singer, or let die that dragon-slayer in the grasses of the marsh? But then I did not know what now I know!"

"And what is it that you know, Iseult?"

She laid her arm upon Tristan's shoulder, the light of her eyes was drowned and her lips trembled.

"The love of you," she said. Whereat he put his lips to hers.

But as they thus tasted their first joy, Brangien, that watched them, stretched her arms and cried at their feet in tears:

"Stay and return if still you can . . . But oh! that path has no returning. For already Love and his strength drag you on and now henceforth forever never shall you know joy without pain again. The wine possesses you, the draught your mother gave me, the draught the King alone should have drunk with you: but that old Enemy has tricked us, all us three; friend Tristan, Iseult my friend, for that bad ward I kept take here my body and my life, for through me and in that cup you have drunk not love alone, but love and death together."

The lovers held each other; life and desire trembled through their youth, and Tristan said, "Well then, come Death."

And as evening fell, upon the bark that heeled and ran to King Mark's land, they gave themselves up utterly to love.

# The Tall Pine-Tree

As King Mark came down to greet Iseult upon the shore, Tristan took her hand and led her to the King and the King took seizin of her, taking her hand. He led her in great pomp to his castle of Tintagel, and as she came in hall amid the vassals her beauty shone so that the walls were lit as they are lit at dawn. Then King Mark blessed those swallows which, by happy courtesy, had brought the Hair of Gold, and Tristan also he blessed, and the hundred knights who, on that adventurous bark, had gone to find him joy of heart and of eyes; yet to him also that ship was to bring sting, torment and mourning.

And on the eighteenth day, having called his Barony together he took Iseult to wife. But on the wedding night, to save her friend, Brangien took her place in the darkness, for her remorse demanded even this from her; nor was the trick discovered.

Then Iseult lived as a queen, but lived in sadness. She had King Mark's tenderness and the barons' honour; the people also loved her; she passed her days amid the frescoes on the walls and floors all strewn with flowers; good jewels had she and purple cloth and tapestry of Hungary and Thessaly too, and songs of harpers, and curtains upon which were worked leopards and eagles and popinjays and all the beasts of sea and field. And her love too she had, love high and splendid, for as is the custom among great lords, Tristan could ever be near her. At his leisure and his dalliance, night and day: for he slept in the King's chamber as great lords do, among the lieges and the councillors. Yet still she feared; for though her love were secret and Tristan unsuspected (for who suspects a son?) Brangien knew. And Brangien seemed in the Queen's mind like a witness spying; for Brangien alone knew what manner of life she led, and held her at mercy so. And the Queen thought: Ah, if some day she should weary of serving as a slave the bed where once she passed for Queen . . . If Tristan should die from her betrayal! So fear maddened the Queen, but not in truth the fear of Brangien who was loyal; her own heart bred the fear.

Not Brangien who was faithful, not Brangien, but themselves had these lovers to fear, for hearts so stricken will lose their vigilance. Love pressed them hard, as thirst presses the dying stag to the stream; love dropped upon them from high heaven, as a hawk slipped after long hunger falls right upon the bird. And love will not be hidden. Brangien indeed by her prudence saved them well, nor ever were the Queen and her lover unguarded. But in every hour and place every man could see Love terrible, that rode them, and could see in these lovers their every sense overflowing like new wine working in the vat.

The four felons at court who had hated Tristan of old for his prowess, watched the Queen; they had guessed that great love, and they burnt with envy and hatred and now a kind of evil joy. They planned to give news of their watching to the King, to see his tenderness turned to fury, Tristan thrust out or slain, and the Queen in torment; for though they feared Tristan their hatred mastered their fear; and, on a day, the four barons called King Mark to parley, and Andret said:

"Fair King, your heart will be troubled and we four also mourn; yet are we bound to tell you what we know. You have placed your trust in Tristan and Tristan would shame you. In vain we warned you. For the love of one man you have mocked ties of blood and all your Barony. Learn then that Tristan loves the Queen; it is truth proved and many a word is passing on it now."

The royal King shrank and answered:

"Coward! What thought was that? Indeed I have placed my trust in Tristan. And rightly, for on the day when the Morholt offered combat to you all, you hung your heads and were dumb, and you trembled before him; but Tristan dared him for the honour of this land, and took mortal wounds. Therefore do you hate him, and therefore do I cherish him beyond thee, Andret, and beyond any other; but what then have you seen or heard or known?"

"Naught, lord, save what your eyes could see or your ears hear. Look you and listen, Sire, if there is yet time."

And they left him to taste the poison.

Then King Mark watched the Queen and Tristan; but Brangien noting it warned them both and the King watched in vain, so that, soon wearying of an ignoble task, but knowing (alas!) that he could not kill his uneasy thought, he sent for Tristan and said:

"Tristan, leave this castle; and having left it, remain apart and do not think to return to it, and do not repass its moat or boundaries. Felons have charged you with an awful treason, but ask me nothing; I could not speak their words without shame to us both, and for your part seek you no word to appease. I have not believed them . . . had I done so . . . but their evil words have troubled all my soul and only by your absence can my disquiet be soothed. Go, doubtless I will soon recall you. Go, my son, you are still dear to me."

When the felons heard the news they said among themselves, "He is gone, the wizard; he is driven out. Surely he will cross the sea on far adventures to carry his traitor service to some distant King."

But Tristan had not strength to depart altogether; and when he had crossed the moats and boundaries of the Castle he knew he could go no further. He stayed in Tintagel town and lodged with Gorvenal in a burgess' house, and languished oh! more wounded than when in that past day the shaft of the Morholt had tainted his body.

In the close towers Iseult the Fair drooped also, but more wretched still. For it was hers all day long to feign laughter and all night long to conquer fever and despair. And all night as she lay by King Mark's side, fever still kept her waking, and she stared at darkness. She longed to fly to Tristan and she dreamt dreams of running to the gates and of finding there sharp scythes, traps of the felons, that cut her tender knees; and she dreamt of weakness and falling, and that her wounds had left her blood upon the ground. Now these lovers would have died, but Brangien succoured them. At peril of her life she found the house where Tristan lay. There Gorvenal opened to her very gladly, knowing what salvation she could bring.

So she found Tristan, and to save the lovers she taught him a device, nor was ever known a more subtle ruse of love.

Behind the castle of Tintagel was an orchard fenced around and wide and all closed in with stout and pointed stakes and numberless trees were there and fruit on them, birds and clusters of sweet grapes. And furthest from the castle, by the stakes of the pallisade, was a tall pine-tree, straight and with heavy branches spreading from its trunk. At its root a living spring welled calm into a marble round, then ran between two borders winding, throughout the orchard and so, on, till it flowed at last within the castle and through the women's rooms.

And every evening, by Brangien's counsel, Tristan cut him twigs and bark, leapt the sharp stakes and, having come beneath the pine, threw them into the clear spring; they floated light as foam down the stream to the women's rooms; and Iseult watched for their coming, and on those evenings she would wander out into the orchard and find her friend. Lithe and in fear would she come, watching at every step for what might lurk in the trees observing, foes or the felons whom she knew, till she spied Tristan; and the night and the branches of the pine protected them.

And so she said one night: "Oh, Tristan, I have heard that the castle is faëry and that twice a year it vanishes away. So is it vanished now and this is that enchanted orchard of which the harpers sing." And as she said it, the sentinels bugled dawn.

Iseult had refound her joy. Mark's thought of ill-ease grew faint; but the felons felt or knew which way lay truth, and they guessed that Tristan had met the Queen. Till at last Duke Andret (whom God shame) said to his peers:

"My lords, let us take counsel of Frocin the Dwarf; for he knows the seven arts, and magic and every kind of charm. He will teach us if he will the wiles of Iseult the Fair."

The little evil man drew signs for them and characters of sorcery; he cast the fortunes of the hour and then at last he said:

"Sirs, high good lords, this night shall you seize them both."

Then they led the little wizard to the King, and he said:

"Sire, bid your huntsmen leash the hounds and saddle the horses, proclaim a seven days' hunt in the forest and seven nights abroad therein, and hang me high if you do not hear this night what converse Tristan holds."

So did the King unwillingly; and at fall of night he left the hunt taking the dwarf in pillion, and entered the orchard, and the dwarf took him to the tall pine-tree, saying:

"Fair King, climb into these branches and take with you your arrows and your bow, for you may need them; and bide you still."

That night the moon shone clear. Hid in the branches the King saw his nephew leap the pallisades and throw his bark and twigs into the stream. But Tristan had bent over the round well to throw them and so doing had seen the image of the King. He could not stop the branches as they floated away, and there, yonder, in the women's rooms, Iseult was watching and would come.

She came, and Tristan watched her motionless. Above him in the tree he heard the click of the arrow when it fits the string.

She came, but with more prudence than her wont, thinking, "What has passed, that Tristan does not come to meet me? He has seen some foe."

Suddenly, by the clear moonshine, she also saw the King's shadow in the fount. She showed the wit of women well, she did not lift her eyes.

"Lord God," she said, low down, "grant I may be the first to speak."

"Tristan," she said, "what have you dared to do, calling me hither at such an hour? Often have you called me—to beseech, you said. And Queen though I am, I know you won me that title—and I have come. What would you?"

"Queen, I would have you pray the King for me."

She was in tears and trembling, but Tristan praised God the Lord who had shown his friend her peril.

"Queen," he went on, "often and in vain have I summoned you; never would you come. Take pity; the King hates me and I know not why. Perhaps you know the cause and can charm his anger. For whom can he trust if not you, chaste Queen and courteous, Iseult?"

"Truly, Lord Tristan, you do not know he doubts us both. And I, to add to my shame, must acquaint you of it. Ah! but God knows if I lie, never went out my love to any man but he that first received me. And would you have me, at such a time, implore your pardon of the King? Why, did he know of my passage here to-night he would cast my ashes to the wind. My body trembles and I am afraid. I go, for I have waited too long."

In the branches the King smiled and had pity.

And as Iseult fled: "Queen," said Tristan, "in the Lord's name help me, for charity."

"Friend," she replied, "God aid you! The King wrongs you but the Lord God will be by you in whatever land you go."

So she went back to the women's rooms and told it to Brangien, who cried: "Iseult, God has worked a miracle for you, for He is compassionate and will not hurt the innocent in heart."

And when he had left the orchard, the King said smiling:

"Fair nephew, that ride you planned is over now."

But in an open glade apart, Frocin, the Dwarf, read in the clear stars that the King now meant his death; he blackened with shame and fear and fled into Wales.

## The Discovery

King Mark made peace with Tristan. Tristan returned to the castle as of old. Tristan slept in the King's chamber with his peers. He could come or go, the King thought no more of it.

Mark had pardoned the felons, and as the seneschal, Dinas of Lidan, found the dwarf wandering in a forest abandoned, he brought him home, and the King had pity and pardoned even him.

But his goodness did but feed the ire of the barons, who swore this oath: If the King kept Tristan in the land they would withdraw to their strongholds as for war, and they called the King to parley.

"Lord," said they, "Drive you Tristan forth. He loves the Queen as all who choose can see, but as for us we will bear it no longer."

And the King sighed, looking down in silence.

"King," they went on, "we will not bear it, for we know now that this is known to you and that yet you will not move. Parley you, and take counsel. As for us if you will not exile this man, your nephew, and drive him forth out of your land forever, we will withdraw within our Bailiwicks and take our neighbours also from your court: for we cannot endure his presence longer in this place. Such is your balance: choose."

"My lords," said he, "once I hearkened to the evil words you spoke of Tristan, yet was I wrong in the end. But you are my lieges and I would not lose the service of my men. Counsel me therefore, I charge you, you that owe me counsel. You know me for a man neither proud nor overstepping."

"Lord," said they, "call then Frocin hither. You mistrust him for that orchard night. Still, was it not he that read in the stars of the Queen's coming there and to the very pine-tree too? He is very wise, take counsel of him."

And he came, did that hunchback of Hell: the felons greeted him and he planned this evil.

"Sire," said he, "let your nephew ride hard to-morrow at dawn with a brief drawn up on parchment and well sealed with a seal: bid him ride to King Arthur at Carduel. Sire, he sleeps with the peers in your chamber; go you out when the first sleep falls on men, and if he love Iseult so madly, why, then I swear by God and by the laws of Rome, he will try to speak with her before he rides. But if he do so unknown to you or to me, then slay me. As for the trap, let me lay it, but do you say nothing of his ride to him until the time for sleep."

And when King Mark had agreed, this dwarf did a vile thing. He bought of a baker four farthings' worth of flour, and hid it in the turn of his coat. That night, when the King had supped and the men-at-arms lay down to sleep in hall, Tristan came to the King as custom was, and the King said:

"Fair nephew, do my will: ride tomorrow night to King Arthur at Carduel, and give him this brief, with my greeting, that he may open it: and stay you with him but one day."

And when Tristan said: "I will take it on the morrow;"

The King added: "Aye, and before day dawn."

But, as the peers slept all round the King their lord, that night, a mad thought took Tristan that, before he rode, he knew not for how long, before dawn he would say a last word to the Queen. And there was a spear length in the darkness between them. Now the dwarf slept with the rest in the King's chamber, and when he thought that all slept he rose and scattered the flour silently in the spear length that lay between Tristan and the Queen; but Tristan watched and saw him, and said to himself:

"It is to mark my footsteps, but there shall be no marks to show."

At midnight, when all was dark in the room, no candle nor any lamp glimmering, the King went out silently by the door and with him the dwarf. Then Tristan rose in the darkness and judged the spear length and leapt the space between, for his farewell. But that day in the hunt a boar had wounded him in the leg, and in this effort the wound bled. He did not feel it or see it in the darkness, but the blood dripped upon the couches and the flour strewn between; and outside in the moonlight the dwarf read the heavens and knew what had been done and he cried:

"Enter, my King, and if you do not hold them, hang me high."

Then the King and the dwarf and the four felons ran in with lights and noise, and though Tristan had regained his place there was the blood for witness, and though Iseult feigned sleep, and Perinis too, who lay at Tristan's feet, yet there was the blood for witness. And the King looked in silence at the blood where it lay upon the bed and the boards and trampled into the flour.

And the four barons held Tristan down upon his bed and mocked the Queen also, promising her full justice; and they bared and showed the wound whence the blood flowed.

Then the King said:

"Tristan, now nothing longer holds. To-morrow you shall die."

And Tristan answered:

"Have mercy, Lord, in the name of God that suffered the Cross!"

But the felons called on the King to take vengeance, saying:

"Do justice, King: take vengeance."

And Tristan went on, "Have mercy, not on me—for why should I stand at dying?—Truly, but for you, I would have sold my honour high to cowards who, under your peace, have put hands on my body—but in homage to you I have yielded and you may do with me what you will. But, lord, remember the Queen!"

And as he knelt at the King's feet he still complained:

"Remember the Queen; for if any man of your household make so bold as to maintain the lie that I loved her unlawfully, I will stand up armed to him in a ring. Sire, in the name of God the Lord, have mercy on her."

Then the barons bound him with ropes, and the Queen also. But had Tristan known that trial by combat was to be denied him, certainly he would not have suffered it.

For he trusted in God and knew no man dared draw sword against him in the lists. And truly he did well to trust in God, for though the felons mocked him when he said he had loved loyally, yet I call you to witness, my lords who read this, and who know of the philtre drunk upon the high seas, and who understand whether his love were disloyalty indeed. For men see this and that outward thing, but God alone the heart, and in the heart alone is crime and the sole final judge is God. Therefore did He lay down the law that a man accused might uphold his cause by battle, and God himself fights for the innocent in such a combat.

Therefore did Tristan claim justice and the right of battle and therefore was he careful to fail in nothing of the homage he owed King Mark, his lord.

But had he known what was coming, he would have killed the felons.


# The Chantry Leap

Dark was the night, and the news ran that Tristan and the Queen were held and that the King would kill them; and wealthy burgess, or common man, they wept and ran to the palace.

And the murmurs and the cries ran through the city, but such was the King's anger in his castle above that not the strongest nor the proudest baron dared move him.

Night ended and the day drew near. Mark, before dawn, rode out to the place where he held pleas and judgment. He ordered a ditch to be dug in the earth and knotty vine-shoots and thorns to be laid therein.

At the hour of Prime he had a ban cried through his land to gather the men of Cornwall; they came with a great noise and the King spoke them thus:

"My lords, I have made here a faggot of thorns for Tristan and the Queen; for they have fallen."

But they cried all, with tears:

"A sentence, lord, a sentence; an indictment and pleas; for killing without trial is shame and crime."

But Mark answered in his anger:

"Neither respite, nor delay, nor pleas, nor sentence. By God that made the world, if any dare petition me, he shall burn first!"

He ordered the fire to be lit, and Tristan to be called.

The flames rose, and all were silent before the flames, and the King waited.

The servants ran to the room where watch was kept on the two lovers; and they dragged Tristan out by his hands, though he wept for his honour; but as they dragged him off in such a shame, the Queen still called to him:

"Friend, if I die that you may live, that will be great joy."

Now, hear how full of pity is God and how He heard the lament and the prayers of the common folk, that day.

For as Tristan and his guards went down from the town to where the faggot burned, near the road upon a rock was a chantry, it stood at a cliff's edge steep and sheer, and it turned to the sea-breeze; in the apse of it were windows glazed. Then Tristan said to those with him:

"My lords, let me enter this chantry, to pray for a moment the mercy of God whom I have offended; my death is near. There is but one door to the place, my lords, and each of you has his sword drawn. So, you may well see that, when my prayer to God is done, I must come past you again: when I have prayed God, my lords, for the last time."

And one of the guards said: "Why, let him go in."

So they let him enter to pray. But he, once in, dashed through and leapt the altar rail and the altar too and forced a window of the apse, and leapt again over the cliff's edge. So might he die, but not of that shameful death before the people.

Now learn, my lords, how generous was God to him that day. The wind took Tristan's cloak and he fell upon a smooth rock at the cliff's foot, which to this day the men of Cornwall call "Tristan's leap."

His guards still waited for him at the chantry door, but vainly, for God was now his guard. And he ran, and the fine sand crunched under his feet, and far off he saw the faggot burning, and the smoke and the crackling flames; and fled.

Sword girt and bridle loose, Gorvenal had fled the city, lest the King burn him in his master's place: and he found Tristan on the shore.

"Master," said Tristan, "God has saved me, but oh! master, to what end? For without Iseult I may not and I will not live, and I rather had died of my fall. They will burn her for me, then I too will die for her."

"Lord," said Gorvenal, "take no counsel of anger. See here this thicket with a ditch dug round about it. Let us hide therein where the track passes near, and comers by it will tell us news; and, boy, if they burn Iseult, I swear by God, the Son of Mary, never to sleep under a roof again until she be avenged."

There was a poor man of the common folk that had seen Tristan's fall, and had seen him stumble and rise after, and he crept to Tintagel and to Iseult where she was bound, and said:

"Queen, weep no more. Your friend has fled safely."

"Then I thank God," said she, "and whether they bind or loose me, and whether they kill or spare me, I care but little now."

And though blood came at the cord-knots, so tightly had the traitors bound her, yet still she said, smiling:

"Did I weep for that when God has loosed my friend I should be little worth."

When the news came to the King that Tristan had leapt that

leap and was lost he paled with anger, and bade his men bring forth Iseult.

They dragged her from the room, and she came before the crowd, held by her delicate hands, from which blood dropped, and the crowd called:

"Have pity on her—the loyal Queen and honoured! Surely they that gave her up brought mourning on us all—our curses on them!"

But the King's men dragged her to the thorn faggot as it blazed. She stood up before the flame, and the crowd cried its anger, and cursed the traitors and the King. None could see her without pity, unless he had a felon's heart: she was so tightly bound. The tears ran down her face and fell upon her grey gown where ran a little thread of gold, and a thread of gold was twined into her hair.

Just then there had come up a hundred lepers of the King's, deformed and broken, white horribly, and limping on their crutches. And they drew near the flame, and being evil, loved the sight. And their chief Ivan, the ugliest of them all, cried to the King in a quavering voice:

"O King, you would burn this woman in that flame, and it is sound justice, but too swift, for very soon the fire will fall, and her ashes will very soon be scattered by the high wind and her agony be done. Throw her rather to your lepers where she may drag out a life for ever asking death."

And the King answered:

"Yes; let her live that life, for it is better justice and more terrible. I can love those that gave me such a thought."

And the lepers answered:

"Throw her among us, and make her one of us. Never shall lady have known a worse end. And look," they said, "at our rags and our abominations. She has had pleasure in rich stuffs and furs, jewels and walls of marble, honour, good wines and joy, but when she sees your lepers always, King, and only them for ever, their couches and their huts, then indeed she will know the wrong she has done, and bitterly desire even that great flame of thorns."

And as the King heard them, he stood a long time without moving; then he ran to the Queen and seized her by the hand, and she cried:

"Burn me! rather burn me!"

But the King gave her up, and Ivan took her, and the hundred lepers pressed around, and to hear her cries all the crowd rose in pity. But Ivan had an evil gladness, and as he went he dragged her out of the borough bounds, with his hideous company.

Now they took that road where Tristan lay in hiding, and Gorvenal said to him:

"Son, here is your friend. Will you do naught?"

Then Tristan mounted the horse and spurred it out of the bush, and cried:

"Ivan, you have been at the Queen's side a moment, and too long. Now leave her if you would live."

But Ivan threw his cloak away and shouted:

"Your clubs, comrades, and your staves! Crutches in the air—for a fight is on!"

Then it was fine to see the lepers throwing their capes aside, and stirring their sick legs, and brandishing their crutches, some threatening: groaning all; but to strike them Tristan was too noble. There are singers who sing that Tristan killed Ivan, but it is a lie. Too much a knight was he to kill such things. Gorvenal indeed, snatching up an oak sapling, crashed it on Ivan's head till his blood ran down to his misshapen feet. Then Tristan took the Queen.

Henceforth near him she felt no further evil. He cut the cords that bound her arms so straightly, and he left the plain so that they plunged into the wood of Morois; and there in the thick wood Tristan was as sure as in a castle keep.

And as the sun fell they halted all three at the foot of a little hill: fear had wearied the Queen, and she leant her head upon his body and slept.

But in the morning, Gorvenal stole from a woodman his bow and two good arrows plumed and barbed, and gave them to Tristan, the great archer, and he shot him a fawn and killed it. Then Gorvenal gathered dry twigs, struck flint, and lit a great fire to cook the venison. And Tristan cut him branches and made a hut and garnished it with leaves. And Iseult slept upon the thick leaves there.

So, in the depths of the wild wood began for the lovers that savage life which yet they loved very soon.

# PART II

They wandered in the depths of the wild wood, restless and in haste like beasts that are hunted, nor did they often dare to return by night to the shelter of yesterday. They ate but the flesh of wild animals. Their faces sank and grew white, their clothes ragged, for the briars tore them. They loved each other and they did not know that they suffered.

One day, as they were wandering in these high woods that had never yet been felled or ordered, they came upon the hermitage of Ogrin.

The old man limped in the sunlight under a light growth of maples near his chapel: he leant upon his crutch, and cried:

"Lord Tristan, hear the great oath which the Cornish men have sworn. The King has published a ban in every parish: Whosoever may seize you shall receive a hundred marks of gold for his guerdon, and all the barons have sworn to give you up alive or dead. Do penance, Tristan! God pardons the sinner who turns to repentance."

"And of what should I repent, Ogrin, my lord? Or of what crime? You that sit in judgment upon us here, do you know what cup it was we drank upon the high sea? That good, great draught inebriates us both. I would rather beg my life long and live of roots and herbs with Iseult than, lacking her, be king of a wide kingdom."

"God aid you, Lord Tristan; for you have lost both this world and the next. A man that is traitor to his lord is worthy to be torn by horses and burnt upon the faggot, and wherever his ashes fall no grass shall grow and all tillage is waste, and the trees and the green things die. Lord Tristan, give back the Queen to the man who espoused her lawfully according to the laws of Rome."

"He gave her to his lepers. From these lepers I myself conquered her with my own hand; and henceforth she is altogether mine. She cannot pass from me nor I from her."

Ogrin sat down; but at his feet Iseult, her head upon the knees of that man of God, wept silently. The hermit told her and re-told her the words of his holy book, but still while she wept she shook her head, and refused the faith he offered.

"Ah me," said Ogrin then, "what comfort can one give the dead? Do penance, Tristan, for a man who lives in sin without repenting is a man quite dead."

"Oh no," said Tristan, "I live and I do no penance. We will go back into the high wood which comforts and wards us all round about. Come with me, Iseult, my friend."

Iseult rose up; they held each other's hands. They passed into the high grass and the underwood: the trees hid them with their branches. They disappeared beyond the curtain of the leaves.

The summer passed and the winter came: the two lovers lived, all hidden in the hollow of a rock, and on the frozen earth the cold crisped their couch with dead leaves. In the strength of their love neither one nor the other felt these mortal things. But when the open skies had come back with the springtime, they built a hut of green branches under the great trees. Tristan had known, ever since his childhood, that art by which a man may sing the song of birds in the woods, and at his fancy, he would call as call the thrush, the blackbird and the nightingale, and all winged things; and sometimes in reply very many birds would come on to the branches of his hut and sing their song full-throated in the new light.

The lovers had ceased to wander through the forest, for none of the barons ran the risk of their pursuit knowing well that Tristan would have hanged them to the branches of a tree. One day, however, one of the four traitors, Guenelon, whom God blast! drawn by the heat of the hunt, dared enter the Morois. And that morning, on the forest edge in a ravine, Gorvenal, having unsaddled his horse, had let him graze on the new grass, while far off in their hut Tristan held the Queen, and they slept. Then suddenly Gorvenal heard the cry of the pack; the hounds pursued a deer, which fell into that ravine. And far on the heath the hunter showed—and Gorvenal knew him for the man whom his master hated above all. Alone, with bloody spurs, and striking his horse's mane, he galloped on; but Gorvenal watched him from ambush: he came fast, he would return more slowly. He passed and Gorvenal leapt from his ambush and seized the rein and, suddenly, remembering all the wrong that man had done, hewed him to death and carried off his head in his hands. And when the hunters found the body, as they followed, they thought Tristan came after and they fled in fear of death, and thereafter no man hunted in that wood. And far off, in the hut upon their couch of leaves, slept Tristan and the Queen.

There came Gorvenal, noiseless, the dead man's head in his hands that he might lift his master's heart at his awakening. He hung it by its hair outside the hut, and the leaves garlanded it about. Tristan woke and saw it, half hidden in the leaves, and staring at him as he gazed, and he became afraid. But Gorvenal said: "Fear not, he is dead. I killed him with this sword."

Then Tristan was glad, and hence-forward from that day no one dared enter the wild wood, for terror guarded it and the lovers were lords of it all: and then it was that Tristan fashioned his bow "Failnaught" which struck home always, man or beast, whatever it aimed at.

My lords, upon a summer day, when mowing is, a little after

Whitsuntide, as the birds sang dawn Tristan left his hut and girt his sword on him, and took his bow "Failnaught" and went off to hunt in the wood; but before evening, great evil was to fall on him, for no lovers ever loved so much or paid their love so dear.

When Tristan came back, broken by the heat, the Queen said:

"Friend, where have you been?"

"Hunting a hart," he said, "that wearied me. I would lie down and sleep."

So she lay down, and he, and between them Tristan put his naked sword, and on the Queen's finger was that ring of gold with emeralds set therein, which Mark had given her on her bridal day; but her hand was so wasted that the ring hardly held. And no wind blew, and no leaves stirred, but through a crevice in the branches a sunbeam fell upon the face of Iseult, and it shone white like ice. Now a woodman found in the wood a place where the leaves were crushed, where the lovers had halted and slept, and he followed their track and found the hut, and saw them sleeping and fled off, fearing the terrible awakening of that lord. He fled to Tintagel, and going up the stairs of the palace, found the King as he held his pleas in hall amid the vassals assembled.

"Friend," said the King, "what came you hither to seek in haste and breathless, like a huntsman that has followed the dogs afoot? Have you some wrong to right, or has any man driven you?"

But the woodman took him aside and said low down:

"I have seen the Queen and Tristan, and I feared and fled."

"Where saw you them?"

"In a hut in Morois, they slept side by side. Come swiftly and take your vengeance."

"Go," said the King, "and await me at the forest edge where the red cross stands, and tell no man what you have seen. You shall have gold and silver at your will."

The King had saddled his horse and girt his sword and left the city alone, and as he rode alone he minded him of the night when he had seen Tristan under the great pine-tree, and Iseult with her clear face, and he thought:

"If I find them I will avenge this awful wrong."

At the foot of the red cross he came to the woodman and said:

"Go first, and lead me straight and quickly."

The dark shade of the great trees wrapt them round, and as the King followed the spy he felt his sword, and trusted it for the great blows it had struck of old; and surely had Tristan wakened, one of the two had stayed there dead. Then the woodman said:

"King, we are near."

He held the stirrup, and tied the rein to a green apple-tree, and saw in a sunlit glade the hut with its flowers and leaves. Then the King cast his cloak with its fine buckle of gold and drew his sword from its sheath and said again in his heart that they or he should die. And he signed to the woodman to be gone.

He came alone into the hut, sword bare, and watched them as they lay: but he saw that they were apart, and he wondered because between them was the naked blade.

Then he said to himself: "My God, I may not kill them. For all the time they have lived together in this wood, these two lovers, yet is the sword here between them, and throughout Christendom men know that sign. Therefore I will not slay, for that would be treason and wrong, but I will do so that when they wake they may know that I found them here, asleep, and spared them and that God had pity on them both."

And still the sunbeam fell upon the white face of Iseult, and the King took his ermined gloves and put them up against the crevice whence it shone.

Then in her sleep a vision came to Iseult. She seemed to be in a great wood and two lions near her fought for her, and she gave a cry and woke, and the gloves fell upon her breast; and at the cry Tristan woke, and made to seize his sword, and saw by the golden hilt that it was the King's. And the Queen saw on her finger the King's ring, and she cried:

"O, my lord, the King has found us here!"

And Tristan said:

"He has taken my sword; he was alone, but he will return, and will burn us before the people. Let us fly."

So by great marches with Gorvenal alone they fled towards Wales.


# Ogrin The Hermit

After three days it happened that Tristan, in following a wounded deer far out into the wood, was caught by night-fall, and took to thinking thus under the dark wood alone:

"It was not fear that moved the King . . . he had my sword and I slept . . . and had he wished to slay, why did he leave me his own blade? . . . O, my father, my father, I know you now. There was pardon in your heart, and tenderness and pity . . . yet how was that, for who could forgive in this matter without shame? . . . It was not pardon, it was understanding; the faggot and the chantry leap and the leper ambush have shown him God upon our side. Also I think he remembered the boy who long ago harped at his feet, and my land of Lyonesse which I left for him; the Morholt's spear and blood shed in his honour. He remembered how I made no avowal, but claimed a trial at arms, and the high nature of his heart has made him understand what men around him cannot; never can he know of the spell, yet he doubts and hopes and knows I have told no lie, and would have me prove my cause. O, but to win at arms by God's aid for him, and to enter his peace and to put on mail for him again . . . but then he must take her back, and I must yield her . . . it would have been much better had he killed me in my sleep. For till now I was hunted and I could hate and forget; he had thrown Iseult to the lepers, she was no more his, but mine; and now by his compassion he has wakened my heart and regained the Queen. For Queen she was at his side, but in this wood she lives a slave, and I waste her youth; and for rooms all hung with silk she has this savage place, and a hut for her splendid walls, and I am the cause that she treads this ugly road. So now I cry to God the Lord, who is King of the World, and beg Him to give me strength to yield back Iseult to King Mark; for she is indeed his wife, wed according to the laws of Rome before all the Barony of his land."

And as he thought thus, he leant upon his bow, and all through the night considered his sorrow.

Within the hollow of thorns that was their resting-place Iseult the Fair awaited Tristan's return. The golden ring that King Mark had slipped there glistened on her finger in the moonlight, and she thought:

"He that put on this ring is not the man who threw me to his lepers in his wrath; he is rather that compassionate lord who, from the day I touched his shore, received me and protected. And he loved Tristan once, but I came, and see what I have done! He should have lived in the King's palace; he should have ridden through King's and baron's fees, finding adventure; but through me he has forgotten his knighthood, and is hunted and exiled from the court, leading a random life . . ."

Just then she heard the feet of Tristan coming over the dead leaves and twigs. She came to meet him, as was her wont, to relieve him of his arms, and she took from him his bow, "Failnaught," and his arrows, and she unbuckled his sword-straps. And, "Friend," said he, "it is the King's sword. It should have slain, but it spared us."

Iseult took the sword, and kissed the hilt of gold, and Tristan saw her weeping.

"Friend," said he, "if I could make my peace with the King; if he would allow me to sustain in arms that neither by act nor word have I loved you with a wrongful love, any knight from the Marshes of Ely right away to Dureaume that would gainsay me, would find me armed in the ring. Then if the King would keep you and drive me out I would cross to the Lowlands or to Brittany with Gorvenal alone. But wherever I went and always, Queen, I should be yours; nor would I have spoken thus, Iseult, but for the wretchedness you bear so long for my sake in this desert land."

"Tristan," she said, "there is the hermit Ogrin. Let us return to him, and cry mercy to the King of Heaven."

They wakened Gorvenal; Iseult mounted the steed, and Tristan led it by the bridle, and all night long they went for the last time through the woods of their love, and they did not speak a word. By morning they came to the Hermitage, where Ogrin read at the threshold, and seeing them, called them tenderly:

"Friends," he cried, "see how Love drives you still to further wretchedness. Will you not do penance at last for your madness?"

"Lord Ogrin," said Tristan, "hear us. Help us to offer peace to the King, and I will yield him the Queen, and will myself go far away into Brittany or the Lowlands, and if some day the King suffer me, I will return and serve as I should."

And at the hermit's feet Iseult said in her turn:

"Nor will I live longer so, for though I will not say one word of penance for my love, which is there and remains forever, yet from now on I will be separate from him."

Then the hermit wept and praised God and cried: "High King, I praise Thy Name, for that Thou hast let me live so long as to give aid to these!"

And he gave them wise counsel, and took ink, and wrote a little writ offering the King what Tristan said.

That night Tristan took the road. Once more he saw the marble well and the tall pine-tree, and he came beneath the window where the King slept, and called him gently, and Mark awoke and whispered:

"Who are you that call me in the night at such an hour?"

"Lord, I am Tristan: I bring you a writ, and lay it here."

Then the King cried: "Nephew! nephew! for God's sake wait awhile," but Tristan had fled and joined his squire, and mounted rapidly. Gorvenal said to him:

"O, Tristan, you are mad to have come. Fly hard with me by the nearest road."

So they came back to the Hermitage, and there they found Ogrin at prayer, but Iseult weeping silently.

# The Ford

Mark had awakened his chaplain and had given him the writ to read; the chaplain broke the seal, saluted in Tristan's name, and then, when he had cunningly made out the written words, told him what Tristan offered; and Mark heard without saying a word, but his heart was glad, for he still loved the Queen.

He summoned by name the choicest of his baronage, and when they were all assembled they were silent and the King spoke:

"My lords, here is a writ, just sent me. I am your King, and you my lieges. Hear what is offered me, and then counsel me, for you owe me counsel."

The chaplain rose, unfolded the writ, and said, upstanding:

"My lords, it is Tristan that first sends love and homage to the King and all his Barony, and he adds, 'O King, when I slew the dragon and conquered the King of Ireland's daughter it was to me they gave her. I was to ward her at will and I yielded her to you. Yet hardly had you wed her when felons made you accept their lies, and in your anger, fair uncle, my lord, you would have had us burnt without trial. But God took compassion on us; we prayed him and he saved the Queen, as justice was: and me also—though I leapt from a high rock, I was saved by the power of God. And since then what have I done blameworthy? The Queen was thrown to the lepers; I came to her succour and bore her away. Could I have done less for a woman, who all but died innocent through me? I fled through the woods. Nor could I have come down into the vale and yielded her, for there was a ban to take us dead or alive. But now, as then, I am ready, my lord, to sustain in arms against all comers that never had the Queen for me, nor I for her, a love dishonourable to you. Publish the lists, and if I cannot prove my right in arms, burn me before your men. But if I conquer and you take back Iseult, no baron of yours will serve you as will I; and if you will not have me, I will offer myself to the King of Galloway, or to him of the Lowlands, and you will hear of me never again. Take counsel, King, for if you will make no terms I will take back Iseult to Ireland, and she shall be Queen in her own land.'"

When the barons of Cornwall heard how Tristan offered battle, they said to the King:

"Sire, take back the Queen. They were madmen that belied her to you. But as for Tristan, let him go and war it in Galloway, or in the Lowlands. Bid him bring back Iseult on such a day and that soon."

Then the King called thrice clearly:

"Will any man rise in accusation against Tristan?"

And as none replied, he said to his chaplain:

"Write me a writ in haste. You have heard what you shall write. Iseult has suffered enough in her youth. And let the writ be hung upon the arm of the red cross before evening. Write speedily."

Towards midnight Tristan crossed the Heath of Sand, and found the writ, and bore it sealed to Ogrin; and the hermit read the letter; "How Mark consented by the counsel of his barons to take back Iseult, but not to keep Tristan for his liege. Rather let him cross the sea, when, on the third day hence, at the Ford of Chances, he had given back the Queen into King Mark's hands."

Then Tristan said to the Queen:

"O, my God! I must lose you, friend! But it must be, since I can thus spare you what you suffer for my sake. But when we part for ever I will give you a pledge of mine to keep, and from whatever unknown land I reach I will send some messenger, and he will bring back word of you, and at your call I will come from far away."

Iseult said, sighing:

"Tristan, leave me your dog, Toothold, and every time I see him I will remember you, and will be less sad. And, friend, I have here a ring of green jasper. Take it for the love of me, and put it on your finger; then if anyone come saying he is from you, I will not trust him at all till he show me this ring, but once I have seen it, there is no power or royal ban that can prevent me from doing what you bid—wisdom or folly."

"Friend," he said, "here give I you Toothold."

"Friend," she replied, "take you this ring in reward."

And they kissed each other on the lips.

Now Ogrin, having left the lovers in the Hermitage, hobbled upon his crutch to the place called The Mount, and he bought ermine there and fur and cloth of silk and purple and scarlet, and a palfrey harnessed in gold that went softly, and the folk laughed to see him spending upon these the small moneys he had amassed so long; but the old man put the rich stuffs upon the palfrey and came back to Iseult.

And "Queen," said he, "take these gifts of mine that you may seem the finer on the day when you come to the Ford."

Meanwhile the King had had cried through Cornwall the news that on the third day he would make his peace with the Queen at the Ford, and knights and ladies came in a crowd to the gathering, for all loved the Queen and would see her, save the three felons that yet survived.

On the day chosen for the meeting, the field shone far with the rich tents of the barons, and suddenly Tristan and Iseult came out at the forest's edge, and caught sight of King Mark far off among his Barony:

"Friend," said Tristan, "there is the King, your lord—his knights and his men; they are coming towards us, and very soon we may not speak to each other again. By the God of Power I conjure you, if ever I send you a word, do you my bidding."

"Friend," said Iseult, "on the day that I see the ring, nor tower, nor wall, nor stronghold will let me from doing the will of my friend."

"Why then," he said, "Iseult, may God reward you."

Their horses went abreast and he drew her towards him with his arm.

"Friend," said Iseult, "hear my last prayer: you will leave this land, but wait some days; hide till you know how the King may treat me, whether in wrath or kindness, for I am afraid. Friend, Orri the woodman will entertain you hidden. Go you by night to the abandoned cellar that you know and I will send Perinis there to say if anyone misuse me."

"Friend, none would dare. I will stay hidden with Orri, and if any misuse you let him fear me as the Enemy himself."

Now the two troops were near and they saluted, and the King rode a bowshot before his men and with him Dinas of Lidan; and when the barons had come up, Tristan, holding Iseult's palfrey by the bridle, bowed to the King and said:

"O King, I yield you here Iseult the Fair, and I summon you, before the men of your land, that I may defend myself in your court, for I have had no judgment. Let me have trial at arms, and if I am conquered, burn me, but if I conquer, keep me by you, or, if you will not, I will be off to some far country."

But no one took up Tristan's wager, and the King, taking Iseult's palfrey by the bridle, gave it to Dinas, and went apart to take counsel.

Dinas, in his joy, gave all honour and courtesy to the Queen, but when the felons saw her so fair and honoured as of old, they were stirred and rode to the King, and said:

"King, hear our counsel. That the Queen was slandered we admit, but if she and Tristan re-enter your court together, rumour will revive again. Rather let Tristan go apart awhile. Doubtless some day you may recall him."

And so Mark did, and ordered Tristan by his barons to go off without delay.

Then Tristan came near the Queen for his farewell, and as they looked at one another the Queen in shame of that assembly blushed, but the King pitied her, and spoke his nephew thus for the first time:

"You cannot leave in these rags; take then from my treasury gold and silver and white fur and grey, as much as you will."

"King," said Tristan, "neither a penny nor a link of mail. I will go as I can, and serve with high heart the mighty King in the Lowlands."

And he turned rein and went down towards the sea, but Iseult followed him with her eyes, and so long as he could yet be seen a long way off she did not turn.

Now at the news of the peace, men, women, and children, great and small, ran out of the town in a crowd to meet Iseult, and while they mourned Tristan's exile they rejoiced at the Queen's return.

And to the noise of bells, and over pavings strewn with branches, the King and his counts and princes made her escort, and the gates of the palace were thrown open that rich and poor might enter and eat and drink at will.

And Mark freed a hundred of his slaves, and armed a score of squires that day with hauberk and with sword.

But Tristan that night hid with Orri, as the Queen had counselled him.


## The Ordeal by Iron

Denoalen, Andret, and Gondoïn held themselves safe; Tristan was far over sea, far away in service of a distant king, and they beyond his power. Therefore, during a hunt one day, as the King rode apart in a glade where the pack would pass, and hearkening to the hounds, they all three rode towards him, and said:

"O King, we have somewhat to say. Once you condemned the Queen without judgment, and that was wrong; now you acquit her without judgment, and that is wrong. She is not quit by trial, and the barons of your land blame you both. Counsel her, then, to claim the ordeal in God's judgment, for since she is innocent, she may swear on the relics of the saints and hot iron will not hurt her. For so custom runs, and in this easy way are doubts dissolved."

But Mark answered:

"God strike you, my Cornish lords, how you hunt my shame! For you have I exiled my nephew, and now what would you now? Would you have me drive the Queen to Ireland too? What novel plaints have you to plead? Did not Tristan offer you battle in this matter? He offered battle to clear the Queen forever: he offered and you heard him all. Where then were your lances and your shields?"

"Sire," they said, "we have counselled you loyal counsel as lieges and to your honour; henceforward we hold our peace. Put aside your anger and give us your safe-guard."

But Mark stood up in the stirrup and cried:

"Out of my land, and out of my peace, all of you! Tristan I exiled for you, and now go you in turn, out of my land!"

But they answered:

"Sire, it is well. Our keeps are strong and fenced, and stand on rocks not easy for men to climb."

And they rode off without a salutation.

But the King (not tarrying for huntsman or for hound but straight away) spurred his horse to Tintagel; and as he sprang up the stairs the Queen heard the jangle of his spurs upon the stones.

She rose to meet him and took his sword as she was wont, and bowed before him, as it was also her wont to do; but Mark raised her, holding her hands; and when Iseult looked up she saw his noble face in just that wrath she had seen before the faggot fire.

She thought that Tristan was found, and her heart grew cold, and without a word she fell at the King's feet.

He took her in his arms and kissed her gently till she could speak again, and then he said:

"Friend, friend, what evil tries you?"

"Sire, I am afraid, for I have seen your anger."

"Yes, I was angered at the hunt."

"My lord, should one take so deeply the mischances of a game?"

Mark smiled and said:

"No, friend; no chance of hunting vexed me, but those three felons whom you know; and I have driven them forth from my land."

"Sire, what did they say, or dare to say of me?"

"What matter? I have driven them forth."

"Sire, all living have this right: to say the word they have conceived. And I would ask a question, but from whom shall I learn save from you? I am alone in a foreign land, and have no one else to defend me."

"They would have it that you should quit yourself by solemn oath and by the ordeal of iron, saying 'that God was a true judge, and that as the Queen was innocent, she herself should seek such judgment as would clear her for ever.' This was their clamour and their demand incessantly. But let us leave it. I tell you, I have driven them forth."

Iseult trembled, but looking straight at the King, she said:

"Sire, call them back; I will clear myself by oath. But I bargain this: that on the appointed day you call King Arthur and Lord Gawain, Girflet, Kay the Seneschal, and a hundred of his knights to ride to the Sandy Heath where your land marches with his, and a river flows between; for I will not swear before your barons alone, lest they should demand some new thing, and lest there should be no end to my trials. But if my warrantors, King Arthur and his knights, be there, the barons will not dare dispute the judgment."

But as the heralds rode to Carduel, Iseult sent to Tristan secretly her squire Perinis: and he ran through the underwood, avoiding paths, till he found the hut of Orri, the woodman, where Tristan for many days had awaited news. Perinis told him all: the ordeal, the place, and the time, and added:

"My lord, the Queen would have you on that day and place come dressed as a pilgrim, so that none may know you—unarmed, so that none may challenge—to the Sandy Heath. She must cross the river to the place appointed. Beyond it, where Arthur and his hundred knights will stand, be you also; for my lady fears the judgment, but she trusts in God."

Then Tristan answered:

"Go back, friend Perinis, return you to the Queen, and say that I will do her bidding."

And you must know that as Perinis went back to Tintagel he caught sight of that same woodman who had betrayed the lovers before, and the woodman, as he found him, had just dug a pitfall for wolves and for wild boars, and covered it with leafy branches to hide it, and as Perinis came near the woodman fled, but Perinis drove him, and caught him, and broke his staff and his head together, and pushed his body into the pitfall with his feet.

On the appointed day King Mark and Iseult, and the barons of Cornwall, stood by the river; and the knights of Arthur and all their host were arrayed beyond.

And just before them, sitting on the shore, was a poor pilgrim, wrapped in cloak and hood, who held his wooden platter and begged alms.

Now as the Cornish boats came to the shoal of the further bank, Iseult said to the knights:

"My lords, how shall I land without befouling my clothes in the river-mud? Fetch me a ferryman."

And one of the knights hailed the pilgrim, and said:

"Friend, truss your coat, and try the water; carry you the Queen to shore, unless you fear the burden."

But as he took the Queen in his arms she whispered to him: "Friend."

And then she whispered to him, lower still:

"Stumble you upon the sand."

And as he touched shore, he stumbled, holding the Queen in his arms; and the squires and boatmen with their oars and boat-hooks drove the poor pilgrim away.

But the Queen said:

"Let him be; some great travail and journey has weakened him."

And she threw to the pilgrim a little clasp of gold.

Before the tent of King Arthur was spread a rich Nicean cloth upon the grass, and the holy relics were set on it, taken out of their covers and their shrines.

And round the holy relics on the sward stood a guard more than a king's guard, for Lord Gawain, Girflet, and Kay the Seneschal kept ward over them.

The Queen having prayed God, took off the jewels from her neck and hands, and gave them to the beggars around; she took off her purple mantle, and her overdress, and her shoes with their precious stones, and gave them also to the poor that loved her.

She kept upon her only the sleeveless tunic, and then with arms and feet quite bare she came between the two kings, and all around the barons watched her in silence, and some wept, for near the holy relics was a brazier burning.

And trembling a little she stretched her right hand towards the bones and said: "Kings of Logres and of Cornwall; my lords Gawain, and Kay, and Girflet, and all of you that are my warrantors, by these holy things and all the holy things of earth, I swear that no man has held me in his arms saving King

Mark, my lord, and that poor pilgrim. King Mark, will that oath stand?"

"Yes, Queen," he said, "and God see to it."

"Amen," said Iseult, and then she went near the brazier, pale and stumbling, and all were silent. The iron was red, but she thrust her bare arms among the coals and seized it, and bearing it took nine steps.

Then, as she cast it from her, she stretched her arms out in a cross, with the palms of her hands wide open, and all men saw them fresh and clean and cold. Seeing that great sight the kings and the barons and the people stood for a moment silent, then they stirred together and they praised God loudly all around.

# Part III

When Tristan had come back to Orri's hut, and had loosened his heavy pilgrim's cape, he saw clearly in his heart that it was time to keep his oath to King Mark and to fly the land.

Three days yet he tarried, because he could not drag himself away from that earth, but on the fourth day he thanked the woodman, and said to Gorvenal:

"Master, the hour is come."

And he went into Wales, into the land of the great Duke Gilain, who was young, powerful, and frank in spirit, and welcomed him nobly as a God-sent guest.

And he did everything to give him honour and joy; but he found that neither adventure, nor feast could soothe what Tristan suffered.

One day, as he sat by the young Duke's side, his spirit weighed upon him, so that not knowing it he groaned, and the Duke, to soothe him, ordered into his private room a fairy thing, which pleased his eyes when he was sad and relieved his own heart; it was a dog, and the varlets brought it in to him, and they put it upon a table there. Now this dog was a fairy dog, and came from the Duke of Avalon; for a fairy had given it him as a love-gift, and no one can well describe its kind or beauty. And it bore at its neck, hung to a little chain of gold, a little bell; and that tinkled so gaily, and so clear and so soft, that as Tristan heard it, he was soothed, and his anguish melted away, and he forgot all that he had suffered for the Queen; for such was the virtue of the bell and such its property: that whosoever heard it, he lost all pain. And as

Tristan stroked the little fairy thing, the dog that took away his sorrow, he saw how delicate it was and fine, and how it had soft hair like samite, and he thought how good a gift it would make for the Queen. But he dared not ask for it right out since he knew that the Duke loved this dog beyond everything in the world, and would yield it to no prayers, nor to wealth, nor to wile; so one day Tristan having made a plan in his mind said this:

"Lord, what would you give to the man who could rid your land of the hairy giant Urgan, that levies such a toll?"

"Truly, the victor might choose what he would, but none will dare."

Then said Tristan:

"Those are strange words, for good comes to no land save by risk and daring, and not for all the gold of Milan would I renounce my desire to find him in his wood and bring him down."

Then Tristan went out to find Urgan in his lair, and they fought hard and long, till courage conquered strength, and Tristan, having cut off the giant's hand, bore it back to the Duke.

And "Sire," said he, "since I may choose a reward according to your word, give me the little fairy dog. It was for that I conquered Urgan, and your promise stands."

"Friend," said the Duke, "take it, then, but in taking it you take away also all my joy."

Then Tristan took the little fairy dog and gave it in ward to a Welsh harper, who was cunning and who bore it to Cornwall till he came to Tintagel, and having come there put it secretly into Brangien's hands, and the Queen was so pleased that she gave ten marks of gold to the harper, but she put it about that the Queen of Ireland, her mother, had sent the beast. And she had a goldsmith work a little kennel for him, all jewelled, and incrusted with gold and enamel inlaid; and wherever she went she carried the dog with her in memory of her friend, and as she watched it sadness and anguish and regrets melted out of her heart.

At first she did not guess the marvel, but thought her consolation was because the gift was Tristan's, till one day she found that it was fairy, and that it was the little bell that charmed her soul; then she thought: "What have I to do with comfort since he is sorrowing? He could have kept it too and have forgotten his sorrow; but with high courtesy he sent it to me to give me his joy and to take up his pain again. Friend, while you suffer, so long will I suffer also."

And she took the magic bell and shook it just a little, and then by the open window she threw it into the sea.

# Iseult of the White Hands

Apart the lovers could neither live nor die, for it was life and death together; and Tristan fled his sorrow through seas and islands and many lands.

He fled his sorrow still by seas and islands, till at last he came back to his land of Lyonesse, and there Rohalt, the keeper of faith, welcomed him with happy tears and called him son. But he could not live in the peace of his own land, and he turned again and rode through kingdoms and through baronies, seeking adventure. From the Lyonesse to the Lowlands, from the Lowlands on to the Germanies; through the Germanies and into Spain. And many lords he served, and many deeds did, but for two years no news came to him out of Cornwall, nor friend, nor messenger. Then he thought that Iseult had forgotten.

Now it happened one day that, riding with Gorvenal alone, he came into the land of Brittany. They rode through a wasted plain of ruined walls and empty hamlets and burnt fields everywhere, and the earth deserted of men; and Tristan thought:

"I am weary, and my deeds profit me nothing; my lady is far off and I shall never see her again. Or why for two years has she made no sign, or why has she sent no messenger to find me as I wandered? But in Tintagel Mark honours her and she gives him joy, and that little fairy bell has done a thorough work; for little she remembers or cares for the joys and the mourning of old, little for me, as I wander in this desert place. I, too, will forget."

On the third day, at the hour of noon, Tristan and Gorvenal came near a hill where an old chantry stood and close by a hermitage also; and Tristan asked what wasted land that was, and the hermit answered:

"Lord, it is Breton land which Duke Hoël holds, and once it was rich in pasture and ploughland, but Count Riol of Nantes has wasted it. For you must know that this Count Riol was the Duke's vassal. And the Duke has a daughter, fair among all King's daughters, and Count Riol would have taken her to wife; but her father refused her to a vassal, and Count Riol would have carried her away by force. Many men have died in that quarrel."

And Tristan asked:

"Can the Duke wage his war?"

And the hermit answered:

"Hardly, my lord; yet his last keep of Carhaix holds out still, for the walls are strong, and strong is the heart of the Duke's son Kaherdin, a very good knight and bold; but the enemy surrounds them on every side and starves them. Very hardly do they hold their castle."

Then Tristan asked:

"How far is this keep of Carhaix?"

"Sir," said the hermit, "it is but two miles further on this way."

Then Tristan and Gorvenal lay down, for it was evening.

In the morning, when they had slept, and when the hermit had chanted, and had shared his black bread with them, Tristan thanked him and rode hard to Carhaix. And as he halted beneath the fast high walls, he saw a little company of men behind the battlements, and he asked if the Duke were there with his son Kaherdin. Now Hoël was among them; and when he cried "yes," Tristan called up to him and said:

"I am that Tristan, King of Lyonesse, and Mark of Cornwall is my uncle. I have heard that your vassals do you a wrong, and I have come to offer you my arms."

"Alas, lord Tristan, go you your way alone and God reward you, for here within we have no more food; no wheat, or meat, or any stores but only lentils and a little oats remaining."

But Tristan said:

"For two years I dwelt in a forest, eating nothing save roots and herbs; yet I found it a good life, so open you the door."

They welcomed him with honour, and Kaherdin showed him the wall and the dungeon keep with all their devices, and from the battlements he showed the plain where far away gleamed the tents of Duke Riol. And when they were down in the castle again he said to Tristan:

"Friend, let us go to the hall where my mother and sister sit."

So, holding each other's hands, they came into the women's room, where the mother and the daughter sat together weaving gold upon English cloth and singing a weaving song. They sang of Doette the fair who sits alone beneath the white-thorn, and round about her blows the wind. She waits for Doon, her friend, but he tarries long and does not come. This was the song they sang. And Tristan bowed to them, and they to him. Then Kaherdin, showing the work his mother did, said:

"See, friend Tristan, what a work-woman is here, and how

marvellously she adorns stoles and chasubles for the poor minsters, and how my sister's hands run thread of gold upon this cloth. Of right, good sister, are you called, 'Iseult of the White Hands.'"

But Tristan, hearing her name, smiled and looked at her more gently.

And on the morrow, Tristan, Kaherdin, and twelve young knights left the castle and rode to a pinewood near the enemy's tents. And sprang from ambush and captured a waggon of Count Riol's food; and from that day, by escapade and ruse they would carry tents and convoys and kill off men, nor ever come back without some booty; so that Tristan and Kaherdin began to be brothers in arms, and kept faith and tenderness, as history tells. And as they came back from these rides, talking chivalry together, often did Kaherdin praise to his comrade his sister, Iseult of the White Hands, for her simplicity and beauty.

One day, as the dawn broke, a sentinel ran from the tower through the halls crying:

"Lords, you have slept too long; rise, for an assault is on."

And knights and burgesses armed, and ran to the walls, and saw helmets shining on the plain, and pennons streaming crimson, like flames, and all the host of Riol in its array. Then the Duke and Kaherdin deployed their horsemen before the gates, and from a bow-length off they stooped, and spurred and charged, and they put their lances down together and the arrows fell on them like April rain.

Now Tristan had armed himself among the last of those the sentinel had roused, and he laced his shoes of steel, and put on his mail, and his spurs of gold, his hauberk, and his helm over the gorget, and he mounted and spurred, with shield on breast, crying:

"Carhaix!"

And as he came, he saw Duke Riol charging, rein free, at Kaherdin, but Tristan came in between. So they met, Tristan and Duke Riol. And at the shock, Tristan's lance shivered, but Riol's lance struck Tristan's horse just where the breast-piece runs, and laid it on the field.

But Tristan, standing, drew his sword, his burnished sword, and said:

"Coward! Here is death ready for the man that strikes the horse before the rider."

But Riol answered:

"I think you have lied, my lord!"

And he charged him.

And as he passed, Tristan let fall his sword so heavily upon his helm that he carried away the crest and the nasal, but the sword slipped on the mailed shoulder, and glanced on the horse, and killed it, so that of force Duke Riol must slip the stirrup and leap and feel the ground. Then Riol too was on his feet, and they both fought hard in their broken mail, their 'scutcheons torn and their helmets loosened and lashing with their dented swords, till Tristan struck Riol just where the helmet buckles, and it yielded and the blow was struck so hard that the baron fell on hands and knees; but when he had risen again, Tristan struck him down once more with a blow that split the helm, and it split the headpiece too, and touched the skull; then Riol cried mercy and begged his life, and Tristan took his sword.

So he promised to enter Duke Hoël's keep and to swear homage again, and to restore what he had wasted; and by his order the battle ceased, and his host went off discomfited.

Now when the victors were returned Kaherdin said to his father:

"Sire, keep you Tristan. There is no better knight, and your land has need of such courage."

So when the Duke had taken counsel with his barons, he said to Tristan:

"Friend, I owe you my land, but I shall be quit with you if you will take my daughter, Iseult of the White Hands, who comes of kings and of queens, and of dukes before them in blood."

And Tristan answered:

"I will take her, Sire."

So the day was fixed, and the Duke came with his friends and Tristan with his, and before all, at the gate of the minster, Tristan wed Iseult of the White Hands, according to the Church's law.

But that same night, as Tristan's valets undressed him, it happened that in drawing his arm from the sleeve they drew off and let fall from his finger the ring of green jasper, the ring of Iseult the Fair. It sounded on the stones, and Tristan looked and saw it. Then his heart awoke and he knew that he had done wrong. For he remembered the day when Iseult the Fair had given him the ring. It was in that forest where, for his sake, she had led the hard life with him, and that night he saw again the hut in the wood of Morois, and he was bitter with himself that ever he had accused her of treason; for now it was he that had betrayed, and he was bitter with himself also in pity for this new wife and her simplicity and beauty. See how these two Iseults had met him in an evil hour, and to both had he broken faith!

Now Iseult of the White Hands said to him, hearing him sigh:

"Dear lord, have I hurt you in anything? Will you not speak me a single word?"

But Tristan answered: "Friend, do not be angry with me; for once in another land I fought a foul dragon and was near to death, and I thought of the Mother of God, and I made a vow to Her that, should I ever wed, I would spend the first holy nights of my wedding in prayer and in silence."

"Why," said Iseult, "that was a good vow."

And Tristan watched through the night.

# The Madness Of Tristan

Within her room at Tintagel, Iseult the Fair sighed for the sake of Tristan, and named him, her desire, of whom for two years she had had no word, whether he lived or no.

Within her room at Tintagel Iseult the Fair sat singing a song she had made. She sang of Guron taken and killed for his love, and how by guile the Count gave Guron's heart to her to eat, and of her woe. The Queen sang softly, catching the harp's tone; her hands were cunning and her song good; she sang low down and softly.

Then came in Kariado, a rich count from a far-off island, that had fared to Tintagel to offer the Queen his service, and had spoken of love to her, though she disdained his folly. He found Iseult as she sang, and laughed to her:

"Lady, how sad a song! as sad as the Osprey's; do they not say he sings for death? and your song means that to me; I die for you."

And Iseult said: "So let it be and may it mean so; for never come you here but to stir in me anger or mourning. Ever were you the screech owl or the Osprey that boded ill when you spoke of Tristan; what news bear you now?"

And Kariado answered:

"You are angered, I know not why, but who heeds your words? Let the Osprey bode me death; here is the evil news the screech owl brings. Lady Iseult, Tristan, your friend is lost to you. He has wed in a far land. So seek you other where, for he mocks your love. He has wed in great pomp Iseult of the White Hands, the King of Brittany's daughter."

And Kariado went off in anger, but Iseult bowed her head and broke into tears.

Now far from Iseult, Tristan languished, till on a day he must needs see her again. Far from her, death came surely; and he had rather die at once than day by day. And he desired some death, but that the Queen might know it was in finding her; then would death come easily.

So he left Carhaix secretly, telling no man, neither his kindred nor even Kaherdin, his brother in arms. He went in rags afoot (for no one marks the beggar on the high road) till he came to the shore of the sea.

He found in a haven a great ship ready, the sail was up and the anchor-chain short at the bow.

"God save you, my lords," he said, "and send you a good journey. To what land sail you now?"

"To Tintagel," they said.

Then he cried out:

"Oh, my lords! take me with you thither!"

And he went aboard, and a fair wind filled the sail, and she ran five days and nights for Cornwall, till, on the sixth day, they dropped anchor in Tintagel Haven. The castle stood above, fenced all around. There was but the one armed gate, and two knights watched it night and day. So Tristan went ashore and sat upon the beach, and a man told him that Mark was there and had just held his court.

"But where," said he, "is Iseult, the Queen, and her fair maid, Brangien?"

"In Tintagel too," said the other, "and I saw them lately; the Queen sad, as she always is."

At the hearing of the name, Tristan suffered, and he thought that neither by guile nor courage could he see that friend, for Mark would kill him.

And he thought, "Let him kill me and let me die for her, since every day I die. But you, Iseult, even if you knew me here, would you not drive me out?" And he thought, "I will try guile. I will seem mad, but with a madness that shall be great wisdom. And many shall think me a fool that have less wit than I."

Just then a fisherman passed in a rough cloak and cape, and Tristan seeing him, took him aside, and said:

"Friend, will you not change clothes?"

And as the fisherman found it a very good bargain, he said in answer:

"Yes, friend, gladly."

And he changed and ran off at once for fear of losing his gain. Then Tristan shaved his wonderful hair; he shaved it close to his head and left a cross all bald, and he rubbed his face with magic herbs distilled in his own country, and it changed in colour and skin so that none could know him, and he made him a club from a young tree torn from a hedge-row and hung it to his neck, and went bare-foot towards the castle.

The porter made sure that he had to do with a fool and said:

"Good morrow, fool, where have you been this long while?"

And he answered:

"At the Abbot of St. Michael's wedding, and he wed an abbess, large and veiled. And from the Alps to Mount St. Michael how they came, the priests and abbots, monks and regulars, all dancing on the green with croziers and with staves under the high trees' shade. But I left them all to come hither, for I serve at the King's board to-day."

Then the porter said:

"Come in, lord fool; the Hairy Urgan's son, I know, and like your father."

And when he was within the courts the serving men ran after him and cried:

"The fool! the fool!"

But he made play with them though they cast stones and struck him as they laughed, and in the midst of laughter and their cries, as the rout followed him, he came to that hall where, at the Queen's side, King Mark sat under his canopy.

And as he neared the door with his club at his neck, the King said:

"Here is a merry fellow, let him in."

And they brought him in, his club at his neck. And the King said:

"Friend, well come; what seek you here?"

"Iseult," said he, "whom I love so well; I bring my sister with me, Brunehild, the beautiful. Come, take her, you are weary of the Queen. Take you my sister and give me here Iseult, and I will hold her and serve you for her love."

The King said laughing:

"Fool, if I gave you the Queen, where would you take her, pray?"

"Oh! very high," he said, "between the clouds and heaven, into a fair chamber glazed. The beams of the sun shine through it, yet the winds do not trouble it at all. There would I bear the Queen into that crystal chamber of mine all compact of roses and the morning."

The King and his barons laughed and said:

"Here is a good fool at no loss for words."

But the fool as he sat at their feet gazed at Iseult most fixedly.

"Friend," said King Mark, "what warrant have you that the Queen would heed so foul a fool as you?"

"O! Sire," he answered gravely, "many deeds have I done for her, and my madness is from her alone."

"What is your name?" they said, and laughed.

"Tristan," said he, "that loved the Queen so well, and still till death will love her."

But at the name the Queen angered and weakened together, and said: "Get hence for an evil fool!"

But the fool, marking her anger, went on:

"Queen Iseult, do you mind the day, when, poisoned by the Morholt's spear, I took my harp to sea and fell upon your shore? Your mother healed me with strange drugs. Have you no memory, Queen?"

But Iseult answered:

"Out, fool, out! Your folly and you have passed the bounds!"

But the fool, still playing, pushed the barons out, crying:

"Out! madmen, out! Leave me to counsel with Iseult, since I come here for the love of her!"

And as the King laughed, Iseult blushed and said:

"King, drive me forth this fool!"

But the fool still laughed and cried:

"Queen, do you mind you of the dragon I slew in your land? I hid its tongue in my hose, and, burnt of its venom, I fell by the roadside. Ah! what a knight was I then, and it was you that succoured me."

Iseult replied:

"Silence! You wrong all knighthood by your words, for you are a fool from birth. Cursed be the seamen that brought you hither; rather should they have cast you into the sea!"

"Queen Iseult," he still said on, "do you mind you of your haste when you would have slain me with my own sword? And of the Hair of Gold? And of how I stood up to the seneschal?"

"Silence!" she said, "you drunkard. You were drunk last night, and so you dreamt these dreams."

"Drunk, and still so am I," said he, "but of such a draught that never can the influence fade. Queen Iseult, do you mind you of that hot and open day on the high seas? We thirsted and we drank together from the same cup, and since that day have I been drunk with an awful wine."

When the Queen heard these words which she alone could understand, she rose and would have gone.

But the King held her by her ermine cloak, and she sat down again.

And as the King had his fill of the fool he called for his falcons and went to hunt; and Iseult said to him:

"Sire, I am weak and sad; let me be go rest in my room; I am tired of these follies."

And she went to her room in thought and sat upon her bed and mourned, calling herself a slave and saying:

"Why was I born? Brangien, dear sister, life is so hard to me that death were better! There is a fool without, shaven criss-cross, and come in an evil hour, and he is warlock, for he knows in every part myself and my whole life; he knows what you and I and Tristan only know."

Then Brangien said: "It may be Tristan."

But—"No," said the Queen, "for he was the first of knights, but this fool is foul and made awry. Curse me his hour and the ship that brought him hither."

"My lady!" said Brangien, "soothe you. You curse over much these days. May be he comes from Tristan?"

"I cannot tell. I know him not. But go find him, friend, and see if you know him."

So Brangien went to the hall where the fool still sat alone. Tristan knew her and let fall his club and said:

"Brangien, dear Brangien, before God! have pity on me!"

"Foul fool," she answered, "what devil taught you my name?"

"Lady," he said, "I have known it long. By my head, that once was fair, if I am mad the blame is yours, for it was yours to watch over the wine we drank on the high seas. The cup was of silver and I held it to Iseult and she drank. Do you remember, lady?"

"No," she said, and as she trembled and left he called out: "Pity me!"

He followed and saw Iseult. He stretched out his arms, but in her shame, sweating agony she drew back, and Tristan angered and said:

"I have lived too long, for I have seen the day that Iseult will nothing of me. Iseult, how hard love dies! Iseult, a welling water that floods and runs large is a mighty thing; on the day that it fails it is nothing; so love that turns."

But she said:

"Brother, I look at you and doubt and tremble, and I know you not for Tristan."

"Queen Iseult, I am Tristan indeed that do love you; mind you for the last time of the dwarf, and of the flower, and of the blood I shed in my leap. Oh! and of that ring I took in kisses and in tears on the day we parted. I have kept that jasper ring and asked it counsel."

Then Iseult knew Tristan for what he was, and she said:

"Heart, you should have broken of sorrow not to have known the man who has suffered so much for you. Pardon, my master and my friend."

And her eyes darkened and she fell; but when the light returned she was held by him who kissed her eyes and her face.

So passed they three full days. But, on the third, two maids that watched them told the traitor Andret, and he put spies well-armed before the women's rooms. And when Tristan would enter they cried:

"Back, fool!"

But he brandished his club laughing, and said:

"What! May I not kiss the Queen who loves me and awaits me now?"

And they feared him for a mad fool, and he passed in through the door.

Then, being with the Queen for the last time, he held her in his arms and said:

"Friend, I must fly, for they are wondering. I must fly, and perhaps shall never see you more. My death is near, and far from you my death will come of desire."

"Oh friend," she said, "fold your arms round me close and strain me so that our hearts may break and our souls go free at last. Take me to that happy place of which you told me long ago. The fields whence none return, but where great singers sing their songs for ever. Take me now."

"I will take you to the Happy Palace of the living, Queen! The time is near. We have drunk all joy and sorrow. The time is near. When it is finished, if I call you, will you come, my friend?"

"Friend," said she, "call me and you know that I shall come."

"Friend," said he, "God send you His reward."

As he went out the spies would have held him; but he laughed aloud, and flourished his club, and cried:

"Peace, gentlemen, I go and will not stay. My lady sends me to prepare that shining house I vowed her, of crystal, and of rose shot through with morning."

And as they cursed and drave him, the fool went leaping on his way.

# The Death of Tristan

When he was come back to Brittany, to Carhaix, it happened that Tristan, riding to the aid of Kaherdin his brother in arms, fell into ambush and was wounded by a poisoned spear; and many doctors came, but none could cure him of the ill. And Tristan weakened and paled, and his bones showed.

Then he knew that his life was going, and that he must die, and he had a desire to see once more Iseult the Fair, but he could not seek her, for the sea would have killed him in his weakness, and how could Iseult come to him? And sad, and suffering the poison, he awaited death.

He called Kaherdin secretly to tell him his pain, for they loved each other with a loyal love; and as he would have no one in the room save Kaherdin, nor even in the neighbouring rooms, Iseult of the White Hands began to wonder. She was afraid and wished to hear, and she came back and listened at the wall by Tristan's bed; and as she listened one of her maids kept watch for her.

Now, within, Tristan had gathered up his strength, and had half risen, leaning against the wall, and Kaherdin wept beside him. They wept their good comradeship, broken so soon, and their friendship: then Tristan told Kaherdin of his love for that other Iseult, and of the sorrow of his life.

"Fair friend and gentle," said Tristan, "I am in a foreign land where I have neither friend nor cousin, save you; and you alone in this place have given me comfort. My life is going, and I wish to see once more Iseult the Fair. Ah, did I but know of a messenger who would go to her! For now I know that she will come to me. Kaherdin, my brother in arms, I beg it of your friendship; try this thing for me, and if you carry my word, I will become your liege, and I will cherish you beyond all other men."

And as Kaherdin saw Tristan broken down, his heart reproached him and he said:

"Fair comrade, do not weep; I will do what you desire, even if it were risk of death I would do it for you. Nor no distress nor anguish will let me from doing it according to my power. Give me the word you send, and I will make ready."

And Tristan answered:

"Thank you, friend; this is my prayer: take this ring, it is a sign between her and me; and when you come to her land pass yourself at court for a merchant, and show her silk and stuffs, but make so that she sees the ring, for then she will find some ruse by which to speak to you in secret. Then tell her that my heart salutes her; tell her that she alone can bring me comfort; tell her that if she does not come I shall die. Tell her to remember our past time, and our great sorrows, and all the joy there was in our loyal and tender love. And tell her to remember that draught we drank together on the high seas. For we drank our death together. Tell her to remember the oath I swore to serve a single love, for I have kept that oath."

But behind the wall, Iseult of the White Hands heard all these things; and Tristan continued:

"Hasten, my friend, and come back quickly, or you will not see me again. Take forty days for your term, but come back with Iseult the Fair. And tell your sister nothing, or tell her that you seek some doctor. Take my fine ship, and two sails with you, one white, one black. And as you return, if you bring Iseult, hoist the white sail; but if you bring her not, the black. Now I have nothing more to say, but God guide you and bring you back safe."

With the first fair wind Kaherdin took the open, weighed anchor and hoisted sail, and ran with a light air and broke the seas. They bore rich merchandise with them, dyed silks of rare colours, enamel of Touraine and wines of Poitou, for by this ruse Kaherdin thought to reach Iseult. Eight days and nights they ran full sail to Cornwall.

Now a woman's wrath is a fearful thing, and all men fear it, for according to her love, so will her vengeance be; and their love and their hate come quickly, but their hate lives longer than their love; and they will make play with love, but not with hate. So Iseult of the White Hands, who had heard every word, and who had so loved Tristan, waited her vengeance upon what she loved most in the world. But she hid it all; and when the doors were open again she came to Tristan's bed and served him with food as a lover should, and spoke him gently and kissed him on the lips, and asked him if Kaherdin would soon return with one to cure him . . . but all day long she thought upon her vengeance.

And Kaherdin sailed and sailed till he dropped anchor in the haven of Tintagel. He landed and took with him a cloth of rare dye and a cup well chiselled and worked, and made a present of them to King Mark, and courteously begged of him his peace and safeguard that he might traffick in his land; and the King gave him his peace before all the men of his palace.

Then Kaherdin offered the Queen a buckle of fine gold; and "Queen," said he, "the gold is good."

Then taking from his finger Tristan's ring, he put it side by side with the jewel and said:

"See, O Queen, the gold of the buckle is the finer gold; yet that ring also has its worth."

When Iseult saw what ring that was, her heart trembled and her colour changed, and fearing what might next be said she drew Kaherdin apart near a window, as if to see and bargain the better; and Kaherdin said to her, low down:

"Lady, Tristan is wounded of a poisoned spear and is about to die. He sends you word that you alone can bring him comfort, and recalls to you the great sorrows that you bore together. Keep you the ring—it is yours."

But Iseult answered, weakening:

"Friend, I will follow you; get ready your ship to-morrow at dawn."

And on the morrow at dawn they raised anchor, stepped mast, and hoisted sail, and happily the barque left land.

But at Carhaix Tristan lay and longed for Iseult's coming. Nothing now filled him any more, and if he lived it was only as awaiting her; and day by day he sent watchers to the shore to see if some ship came, and to learn the colour of her sail. There was no other thing left in his heart.

He had himself carried to the cliff of the Penmarks, where it overlooks the sea, and all the daylight long he gazed far off over the water.

Hear now a tale most sad and pitiful to all who love. Already was Iseult near; already the cliff of the Penmarks showed far away, and the ship ran heartily, when a storm wind rose on a sudden and grew, and struck the sail, and turned the ship all round about, and the sailors bore away and sore against their will they ran before the wind. The wind raged and big seas ran, and the air grew thick with darkness, and the ocean itself turned dark, and the rain drove in gusts. The yard snapped, and the sheet; they struck their sail, and ran with wind and water. In an evil hour they had forgotten to haul their pinnace aboard; it leapt in their wake, and a great sea broke it away.

Then Iseult cried out: "God does not will that I should live to see him, my love, once—even one time more. God wills my drowning in this sea. O, Tristan, had I spoken to you but once again, it is little I should have cared for a death come afterwards. But now, my love, I cannot come to you; for God so wills it, and that is the core of my grief."

And thus the Queen complained so long as the storm endured; but after five days it died down. Kaherdin hoisted the sail, the white sail, right up to the very masthead with great joy; the white sail, that Tristan might know its colour from afar: and already Kaherdin saw Britanny far off like a cloud. Hardly were these things seen and done when a calm came, and the sea lay even and untroubled. The sail bellied no longer, and the sailors held the ship now up, now down, the tide, beating backwards and forwards in vain. They saw the shore afar off, but the storm had carried their boat away and they could not land. On the third night Iseult dreamt this dream: that she held in her lap a boar's head which befouled her skirts with blood; then she knew that she would never see her lover again alive.

Tristan was now too weak to keep his watch from the cliff of the Penmarks, and for many long days, within walls, far from the shore, he had mourned for Iseult because she did not come. Dolorous and alone, he mourned and sighed in restlessness: he was near death from desire.

At last the wind freshened and the white sail showed. Then it was that Iseult of the White Hands took her vengeance.

She came to where Tristan lay, and she said:

"Friend, Kaherdin is here. I have seen his ship upon the sea. She comes up hardly—yet I know her; may he bring that which shall heal thee, friend."

And Tristan trembled and said:

"Beautiful friend, you are sure that the ship is his indeed? Then tell me what is the manner of the sail?"

"I saw it plain and well. They have shaken it out and hoisted it very high, for they have little wind. For its colour, why, it is black."

And Tristan turned him to the wall, and said:

"I cannot keep this life of mine any longer." He said three times: "Iseult, my friend." And in saying it the fourth time, he died.

Then throughout the house, the knights and the comrades of Tristan wept out loud, and they took him from his bed and laid him on a rich cloth, and they covered his body with a shroud. But at sea the wind had risen; it struck the sail fair and full and drove the ship to shore, and Iseult the Fair set foot upon the land. She heard loud mourning in the streets, and the tolling of bells in the minsters and the chapel towers; she asked the people the meaning of the knell and of their tears. An old man said to her:

"Lady, we suffer a great grief. Tristan, that was so loyal and so right, is dead. He was open to the poor; he ministered to the suffering. It is the chief evil that has ever fallen on this land."

But Iseult, hearing them, could not answer them a word. She went up to the palace, following the way, and her cloak was random and wild. The Bretons marvelled as she went; nor had they ever seen woman of such a beauty, and they said:

"Who is she, or whence does she come?"

Near Tristan, Iseult of the White Hands crouched, maddened at the evil she had done, and calling and lamenting over the dead man. The other Iseult came in and said to her:

"Lady, rise and let me come by him; I have more right to mourn him than have you—believe me. I loved him more."

And when she had turned to the east and prayed God, she moved the body a little and lay down by the dead man, beside her friend. She kissed his mouth and his face, and clasped him closely; and so gave up her soul, and died beside him of grief for her lover.

When King Mark heard of the death of these lovers, he crossed the sea and came into Brittany; and he had two coffins hewn, for Tristan and Iseult, one of chalcedony for Iseult, and one of beryl for Tristan. And he took their beloved bodies away with him upon his ship to Tintagel, and by a chantry to the left and right of the apse he had their tombs built round. But in one night there sprang from the tomb of Tristan a green and leafy briar, strong in its branches and in the scent of its flowers. It climbed the chantry and fell to root again by Iseult's tomb. Thrice did the peasants cut it down, but thrice it grew again as flowered and as strong. They told the marvel to King Mark, and he forbade them to cut the briar any more.

The good singers of old time, Beroul and Thomas of Built, Gilbert and Gottfried told this tale for lovers and none other, and, by my pen, they beg you for your prayers. They greet those who are cast down, and those in heart, those troubled and those filled with desire. May all herein find strength against inconstancy and despite and loss and pain and all the bitterness of loving.

# THE COMING OF THE LIGHT
## by Phyllis Ann Karr

*Phyllis Ann Karr (1944– ), is a noted Arthurian student, and the author of an excellent historical Arthurian mystery,* The Idylls of the Queen *(1982). She was present in* The Pendragon Chronicles *with "The Lady of Belec". For the following new story, she considers the Christian-heathen conflict between Britons and Saxons, and raises the question of where real Christian love existed.*

God All-Father had hung nine nights in the Tree. Ulfric son of Osric and Elwyn had spent many more nights than nine balanced in the branches of high trees all across this uncultivated wilderness of a land, but never more than one night in the same tree. And never a night beneath a heathen roof, until the morning he woke and heard the hunting party beneath him.

It was long after the season of harvest, and the branches were all but bare. The wonder was that the savages had not seen him yet. Feeling that at any moment one of their rare upward glances would fly in his direction, Ulfric huddled into the tree's great crotch as deeply as he could fit and stared down at them.

He understood their barbaric language well enough to learn what hunting party it was, and who was with them. That same bloody war chieftain, less man than monster, in whose name the murderers had struck.

360

All-Father! Ulfric thought, feeling the hour of his fate tighten around him. I am not yet ready!

But when would he be ready, if not now? In another nine nights times nine, with the strength of his fifteen summers still further sapped by winter's frozen famine? Was he not readier now than they had been, the whole family of them—Father and Mother, Uncles and Aunt, Brother and Sister, Chatwin with his bride and their baby daughter—eleven homesteaders in all, counting Ulfric—ten of them dead in a burned steading and the last one left for dead when the raiders passed on.

They should have been more ready. They had been warned: beyond such-and-such a boundary, the barbarians have made it their "law" that no cultivated folk shall go. But there lay the land, all forest and waste, inviting people and the plough to turn it into fair field and fragrant pasture, smiling beneath All-Father's sun. And Thane Osric had always held that even the natives of this wilderness, if offered friendship in peace, would respond like human men and women.

Thane Osric had been wrong.

For what else have I come this distance, Thane Osric's son thought with the wry fatalism of a cultivated and a realistic man, if not to avenge our family upon this fenris-wolf? Even though it cost me my life . . . what else is this life of mine worth?

Waiting and watching, he held his knife at the ready and, when at length he saw his chance, let fly with it.

He had enough throwing skill to keep himself alive on the flesh of forest beasts; but this morning he was cramped and shaky from excitement and eagerness, atop a hard night's rest. And, truth to tell, he had too often gone hungry since the bloodbath. His blade struck the band of the enemy's golden crown and flipped into the earth beyond, leaving a small dent in the metal and surely a large bruise beneath, but doing no further damage except to alarm the horses, hounds, and hunters.

Shouts of "There! Up there!" filled the air, and within moments Ulfric was brought to earth and knocked senseless.

He awoke chained in sticky and vile-smelling blackness, with a little moldy straw between him and the dank cold stones. The rust of his shackles chafed his skin, and the only sound besides the scurrying of vermin was a distant dripping of water or other liquid. That dripping, with his thirst and hunger and the need of his body to relieve itself, formed his only means for measuring time. He ached in muscle, bone, and head, with here and there an angry throbbing; and he thought he felt a fever. Yet all this was comfort compared with what he would feel when they remembered him, for these savages had tortures to make a man pray for the blood eagle as a mercy.

He had counted many thousand drops, sometimes dozing off at his task, and had been forced, despite his thirst, to empty his bladder twice into the noises of the vermin which at other times he had to beat off with his arms, legs, and chains, when at last there came the dull sound of approaching footsteps, accompanied by distant torchlight and an occasional soft curse in the barbaric tongue.

Then, Saxon though he was, Ulfric the son of Osric had work to suppress a shudder, to remind himself that any execution at the savages' hands, no matter how prolonged, was preferable to a still more lingering death of starvation and vermin bites in the dank darkness; and that even if it were not, he remained a thane's son and owed it to his heritage to die with heroism.

Slowly, he stood, in order to meet his captors on his feet and face to face.

He thought that surprised them: an old man wearing a shaven white scalp and a long black garment, and carrying a wooden and silver "cross," that favorite symbol of the savages' superstition that looked so much at first glance like a Thor's Hammer; a younger man who wore a garish long tunic over linked metal and carried a sword; and a third, in a short tunic, who stood a little aside, holding the torch.

The swordsman flourished his weapon and said, "Ask him why he tried to kill our noble king."

The man with shaven head turned to Ulfric and repeated the question in vilely garbled Saxon.

Ulfric thought of answering in the barbarian tongue, but decided not to dirty his mouth. Without betraying that he had understood the first speaker, he said in his own language, "Your king is a foul murderer."

Turning to his comrades, the blackrobe rendered Ulfric's statement as, "He calls our king a sinful killer."

The man with the torch muttered, "He has a devil!" and used his free hand to make the savages' favorite superstitious gesture over his forehead, shoulders, and chest. The swordsman scowled and lifted his weapon as if to strike. Ulfric stared back at him and did not flinch.

"One moment, I pray you, Sir Gareth!" the blackrobe said in the barbarian tongue, putting out one hand. "Are we not all of us poor sinners?" Turning again to Ulfric, he asked in his stumbling Saxon why the prisoner had spoken as he had.

Because of the questioner's poor Saxon, Ulfric chose simple words. "In the name of your king, a war party came down and murdered all our household, who were four peaceable men and three women grown, besides my younger sister and brother, and a baby girl half a year in age. And we were no warriors, but peace-loving farmers! Could I kill your king with all his bloody men, I would do it at once."

Instead of translating, the blackrobe told his companions, "This youth has appealed to the high king's justice."

There was grumbling and argument, but in the end the torch-bearer brought forward a bunch of keys and unlocked Ulfric's shackles. He and the swordsman laid strong hold on Ulfric's arms, and between them they marched him along passageways, up flights of stairs, and along more passageways, the blackrobe following, until at length they emerged in a large stone chamber where many men sat around a great table.

Although somewhat lighter than the dungeon, this chamber was almost equally chill and dank, despite the tapestries—bar-baric but colourful—which swayed softly in the drafts along the walls. The floor was deep in straw not quite as moldy as that of the dungeon, yet fuller of fragments of food and bone and the droppings from grease lamps and candles both tallow and wealthy waxen. Of the droppings, too, of dogs and hounds, who here took the place of the vermin, as wholesomely as if in a cultivated house.

The table was a ring of wood joined into a single piece, a circle with seats placed only around the outside, and with one break in the side nearest the door, so that the savages' slaves and servitors could carry food and drink to those that feasted. No one ate at present, nor was any food upon the table; but several men sat with drinking vessels before them.

Many as the men seemed who sat there, Ulfric soon saw that there were empty chairs for many more.

His guards thrust him through the servitors' opening and stood with him in the open center of the table, directly in face of the barbarian chieftain himself. Yes, there he sat, this man who commanded murders, whose name caused fear, at his ease in a chair with higher armrests and, by his seeming height, heavier cushions than any of the others. His beard hung long and grizzled and still becrumbed from his last meal. The gem-encrusted gold of his crown gleamed wistfully on his silvering head, as if, being a piece of fine old artistry, it could wish itself encircling a worthier brain; and from beneath its lower edge on one side, Ulfric saw with satisfaction, showed the bottom of a great purple bruise.

"Well?" the old chieftain asked wearily. "Why have you brought him here? Hang him and be done with it."

Sir Gareth, the swordsman who held Ulfric's right arm, said: "This is the one who tried to kill Your Grace yesterday in the woods."

"So? Then draw and quarter him and up on the outer walls with his head and members as a warning to others. Now go." As if shooing away flies, the king waved one heavily jeweled hand.

"But, my lord," the blackrobe protested, stepping in front of Sir Gareth, "he has appealed to Your Grace's mercy."

"I have not!" the prisoner cried proudly. And then, seeing in the sudden hush how he had betrayed his understanding of the barbarian tongue, he squared his shoulders and went on, this time in their own language so that the man with the shaven head could no longer twist his meaning, "I have called you a bloody murderer, you king of barbarian savages, and I call you the same name again, to your face. You are bloody murderers, you and all your men, and I wanted justice for the murders of all my family and farmstead, and for the pain of them who were raped and tortured before they died!"

Angry voices filled the room before he finished, but the chieftain stilled them by raising one hand as though bored, and saying, "Skin him first, and it may be as well to salt him a little afterwards, before hanging him. Or sear him, it makes a better show and gives our people all the more heart. Now leave us in peace."

"One moment, my lord," said a sharpfaced dark man, also with hair more silver than black, who sat far to one side but spoke with more authority than his distance from the king would have suggested.

"As you will, Sir Kay," the king replied with a small sigh.

Looking closely at Ulfric, Sir Kay went on, "There are knights riding about committing murders who are none of our people, boy. These men that attacked your steading—can you tell us what their shields looked like?"

"There were nine of them," Ulfric replied. "Nine armoured raiders, all of them mounted in your savage manner of warfare, against five peaceable farm men—including myself—with my mother, my aunt, and Chatwin's young wife, and three children, one of them still in her cradle. Your people plucked her out of it and one of them threw her into the air for two others to swop their swords at her as she fell. And he that led these raiders carried a white shield with three bands the color of dark blood."

"Sir Lancelot!" The name went up from mouths all around the table. "Our great Sir Lancelot! The pride of all our company!"

"It is clear enough," said the king. "If Sir Lancelot and his party attacked you, he must have had good cause."

A man on the other side of the table from Sir Kay, one whose hair had hardly yet begun to silver, said: "Even if that good and noble cause was simply another of the great Sir Lancelot's famous battle rages."

"Silence, Mordred!" said Sir Gareth. "No man speaks ill of my lord Sir Lancelot in my presence!"

"Four farm men dead," said Sir Kay, "three women, two children, and an infant. And one halfgrown boy remains to tell the tale. I suppose they must have left you for dead, lad?"

"My name is Ulfric, the son of Thane Osric and Elwyn his good wife, nephew to Adalard, Sibert, and Edmonda, older brother to Elga and Norbert, thane's son to Chatwin, Ortrude, and tiny Mayda who was darling to us all. And all of us peaceable people who had never harmed any of you, but only taken a hide of wild land to turn into a fair new farm."

The king nodded complacently. "On the wrong side of the line, you must have been."

Sir Kay said, so sarcastically he might almost have been a cultivated man, "After so noble a deed, it will be a wonder if the great Lancelot should fail in his quest for the Grail."

"We had never taken that, whatever it is!" said Ulfric. "We had taken nothing at all except a hide of good land that you were leaving waste and unused when, by Freya's hand and ours, it could have blossomed and borne fruit."

"Be quiet, boy," said the blackrobe. "In your unchristened paganhood, you understand nothing. The Holy Grail is not a thing that can be taken or held by any human hand. It is one of the highest and holiest visions man may achieve in this mortal life."

Sir Kay asked, "When did this happen to your people, Ulfric son of Osric?"

"Between the times of planting and haymaking last past."

"Soon after they struck out," Sir Kay said softly. "The boy has been a wandering outlaw for half a year."

"No christened soul may meddle with any man who goes in quest of the Holy Grail," the king said with another nod. "And, in any case, my good Sir Lancelot and his companions have only cleaned out one more nest of Saxons, for which they must be praised. But you may give the boy a simple hanging."

Ulfric's pride blazed forth. "I never asked for your mercy, king of savage barbarians."

The king said, still sounding bored, "Take him away."

"Wait." Sir Kay stood up. "The lad has courage, and we will have empty places in plenty by the time this general Grail Quest is ended."

Sir Gareth cried, "Do you say we should test this Saxon for a place in our company, Sir Kay?"

"I say that he shows as much promise as you showed when I tested you, Gareth Fairhands. And as Tor and Tattercoat showed when I tested them."

"He is unchristened," said the king.

"So was our good Sir Palomides," replied Sir Kay.

The man called Mordred stood up. "Let me test this one, Sir Seneschal," he said lazily, winking across the table to Sir Kay. That wink made Mordred's next words an insult aimed less at his fellow barbarian than at the small, helpless, dead babe: "At your age now, the tiny Mayda could have defeated you. I do not suppose, Saxon farmer," he went on, as Ulfric glared at him, "that you have the art of jousting on horseback?"

"When we fight, we fight like men, on foot."

Mordred smiled. "We need not lead out the horses, then. We may proceed directly to the footwork. Unless you would rather hang in peace at once and be done with it, Saxon."

"Farmer that I am, I would fight every man of you and kill you all if I could!"

"One will be enough for today," Mordred said, and threw a glance that seemed mostly of hate, yet tangled with a strange strand of love, at his chieftain.

Showing no awareness of Mordred's glance, the king nodded a half-willing consent to his proposal and Sir Kay's, and the whole company moved their prisoner, none too gently, outside into an open field.

Here, as Ulfric blinked in the sunlight that seemed so bright and blessed after his long hours in the dungeon, they put one of their awkwardly styled shields upon his left arm and an iron cap upon his head. Then they formed a ring around him and Mordred, who had put on a similar cap and shield, and who held two swords.

They had brought a chair outdoors for their chieftain, who sat at the upper end of the ring as if in court. When everything seemed ready to their satisfaction, Mordred put one of the two swords down upon the autumn-brown grass in the center of the fighting field and stepped a few paces back, balancing the other sword in his right hand.

Ulfric saw the disadvantage he stood in. Half starved and parched from his day and night in the dungeon, he was also weakened in many ways—even if toughened in a few—by his months of wandering the wilderness. And, while his father and uncles had snatched some time for teaching him rudiments of battle, by far the most of their life had gone into farmwork. Had their aim not been to live in peace and Freya's plenty? Had the grown farmers themselves not allowed their fighting skills to rust, Thane Osric thinking to need them no more henceforward unless against the stray four-footed forest beast? Mordred would be fresh, well fed, and a warrior trained and long exercised in the arts of battle as the barbarians practice it. Even the sword felt strange in Ulfric's hand, unlike the style he had used in his few hours of practice. Nor had the young Saxon ever killed any human creature before, though he had tried on two occasions—during the massacre of his family, and again as he crouched in the tree taking aim at the savage king. Mordred must have killed many times in combat, fair or foul.

But Ulfric had his hatred, his thirst for revenge, and his long heritage as a cultivated man. And if, up until a certain moment, Mordred had seemed perhaps the best of the barbarians after Sir Kay, he had broken the illusion of humanity when he made sport of tiny Mayda. Ulfric had nothing to lose, and could he kill even one of the barbarians—if not their king, or Sir Lancelot, or one of Sir Lancelot's marauders, then at least this Mordred—he felt he could face whatever pains they put him to afterward.

He and Mordred began to circle each other, approaching, withdrawing, first one and then the other lifting his blade as if measuring for a blow, but leaving it unstruck as the other weighed his own weapon to meet it. A single blow, well struck, would end the battle—could end the need for anything after the battle, as the sharp, heavy blade sliced through muscle and gristle, sinew and bone cleanly as a cleaver through a cow's carcass on butchering day.

Mordred might be waiting his chance for just such a blow. Or he might be circling for the simple, catlike joy of the game. Surely he could not fear the farmboy . . . or why begin by baiting him into this battle?

At last Ulfric rushed, heaving up his blade to aim a blow at the barbarian's neck.

Mordred caught it on the flat of his own sword, smiled, said, "Lesson one, boy: never let your plan show in your face," and pushed him back with his shield so forcefully that Ulfric staggered and almost fell. Mordred could have finished it easily then; but he did not, instead waiting until Ulfric had regained his balance.

They circled once more, Mordred's words echoing in Ulfric's brain. Those words brought back the face of his father, who had told him much the same thing. Memory of his father brought back the berserk rage, and he rushed again, so quickly that he himself had hardly time to know what he was about, much less show it in his face.

Mordred answered with an impact of his shield to Ulfric's chest that knocked the Saxon off his feet and the sword out of his hand.

"Lesson two," said Mordred, stepping up to straddle him with swordpoint to throat, "*have* a plan, though you keep it hidden."

Expecting death, Ulfric stared up steadily into his enemy's eyes. Mordred coolly stepped back and stood several paces away, as if waiting.

A wound worn in the back marked a man a coward, since few ever asked whether the wound had been dealt in treachery. Fearing some such trick from the man who had mocked a baby's murder, Ulfric moved warily, keeping one eye on Mordred the whole time he was recovering his sword; but the barbarian never stirred.

To have been at Mordred's mercy twice, and still to breathe . . . Ulfric had assumed this "test" to be but another cruel joke or, at best—having been proposed by Sir Kay, the one among them all who showed a shred of something that might be called honor—a comparatively quick and honourable execution. Now he began to wonder if it were indeed what Sir Kay had called it, if the man intended to save his life by making him one of this company, by trickery if need be; if that wink had meant that Mordred understood the older man and promised to let the Saxon pass the test.

Even if that were the case, Ulfric son of Osric scorned to become one of these fenris-wolves. Better death. Hardly had his hand closed round the weapon's grip, than Ulfric changed his speed. Springing up from his crouch, he hurled himself across the open space with one fierce shout, to knock his enemy's sword askew before it was half lifted. Thrusting Mordred down with his shield, as Mordred had thrust him on his first rush, he used a second stroke to bat the sword out of Mordred's hand completely.

Now their places were changed and it was the Saxon who stood, panting, with his sword's point at his foeman's throat.

"Ah!" said Mordred. "At last. Lesson three, Saxon: never leave the serpent alive to strike again, and damn Fate and prophetic dreams."

Yet Ulfric hesitated. Not from lack of stomach. He had often helped in the butchering, and were not the beasts they slaughtered for food better creatures and worthier of life than these murdering barbarians? No: he hesitated because, by the eager gleam in Mordred's eyes—their color so much like his chieftain's—Ulfric read the riddle of his last few words. Mordred *wanted* to die, wished for death as for a freedom-bringing friend.

And then? Even if Sir Kay were a man of honor, he could not have meant this test to go to the death of his comrade, or he himself would not have survived those earlier testings they had spoken of. So soon as Mordred was slain, the rest of the ring would close in and hew his slayer down like a tuft of hay. No matter. It would be a more honorable death, and quicker and cleaner, than any other Ulfric could hope for at their hands.

But to kill only Mordred, who wanted to die, who had tricked Ulfric into place for giving him his wish . . . after all, that might be very little, and Mordred scarcely remembered longer than Ulfric himself, among these savages. While to put an end to their bloody chieftain—Aye, that would give his own death a meaning for all his people.

Measuring the distance with his side vision, Ulfric saw that the battle had brought them close enough. That was surely a sign from the All-Father. Whirling suddenly with sword held high, he threw himself at the throne.

An instant of fright on the old king's face—and at once half a dozen weapons interposed, while another dozen arms dragged Ulfric back, disarmed him, and wrestled him down.

"You see, Kay," said the king, rubbing his unharmed neck, "we cannot trust these Saxon dogs. Skin him and salt him."

Holding up one hand, Sir Kay turned to look at Ulfric. With sorrow in his voice, he said, "*Why*, lad? Why that trick, when we had given you a chance?"

"Who would not strike off the head of the wolf that murders the flock?"

"By my soul!" came Mordred's mocking voice, "the Saxon has ideals. He would lay down his life for his own kind. In his own way, he seeks the Grail!"

"It is no such thing," said the king. "He seeks the death of Christians."

Only to belie the king, Ulfric spoke while he still had voice. "If the freedom of my own folk to farm their land without fear is what you call the Grail, then, yes, I seek the Grail!"

"Do you hear?" said Mordred. "He is indeed in quest of the Holy Grail, and no Christian soul may offer him harm!"

Many voices shouted protest, but the blackrobe, who had watched wordlessly since coming out of doors, lifted his cross and cried, "Think on the merciful Christ, who bled into the Grail for all alike!"

"Think on those who bled before Ossa's Saxons on Badon Hill!" Sir Gareth shouted back.

Sir Kay looked at the king and said, very deliberately, "Think of Lyonor's son Bohart, who lusted for your crown, foster brother, and lies in a hidden grave. You owe me a fairly large debt for Bohart."

So Ulfric learned both Sir Kay's relationship to his chief, and the source of his power.

"What do you want, Kex?" the king asked almost plaintively. "The life of this young Saxon dog?"

"I never understand which you mean to insult," Sir Kay complained with an ironic smile, "the Saxon or the dog." Then, serious again, and sparing a glance for Sir Gareth, "Badon Hill was an honest battle, and Ossa an honest commander of honest warriors. What happened at this lad's hearth was akin to murder. I say that he had some justice in seeking revenge, and that he has as much right as any of us to go in quest of the Grail."

For a few heartbeats, Sir Kay and the king stared hard into each other's eyes. Then the king's drooped. Jerking his face up again, he looked around at all his people, raised both arms, and said, "Let us argue this in full court, around my table. For now, return the Saxon to his cell."

So, fast as foot could stumble, Ulfric found himself once again in the rank blackness, measuring his wait by counting the drips of distant liquid.

There he sat, holding his thoughts as far as possible from the horrors of his past half year, present prison, and coming doom, until, bit by bit, his mind slipped back to Thane Osric's steading when all of them were still alive, he and all his father's household, toiling side by side each day, feeding on the fruits of their toil and Freya's bounty, looking forward in hearty hope to the time when theirs would be one steading among many. The memories grew sharper, more solid than the stones of the cell, so real that he felt he could step through into them . . .

He had stepped through, and now it was summer once more, a summer following that in which the raiders had *not* come, a bright day in early summer when he sat on a tuft, swallowing cool ale in a respite from the haymaking, and cheered tiny Mayda's toddling steps through the stubble. As she stumbled towards him, she grew taller, older, more graceful, until, reaching him, she stood a proud young woman, with wheat-gold hair hanging free to her waist. Standing beside her, he took her freely offered hand into his own.

And then it seemed that they were soaring together, hawklike, over this Angle-land tamed by Saxon settlement and flowering beneath Saxon cultivation, wastes cleared away and fields springing forth with the promise of rich harvests of every kind of crop, sheep and kine of every sort browsing their fill in rolling pastures, houses raised with the sturdiest carpentry and decked with the most skillful woodcarving, singers and storytellers feeding minds and souls as lavishly as the farmland fed bodies, free folk meeting to govern themselves in fair and equal moot . . . the land as it would someday become; for though Thane Osric's household and others of the first wave were washed out in blood, still more of their people would follow, more and more, pushing back the unjust and arrogant boundary until it broke altogether, overwhelming the savages in a bounteous tide of settlement and cultivation . . .

A hand shaking his shoulder brought him reluctantly back. Opening his eyes, he exchanged the fair vision for a view of Mordred's face.

"He still lives," Mordred called to a pair of comrades waiting at the door, one holding the torch and the other a drawn sword. Then, unlocking the shackles that held Ulfric's legs to the floorstone, though not the ones that linked his wrists one to the other, Mordred muttered, "He is ready to state his royal decision. However that goes, Saxon, it may comfort you that in leaving me alive, you likely helped your own people's cause more than you guess."

As Ulfric stared at him he went on, seemingly more to himself than to the prisoner,

"He dreamed at my birth that I would destroy him, and murdered more babes than Herod, trying to destroy me first. He no longer dares anything so obvious. Not after all those babes. Nor after Bohart. And so we circle each other like wary old hounds, waiting for the prophecies to fulfill themselves."

Whoever or whatever "Herod" was. Some monster of the savages' superstition, maybe. Or, considering what they had done to Mayda, some hero. What better stuff had they for heroes? these pitiful beings so bound into their barbarism that they preferred using wild butchery to welcoming cultivation. Could they even glimpse the futility of their desperation? Yes, the Norns might indeed have saved this monstrous king from rightful vengeance for the sake of delivering him to treachery. And, with the savages divided among themselves, their night could not last forever. Already in his dream Ulfric had witnessed the coming dawn.

Filling his heart with these things, he let them bring him back to the room of the round table and stand him in its open center. This time the king sat with the familiar blackrobe standing at his left shoulder, and a tall, sternfaced man bearing a golden crook and wearing garments that blazed with barbaric splendor standing at his right.

"Dubric our bishop," the king began, scowling, "agrees with Amustans our chaplain. Any man has the right to quest for the Holy Grail, even a pagan Saxon. But we make this condition: let him never presume to take up arms like a Christian knight, nor ever carry any weapon or bladed tool larger than a small knife to cut his meat."

"Well?" Sir Kay asked Ulfric. "Will you agree to escape torture and death on those terms?"

"What is it to me?" Ulfric answered, wondering idly which of the two at the king's back was "bishop" and which "chaplain," and what power these new words signified. No matter. "Yes, I agree. Maybe I will even find your Grail where you have failed."

Mordred unlocked the chains from his wrists. The king, with a look of disgust, flicked a tiny knife to the floor at his feet, saying, "For your meat."

Hunkering proudly, Ulfric fished the knife out of the straw. Its blade was scarcely as long as his little finger. He scorned to ask how they expected him to get his meat.

Sir Kay held out a folded parchment and said, "Here. Show them this, tell them you want to find the Holy Grail, and nobody will refuse you a meal or two."

From no other man of that company would Osric's son have accepted such a token. Even taking it from Sir Kay's hand, he uttered no thanks: it was enough that he refrained from voicing the thought that he would rather grub for roots and hunt with stones than trust himself to the natives.

One thing more, however, remained for him to say aloud.

Before marching out alone into the wilderness that would one day flower beneath Saxon cultivation, he turned and made his final statement to the barbarian chieftain:

"Someday, King Arthur, you will be nothing but a name to frighten little children with, when my people have finally brought light to this dark land."

# TOLD BY MOONLIGHT
## by Darrell Schweitzer

*Darrell Schweitzer (1952–) is a prolific American writer and critic, and currently editor of the magazine* Weird Tales. *He was represented in* The Pendragon Chronicles *with "Midnight, Moonlight, and the Secret of the Sea", a rather melancholy tale of the hapless wanderings of the dispossessed knight, Sir Julian. That same atmosphere permeates "Told By Moonlight", which was specially written for this volume, and looks behind the facade of the dream-world of Camelot to the nightmares beyond.*

"You there! Are you a lunatic, or a ghost?"

He emerged from a dream of rage and pain, from a maelstrom of screaming faces and crashing metal, into a cool, still twilight. He staggered at first, then found his footing, and made his way over mossy stones, up a steep, wooded hillside.

"It's certainly a fit season for lunatics!" the voice cried again.

The full moon had already risen. Below, and far to the horizon, the towns of the plain flickered like votive candles.

He reached a round, clear plateau, and stepped out onto the grass, into moonlight so bright he could almost see colors.

"Oh! I hope you are merely mad, and not an uncanny thing, for I am much afraid of ghosts, of my own dead, whose deaths I have caused, and they torment me always. But you, fellow madman, have come to comfort me."

The source of the voice was very near. Hands remembered sword, drew blade. He whirled, and spoke at last, "Show yourself."

Something scrambled toward him out of the underbrush, perhaps a huge badger or a small bear, dark, matted, waddling, sloppy; no, he realized with some shock, a *man*, the filthiest, raggedest specimen he had ever seen, only once rising from all fours to sniff the air.

The thing grovelled at his feet, clawing the earth.

"I asked you, good sir," it said, "what you are, madman, specter, or . . . a true knight."

Further shock: he did not *know*, and could not reach more than a few minutes in his memory, to his arrival here, as if it were a birth.

"What about you? Are you a troll?"

The filthy one stood up straight, brushed himself perfunctorily, and executed a stately bow.

"No, I am most definitely a lunatic, at your service, sir."

He put his sword away, stroked his chin, and laughed softly. "An amusing riddle. How does a madman know he is mad? Surely only a sane man may recognize a lunatic, who regards himself as sane with the utmost conviction. Therefore, riddle me."

The madman tilted his head sideways, smiled ingratiatingly, then whirled about in a kind of dance. "Oh, how clever you are, how sharp. Be not cruel; seek no advantage over my poor, weak, diseased, rattled wits. Say you are a brave knight and true, that you have come here to comfort me, to tell me stories of chivalry. This is the time for it, yes, and this is the place."

He took the madman firmly by the arm. "You haven't answered my question."

"Nor you mine. Let me merely say that I have been mad before, that once I grazed these hills like a beast, naked, like King Nebuchadrezzar when the Lord God smote him. Therefore I recognize madness from personal experience."

"Ah."

"Will you come into my moonlight bower, sir? It is made entirely of moonbeams. I sit here of nights, weaving them." The madman tried to drop to all fours again.

The other held the madman firmly. "No. Walk like a man."

"You are kind, yes, kind, or maybe you are cruel, for by clearing away my madness you might cause me to remember who I was."

"Who?"

"Look! There! It begins!"

From either side of the flat hilltop, two mounted knights appeared, spears and visors lowered, pennons and ribbons streaming as they charged one another in absolute silence, colliding, vanishing like a burst bubble.

"Now sit," said the madman, easing the other to the ground, "and I shall say that thou art a knight of great worship—remember that phrase; we used it a lot in the old days—Ah, what a sound! *Great worship*. Yes. Look here. Knock! Knock! You're wearing armor. But it is dented and worn and—Oh!—smeared with blood. Look how your greave is hewn away, and there is a great black wound on your calf. And here, a greater wound yet."

He watched the madman probing through a huge hole in his breastplate, but there was no sensation inside.

"These have a story to tell," said the madman.

"I do not know it."

"Not yet. I shall start then, with another story. Very well. Hark! When King Arthur, the greatest, bravest, truest knight that ever lived—"

"Of . . . great worship . . ."

"Yes! Exactly! Now you're getting it! Anyway, when Arthur the King had gathered all his worshipful knights in Camelot and seated them in their places at the Round Table, and declared a great feast to celebrate his triumph over the Five Kings—then a Lady From Under the Hill came into the hall bearing two coffers. 'This, Sir King,' says she, holding up the first, 'contains a wondrous prize for any knight, which is honor.' So the King reached for it. She drew it away. 'Ah, but *this*,' says she, offering the second beside the first, 'contains another prize, which is wisdom.' 'I'll take both,' says the King. 'I offer only one,' says she. 'You have to choose.'"

The madman paused in his telling.

"So what did the King do?"

"*I* don't know. My brains are addled! It's a riddle."

He rose to his feet, drawing out his sword. "You waste my time, chattering magpie. I am greatly minded to have your noisy head off."

"Now *that* would be an original solution to the riddle! Not even Arthur thought of that."

"A true knight would choose honor."

"A true knight would have honor already. And many's the fool who went to his death honorably, but unwisely."

"Let him choose wisdom them. I grow impatient with this."

"Many's the tragic man who learned wisdom when it is too late, and merely dies knowing that his wrongs are irreparable."

He prodded the madman under the chin with his sword.

"Now I command you tell me, which did Arthur choose?"

"Perhaps neither. Perhaps he could not and that was the undoing of him. It's only a story, and stories are only as true as we make them. Ask . . . ask . . . any of these others. They all have stories to tell . . ."

"Others?"

"Look about you."

They were no longer alone on the plateau. A numerous host of lords and ladies rode on horseback out of the moonbeams, parading around and around in utter silence.

He reached out to touch them, and they vanished.

"Sit beside me once more," said the madman, "and tell your own story."

He sat, sword across his knees. "I am greatly afraid. My story is of a son who loved his father and hated him, who slew his father and was slain by him, who died and is not dead, even as his father died and is not dead."

The madman put a hand on his shoulder to comfort him. "That is a mighty riddle indeed, written, I think, in blood. As is mine own tale, concerning a friend who was not a friend, the truest knight in all the world who was also a vile traitor, a sinner who worked holy miracles, a lover who brought only shame to his beloved, dying but never quite dead—Oh, I too am afraid. Help me, Sir Knight! I think I am ceasing to be mad!"

"I think I am beginning to remember."

They two embraced, and wept like children who had been beaten.

"Let us go inside now," said the ragged man. "Let us no longer tarry."

Now the plateau filled with golden mist, rising out of the ground to the level of their shoulders as they sat there, so their heads alone seemed to float in a sea of brilliant, luminous smoke. And as they watched, five black points emerged, tearing the mist apart, rising up like the fingers of an enormous, mailed hand; five towers, then battlements and walls revealed, a strong castle, its gate open, portcullis raised like the teeth of a waiting mouth; dark, empty, awash in golden mist, touched by moonlight, but a lifeless thing of vacant windows and silence.

"I like this not."

"Nor I," said the madman. "Still, we must go in. Know you not this castle? It is Camelot."

"I never saw it thus."

No sentries challenged them. His iron shoes echoed in the

inner court. Barefoot, the madman padded softly behind him. They searched many chambers, and found the skeletons of ladies reposing there amid cobwebs and dust. In the great feasting hall, the Round Table shone like a ring cut out of the face of the moon, brilliant and gleaming, but the knights gathered there were corpses.

The madman whimpered. They made a slow circuit: here, a youth cleft through the brainpan, and here a grizzled man with an arrow in his heart; and another, so torn apart by beasts and trampled by horses that he was in no wise recognizable even as a man, but for the emblem on his bloodied surcoat; and so on, a blond boy with his throat cut, one eye perfectly blue like a gem, the other torn away by crows; a grim-browed, stout warrior impaled on a spear.

Amid them all, King Arthur sat, weeping tears of blood.

The knight knew him. He was certain that the madman at his side did too, and was no longer mad. This was the truth. This was the ending. The cataclysmic memories returned.

"My father," said the knight softly.

"My friend," said the madman, clearly and distinctly.

Neither could meet the King's gaze. Instead they regarded their own reflections, and his, in the polished tabletop.

King Arthur said, "So it is you."

Then in a thunderclap the hall and the castle were gone, and the knight was screaming and the madman screaming back as they rolled over and over across the grass in the moonlight, hands at throats, clawing at faces.

"You are my foe!" said the madman.

"And you are mine!"

"You are *Mordred*, monster of incest, betrayer—"

"My birth was not my own choosing. You, *Lancelot*, purest of men, betrayed him also—"

They lay in one another's arms.

"Oh, comfort me!"

"Help me to be mad again!"

"Help me to forget!"

"Riddle me! Riddle me! Which did Arthur choose?"

"I think he could not choose, and that was his undoing."

As the moon set in the west, they two sat together, among the fallen, mossy stones of Camelot at the edge of the plateau, gazing out over the plain.

"Not all the stories are true," said the madman, mad once more. "Not all of them ended the way the books tell. None of that odor of sanctity for Lancelot. No, he lingers, waiting for Arthur to rise from the sleep of Avalon."

"And Mordred too. Was he not also carried from the field of Camlann to be healed? One of the queens in the boat was Morgause, his own mother. She would not have left him."

"I think we live on in Arthur's dream, so that we may be there on the day of his return."

"But for what purpose? To murder or to embrace? To be revenged or reconciled?"

"Ah, riddle me, riddle me."

# THE QUIET MONK
## by Jane Yolen

*Jane Yolen (1939–) is probably better known for her many children's books, but she is an equally gifted writer of adult fantasy. She was present in* The Pendragon Chronicles *with "The Dragon's Boy", a story from Arthur's childhood. Here we move beyond Arthur's death, into the lingering limbo of Sir Lancelot's fate.*

*Glastonbury Abbey, in the year of Our Lord 1191*

He was a tall man, and his shoulders looked broad even under the shapeless disguise of the brown sacking. The hood hid the color of his hair and, when he pushed the hood back, the tonsure was so close cropped, he might have been a blonde or a redhead or gray. It was his eyes that held one's interest most. They were the kind of blue that I had only seen on midsummer skies, with the whites the color of bleached muslin. He was a handsome man, with a strong, thin nose and a mouth that would make all the women in the parish sure to shake their heads with the waste of it. They were a lusty lot, the parish dames, so I had been warned.

I was to be his guide as I was the spritest of the brothers, even with my twisted leg, for I was that much younger than the rest, being newly come to my vocation, one of the few infant oblates who actually joined that convocation of saints. Most left to go into trade, though a few, it must be admitted, joined the army, safe in their hearts for a peaceful death.

Father Joseph said I was not to call the small community "saints," for sainthood must be earned not conferred, but my birth father told me, before he gave me to the abbey, that by living

380

in such close quarters with saintly men I could become one. And that he, by gifting me, would win a place on high. I am not sure if all this was truly accomplished, for my father died of a disease his third wife brought to their marriage bed, a strange wedding portion indeed. And mostly my time in the abbey was taken up not in prayer side by side with saints but on my knees cleaning the abbot's room, the long dark halls, and the *dortoir*. Still, it was better than being back at home in Meade's Hall where I was the butt of every joke, no matter I was the son of the lord. His eighth son, born twisted ankle to thigh, the murderer of his own mother at the hard birthing. At least in Glastonbury Abbey I was needed, if not exactly loved.

So when the tall wanderer knocked on the door late that Sunday night, and I was the watcher at the gate, Brother Sanctus being abed with a shaking fever, I got to see the quiet monk first.

It is wrong, I know, to love another man in that way. It is wrong to worship a fellow human even above God. It is the one great warning drummed into infant oblates from the start. For a boy's heart is a natural altar and many strange deities ask for sacrifice there. But I loved him when first I saw him for the hope I saw imprinted on his face and the mask of sorrow over it.

He did not ask to come in; he demanded it. But he never raised his voice nor spoke other than quietly. That is why we dubbed him the Quiet Monk and rarely used his name. Yet he owned a voice with more authority than even Abbot Giraldus could command, for *he* is a shouter. Until I met the Quiet Monk, I had quaked at the abbot's bluster. Now I know it for what it truly is: fear masquerading as power.

"I seek a quiet corner of your abbey and a word with your abbot after his morning prayers and ablutions," the Quiet Monk said.

I opened the gate, conscious of the squawking lock and the cries of the wood as it moved. Unlike many abbeys, we had no rooms ready for visitors. Indeed we never entertained guests anymore. We could scarce feed ourselves these days. But I did not tell *him* that. I led him to my own room, identical to all the others save the abbot's, which was even meaner, as Abbot Giraldus reminded us daily. The Quiet Monk did not seem to notice, but nodded silently and eased himself onto my thin pallet, falling asleep at once. Only soldiers and monks have such a facility. My father, who once led a cavalry, had it. And I, since coming to the abbey, had it, too. I covered him gently with my one thin blanket and crept from the room.

In the morning, the Quiet Monk talked for a long time with Abbot Giraldus and then with Fathers Joseph and Paul. He joined us in our prayers, and when we sang, his voice leaped over the rest, even over the sopranos of the infant oblates and the lovely tenor of Brother John. He stayed far longer on his knees than any, at the last prostrating himself on the cold stone floor for over an hour. That caused the abbot much distress, which manifested itself in a tantrum aimed at my skills at cleaning. I had to rewash the floor in the abbot's room where the stones were already smooth from his years of penances.

Brother Denneys—for so was the Quiet Monk's name, called he said after the least of boys who shook him out of a dream of apathy—was given leave to stay until a certain task was accomplished. But before the task could be done, permission would have to be gotten from the pope.

What that task was to be, neither the abbot nor Fathers Joseph or Paul would tell. And if I wanted to know, the only one I might turn to was Brother Denneys himself. Or I could wait until word came from the Holy Father, which word—as we all knew full well—might take days, weeks, even months over the slow roads between Glastonbury and Rome. If word came at all.

Meanwhile, Brother Denneys was a strong back and a stronger hand. And wonder of wonders (a miracle, said Father Joseph, who did not parcel out miracles with any regularity), he also had a deep pocket of gold which he shared with Brother Aermand, who cooked our meagre meals. As long as Brother Denneys remained at the abbey, we all knew we would eat rather better than we had in many a year. Perhaps that is why it took so long for word to come from the Pope. So it was our small convocation of saints became miners, digging gold out of a particular seam. Not all miracles, Father Joseph had once said, proceed from a loving heart. Some, he had mused, come from too little food or too much wine or not enough sleep. And, I added to myself, from too great a longing for gold.

Ours was not a monastery where silence was the rule. We had so little else, talk was our one great privilege, except of course on holy days, which there were rather too many of. As was our custom, we foregathered at meals to share the day's small events: the plants beginning to send through their green hosannahs, the epiphanies of birds' nest, and the prayerful bits of gossip any small community collects. It was rare we talked of our pasts. The past is what had driven most of us to Glastonbury. Even

Saint Patrick, that most revered of holy men, it was said came to Glastonbury posting ahead of his long past. Our little wattled church had heard the confessions of good men and bad, saints of passing fairness and sinners of surprising depravity, before it had been destroyed seven years earlier by fire. But the stories that Brother Denneys told us that strange spring were surely the most surprising confessions of all, and I read in the expressions of the abbot and Fathers Joseph and Paul a sudden overwhelming greed that surpassed all understanding.

What Brother Denneys rehearsed for us were the matters that had set him wandering: a king's wife betrayed, a friendship destroyed, a repentance sought, and over the many years a driving need to discover the queen's grave, that he might plead for forgiveness at her crypt. But all this was not new to the father confessors who had listened to lords and ploughmen alike. It was the length of time he had been wandering that surprised us.

Of course we applauded his despair and sanctified his search with a series of oratories sung by our choir. Before the church had burned down, we at Glastonbury had been noted for our voices, one of the three famed perpetual choirs, the others being at Caer Garadawg and at Bangor. I sang the low ground bass, which surprised everyone who saw me, for I am thin and small with a chest many a martyr might envy. But we were rather fewer voices than we might have been seven years previously, the money for the church repair having gone instead to fund the Crusades. Fewer voices—and quite a few skeptics, though the abbot, and Fathers Paul and Joseph, all of whom were in charge of our worldly affairs, were quick to quiet the doubters because of that inexhaustible pocket of gold.

How long had he wandered? Well, he certainly did not look his age. Surely six centuries should have carved deeper runes on his brow and shown the long bones. But in the end, there was not a monk at Glastonbury, including even Brother Thomas, named after that doubting forebear, who remained unconvinced.

Brother Denneys revealed to us that he had once been a knight, the fairest of that fair company of Christendom who had accompanied the mighty King Arthur in his search for the grail.

"I who was Lancelot du Lac," he said, his voice filled with that quiet authority, "am now but a wandering mendicant. I seek the grave of that sweetest lady whom I taught to sin, skin upon skin, tongue into mouth like fork into meat."

If we shivered deliciously at the moment of the telling, who can blame us, especially those infant oblates just entering their manhood. Even Abbot Giraldus forgot to cross himself, so moved was he by the confession.

But all unaware of the stir he was causing, Brother Denneys continued.

"She loved the king, you know, but not the throne. She loved the man of him, but not the monarch. He did not know how to love a woman. He husbanded a kingdom, you see. It was enough for him. He should have been a saint."

He was silent then, as if in contemplation. We were all silent, as if he had set us a parable that we would take long years unraveling, as scholars do a tale.

A sign from his mouth, like the wind over an old unused well, recalled us. He did not smile. It was as if there were no smiles left in him, but he nodded and continued.

"What does a kingdom need but to continue? What does a queen need but to bear an heir?" He paused, not to hear the questions answered but to draw deep breath. He went on. "I swear that was all that drove her into my arms, not any great adulterous love for me. Oh, for a century or two I still fancied ours was the world's great love, a love borne on the wings of magic first and then the necromancy of passion alone. I cursed and blamed that witch Morgaine even as I thanked her. I cursed and blamed the stars. But in the end I knew myself a fool, for no man is more foolish than when he is misled by his own base maunderings." He gestured downward with his hand, dismissing the lower half of his body, bit his lip as if in memory, then spoke again.

"When she took herself to Amesbury Convent, I knew the truth but would not admit it. Lacking the hope of a virgin birth, she had chosen me—not God—to fill her womb. In that I failed her even as God had. She could not hold my seed; I could not plant a healthy crop. There was one child that came too soon, a tailed infant with bulging eyes, more *mer* than human. After that there were no more." He shivered.

I shivered.

We all shivered, thinking on that monstrous child.

"When she knew herself a sinner, who had sinned without result, she committed herself to sanctity alone, like the man she worshipped, the husband she adored. I was forgot."

One of the infant oblates chose that moment to sigh out loud, and the abbot threw him a dark look, but Brother Denneys never heard.

"Could I do any less than she?" His voice was so quiet then, we all strained forward in the pews to listen. "Could I strive to forget my sinning self? I had to match her passion for passion, and so I gave my sin to God." He stood and with one swift, practiced movement pulled off his robe and threw himself naked onto the stone floor.

I do not know what others saw, but I was so placed that I could not help but notice. From the back, where he lay full length upon the floor, he was a well-muscled man. But from the front he was as smoothly wrought as a girl. In some frenzy of misplaced penitence in the years past, he had cut his manhood from him, dedicating it—God alone knew where—on an altar of despair.

I covered my face with my hands and wept; wept for his pain and for his hopelessness and wept that I, crooked as I was, could not follow him on his long, lonely road.

We waited for months for word to come from Rome, but either the Holy Father was too busy with the three quarrelsome kings and their Crusades, or the roads between Glastonbury and Rome were closed, as usual, by brigands. At any rate, no message came, and still the Quiet Monk worked at the abbey, paying for the privilege out of his inexhaustible pocket. I spent as much time as I could working by his side, which meant I often did double and triple duty. But just to hear his soft voice rehearsing the tales of his past was enough for me. Dare I say it? I preferred his stories to the ones in the Gospels. They had all the beauty, the magic, the mystery, and one thing more. They had a human passion, a life such as I could never attain.

One night, long after the winter months were safely past and the sun had warmed the abbey gardens enough for our spades to snug down easily between the rows of last year's plantings, Brother Denneys came into my cell. Matins was past for the night and such visits were strictly forbidden.

"My child," he said quietly, "I would talk with you."

"Me?" My voice cracked as it had not this whole year past. "Why me?" I could feel my heart beating out its own canonical hours, but I was not so far from my days as an infant oblate that I could not at the same time keep one ear tuned for footsteps in the hall.

"You, Martin," he said, "because you listen to my stories and follow my every move with the eyes of a hound to his master or a squire his knight."

I looked down at the stone floor unable to protest, for he was right. It was just that I had not known he had noticed my faithfulness.

"Will you do something for me if I ask it?"

"Even if it were to go against God and his saints," I whispered. "Even then."

"Even if it were to go against Abbot Giraldus and his rule?"

"Especially then," I said under my breath, but he heard.

Then he told me what had brought him specifically to Glastonbury, the secret which he had shared with the abbot and Fathers Paul and Joseph, the reason he waited for word from Rome that never came.

"There was a bard, a Welshman, with a voice like a demented dove, who sang of this abbey and its graves. But there are many abbeys and many acres of stones throughout this land. I have seen them all. Or so I thought. But in his rhymes—and in his cups—he spoke of Glastonbury's two pyramids with the grave between. His song had a ring of Merlin's truth in it, which that mage had spoke long before the end of our tale: '*a little green, a private peace, between the standing stones.*'"

I must have shaken my head, for he began to recite a poem with the easy familiarity of the mouth which sometimes remembers what the mind has forgot.

A time will come when what is three makes one:
A little green, a private peace, between the standing stones.
A gift of gold shall betray the place at a touch.
Absolution rests upon its mortal couch.

He spoke with absolute conviction, but the whole spell made less sense to me than the part. I did not answer him.

He sighed. "You do not understand. The grave between those stone pyramids is the one I seek. I am sure of it now. But your abbot is adamant. I cannot have permission to unearth the tomb without a nod from Rome. Yet I must open it, Martin, I must. She is buried within and I must throw myself at her dear dead feet and be absolved." He had me by the shoulders.

"Pyramids?" I was not puzzled by his passion or by his utter conviction that he had to untomb his queen. But as far as I knew there were no pyramids in the abbey's yard.

"There are two tapered plinths," Brother Denneys said. "With carvings on them. A whole roster of saints." He shook my shoulders as if to make me understand.

Then I knew what he meant. Or at least I knew the plinths to which he referred. They looked little like pyramids. They were large standing tablets on which the names of the abbots of the past and other godly men of this place ran down the side like rainfall. It took a great imagining—or a greater need—to read a pair of pyramids there. And something more. I *had* to name it.

"There is no grave there, Brother Denneys. Just a sward, green in the spring and summer, no greener place in all the boneyard. We picnic there once a year to remember God's gifts."

"That is what I hoped. That is how Merlin spoke the spell. *A little green. A private peace.* My lady's place would be that green."

"But there is nothing there!" On this one point I would be adamant.

"You do not know that, my son. And my hopes are greater than your knowledge." There was a strange cast to his eyes that I could just see, for a sliver of moonlight was lighting my cell. "Will you go with me when the moon is full, just two days hence? I cannot dig it alone. Someone must needs stand guardian."

"Against whom?"

"Against the mist maidens, against the spirits of the dead."

"I can only stand against the abbot and those who watch at night." I did not add that I could also take the blame. He was a man who brought out the martyr in me. Perhaps that was what had happened to his queen.

"Will you?"

I looked down the bed at my feet, outlined under the thin blanket in that same moonlight. My right foot was twisted so severely that, even disguised with the blanket, it was grotesque. I looked up at him, perched on my bedside. He was almost smiling at me.

"I will," I said. "God help me, I will."

He embraced me once, rose, and left the room.

How slowly, how quickly those two days flew by. I made myself stay away from his side as if by doing so I could avert all suspicion from our coming deed. I polished the stone floors along the hall until one of the infant oblates, young Christopher of Chedworth, slipped and fell badly enough to have to remain the day under the infirmarer's care. The abbot removed me from my duties and set me to hoeing the herb beds and washing the pots as penance.

And the Quiet Monk did not speak to me again, nor even nod as he passed, having accomplished my complicity. Should we have known that all we did *not* do signaled even more clearly our intent? Should Brother Denneys, who had been a man of battle, have plotted better strategies? I realize now that as a knight he had been a solitary fighter. As a lover, he had been caught out at his amours. Yet even then, even when I most certainly was denying Him, God was looking over us and smoothing the stones in our paths.

Matins was done and I had paid scant attention to the psalms and even less to the antiphons. Instead I watched the moon as it shone through the chapel window, illuminating the glass picture of Lazarus rising from the dead. Twice Brother Thomas had elbowed me into the proper responses and three times Father Joseph had glared down at me from above.

But Brother Denneys never once gave me the sign I awaited, though the moon made a full halo over the lazar's head.

Dejected, I returned to my cell and flung myself onto my knees, a position that was doubly painful to me because of my bad leg, and prayed to the God I had neglected to deliver me from false hopes and wicked promises.

And then I heard the slap of sandals coming down the hall. I did not move from my knees, though the pains shot up my right leg and into my groin. I waited, taking back all the prayers I had sent heavenward just moments before, and was rewarded for my faithlessness by the sight of the Quiet Monk striding into my cell.

He did not have to speak. I pulled myself up without his help, smoothed down the skirts of my cassock so as to hide my crooked leg, and followed him wordlessly down the hall.

It was silent in the dark *dortoir*, except for the noise of Brother Thomas's strong snores and a small pop-pop-popping sound that punctuated the sleep of the infant oblates. I knew that later that night, the novice master would check on the sleeping boys, but he was not astir now. Only the gatekeeper was alert, snug at the front gate and waiting for a knock from Rome that might never come. But we were going out the back door and into the graveyard. No one would hear us there.

Brother Denneys had a great shovel ready by the door. Clearly, he had been busy while I was on my knees. I owed him silence and duty. And my love.

We walked side by side through the cemetery, threading our way past many headstones. He slowed his natural pace to my limping one, though I know he yearned to move ahead rapidly. I thanked him silently and worked hard to keep up.

There were no mist maidens, no white robed ghosts moaning aloud beneath the moon, nor had I expected any. I knew more than most how the mind conjures up monsters. So often jokes had been played upon me as a child, and a night in the boneyard was a favorite in my part of the land. Many a chilly moon I had been left in our castle graveyard, tied up in an open pit or laid flat on a new slab. My father used to laugh at the pranks. He may even have paid the pranksters. After all, he was a great believer in the toughened spirit. But I like to think he was secretly proud that I never complained. I had often been cold and the ache settled permanently in my twisted bones, but I was never abused by ghosts and so did not credit them.

All these memories and more marched across my mind as I followed Brother Denneys to the pyramids that bordered his hopes.

There were no ghosts, but there *were* shadows, and more than once we both leaped away from them, until we came at last to the green, peaceful place where the Quiet Monk believed his lost love lay buried.

"I will dig," he said, "and you will stand there as guard."

He pointed to a spot where I could see the dark outlines of both church and housing, and in that way know quickly if anyone was coming toward us this night. So while he dug, in his quiet, competent manner, I climbed up upon a cold stone dedicated to a certain Brother Silas, and kept the watch.

The only accompaniment to the sound of his spade thudding into the sod was the long, low whinny of a night owl on the hunt and the scream of some small animal that signaled the successful end. After that, there was only the soft *thwack-thwack* of the spade biting deeper and deeper into the dirt of that unproved grave.

He must have dug for hours; I had only the moon to mark the passage of time. But he was well down into the hole with but the crown of his head showing when he cried out.

I ran over to the edge of the pit and stared down.

"What is it?" I asked, staring between the black shadows.

"Some kind of wood," he said.

"A coffin?"

"More like the barrel of a tree," he said. He bent over. "Definitely a tree. Oak, I think."

"Then your bard was wrong," I said. "But then, he was a Welshman."

"It is a Druid burial," he said. "That is what the oak means. Merlin would have fixed it up."

"I thought Merlin died first. Or disappeared. You told me that. In one of your stories."

He shook his head. "It is a Druid trick, no doubt of it. You will see." He started digging again, this time at a much faster pace, the dirt sailing backwards and out of the pit, covering my sandals before I moved. A fleck of it hit my eye and made me cry. I was a long while digging it out, a long while weeping.

"That's it, then," came his voice. "And there's more besides."

I looked over into the pit once again. "More?"

"Some sort of stone, with a cross on the bottom side."

"Because she was Christian?" I asked.

He nodded. "The Druids had to give her that. They gave her little else."

The moon was mostly gone, but a thin line of light stretched tight across the horizon. I could hear the first bells from the abbey, which meant Brother Angelus was up and ringing them. If we were not at prayers, they would look for us. If we were not in our cells alone, I knew they would come out here. Abbot Giraldus might have been a blusterer but he was not a stupid man.

"Hurry," I said.

He turned his face up to me and smiled. "All these years waiting," he said. "All these years hoping. All these years of false graves." Then he turned back and, using the shovel as a pry, levered open the oak cask.

Inside were the remains of two people, not one, with the bones intertwined, as if in death they embraced with more passion than in life. One was clearly a man's skeleton, with the long bones of the legs fully half again the length of the other's. There was a helm such as a fighting man might wear lying crookedly near the skull. The other skeleton was marked with fine gold braids of hair, that caught the earliest bit of daylight.

"Guenivere," the Quiet Monk cried out in full voice for the first time, and he bent over the bones, touching the golden hair with a reverent hand.

I felt a hand on my shoulder but did not turn around, for as I watched, the golden skein of hair turned to dust under his fingers, one instant a braid and the next a reminder of time itself.

Brother Denneys threw himself onto the skeletons, weeping hysterically and I—I flung myself down into the pit, though it was a drop of at least six feet. I pulled him off the brittle, broken bones and cradled him against me until his sorrow was spent. When I looked up, the grave was ringed around with the familiar faces of my brother monks. At the foot of the grave stood the abbot himself, his face as red and as angry as a wound.

Brother Denneys was sent away from Glastonbury, of course. He himself was a willing participant in the exile. For even though the little stone cross had the words HIC JACET ARTHURUS REX QUONDAM REXQUE FUTURUS carved upon it, he said it was not true. That the oak casket was nothing more than a boat from one of the lake villages overturned. That the hair we both saw so clearly in that early morning light was nothing more than grave mold.

"She is somewhere else, not here," he said, dismissing the torn earth with a wave of his hand. "And I must find her."

I followed him out the gate and down the road, keeping pace with him step for step. I follow him still. His hair has gotten grayer over the long years, a strand at a time, but cannot keep up with the script that now runs across my brow. The years as his squire have carved me deeply but his sorrowing face is untouched by time or the hundreds of small miracles he, all unknowing, brings with each opening of a grave: the girl in Westminster whose once blind eyes can now admit light, a Shropshire lad, dumb from birth, with a tongue that can now make rhymes.

And I understand that he will never find this particular grail. He is in his own hell and I but chart its regions, following after him on my two straight legs. A small miracle, true. In the winter, in the deepest snow, the right one pains me, a twisting memory of the old twisted bones. When I cry out in my sleep, he does not notice nor does he comfort me. And my ankle still warns of every coming storm. He is never grateful for the news. But I can walk for the most part without pain or limp, and surely every miracle maker needs a witness to his work, an apostle to send letters to the future. That is my burden. It is my duty. It is my everlasting joy.

The Tudor antiquary Bale reported that "In Avallon in 1191, there found they the flesh bothe of Arthur and of hys wyfe Guenever turned all into duste, wythin theyr confines of strong oke, the boneys only remaynynge. A monke of the same abbeye, standyng and behouldyng the fine broydinges of the womman's hear as yellow as golde there still to remayne, as a man ravyshed, or more than halfe from his wyttes, he leaped into the graffe, xv fote depe, to have caughte them sodenlye. But he fayled of his purpose. For so soon as they were touched they fell all to powder."

By 1193, *the monks at Glastonbury had money enough to work again on the rebuilding of their church, for wealthy pilgrims flocked to the relics and King Richard himself presented a sword reputed to be Excalibur to Tancred, the Norman ruler of Sicily, a few short months after the exhumation.*

# THE SAD WIZARD
## by John T. Aquino

*We conclude our journey through* The Camelot
Chronicles *with a reflective tale by a young
American writer, John Aquino. He takes us to
the Middle Ages of Elizabethan England, where
the Arthurian legend underwent a revival, and
tells of how Merlin sought to recreate another
Arthurian age.*

"In the instant of a breath, by witches' wish, fast to the feet of a crisp crow,
past millions of miles of fields and seas, you fly, gentle, to me. I have seen you.
Eons have I waited. 'Fore creeds and laws, church with cross and spite, books
not drawn, and trips for pleasure, always I. Come to me. Live my spell. I will
fill your form with life and through you, at least, I will leave here."

Until he was born, James Bolt, like all babies, had been the darling
of the gods. He was then plucked out, christened, and educated.
But he continually, though unknowingly, strove to preserve his
faerie thoughts. When he could read, he neglected the political
speeches and articles his father tried to use as primers and read
of Venus and Adonis in a quarto translation of Ovid, of Arthur
and his knights and their dream of Camelot, and other paeans to
gallantry and magic. Through the poems of Wyatt and Howard,
James learned, through the spell of words, that trees do talk, birds
do mourn the dead, and hearts do cry. James's father's tutoring,
however, soon buried these thoughts deep in James's soul.

James learned that he was of a noble family—a family of which
few people had ever heard. Queen Elizabeth had knighted James's
father for his bravery in the Irish wars, but two years later had
him thrown out of a royal reception for being unknown to her.

393

James took his father's place at court, in the back. His duties at court were not taxing. He dressed in finery, he listened to politics and policy, and he awaited the opportunity to fight in great wars—wars that the queen predicted would never come. Mostly, he spent his time writing poetry, last vestige of his youth's desire, to a young lady-in-waiting named Elizabeth or Beth, whose eyes and hair were the brown of a walnut's heart and whose smile was subtle.

XXXI.

> When I walk upon the beach alone
> And count the ways I love thee true,
> Even the gulls cry that you are mine own
> And waves murmur gentle thoughts of you.
> To lose you, love, would mean my death,
> My lovely, saintly, godly Beth.

James thought that it was shyness that caused Beth not to reply or acknowledge. He continued writing.

CXV.

> For Beth, my love,
> I send this dove
> As a symbol of my loving,
> Like a flameless light
> Or a starless night
> Or pewter in need of rubbing.
> Nothing will stop me, not even death,
> Come to me, come to me, come to me, Beth.

Beth did not come to him. The night after she received this poem, Beth's two brothers, Basil and George, followed James home, knocked on the door, criticized the meter of his verse, then beat him up.

James was stricken for days with grief and shame. As always, he put his feelings into poetry:

> When love is gone, then life is lost,
> Like budding spring to killing frost.
> Farewell meaning, farewell soul,
> I will vanish to my hole.

And so, James walked and walked, searching for a hole where he could hide. He wandered through forests and streams, valleys and hills. He did not look where he was going, mostly because he was searching for a rhyme for "lifeless."

It was a summer day in the truest sense, for everything seemed the sum of its parts. A tree's leaf did swell with the throbbing of its cells and threads, its bark did glisten with the wet of morning dew, its roots strained and pushed forward for another inch, another inch. A fisherman on the beach mending his net whistled as James passed him, singing a hymn to his lips that pursed, to his lungs that pushed the breath, to his brain that made the tune. But James ignored the tree and the man, thinking only of "lifeless, strifeless, titheless."

He walked past a woman with two children on her knees nursing still another in the shade of a beached ship, three children playing with a ball in a graveyard over the remains of poets and mathematicians, and an old man sitting in a chair, slowly closing his eyes forever, watching the endless flight of a gull.

He passed ships and homes, fields empty and with flower, stones of towers that fell with Rome. Hours had flown by so quickly that soon they were without meaning. In the middle of a field, barren except for florid turfs of wild grass, there was a tall mound, perhaps the shovel leavings of graves, or perhaps a grave itself, or the tenth layer of a deceased civilization that both dwelt with toads and soared with angels. It was solid, rockish, perhaps a star from the inky black which fell solely to sink itself in earth's crust.

James walked right toward it. For some reason, he could not get his poem right. He tried it aloud:

> "Thy lack of care has sapped my breath
> And made me all but lifeless.
> I think that I would take my life,
> But alas I find me knifeless."

"For the sake of Bran, wretch," cried a voice from the mound, "that not only kills the meter but the sense!"

James walked to the mound to see who was speaking.

"If you must finish it, and I don't see why you should," the voice continued, "this is the way:

> My breath is sapped, my vision fades,
> My arm hangs limp and lifeless.
> You are to blame, most wicked maid,
> For 'tis you who left me wifeless."

James came to the other side of the mound and found an opening. He went into frigid darkness and with his first step found more room than the outside shell showed. He came ten feet forward and found a grating of wrought iron. Through the bars he could see a figure, stooped and cloaked, sitting behind a gray stone construction that could have been an altar. What light there was came from a candle on a stack of books to James's left, just within his line of vision.

"Come in," said the figure. "The gate will open—for you."

James touched the bars, which jumped at his touch. James came freely into the room and was greeted by the smell, not of rot and age, but of fresh jasmine newly cut.

"I hope you do not mind my improvement on your rhyme, but I really cannot stand a shattered iam."

"Who are you?" James asked in wonder.

"I am—a magician," said the cloaked man. "Of sorts," he added.

"Are you?" James said earnestly, but with just a touch of skepticism. "How shall I win her?"

The ancient voice crackled in laughter. "So abrupt. So to the point. The lady Beth," he sighed. "If you must win her," he said, "have your poems printed."

"Printed?"

"Yes. A limited run, a thousand copies or so. A suitable Latin title, 'Poetae Elizabethae,' or something like that."

"I see," James said excitedly. "Then she will see my love by my spreading it to the world. I will make her famous. Then others will tell her I love her."

"Yes, yes," said the old man. "For a printer, William Jaggard is not bad, I hear—very cheap—though I would not like to have him over for dinner."

"I will do it," James said breathlessly. "Thank you, sir. Bless you," he shouted, running mindlessly into the darkness.

"Bless yourself," the old voice laughed after him. "And, when you talk to Philip Henslowe, keep saying 'four pounds three!'"

The reaction to "Poetae Elizabethae" was almost immediate. The day Jaggard's edition was issued, Basil and George drew swords on James as he was coming out of the Mermaid's Tavern. James was never skilled at swords, but their laughter at James's awkwardness made Basil and George careless. Basil was trampled by a runaway carriage and George, trying to hack

James in half, wrapped his sword around a post and plunged the blade into his own shoulder.

James was acclaimed a hero. There was even a ballad written about "Lucky Jim, or How the Gods of Chance Caused a Man to Be Saved for His Lady." This gave Jaggard the printer an idea. He called James in.

"Look, my boy," he said in a whisper while continually glancing over his shoulder, "you take these poems you have written about this Beth, the ballad, the first act of *Hamlet* but cut out the ghost, the third act of *Romeo and Juliet*, act five of *Henry V* when he woos the French queen, mix it together in sequence, and we have one hell of a play! Of course, a play has to be performed. Philip Henslowe runs a theater— "

Philip Henslowe was a very short man who sat on a very high stool writing in a ledger. He had a huge mole in the center of his forehead, hair only on the back of his head, and a huge belly from sitting.

"Jaggard," he screeched from the depth of his hose, "gave me your play. It sounds familiar to me, and the rhymes are sometimes harsh to my ears, but there is the stuff of greatness in it, somewhere." Some men entered the room as Henslowe was speaking. "Still, it needs some work—all plays do. We often share tasks here; Dekker, Shakespeare, and Jonson here will shape it up. And," he thumbed sloppily through his ledger, "for your work we will give you—two pounds."

James found himself shouting the old man's words. "Four pounds, three."

Henslowe's ledger fell from his desk. There was mumbling from the men in the shadows of the room: "Of all the gall! Young scallion! Look at Henslowe!"

The fat man said nothing, as if waiting for James to talk. Then, when James just stood there, he smiled suddenly. "Perhaps," Henslowe chewed his lip, "two, six?"

"Four pounds, three!"

"Three!"

"Four pounds, three!"

"Three, six!"

"Four pounds, three!"

"Done! Done!"

The shadowy figures behind Henslowe bowed to James, and he in return bowed back.

*Love's Cup, or Persistency Rewarded,* as the play was finally called, opened at the Swan Theater and was well received. Beth was in the audience, as was her father. There was acted the tale of James who was all but driven to madness for love of Beth. But the two are kept apart by differences between their families. He kills her two brothers in a duel, then wins her love by his clever discourse and his beautiful poems.

After seeing the play, Beth's father disowned her and drove her in the rain from his home. "Out, out you thing to be maligned!"

"But father," she said, "he was nothing to me. He made it up in his fancy."

"Nonsense!" he cried. "How could he have made it all up in his head?"

Beth fled. And she went to the only refuge she knew, to a man who claimed to adore her and who was, after all, the cause of her troubles.

Three days later, James and Beth were married by a half-sober minister ten miles from London. The total cost to James, including coach, lodging, the minister's fee, and the minister's drink, was four pounds, three.

Two weeks later, in the middle of the night, James awoke, thinking of the old man in the cave. He took himself from Beth's arms and wandered in darkness and fog in search of the cave in the barren field.

"Old man!" he cried aloud as he walked. He did not know the time or where he was going or why there was suddenly fog in an evening that had been clear and bright. "Old man!" he cried.

"Here I am," said the voice. "By an astounding coincidence, you are exactly 3.6 meters from the gate now. Take three giant steps forward."

James did as he was told and, though he could not see, heard the sharp ring of the gate flying open. James took another step forward and saw—the cloak had fallen to the old man's shoulders. His face seemed to James gentle and loving. The old man's beard was soft and silken; his smile warm and magically beneficent.

"Who are you, old man," James said softly but firmly. "I had almost convinced myself that I had dreamed you. But you knew Beth's name and I had not told you. You knew about the four pounds, three, and you probably knew what would happen if I had my poems printed."

"Probably is for historians," the old man laughed.

"And tonight, I—I heard you call me."

"That is because I did."

"But—how?" James stammered foolishly.

"Come here," the old man said, extending his arm. "Come around and see my pool of tears."

"Your what?"

"My crystal pool. Cried of my own tears."

James came forward and saw on the marble, altar-like structure a perfectly circular pool of water. It was completely flat; there was no depth to it. As he looked, James saw a milky cloud form in the pool, though the movement did not disturb its surface. In a second, the cloud disappeared and within the pool's confines James saw Beth lying asleep on their bed, wearing the white linen bed-sheets that he had bought for her last Wednesday, an empty space beside her where he had lain.

"But that's Beth, my wife!" James marveled.

"Yes, you must be thinking of her," the old man said calmly.

"I was. I was wishing she were with me. But how can it be?"

"Why, my tears were magic, of course. Consequently— "

"Who are you?" James demanded.

"Oh, I have many names." The old man produced a metal wand from nowhere and stuck and stirred it in Beth's image as if he were mixing batter. Beth's form was whipped away. "Some call me devil's son, some the god of the sky. Jupiter, Myrddin, Merlinus, Merlin— "

"Merlin! King Arthur's Merlin! The Magician! Yes, you said you were a— "

"Of sorts." The old man cut him off hastily. "The term 'magician' is much too limited. I have seen the dawn of creation and the dusk of humanity. To me, time is a whirlwind in which I walk. I have tossed thunderclaps at hysterical Athenians, charmed witless Celts with sleight-of-hand and hymns. Imprisoned here by the witch Nimue whom I stupidly coveted, I have been somewhat less active than before, but for my amusement I have breathed melodies into the air, then blown them into the minds of Palestrina and Henry VIII, and for isolated moments shared the minds of Gregory, Nennius, Chaucer, Malory— "

"Some of them I have heard of, but— "

Merlin leaned forward and began to speak persuasively to James, moving the wand here and there for emphasis. But his manner was still calm, logical, as if his statements were facts beyond denial. "I am here now, but in a few seconds I may be strolling through the streets of London, in a hundred years I will be standing on a hill watching the flames of Montezuma's castle and discussing gravitational force with

Isaac Newton—but only because I had gone there before, when I was free."

"I don't understand you," James said, his voice an anxious whine. "I know nothing of walking in time or of this Newton. What of me, me and Beth? What are we to you?"

Merlin stared at James, as if slightly annoyed at the interruption to his autobiographical discourse. "Your Beth means nothing to me. And soon will mean nothing to you. You will not stay with her long."

"That's rubbish. I will never leave my Beth. Never."

"Never?" Merlin asked coolly. "Not even for power. For the rule of England and beyond. Not even for wealth beyond the dreams of a Getty or a Mellon. You will leave her. Tomorrow, as a matter of fact. I know because I have walked in time. I also know because I will cause you to. I cannot wait for that day when I am free and Nimue and I will walk through the ruins of Bristol hand in hand. I still have power to influence life. I still have a destiny. I have chosen you, young man. You will leave your Beth, your moment's pleasure. You will do it because I tell you. And then you will become the new Arthur, King of England, and master of the Round Table!"

"You are mad!" James shouted at him. "Undeniably mad. You have escaped from the care of monks and hidden in this cave. I have been listening to a madman."

James turned to go. Merlin did not move. "You cannot leave me. You are mine. You have always stayed."

James took another step. He felt a blow to his head and then a rush of sound to his ears, like thunder. He looked before him and saw scores of people seated in rows, beating their hands together. He looked to his left and right and saw beside him men dressed in Roman togas, smiling, and bowing toward the rows of people. James was in another time, another place. It was 1864, at a performance of *Julius Caesar* in Washington, D.C., starring for their only time together, Julius, Edwin, and John Wilkes Booth. James found himself bowing with them and smiling. The one to James's left, a short man with a drooping mustache, noticed James. "Who are you?" he said in a hoarse whisper.

"I am James Bolt in the time of Elizabeth of England and have been sent here by Merlin the magician."

And then James was gone.

"Julius," John Wilkes Booth said to his brother, who was once again next to him, "Now I am sure that I am mad."

James was back again in Merlin's cave.

"Who am I?" Merlin asked, standing behind him.

James thought to himself. His life at court had brought him obscurity and heartbreak. Ten minutes with an old man who claimed to be a Celtic myth had brought him success. He was no longer to be stuck in the back of court, but was now the hero of a storybook—the new Arthur. His old life was returning to him.

"Who am I?" repeated the old man. "Or do you require further proof? Prehistoric times? The Battle of Dunkirk? The exploration of the planet Pluto?"

"You are Merlin the magician," James responded weakly, staring ahead.

"Will you listen to what I have to say?"

"Yes," said James in a somewhat firmer voice.

"Fine," said Merlin, drawing near. "But then, I knew you would. I will banish your inhibitions and mold you into history. I am very sorry that I could not let you remain at the play longer. It is really quite a performance. The Booths have a natural flair for theatrical verisimilitude. But we have more important things to be concerned about. Here." He handed James a gold coin which glistened and seemed new, though the words, "Arturus Rex," dated it as 1000 years old. "Now you will think of me even when you are not here."

"Will—Beth be all right?" James asked.

"She will fare well for herself. But come. With my help, you will become the queen's lover and then consort of England!"

"The queen's— " James started, but did not finish, for his head was still spinning. He could only say in argument, "But she is sixty!"

"Fifty-nine," said Merlin.


Beth was just awakening when James returned. "My dearest," she said, startled. She pulled the sheet from her and ran to him naked. She pressed her body to his, standing on her bare tip-toes to kiss him. "Where have you been, my love?"

James slithered from her and walked around the bed. "Beth, I have something to say to you. Sit down." He sat on the bed and waited for her. Beth looked at him for a while in some astonishment, then finally came forward and sat next to him.

"Beth, tonight I have had the most wonderful experience of my life."

"And I also, my beloved."

"No, no, Beth," he said with his eyes closed in annoyance. "You do not understand. Ever since—ever since I was a little boy, I've wanted to ride with the knights, to right wrongs, to charm fair damsels with my deeds and verse, to do good. Now, I have achieved some success with my verse, as you will surely attest— "

Beth said nothing, but only looked at her feet.

"But my father wanted me to serve at court. And he was right, in a way; to do good, one must have power. But I am nothing at court. Only now—tonight—here, let me show you." He fumbled in his pockets and produced the coin Merlin had given him.

"You met a numismatist?"

And James told her of his meetings with Merlin. "And I must leave you," he said at the end. "Merlin insists. I must make love to the queen. Well, what do you think?"

Beth said nothing for a moment. She bent down and seemed to pick something up. She moved toward him. "I can sum up what I think in six words, James. 'My father,' 'my purity,' and 'my love.'" She whipped it around from behind her back and smacked him squarely in the forehead with their bed-pan.

His senses returned just in time to see Beth, fully attired, heading through the door.

"You'll think about it differently when I become king!" he shouted after her.

James's conquest of the queen was gradual. At first, on Merlin's advice, he merely smiled at her politely as she passed by his position at court. After a summer rain, she almost slipped on a wet stretch of ground, but James was close by and caught her hand and held her upright (Merlin had arranged the thunderstorm just by thinking about it). Later, the queen asked for a member of the court who spoke Spanish to deal with an ambassador from the court of Francis I. James volunteered, then ran to Merlin's cave where the magician gave him a one-night course in Spanish by means of words written on little cards. James received the commission and performed brilliantly ("The queen cannot forgive wrongs so clumsily executed."). Soon, he was given more and more commissions from the queen. One night, she asked him to her royal apartments to commend him.

"You know," he told her sheepishly, "I wrote 'Poetae Elizabethae' for you." The queen blushed and asked him to stay and tell her more.

"Am I very old?" she asked as he held her.

He ran his hand over her body. She was firm and fair, despite her years. "No. You are very young. And very wise."

"Let me teach you," she said.

Two years passed. Philip Henslowe spent less and less time running his theater; his belly was draining his life. William Jaggard continued his somewhat larcenous printing practices. He was jailed several times, but never for long. Beth, to avoid politically motivated imprisonment due to James's liaison with the queen, went to America and worked with the missionaries. Merlin told James that by his thoughts he had washed Beth's mind of hurt and shame and that she was quite content and no longer thought of James. James did not enjoy being forgotten, but then there was so much else to enjoy. His "Poetae Elizabethae" went into twelve printings, though James wrote no more. His position at court was enviable. He learned to eat snails. And he grew a fashionable beard.

James was sitting in Merlin's cave, tossing the coin Merlin had given him. "I am really the queen's puppy dog," James told Merlin, who was sitting before his crystal pool and staring into it sullenly. "She has a vein or something, and she is too old. But she says I give her energy. And look at me!" James laughed and stroked his beard and touched the rich braid on his shoulders and wrists. "Captain of the Queen's Guards, Diplomatic Liaison with Spain and Italy, Member of the Queen's Council— "

"Have you asked her to make you consort?" Merlin interrupted him.

"Repeatedly," James said as he rose. "She has told me that if I ask her that one more time she will have my head."

"Then it is time to move. Come here. Look into my pool."

James leaned over and saw in the pool the queen's carriage leaving the palace. "Yes," said James. "She is on her afternoon ride."

"Is the guard loyal to you?"

"Of course."

"Muster them, order them to capture her carriage and hold the queen. Give her one last chance to make you consort. If she will not, then you will take the crown."

"Are you mad? The people will not support— "

"The support of the people has never been necessary in government. I brought England Arthur and a score of years of enlightened peace that is still lauded and treasured in book and song. Arthur was but a boy, like you, but together we eliminated discordant bands, and joined the warring factions of Britannia into a cohesive, harmonious whole governed by justice and reason. It takes courage merged with wisdom."

"But why?" James asked. "What is she doing wrong?"

"Nothing," Merlin said simply, "except that she has no son. Before she dies, *now* is the time to plot England's path."

In spite of his father, James had never really understood politics. What Merlin said made sense. He had heard talk of the lack of an heir at court, but he had not listened closely.

"But she will fight, will she not? She is a proud woman."

"You may have to banish her," said Merlin, stirring the image in his pool with his metal wand. "Perhaps all of your women will end up in America."

The queen's carriage was red and gold and black. It hobbled and weaved on the road to Saint Alban's, a pleasant and reassuring sight to those it passed. Suddenly, from a cluster of trees at the road's fork, darted James and the Queen's Guards, their rapiers high and flashing in the sun. "No harm to the queen!" James shouted in shrill voice. He held Merlin's coin tight in his hand.

The queen's escort of five turned and watched in amazement as the queen's own guard swept like a Mongol horde upon them. Then, with lightning precision, they drew their swords, told the coachman to speed the queen to safety, and prepared to fulfill their duty, heroically and bloodily.

"Stop!" cried the queen from her carriage window. The coachman pulled the carriage slowly and cautiously to a halt. "Drop your swords. Drop them, I say! You are to offer no resistance, do you hear?"

Captain James Bolt and the guard circled the carriage, the queen's escort sitting on their horses in a humiliated and dejected manner. "Yahoo!" they cried at their victory. "Hi lo! I lo! Hilooo!"

James rode up to the carriage and opened its door. The queen was sitting calmly amidst the upholstery of blue and red velvet. "Well, Captain Bolt, we seem to have misjudged you all this time. Are we under arrest?"

"Actually," James said conversationally, using the words Merlin had given him, "you left for your ride before I had the chance to ask you a question. Will you make me consort?"

"No," she said harshly. "Better men than you have asked. It would be an insult to them and their memory to accept you."

James's pride caused his spine to arch and his voice to go strident again. "If you will not let me help you guide England, then I will take it from you and show you how to rule."

The queen smiled. "What can you give England, Captain Bolt, that I cannot?"

James smiled in return. "Magic. Courage merged with wisdom."

"I see. Well, Captain Bolt, for better or worse, England shall avoid your governance." She leaned forward and shouted into the open air to her left: "Take them!"

From the trees to both sides of the carriage rode over a hundred soldiers selected from the veterans of the Irish wars, their rapiers continually weaving and flashing. James and the guard had their weapons at their sides; they were unprepared.

James fumbled for his sword as his first lieutenant fell beside him, a gash in his throat; then others were hacked to death before they could draw or shift for position. Then a grizzled old man, whom James recognized as an old friend of his father, a man who had taken the young James on his knee and predicted a great future, moved his horse slowly toward James, his sword pointed in ritual fashion at James's heart. James tried to dodge the blade, but the old man was quick; the blade shot deep into his arm.

James dropped from his horse and joined his men there. The ground was red and wet. James dragged himself up and saw that the veterans had dismounted and surrounded him. He heard the queen's voice, "Hold! Save him for the Tower!" The veterans moved so that she could see him and he her.

"As I told you, James, better men than you. Many are still of the opinion that a woman is easy prey for a man. You were a pleasure, James, but like all pleasures there soon becomes too much of you. And so now, eat England's dirt."

In the Tower, James sat and thought of what he had done. He thought of the beauty in life he had never studied. He thought of Beth and how he wished that she were there—if only for him to look at and write about as he had when they were both at court. Perhaps, he mused, it would have been better for them both if they had never met.

James felt like writing again. He was of some importance, so many from the court saw to his needs from time to time—Raleigh, Cecil, Essex. Essex, young like James, gave him pen and paper and a mug of stout he smuggled in. On a scrap of paper, that would not be found until years later by a young boy from

Wisconsin playing with the Tower's cracks, James Bolt wrote his last poem:

> *When God peers down from his heavenly throne,*
> *Midst angel psalm and penitent moan,*
> *'Tis humbly I'll address his majesty,*
> *"'Twas tragic circumstance brought me to thee.*
> *Wrong hopes, wrong dreams, wrong time,*
> *wrong place*
> *Robbed my life, sucked forth my grace.*
> *A hapless, stupid suppliant am I.*
> *But at least, dear God, I now know why."*

"Not bad," said a voice from his mug of stout. "At least your rhymes have improved." Reflected there in the stout was Merlin's face.

James was not particularly impressed or surprised. "Speaking from your crystal pool, I see. If my rhymes have improved, old man, it was done without thee."

"That is false," Merlin protested. You are better than when I found you. You will die with nobility and dignity. You were never meant for politics. But you will die well."

And still, in spite of the resentment he felt, James found Merlin's face to be kind and loving—though now somewhat sad and confused.

"Yes. It is knowing how well you will die that has made it easier for me to . . . deceive you." The stout seemed to ripple as Merlin shrugged. "You—each person—is but a brief flash of light in the vast movement of time. I know this to be true. Some of us are of no importance ourselves. Sometimes the higher, more important good must be served. This is why you must be— "

"Sacrificed," James said.

"Yes. Because someone else, who will gain in importance and favor from your demise, will be England's might, the new Arthur—for a while."

"Who?" James asked, suddenly earnest.

"You will see," said Merlin's face, vanishing into foam.

"You were talking to someone?" asked Lord Essex entering the cell.

"Praying to my god, I suppose," said James.

"They are ready," Essex said.

And they took James Bolt to a hastily constructed scaffold, before a throng of six men and two women. He submitted without a word, knelt down, and placed his head on a block wet with morning dew. When the blade fell, he was staring at Lord Essex, who was acting as Marshall, and who was holding in his hand a golden coin like the one Merlin had given James.

The next thing James knew, he was walking in a land with no boundaries, no sky, no color, though there was music in the humming and whispering of a million voices.

Standing, waiting for him, was a shortish man dressed in a black robe and hood, though the hood did not obscure his face, which was gaunt. His eyes were black and beady, and he was smiling, a half-smile such as those of either bemusement or guile.

"Welcome, Brother James. We have been waiting for you."

"Who are you?"

The man started walking, and James walked with him. "My name really depends on what literature you read. To some I am Belinus, I am Pluto, I am Dis, Hades, Mephistopheles— "

"Am I in Hell, then?"

"No. You are dead. That is all you need to know."

"Where are you taking me?"

"To where you will be."

They walked for a while in silence.

"And what of Merlin?" James asked. "And Essex?"

"Do you really care?"

"As an observer I am interested."

"Good answer," said the short man, "for that is exactly what we are." He stopped and turned to look James face to face. "Gaze into my eyes."

And James looked into the reflection of the man's black eyes, and soon, as the eyes clouded, then cleared, he saw Essex in Merlin's cave and Merlin embracing him; he saw Essex in the queen's lap; he saw Essex riding through the streets of London trying to rally the populace to his side in his quest for the crown, but windows closed and Essex, alone, was arrested and later executed on the same scaffold where James had knelt and bowed.

"And so," James said, "Essex does not rule."

"No."

"Merlin did not— "

"No," said the short man as they resumed walking. "Merlin is a strange case. He really, imprisoned as he is, has little influence in the course of things, except that he adds some color and some motivation."

"What of Merlin?" James asked.

"He will be free one day, and he and Arthur will ride again to cure the world's wrongs. Until then, he will continue to meddle from time to time, but not have the effect he would like."

"He must know that he will not succeed."

"He should know. It is sad to think of him trying again and again, with failure inevitable, to recapture with young men like you his moment of glory with Arthur and the Round Table. But he must try."

"Do you expect me to feel sorry for him?" James said bitterly.

"I expect you to feel nothing," the short man said. "You are dead."

James walked—and saw that they were walking in a valley of the truest green color, the purest air that he had ever breathed with the scent of flowers that became honey in his mouth. And there in the valley, James saw men riding in festive games. In the clear air, their standards were plain to James.

"Arthur and his knights," James said in wonder.

"Yes," said the short man with his half-smile. "After the way Merlin used you, it was the least we could do. When Arthur rides again, you will ride with him. It is not necessarily reward here in Avalon, but we thought that it was fitting."

James and the short man walked toward Arthur and his knights, and they did not hear a distant murmur.

*"In the instant of a breath . . ."*

# APPENDIX:

# MOUNTAINY MADNESS
by Theodore Goodridge Roberts

*In* The Pendragon Chronicles *I included "For to Achieve Your Adventure", one of the Sir Dinadan stories by Theodore Goodridge Roberts (1877–1953). Roberts had planned to have these stories collected into bookform, but died before that was accomplished. He was also planning a novel about the early life of Sir Dinadan. He had only completed a draft of the first chapter before he died. This draft was deposited at the University of New Brunswick where it lay until I made enquiries, and the University kindly sent me a copy. The story remains in its first-draft state and is not in a sufficient finished form to include in the body of the anthology, but I append it here for Arthurian scholars, as a fascinating tidbit for a book that might have been.*

# I

*An Episode in the Early Career of Sir Dinadan of the Qursts.*

He rode in a high and unpeopled wilderness in the fall of the year, and was painfully conscious of the desolation of place and season. All the tales that he had ever heard of the witches and warlocks of these wild pastures and darkling glens came back to his mind. Why was he here, two days' march from the strong walls and red hearths, the plough-lands and little river meadows, the crofts and apple-yards, the stir and laughter of his lordship of Hunderholt? Why? Because his wife, the Dame Ashar, had cried shame upon him that he should lose a score of his beeves every year to the masterless mountainy men of the wilderness. He was more afraid of the dame than of witches and warlocks and masterless mountaineers.

A great man was Sir Hew, Knight of the Stooping Falcon and the lord of Hunderholt. Wide were his lands, ancient and earlish was his blood; and in his young manhood he had cut a dash at the court of King Uther Pendragon. He had suffered a painful and unsightly bashing-in of his physiognomy at the hands of an Irish knight, after which he had retired to the quiet and security of his remote barony, the place of his nativity and the cradle of his fathers. After a year of furious pursuit of wolves and tusky wild pigs and wilder mountainy men, and another year of sulking and lonely drinking, he had dashed forth one night of gusty rain and taken to wife the daughter of the wildest of the neighbouring mountain chieftains: and ever since then—for a matter of twenty years—he had been sinking contentedly deeper and deeper into rustic, uncouth, mountainy ways of living and thinking.

Sir Hew did not ride alone. He was attended by a huntsman, a herdsman, half a dozen hairy tribesmen and two couples of leggy hounds. He bestrode a shaggy pony. He was garbed in homespun wool, home-tanned leather and a cloak of wolf skins. His quality was to be distinguished from that of the huntsman, who also bestrode a shaggy pony, by the mild but unmistakable authority of his glance and the golden brooch and heron feather in the front of his leathern cap.

Sir Hew drew rein, unslung a leather bottle from his saddle-bow, tipped it to his pursed lips for a long swig, then passed it on its way even to the hairiest and humblest member of his retinue. It was lighter by the time it was back in the lordly hand. He returned it to its place and rode on. He drew rein again, abruptly, raised and extended a massive arm and pointed a finger.

"D'ye see it?" he cried, in a startled yet challenging tone of voice.

They all looked, and they all saw it. What they saw was a large white horse, but only the huntsman recognized it as such. The herder and the heather-jumpers, never having seen anything of the kind before except mountain ponies, emitted uncouth sounds of awed astonishment through their whiskers.

"A proper war-horse!" exclaimed the huntsman.

"Right!" cried Sir Hew, in rising excitement. "A knightly charger, such as I myself was wont to fork in braver days. Four such have I bestrode in a single day's joustings, and winded them all with my prodigious onsets and cavortings and the weight of my arms and harness. But where is the rider? 'Twill be an errant knight, with seven adventures to achieve; or a questing knight pledged to fetch home the skin of a dragon, that his lady may wear gloves and slippers of unique material—but right welcome will he be to me, whatever his particular form of madness! 'Tis twenty years since I last set eyes on a gentleman of fashion and chivalry, of polish and parts, unhorse me else!"

The great white horse grazed at his pleasure among frost-nipt fern and out-thrusts of granite as sharp and grey as old shoulder-blades, on a hillside beyond a long and narrow lake. On the nearer side of the lake, the ground fell away as steeply, and as rockily and fernily, as it rose on the farther side.

Sir Hew and his followers advanced at an improved pace, eager to round the nearer end of the mere and solve the mystery of the riderless charger. They had not gone half a mile before they came face to face with the unhorsed one himself. He was very young, and a stranger to the Lord of Hunderholt. He walked all unarmed, in rumpled linen and iron-rubbed leather, slowly and with a detached and aimless air. He seemed not to perceive the approaching company. Sir Hew drew rein at ten paces distance and addressed the stranger.

"Fair Sir, welcome to our poor mountains."

The stranger halted and stared blankly at the large man on the small horse. He sighed, but said no word.

"How fares your knightly quest?" inquired Sir Hew.

The stranger pressed a hand to his brow; and still he spoke no word.

"The devil!" exclaimed the mountain lord. "I see the marks of breastplate and thigh-guards on your jerkin and breeks, and so I know you for a knight at arms. And I see your admirable horse. But what are you doing here in this distressing wilderness, in this comfortless season, if not engaged on a knightly quest?"

"A quest?" queried the other, dazedly. "Yes, a quest—but I seem to have forgotten the particulars."

Sir Hew dismounted, advanced and gazed keenly into the stranger's face.

"Where are your arms and armour? Did wild fellows in wolf skins, such as these, reduce you to this plight? Or did something worse befall you?—something of deviltry—or bewitchment?"

The stranger began to speak, gazing vacantly into space the while. His voice was heavy with unshed tears, his eyes were dark as the depths of a mountain tarn. Thus he spoke:- "she found me roots of relish sweet, and in language strange she said, I love thee true."

"God save us!" exclaimed Sir Hew; and he and the huntsman and the herder made the sign of the Cross; and the mountainy men, less enlightened though equally apprehensive of evil, made older signs to other gods. But the stranger spoke on.

"I saw pale kings and princes and pale warriors—death-pale were they all. I saw their starved lips in the gloom and I awoke on the cold hill-side."

This was too much for the Knight of the Stooping Falcon. With a cry of protest and dismay, he seized the stranger by the shoulders with both big hands and shook him until the bewitched words were flapped and broken to silence between the jiggling jaws. Then he called for the leather bottle. Still gripping the mazed and now breathless youth with his left hand, he poured several ounces of Dame Ashar's potent yet mellow honey-brew between the unprotesting lips.

"Gramercy!" gasped the stranger.

Now they all went in search of the stranger's arms and harness. Sir Hew went forward afoot, and the stranger moved beside him with the veiled, fixed eyes of a sleep-walker and the wavering feet of a tippler. The mountain men quartered the rough hillside like dogs; and it was not long before one of them checked suddenly, uttered a wild shout and pointed a finger. The others hurried up. There in a ferny hollow lay the knightly harness, all complete. But the shine of its smooth plates and cunningly welded chain-pieces had been darkened and dimmed by dews and frosts. The casque, with its bedraggled plume, lay a spear-length to one side; and a spider had spun her web under the raised vizor. The shield lay face-down in the ferns. Sir Hew stooped to the shield and turned it over—but its face was as plain as its back and told him nothing. He was disappointed, for even in Pendragonian times, before the first conscious conception of the art and science of heraldry, most knights bore a device or badge of some sort on their shields—such as Sir Hew's own stooping falcon, King Uther Pendragon's charging ram, the coiled viper of Sir Owen of the Bogs and the broken spear of the young Prince of North Galis.

A few minutes later, in a tangled thicket of bramble and thorn, they found the saddle and trappings of oriental leather and workmanship, a two-handed sword and an iron-headed spear of ash. Sir Hew, fired by brave memories, hefted the great sword, then whirled it about his head with one hand, while the hairy mountainy men expressed their wonder and admiration by yelping wildly and leaping high in the air. The stranger paid no attention, gazing blankly to his front. The huntsman rode around the lake and brought in the war-horse and saddled him. Prompted by Sir Hew, the stranger mounted, without protest and equally without enthusiasm.

"Now home to Hunderholt!" cried Sir Hew, forking his pony; and he muttered, "This will take the dame's mind off the lost oxen—a bewitched young questing knight; and if she expects me to run the risk of bewitchment myself, all for the sake of a few tough steers—well, she'll have to get over it as best she can!"

This encounter with the knightly though unresponsive stranger, and with the great horse and the knightly gear, had set the heart and brain of the retired knight afire with the old impulses and dreams of youth and chivalry and liberty.

They faced about and moved southward at a brisk pace. The sun sank and the frost struck. Sir Hew called a halt at a deserted hut of sticks and stones and wild thatch, in a glen that was all but choked by stunted oaks and firs. The running mountainy men gathered fuel, made a fire, gathered dry fern and heather for beds. The white war-horse and the ponies were unsaddled and tethered close at hand. The carcass of a young sheep was laid to the fire on a long iron rod. Sparks flew aloft like swarms of golden bees and jumping red flames painted the wavering walls of the night. The mountaineers skipped in and out of the heat and glare like hairy devils, feeding the fire and twirling the blistering mutton. The knights sat hunched in their cloaks, just far enough away for comfort without danger of scorching. Sir Hew talked of jousts with blunted spears and with pointed spears, in all of which other knights had come off second best. The stranger said not a word, paid no heed. Sir Hew named great names—but for all the effect they had upon the stranger, they might as well have been of cats and mice. The mutton fell into the flames, and the skipping fellow who rescued it caught afire and lost all the hair off his wolf-skin shirt and kilt, inspite of his desperate skipping. The laughter of his lord and his fellows rang high in the still and frosty night; and before that gust of mirth was spent, even as it began to thin and sink, the stranger threw back his head and burst into prodigious guffaws. The stranger laughed loud and high and long, to the astonishment of the company, even of the two couples of hounds. He laughed until he was breathless; then Sir Hew smote him on the back, whereupon he became as silent as the grave again and resumed his staring into the fire with haunted eyes.

The huntsman produced loaves of barley bread and passed them round. Then he served the scorched sheep, offering his lord and the stranger the first goes at it. The younger knight would have none of it: but Sir Hew hacked with a heavy hand, saying that young mountain mutton was almost as much to his taste as mountain venison. When Sir Hew unstoppered the great leather bottle and passed it into the bemused knight's hands—well, that was another story!

"Thank God you are spared your thirst!" said the hospitable lord of Hunderholt.

The huntsman, herder and wild hillsmen washed down their bread and mutton with mountainy mead, a secondary but no mean tipple.

The hounds grabbed all discarded ribs and shank-bones; and the cracking and crunching of the same between pointed fangs sounded louder than the cracking and snapping of the eager fire.

At last Sir Hew licked his fingers conclusively, wiped them on the lining of his cloak and burst into song. He sang of hunting wild, acorn-fed swine and stags of twenty tines and man-eating wolves. He sang of feasts and frollicks, burdened platters, spicey puddings, brimming horns and bellied bottles; and the hounds and the hairy villeins howled lustily in the chorus. At the end of the twenty-first stanza, the good knight seized the leather bottle and tilted it against his lips; and dumbfounding was his surprise, and staggered was the look he turned upon the stranger, when he discovered that no more of that mellow liquor remained than what he could dispose of easily in two gulps.

And now the woebegone stranger, (slightly flushed of face), piped up a lugubrious air in a voice to match. Sir Hew grunted, then shivered. The mountainy men rolled their eyes and threw fresh fuel on the snoring fire.

"I met a lady in the meads,
    Full beautiful, a fairy's child.
Her hair was long, her foot was light,
    And her eyes were wild.

"I set her on my pacing steed,
    And nothing else saw all day long,
For sideways would she lean and sing
    A fairy's song."

At this point, the leggy hounds sat down on their tails, lifted their quivering snouts to the stars and howled and howled.

"I made a garland for her head,
    And bracelets too, and fragrant zone.
She looked at me as she did love,
    And made sweet moan."

Here Sir Hew heaved a sigh from depths even farther down than the bottom of his romantic heart, the hounds howled again and the simple mountaineers made propitiating signs to ancient, outlawed gods.

"And there we slumbered on the moss;
    And there I dreamed—ah, woe betide!—
The latest dream I ever dreamed
    On the cold hill-side.

"I saw pale kings and princes too,
    Pale warriors—death-pale were they all—"

This was too much for the company. The villeins sprang suddenly into action, feeding dry heather and fern and forest branches to the fire; and Sir Hew laid hold of the stranger and shook him violently, crying, "God defend us all! What devil's rigmaroll is this? Enough, enough! This is no place for such—such fancies."

The young knight was silent. The hounds ceased their starward howling. Sir Hew, chilled in marrow and spirit as if by a cold wind on his spine and a ghostly breath of the nape of his neck, shivered and glanced fearfully around.

"From witches and wizards and long-tailed buzzards and all

creeping things that crawl in hedge-bottoms, O Lord deliver us," he mumbled.

His eyes, uneasily rolling, became fixed upon the huntsman. The huntsman was pointing at something, with extended arm and quivering finger. Sir Hew looked. A shadow? The hounds looked, and instantly shrank and cowered, with trembling bellies against the sod and rough hackles on end. It moved. It advanced from the outer gloom. It was not a shadow. It was an old man in a long gown and long, snowy beard, with a shepherd's crook in his right hand. The mountainy men muttered half-forgotten prayers to wild, cruel, outlawed mountain gods.

"Long life to you, noble lord of Hunderholt," said the intruder, in a strong voice.

"Gramercy! Gramercy!" stammered Sir Hew. "Refresh yourself, ancient sir. Sit down. Have a drink. Have a snack. Mead and mutton. Make yourself at home, honourable ancient. Glad to see you."

But his voice gave the lie to the glib assurance of his words, for his teeth were rattling. He was afraid. There was no blinking the queerness of the old man's sudden appearance at the edge of fire-shine, nor of the fact that these mountains were the ancient home and playground of old heathen demigods and warlocks and magicians. His own grandfather, Sir Ouffer of the heavy sword, had once heard the goat-hoofed god Pan playing on his pipes of reeds withing a few miles of this identical glen.

The intruder dismissed the invitation to eat and drink with a curt gesture of the left hand, and moved around the fire and gazed keenly into the face of the younger knight.

"I overheard your dolorous ditty, young sir," he said. "It is an ancient piece, of ancient and mystical inspiration; and I should be glad to know where you learned it."

The youth did not acknowledge this address by so much as the flicker of an eye-lash, but continued to gaze at the glowing heart of the fire.

"Hah!" exclaimed the other. "You are pleased to ignore this poor old shepherd. Hark to me, Dinadan. A mystery and a stranger you may be to good Sir Hew, but you are neither to me. Sir Dinadan of the Quest, the fifth son of a poor knight of Kent, and knighted yourself but three months ago at Westminster, by King Uther Pendragon, in recognition of the glee you made in honour of the Queen of Ireland."

The bemused one pressed a hand to his brow, sighed but uttered no word.

"What is the high quest on which you rode away so bravely from King Uther's court?" asked the old man.

"I have forgotten it," sighed the young knight.

"Nor will you ever remember it," said the other—"never, until the last illuminating gleam strikes your heart and brain. You shall ride through this mortal life on two quests, the first forgotten, the second remembered but forever lost."

He ordered the huntsman to fetch the young knight's shield. The shield was laid at his feet, face upward. He knelt and fell to rubbing the dim iron plates with the tail of his russet gown. Sir Hew and Sir Dinadan arose and stood over him, peering curiously. The huntsman, the herdsman and the wild mountain men crowded round. The ancient one rubbed and rubbed, hissing the while through his teeth like a varlet grooming a horse. He rubbed the entire surface of the shield over and over, now with a circular motion, now back and forth, now up and down. At last he withdrew his hand and squatted back on his heels.

"There! Do you see it?"

"I see it—something glimmering," whispered Sir Hew. "It takes shape, brightening as if through thinning fog. Horse and rider. They gleam and glow. They move, yet remain fixed in the centre of the shield. And now letters appear—words—words flickering and shining like fire."

"Read the words, noble lord."

"Latin," said Sir Hew. "'Expectans equito.' Which is to say—ahem!—something about a horse. I have neglected my Latin, of late. But it looks simple enough. 'Expectans equito.' I am expecting a horse. Or, I await my horse. Something of the sort—roughly speaking."

"Very roughly," said the old man. "The correct British of it is 'Waiting, I ride.' Do you grasp that, Sir Dinadan? 'Waiting, I ride.' It is written. It is on your shield, in imperishable letters. And long shall be the waiting, I promise you; and long and weary the riding, O Sir Dinadan of the two quests!—of the forgotten quest and the hopeless quest. And at the end, what will you find? Nothing that you have not carried all the way in your own heart."

He chuckled, turned abruptly, stepped one pace—and vanished.

Sir Hew stood gaping at nothing, with sweat of unearthly fear prickling and running on his brow. The young knight stood with bowed head, gazing down at the glimmering device on his shield. The big hounds cowered against the knightly legs. The fellows in wolf-skins babbled scraps of prayer to the cruel and crafty gods of their fathers. Sir Hew swabbed his brow with a shaking hand, squared his heavy shoulders, drew a full breath.

"Merlin!" he whispered. "Who else but that mighty warlock, older than antiquity? My old grandsire held him to be the master wizard of the world."